EVERY SKY A GRAVE

ASCENDANCE SERIES BOOK ONE

EVERY SKY A GRAVE

A NOVEL

JAY POSEY

Skybound Books / Gallery Books

New York   London   Toronto   Sydney   New Delhi

Skybound Books / Gallery Books
An Imprint of Simon & Schuster, Inc.
1230 Avenue of the Americas
New York, NY 10020

First Skybound Books/Gallery Books hardcover edition July 2020

SKYBOUND BOOKS/GALLERY BOOKS and colophon are registered trademarks of Simon & Schuster, Inc.
Skybound is a registered trademark owned by Skybound, LLC. All rights reserved.

For information about special discounts for bulk purchases, please contact Simon & Schuster Special Sales at 1-866-506-1949 or business@simonandschuster.com.

The Simon & Schuster Speakers Bureau can bring authors to your live event. For more information or to book an event, contact the Simon & Schuster Speakers Bureau at 1-866-248-3049 or visit our website at www.simonspeakers.com.

Interior design by Davina Mock-Maniscalco

Manufactured in the United States of America

10   9   8   7   6   5   4   3   2   1

Library of Congress Cataloging-in-Publication Data has been applied for.

ISBN 978-1-9821-0775-8
ISBN 978-1-9821-0776-5 (ebook)

For Jennifer, who holds our world together

Respect for the word is the first commandment in the discipline by which a man can be educated to maturity—intellectual, emotional, and moral.

Respect for the word—to employ it with scrupulous care and an incorruptible heartfelt love of truth—is essential if there is to be any growth in a society or in the human race.

To misuse the word is to show contempt for man. It undermines the bridges and poisons the wells. It causes Man to regress down the long path of his evolution.

—Dag Hammarskjöld, *Markings*

ONE

Elyth *knew* this world, as sure as she knew her own name.

She held the earth loosely clasped in her left hand, felt its damp weight, its sponged texture cold with the night. She knew this soil, knew the life it gave, the story it told, and the doom it now bore. She had come to know it well over weeks of reconnaissance, sweat-grimed days and nights spent on the trail of her deadly mark, learning its ways and its weaknesses.

But the time for stalking her prey was finished. Elyth had all she needed to complete the kill.

When her work was done, the planet Revik would lie dying at her feet. And none would be the wiser that an assassin of worlds had been visited upon them.

She raised her monocular to her eye, swept the view smoothly from left to right and back again. Through its lens the numerous guards shone like tongues of pale fire flickering along the walls and interior of the palace, some five hundred yards distant. Crouched at her hidden vantage point, Elyth noted the passing of a pair of watchmen by the main gate at the target site below. It was her third night of observation; she had the rhythm of the place now, its breath and its heartbeat.

A quick glance at the sky. Two moons highlighted the seams between the densely packed clouds drifting like ice floes in a lazy current over-head; the third moon was too weak and distant to make itself known. And though she couldn't see it, Elyth knew between the moons and the clouds lay an armada. Five thousand Ascendance ships, oblivious to her presence on Revik and yet each utterly dependent on her success.

She returned her monocular to its housing at her belt, then re-moved a small pouch from an inner pocket in her vest. Into it, she let fall the handful of soil she'd gathered. A keepsake; a reminder of what once had been, before her coming to this world.

Time to work.

Elyth sealed the pouch of soil and replaced it inside her vest, then wiped her palms on her pants and stood from her crouch. Roughly three hundred yards of untamed land separated her from the border of the cultivated palace grounds, followed by two hundred yards of open space to her target. She drew on her gloves and slipped her mask over her face, concealing the last bits of exposed skin and cloaking herself fully in the smoked gray-blue of her infiltration attire. So clad, she slipped from her elevated position and began her approach.

Locals called the mountain Heifeld, but its true name was much longer and harder to pronounce, and carried within it all the weight and force of the truly ancient. Elyth had discerned that name in her careful interrogation of the land; the twin-peaked, green-gray mountain had become her ally and also her point of attack. A shallow saddle separated her from the lower but larger, flatter peak, where her target sat: the re-gional governor's multitiered, multiwalled summer palace.

As impressive as the structure was, though, Elyth's actual mark was what lay beneath; one of Revik's most potent threadlines. A planetary nerve cluster near the surface with deep-run roots, concentrated into a focal point less than a hundred yards in diameter. Humans seemed in-tuitively drawn to such places of power, even when oblivious to their ecological significance.

Many worlds had died by Elyth's hand, almost all their deaths wrought in the midst of some thriving city, or imposing government complex, or protected sacred ground.

She made her way down the mountainside and across the saddle, ever watchful. The saddle was peppered with spearlike pines and Revik's peculiar wispy red-hued firs, and carried a dense, earthy scent; she had to mind her footing as she picked her way across the needle-blanketed terrain, dotted with its little fractal forests of moss.

As she approached the edge of the forest, she paused within its dark borders to take final stock of her target. The palace was mostly unlit, save for the pools of orange from security lights at regular intervals along the walls. There were six of these, each roughly twelve feet high, separating the center-most residential building from the outer grounds. Based on her estimate of the threadline's size, she judged that she'd have to get beyond at least the fifth wall to carry out her strike. That was a lot of walls to put between her and her escape.

One thing at a time. She'd get within the minimal kill zone and evaluate from there.

She emerged from the tree line and crept shadowed across the open ground toward the eastern side of the palace, pausing whenever guards patrolled into view. Once she reached the outermost wall, she crouched at its base. Its stacked stones were irregular and rounded in the traditional fashion of the region, leaving enough useful gaps for Elyth's skilled hands and feet. She spidered to the top, laid flat on the wide surface for two breaths to ensure no personnel were immediately below, then slipped over and down the opposite side.

The grounds within the walls had the marks of having been well manicured. Curving paths of hand-laid stone flowed over lush, pale yellow grass, like wide rivers amid prairie; pocket gardens dotted the landscape. But to Elyth's careful eye, signs showed of disorder seeping in at all the edges. The height of the grass was uneven, overdue for cutting, and the once sharp borders of path and garden had grown fuzzy and indistinct. Elyth navigated from shadow to shade; the second and third walls were as easily overcome as the first.

Reaching the fourth took more care. The previous grounds had been decorative but largely transitional spaces, but here between the third and fourth walls they opened up in a meandering way, punctuated with small structures. From Elyth's previous observation, she'd gathered these were workshops and general quarters for palace staff. There was little activity but the broken sight lines and patchwork shadows slowed her progress. Patrols moved over the grounds, emerging from blind corners or materializing piecemeal out of the scattered cover of sculpted trees and hedges.

Elyth's previous patient reconnaissance repaid her; instinct cautioned her to pause, or spurred her to move before she had fully scanned for trouble. Some part of her subconscious fed her patterns of movement that she could not have described, and led her safely undetected to the farther wall.

It was between the fourth and fifth walls that her danger heightened. Sentries patrolled in greater numbers, and in crisscrossing patterns. The increased activity spoke of increased importance; indeed, the various buildings she could see were larger, more ornate.

She navigated her way through the patrols, but as she approached the fifth wall she was forced to stop. Eight pairs of sentries were stationed in a shallow zigzag pattern, each within constant sight of at least two others. Elyth studied them for a time, watching to see which pairs were silent and which were prone to conversation, where focus was strong and where it was weak. As was human tendency, they'd positioned themselves close to or under lights; the gaps between left narrow channels of darkness with little room for error.

She identified her best point of access between two of the chattiest sets of guards. It would be close and nothing was ever certain, but if she stayed low enough, Elyth felt she could slip through unnoticed. She went down on her belly, pressed into the soft grass, and began a slow crawl along a seam of darkness. Her path took her closer to the forward-most pair of sentries; as she neared, she picked up a portion of their conversation.

"—besides, blockades already failed at three other worlds," one sentry, a woman, was saying. "We got another two weeks at most."

They spoke casually, in the informal Low Language.

"Two weeks is pretty optimistic. I say another month," the other sentry, a man, replied. "But you're right, they can't sustain the blockade. The Ascendance has no power left. Its doctrine is poison."

"Its structure corrupt," the first sentry replied.

"Its truth has failed. It falls, as it must," the man answered. "And when it is gone, our righteousness will prevail."

The last part of the exchange sounded rehearsed, robotic in its delivery. A liturgical call-and-response, thoughtlessly practiced and repeated. To untrained ears, the peculiar quality of their speech would have gone unnoticed; but to Elyth, whose life had been devoted to art and skill in the Language, their words dripped and seethed, acidic at the edges, caustic to the mind. Though she could understand every word they spoke, she heard how distorted the intent behind them had become. What the man had called righteousness was nothing more than his personal thirst for vengeance, with himself envisioned as holy judge. Their poisoned delusion angered Elyth.

Here, between these two guards, the danger that Revik posed was laid bare. It was not the speaking out against the Ascendance that had led to Elyth's deployment; she herself had mixed feelings about the Grand Council and its leadership. But here, on Revik, the Language had been intentionally corrupted, purposefully shaped toward destructive ends.

Left unchecked, that corruption could and would spread to neighboring worlds. Tragic though it was, Revik's demise would ensure the safety of thousands of planets, and many billions of human lives.

It was the Language that united them. It was the Language that had lifted the human race from the dust and granted them the stars as inheritance. There was power within its words. Every citizen of the Ascendance was meant to guard it. Instead, these remaining citizens of Revik had twisted it, distorted it to portray themselves enslaved; in truth, they were a free people grasping for nothing more than the freedom to destroy themselves.

She continued past and behind them, escaping their notice. Another fifty feet and she would be at the base of the wall. But as she was crossing that final stretch, fortune turned against her.

Without warning, one of the guards broke from his place and began crossing the grounds toward another pair, with Elyth caught between. He'd been standing in one pool of light and was heading toward another, so she knew his unadjusted vision would grant her some extra concealment. But he was going to pass within just a few feet of her, and she couldn't leave the matter to chance.

Her hand found its way to the collapsed baton on her belt. A single strike could fell him easily enough. But the aftermath might be unmanageable.

As he closed within twenty feet of her, many possibilities were contained within those next few seconds. Elyth needed one specific possibility to manifest.

She would call it forth.

The technique was approved by the policy of her House, though only in limited circumstances and under strictest control. One could not twist the fabric of reality far before its warped threads would draw others best left undisturbed. But human perception was the easiest of all domains to influence and manipulate. She paused a moment to clear her mind, to fashion the words first within before she breathed them into existence. Then, with all focus and attention bent on that single sentry, she spoke.

But her words were not of the common dialect. Now, she employed the secret tongue that undergirded it all, the foundation upon which the Language and indeed the cosmos itself had been constructed. She spoke a sealing phrase to draw upon the hidden Deep Language.

"A shadow upon emptiness; the many darknesses are one," she said, her words a barely voiced whisper. And then to the man, *"Though you see me, you do not perceive."*

The guard reacted at the sound; his head pitched up as he brought his gaze from the ground in front of him to the place where Elyth lay. His features were too cloaked in darkness for her to see clearly, but she could feel his eyes upon her.

And the next moment, she felt his gaze slide over and past her. He continued his path in front of her, oblivious, close enough that she could have stretched out and snatched his ankle had she desired. When he was three paces past, she drew up into a low crouch and made her way as quickly as she dared to the wall, cycling her attention between her destination, the sentry she had dodged, and the other guards still standing at their posts. She paused at the base of the wall, pressed her shoulder to it while she surveyed the grounds. The wandering sentry reached his companions, and the three of them engaged in some quiet huddle of conversation. Everything else continued as it had before, with no sign that her passage had disturbed any of the sentries' natural rhythm.

Assured that her crossing had gone unmarked, Elyth quickly cleared the fifth wall and lowered herself into the inner court, the central hub of the summer palace. There remained ahead of her only one final wall cordoning off the governor's personal residence from the rest of the grounds. Whether by design or intuition, the extravagant home was very nearly centered above Elyth's target threadline. She was tempted to breach that area, to infiltrate the place the governor considered most secure, only to prove to herself that she could.

But the threadline was wide enough that she could do her work here without any loss in efficacy, and there was no need to put yet another wall between herself and her escape. With mild reluctance, she set to scouting the various outbuildings between the walls.

There were a number of these, many of which after investigation she determined had been converted to temporary quarters for what she assumed were the governor's most loyal supporters. Elyth circled the innermost wall, looking for a location that would provide her sufficient security for this most delicate part of her operation. Once she began the process, she couldn't afford to be interrupted.

On the side of the palace opposite her initial approach, she found a tall single-story building, a wide and long rectangle, like a warehouse. She crept across an open stretch of ground to it and knelt down by its outer wall, on the darkest end. A high slat window or vent sat above her, roughly ten feet above the ground and set back slightly in the wall. Elyth stepped away, then made a quick dash forward and leapt up, boosting herself with a light step off the building exterior. She caught the narrow lip of the window's housing with her fingertips and drew herself up enough to peek inside. The darkness within was nearly complete, save for a weak glow from somewhere near the main entrances and a pair of squared patches in the roof where the gloom clung less thickly to the ceiling. Skylights, maybe. She lowered herself back to the full extent of her arms, and then dropped softly to the ground.

She looked up, evaluated the roofline. It arced gracefully over the width of the building, coming no lower than perhaps fifteen feet from the ground at either end. The exterior walls were smooth, with no obvious protrusions. Climbing wasn't an option, at least on this end. She

peeked around the corner and spotted two large double-door entrances, each stretching nearly to the roofline in height and twice as
wide. A third door of normal size sat under a light between the two
bays. Between her and the first bay door, however, sat several crates
haphazardly stacked near the storehouse, backlit by a light source farther beyond.

Though the central door promised the easiest access, Elyth hadn't
seen enough of the interior to feel secure entering that way.

She picked her way to the crates.

There were five of them, metal cubes about four feet to a side, and
arranged as though they'd been hastily dumped. Elyth glanced up,
judged the distance between the top crate and the edge of the roof. Significant for a standing jump, but not impossible. She scrambled on top
of the crate and wasted no time.

Elyth leapt, stretched out, and caught the rounded edge of the roof;
she pendulumed toward the building then out again, and used the momentum to accelerate her pull up and over the edge. Once on the roof,
she padded in a low crouch to the nearest skylight opening. There she
drew out her monocular and switched it to light amplification, no magnification.

It was a warehouse indeed. Like the surrounding grounds, it too
showed signs of creeping disarray. From what she could see, the outer
aisles were in good order. But closer to the loading bay doors the lines
became less regular, until there, closest to the front of the building, it
appeared as though large loads had been shoved into careless piles.
Whatever the case, she saw no sign of personnel inside. Still, from her
vantage she couldn't see the source of the interior light and that made
her wary of trying the front door.

The skylight wasn't sealed; scratches at the rear corner showed wear
from moving on hinges. After a few moments Elyth located a mechanism that raised and lowered the large pane, enabling it to double as a

vent; another half minute of work, and she'd bypassed the circuitry and then manually lifted the pane wide enough to gain entry.

High rafters ran along either side of the skylight, but the gap was too great to manage safely. From a pouch strapped to her leg, Elyth removed a small black cylinder about the size of her fist. With the press of a button the top unfurled into a many-fingered hand, each digit willowy and delicate by look. She tugged the upper section free and ran it to the edge of the skylight; a spider-threaded line spooled out behind. When the fronds of the device met the lip of her entry point, she squeezed the handle, and those willowy fingers folded in, grasping the edge from many angles with all the strength of the roots of an ancient oak. The cylinder she hooked onto a small loop on the front of her belt; together the system acted as line and harness.

Secured, Elyth lowered herself through the skylight, feeding out enough line to swing over to the rafter. Crouched there, she unhooked the device from her belt and deactivated the grasping mechanism; it fell free from the skylight and zipped quietly home, its blossom folding neatly closed once back in place. She held position there, perched above the warehouse floor, scanning. And finally, she could see where the sole light was coming from. A guard was posted in a small alcove to one side of the main entrance. But she was committed now; she'd have to see it through.

Elyth navigated her way along and down the support structure to the floor below. For a few minutes, she crept along the long aisles and the incongruous combination of neat stacks and careless piles, evaluating it all for a secure strike point. The single guard didn't appear to have any intention of leaving his station, but she couldn't leave it to chance. She would need every ounce of focus for the task at hand.

On the end of the warehouse opposite from the guard, Elyth discovered a door, sealed by a simple passcode lock. Neither light nor sound came from behind, and she guessed it was some sort of storage closet. She scanned the lock with a device from her vest, which after a moment fed her the proper sequence. Elyth punched in the code and eased the door open.

The room was completely dark; she drew out her monocular and scanned the interior. It was roughly six feet wide and perhaps ten feet deep, filled with racks of various cleaning supplies and other goods without clear markings. Elyth slipped inside and closed the door quietly behind her. Judging from the amount of dust gathered on all but the shelves closest to the door, it appeared it'd been some time since the room had seen any regular use.

With the door shut, she decided it was safe to risk a little light of her own, and put her monocular away. She switched on the personal light mounted on her vest and its red-filtered beam cast a wide pool of ember-glow light; in the back corner of the room, she carefully cleared some space for herself to work. She didn't need much.

Once that was done, she switched off her light, settled herself with a deep breath and exhale and, there, finally, delivered her message. The technique was called Revealing the Silent Gate. It began with *ahn*, the first letter of the Language, and its hand sign.

"*From the void, all come,*" Elyth said, uttering the sealing phrase in the Deep Language, "*to the void, all return.*"

And then wielding the true speech of the universe, known only to and guarded by the select few of her House, she spoke death.

She spoke to the planet directly, intimately, to the complex network of shifting energies and ecosystems that some might call its spirit. It had taken her weeks of careful communion with the world to learn its innermost workings. Now, she spoke of its mountains, and its rivers, and its moss-wrapped forests. She spoke of its ice-white skies, its sun-forsaken deep. And in the Deep Language of the cosmos, she described its collapse.

Revik had fire in its heart, rivers of magma in its veins that had long stayed their course far beneath the surface. Too long. They were the planet's great vulnerability, and these Elyth called by name and stirred to action. She pictured them in her mind, held the whole world in her mind's eye, a spectral globe hovering before her. Within it, she saw the fractures form that would over time grow to great rifts; and these images she described in the Deep Language. It was the end of the world as it would be, one that existed within the planet's natural processes, given enough time. But Elyth was drawing it out from the distant future, into the now. There, in a storage closet in a warehouse, the infinite stretched down to kiss the finite, and she was its bridge. Her body trembled from the focus and exertion it took to keep herself anchored.

Using the hand signs associated with each letter, Elyth ran through the full protocol, speaking to each basic element of Revik's composition, each portion of its ecosystem and the part it would play in relation to the other. There was no power in the gestures; the signs were merely a physical mnemonic, a checklist embodied. It was the universe alone that carried the power of her craft, and the Deep Language was its access.

Around her, the familiar feeling embraced her; a crackling, an ocean foam of possibilities as light and space and time bent around her, warping, roiling. Even in the darkness, she could see multicolored glints and black sparks darker than even the absence of light that surrounded her. Galaxies and black holes; the material of the cosmos, manifest in microscale. Or perhaps her being had expanded to something the mere universe could no longer contain.

Her body vibrated with a manic energy, a buildup of static charge before the lightning strike. Exhilarating. Terrifying.

In the final sequence, Elyth held her hands one above the other, palms facing but separated, as though holding the globe of the world between. The air between them felt dense, heavy. And then she raised her hand above her head, and repeated the sealing phrase.

"From the void, all come; to the void, all return."

As the last words left her mouth, she dropped to a knee and brought her hand down, striking the floor with a heavy palm. The power flowed from the infinite beyond, through her, into the planet; the work of a thousand millennia compressed into a single moment, focused through a point the span of her palm. And that power raced along the threadline, a nerve carrying its pain to the planet's roots where it would radiate out again through every facet of the world.

There was no outward sign, no quaking of the earth, no thunderous blast, no smoke-billowing mountain; but Elyth knew the change as surely as she could know the soul-broken eyes of a mother bereaved. This was a hearty world. On a human scale, its death would be gradual. Perhaps as much as a standard Ascendant year before its surface became toxic to human life. But on a cosmic time frame, its end would be as swift and sudden as an instant.

From that moment on, Revik sped toward death.

She remained there on her knee for several minutes, too disciplined to let herself sink to the floor, but not yet capable of standing. The discharge of power combined with the exertion of the process left Elyth drained and hollow. Reaching out to seize the raw material of the cosmos, to serve as a conduit through which it could flow, exposed her to the mind-breaking gulf separating her tiny existence from that limitless, formless potential. To touch the infinite was to come fully awake to one's own utter limitation. It was no small thing to bear. No matter how many times she'd gone through the process, she'd not yet been able to overcome the fear that one day she might not make it back from that place.

Without conscious thought, Elyth's body carried out its routine for recovery; a set of breathing cycles designed to draw her awareness back to the reality of her physical form, of the concrete nature of her surroundings, and of each individual moment of the present. Gradually the procedure recentered and anchored her sense of being, just as it had been created to do.

But too, as the cosmic horizon receded, the personal, emotional weight of the act bore down upon her. She knew the justness of the sentence she had carried out. The loss of Revik was a surgeon's cut, the death of one cell sacrificed to protect all those around it. But to call forth such precise, intimate destruction, Elyth had to know the planet, and in knowing the planet, she had come to love it. She recognized what made Revik unique, and though she saw how it had been irrevocably corrupted by its inhabitants, she knew too what a precious treasure it had once been. Most if not all of the humans could be saved; the planet would bear the cost. And there was no way to harden oneself against killing a thing beloved.

Elyth would grieve, and deeply. But not right now.

She eased herself up to standing, tested her balance for a moment. The trembling had ceased. She clenched her hands to fists and then opened them again. There was strength in them still, though she felt empty in her core. Strength enough to make it back to her ship, off world, and back into the embrace of the Ascendance, and of her Order. All that stood between her and a much-needed and much-deserved recovery was a series of walls and a few dozen sentries.

Elyth slipped out into the warehouse, made her way past the lone, dozing guard, and exited through its ground-level entryway. She followed roughly the same track as she'd taken on her way in, modifying it as the movement of patrols dictated. It all seemed easy enough, until her ascent up the first of the five walls. Even with the relatively easy climb, she felt the weakening in her grip. The hit was taking its toll and Elyth knew from much experience that her scant remaining stamina would fade ever more rapidly.

At the top of the wall, she decided to conserve what energy she could. Instead of climbing down the opposite side, she made use once more of her support line, affixing its plant-like grasp to the rounded edge of the wall and allowing its line to lower her to the ground below.

The sky was beginning to gray into its first signs of dawn, granting a bare, soft edge of light to the compound. Above her, the clouds had begun to spread and separate subtly but consistently across the expanse. The gradual increase in visibility was both a blessing and a curse; easier to spot potential danger, but that ran true in both directions.

Thankfully, navigating the line of guards that had been her great challenge during infiltration proved less difficult a task on the way out; the line had deteriorated, the sentries forming small clusters of idle chatter. A sure sign that the night's shift was drawing to a close. With careful steps and watchful eyes, she slipped from wall to wall, a moon shadow brushing lightly over the earth.

At each wall, Elyth repeated the process of scaling up and then using her line to descend the opposite side. And though each climb took more effort than the one previous, by the time she'd reached the outermost wall, she'd gotten the rhythm of the sequence so well that she barely had to pause at the top before she could roll over the edge and enjoy a precious few moments of rest as the device lowered her gently to the ground.

It was the mastery of that routine that caused her the trouble.

Her feet had just touched down outside the complex when, as her focus was on her climbing aid to retract its line, a motion in her peripheral vision drew her attention. She snapped her head in its direction then froze. Three sentries were standing no more than twenty feet away. Their line ran diagonally away from her, a few feet between each man and the farthest perhaps thirty feet distant. Fortunately none were looking her direction, but from their stances it was obvious that she couldn't expect them to remain that way for long.

How foolish. She'd climbed over the wall in the exact same location that she'd initially infiltrated; all her previous observation had shown it to be consistently clear of patrols. She had acted on what she'd expected, rather than on what was actually there. It would have cost her a few seconds only. Now, the cost would be somewhat higher.

The motion she had seen had been the nearest guard turning his head, undoubtedly in reaction to the sound of her quiet descent, though it hadn't yet occurred to him that any danger could possibly be coming from behind. And though the security she'd so expertly evaded thus far had seemed inattentive, she saw now in this man's taut posture how quick the response to a threat could be. She knew without a doubt that a single warning raised would activate the entire compound, swarming the grounds and surrounding lands with searchers, both man and machine.

The sun would be cresting the horizon soon enough, and Elyth still had need of what little remained of the night's veil; too much hostile ground lay between her and her escape to wait. There wouldn't be time to hide the bodies.

Without further thought, she launched from her crouch by the wall. The first man she took with a swift blow to the base of the skull. As he pitched forward, Elyth grabbed the back of his collar with one hand and his belt with the other, controlling his fall to limit the sound. The second man was just turning when Elyth reached him, close enough to see his eyes narrowed in confusion. Before they could widen, Elyth's baton found its mark just below his left ear, near the jawline. There was no time to catch him as he fell.

The third guard was a man of powerful stature; already he was turned toward her, rapidly processing the scene as his second companion hit the ground. Elyth knew she couldn't close the distance in time. His mouth was opening, his hands streaking toward the weapon on his belt.

But Elyth was faster.

In her mind's eye, she saw the baton leave her hand and strike its target; in the next instant, it was so. The baton impacted the guard's solar plexus, momentarily stealing his breath and stumbling him a step. Whatever weapon he'd been trying to draw fumbled to the ground. Elyth was on him three steps later, swatting away his attempt at a defense. She darted the edge of her hand into his Adam's apple, stunning the vocal cords, and with a twisting step flowed around and behind him. In the next moment, she snaked her arm around his neck and dropped backward to the ground, dragging him down with her. As she locked her legs around his waist, the man writhed, attempted to pry her arm away from his trachea, and his great strength made itself known.

Elyth clung close and tight in the chaos, reflexively reacting to every shift in the man's weight and power. And in that violent embrace, the heat of his body, the scent of his sweat-sheened skin, the pulsing blood flow within the vise of her arm, all spoke of the terror of death upon him, and his life's thrashing struggle against it.

But neither his strength nor his will were sufficient to overcome her skill and technique.

It took only a few seconds before the man's flailing weakened, and fewer after until it ceased completely. Elyth counted to five before she dared release the hold and then slumped him to one side. He would wake again in ten or twenty seconds, sluggish and confused. It would give her a head start, but not enough to cover the distance to the tree line. If they gave chase, she'd never make it off the planet. She glanced down at the man next to her. A killing blow would be nothing now; as simple as crushing a bug.

But as she looked at the fallen sentry, other faces flashed in her mind. In her youth, she had taken lives rashly, painful mistakes of judgment. Elyth knew nothing of the man; why he had chosen to side with the governor's doomed bid for power, or how deep his indoctrination ran. Maybe he was a true believer. Or maybe he was an innocent man, just trying to survive. None of her Order would fault her for his death. But here, now, with the man helpless, at her utter mercy, the fact that no authority would hold her accountable seemed insignificant.

And during those seconds of consideration, she came to recognize the opportunity he presented. A minor risk, but worth it. If it worked.

She recovered her baton and located the guard's weapon. It was a small kinetic gun. She threw the weapon far away, then moved quickly back to the wall and scaled it as fast as her wearied fingers would allow.

At the top, she paused, dropped onto her belly, and dangled her legs over the interior side, watched the third sentry intently in the ever-growing light of approaching dawn. Any moment.

And there. He stirred briefly, then lay still again. A few moments later, he began to recover himself in earnest, and pushed up unsteadily, glancing about as though he'd expected to find himself home in bed.

And then the realization fell upon him with all its weight, and his searching became sharp, just shy of frantic. Elyth waited until the moment the guard's eyes found her, and then swiftly lowered herself over the edge of the wall back into the interior of the complex. She didn't drop all the way to the ground, though. Instead, she hung there by the edge, gritting her teeth against the weakness in her grip, listening to the activity on the other side. The man tried to cry out, but the damage she'd inflicted on his vocal cords rendered the call hoarse and ineffective. An instant later, the man's heavy footsteps signaled his rush to the nearest help.

When her path was clear, Elyth stared through a fog of exhaustion for just a moment, willing herself to move before she found strength enough to drag herself back over. She didn't even bother to try descending the opposite side with any grace or control, only lowering herself far enough to minimize the chance of breaking an ankle before dropping to the ground. She rolled with the impact and came up run-ning, passing the two guards who still lay unconscious.

She had crossed just over half the distance to the tree line when she heard the alarm go up behind her. If her ruse had worked, however, she knew the immediate focus would be on securing the palace grounds themselves. Hopefully the distraction would give her the time she needed to recover her ship and escape the planet.

Elyth reached the tree line and pushed on as fast as the difficult terrain and her heavy legs would allow. Five miles separated her from the craggy and barren hollow where her small vessel lay concealed. By the time she reached it, she barely had strength left to climb into the cockpit.

It wasn't until she was airborne and climbing steadily out of the at-mosphere that Elyth allowed herself to believe she had truly escaped. She let out a deep exhale then and gave herself permission to feel the full weight of the weeks she had endured on Revik, the part she had played in its inevitable and coming demise, and the exhaustion that laid heavy upon her.

And it was in that moment of mingled relief and utter depletion that she realized a priority transmission had come through while she'd been away from the ship; its header markings and encryption protocols declared its origins to be directly from the Order of the Mind, the high-est order of Elyth's House.

She flicked the message open, skimmed it with anxious eyes. It was terse, but the brevity did not rob it of its weight.

Immediate recall. Revik operation to be passed over.
Return to the Vaunt by fastest possible method.

Passed over. The phrase whipped her with an ice-wind dread. At best, it meant another of her Order was being deployed to complete the mission in her place, due to some unknown failing on her part.

At worst, it might mean she had just killed a planet that should have been spared.

Nausea seized her at the thought, swirled her emotions. If the beauty of Revik could have been preserved after all . . . but she closed her eyes and steadied herself.

Elyth had completed the task as it had been placed before her. There was no way to discern the intent behind this new directive, nor to determine why it had arrived so late. Allowing her imagination to fill in gaps was neither wise nor beneficial. Any answers she might receive would come no sooner than her return. She was already doing all she could.

She marked the message received and closed it, sealing it to oblivion; once read, such transmissions from the Advocates of the Mind dissolved to leave no trace.

If only the same could have been said for the impact of the message.

As the sky darkened around her beyond the cockpit, so too did Elyth's thoughts. Despite her attempts to settle herself, the communication had robbed her of any sense of accomplishment. Instead of a work completed, Revik was now a question posed. And while her ship carried her back into the safety of the Ascendance armada, her mind grappled with the unforeseeable new trial that awaited her return to the grand vaulted city of her Order.

TWO

The baton streaked in from Elyth's right, a low feint emerging suddenly as a sharp-angled strike aimed at her temple. She stepped into the attack, checked her opponent's wrist with her off hand at the last possible moment, and in the same motion jabbed her own baton forward in a counterstrike. But Nyeda anticipated the thrust, twisted, flowed around to Elyth's left, and caught hold of her elbow.

Elyth felt the joint lock unfolding. Instead of resisting, she waited the half breath it took for Nyeda to commit, and then settled back and dropped her hips, gaining the leverage she needed to trap Nyeda's hand mid-technique.

Nyeda was quick, but Elyth's footwork was better, and a moment later, Elyth escaped the hold and tipped the now-unbalanced woman down to the ground shoulder first. Elyth followed the momentum, used her body weight to pin Nyeda down. Beneath her, the older woman slackened, momentarily caught off guard and stunned. Elyth shot her hand around to secure a choke; she had her now.

So she thought.

An instant later, Nyeda shifted and rolled, her body trapping

Elyth's ankle and bringing her to the ground. The woman's baton arced. Elyth's arms were too tangled.

The impact caught her on the collarbone, the dull *thunk* reverberated down through her spine; for a brief moment, the sound was worse than the pain.

And then, all was still while Elyth lay on her back, panting, sweating, suffering the consequence of her mistake. She knew exactly what that mistake had been. In retrospect, she'd felt it, knew her feet had been too close to Nyeda, how she should have adjusted and sprawled more, before she'd gone for the choke. But she'd missed it in the moment, or ignored it; Nyeda's momentary relaxation had thrown her off, made her overconfident.

Nyeda's face appeared above her.

"Sloppy," the older woman said, looking down on her sternly. "Should have sprawled more."

Elyth nodded. And Nyeda's helping hand appeared, offering to pull her once more to her feet.

"Trouble focusing?" Nyeda asked, as Elyth rolled up and took her hand.

"No," Elyth answered, standing. "At least, I didn't think so. Just not quite fully back in my body yet."

"It's still early."

"I feel the loss, Nyeda," Elyth forced herself to say. It was a confession she would have preferred to leave unspoken. But she knew the dangers of her currently vulnerable state. Putting on a brave face for others was on the same path as deceiving herself.

"As you will, my sister," she answered. "Is it overwhelming?"

Elyth shook her head. "Manageable. But this depth of longing is usually gone by now."

"Then you're a quicker healer than most." Nyeda put her hand on Elyth's shoulder, softening from combat instructor to spiritual advisor.

"Each time is unique. Each its own process for you to discover, to pass through, and from which to emerge. And you *will* emerge."

Elyth acknowledged the encouragement with a nod.

"Again?" she asked, ready for another round. But Nyeda shook her head.

"I know you hate to end on a loss, but we've already gone longer than we should have. And this was supposed to be a light day."

"Yeah, I know," Elyth said. "That's why I was taking it so easy."

"Mmm-hmm," Nyeda said. She patted Elyth's cheek with a perfect blend of affection and sarcasm and then gathered the training batons. "Then you should have no trouble settling yourself."

Elyth nodded but didn't hide her disappointment. Tired as she was, she preferred the demands of full-contact sparring to the forced leisure, where her mind could wander where it would. Even knowing its importance to her recovery, it was difficult to endure.

"And double the time today," Nyeda added. "You need it."

Elyth barely contained a groan as she moved to the center of the room and began her meditative routine.

The private training room off the living area of her main residence was spartan; twenty feet long and half as wide, furnished with a dense mat, a simple rack to hold a few training weapons, and little else. Still, Nyeda made herself busy tidying it, keeping her actions so quiet and unobtrusive that it would have been easy to forget she was there. And yet, for all the passivity of the older woman's presence, Elyth knew well how attentive she was to everything around her. Nyeda was keeping a close eye on her, though Elyth felt no sense of being watched. It took years to master such alertness, effortless and relaxed.

Elyth held the initial position, Silence Unveils the Heavens, for twice its normal duration as Nyeda had directed. She stood tall, head tilted slightly backward as though gazing at a star-strewn sky, feeling the stretch through her core, willing the exertion to exorcise the vibrating energy buried within her bones.

It'd been six days since her return to the Vaunt and despite the apparent urgency of the transmission she'd received, she'd been immediately sent into the ritual seclusion that awaited any Advocate of the Voice returning from a successful operation. She knew she couldn't speak of the message she'd received, not until the appropriate audience was given. It was often the way of things. Hers was to operate in uncertainty; the expectation was for patience until further revelation was deemed proper and necessary, if ever. A lifetime of practice had not yet made it any easier to bear.

She took a deep breath and controlled the exhale as she transitioned to the next pose, Arrow Seeks the Heart. A deep lunge forward, one hand extended like a spear-thrust before her.

After the killing of a planet, Advocates of the Order of the Voice were cloistered for a full thirty days of recovery. Given the amount of time that had passed without news, Elyth struggled to resign herself to the idea that she would learn nothing until she had completed the full healing cycle. Another twenty-four days. She acknowledged the frustration that bubbled up at the idea and then allowed it to dissipate.

She moved into the anchoring pose Warrior Summits the Mountain, her feet wide apart, arms raised and out as though embracing the sky.

Normally the pose felt triumphant. Today, her mind would not quiet. Questions nagged; impatience prowled beneath the surface of her every activity.

Watcher Greets the Storm. She clenched one hand into a fist and held it close to her body, the other arm she extended partially, palm upraised as though catching the first drops of rain. *Fitting*, she thought. The pose was symbolic of having done all one could to prepare, and bravely facing that which could not be controlled. In that moment, she didn't feel she was meeting either criterion fully.

A trace of a thought drifted like an echo of smoke, a vague sadness and longing; the ache for something which she had glimpsed, yet could never possess. It was the call of the Deep; the echo of the infinite. Equal parts dream and memory, half-formed. Of this too Elyth took note, and allowed the mist-musing to flow past without attempt to grasp or pursue. Gently, she returned her focus to sensation; the floor, the trembling, the beaded sweat. Reminded herself that this was what it was to have a body, to be in a place, to exist and give form to her own tragic limitation.

Elyth transitioned into the most challenging stance: a deep squat, with her body bent forward and her arms extended as far behind her as she could manage. Titan Bears the World. The muscles in her legs trembled with the strain as she stretched the stiffness from her back and shoulders; she cupped her hands, imagining the sphere of a planet resting upon them, noticed the warmth of the blood flowing through her palms. As she inhaled deeply, her abdomen pressed down into the tops of her thighs. Her feet, flat and firm on the floor, drew from the stability of the world beneath, felt the anchoring weight of its substance. Each of these sensations she noted in passing, observing without judgment. Or at least attempting to.

The truth was it left a scar each time she took a world. Or rather a deep wound that would never fully heal. The melancholy would linger, grief would reemerge and subside in its own time. But Elyth knew she must not seek to return to it, must not rehearse the loss, or comfort herself with the familiar pain. She had been warned where that path led. And she had seen it for herself, when other Advocates, beloved sisters, had chosen to walk it, and had lost themselves within it.

She moved to her next-to-last position, Orual Releases the Dove, a standing pose with her hands in front of her, palms cupped together and angled toward the ceiling. Relaxation flooded her body, gentle relief from Titan Bears the World.

And with the release of tension, Elyth imagined herself releasing also the guilt she felt for the death of Revik. It was heavier upon her than she wanted to admit, and she realized now in this quiet moment how she'd been avoiding reflecting upon it.

She reminded herself that she was not solely responsible for Revik's ultimate fate. She was merely the final point of a process that began long before, one in a chain whose links were of numbers untold; the tip of a finger at the end of the Ascendance's godlike reach. Before she had been deployed, there had been many attempts to set the world on a better course, ample opportunity for a better outcome. In the end, her actions were a mercy, a difficult act for a greater good; it was the burden she and her sisters willingly bore for the greatest good.

Elyth told herself all these things while physically embodying the act of letting go. It wasn't that simple. But the mindful practice of it would in time help make the release a reality.

She completed the sequence with the final pose, head bowed, hands clasped in front of her. Servant Awaits with Gratitude. This she held for a full two minutes, and when she reached the end of the count, felt a mild reluctance to return to the world beyond herself. As invigorated as she was, the idea of interacting with others seemed now like an intrusion upon a sacred silence. But she knew she couldn't allow herself to nurse the desire to withdraw.

"I think I'll record the history this morning," she said.

She had not felt strong enough to do so before. But this morning, the memory was fresh enough to be captured and distant enough to withstand without tipping over the edge.

"There's no rush," Nyeda answered. "And you must allow yourself to rest, Elyth."

"I'll rest easier when the memories are on the page."

Nyeda regarded her carefully for a few moments; Elyth could see the woman weighing the options. Nyeda was her keeper for the duration of the recovery; "sitting watch" they called it. A sacred service within the House. It was her duty to watch and guard all aspects of Elyth's well-being during her recovery, to be counselor and trusted advocate. And to protect her from herself, should the need arise.

Finally, Nyeda nodded, and the two retired to the adjoining parlor. The training area was separated from the rest of Elyth's private apartment by a large sliding screen. The room on the other side was a more intimate space, furnished with a divan and a pair of comfortable chairs arranged around a plush circular rug. Against one wall sat a large bookcase, and along the adjacent wall by a large window were Elyth's small desk and accompanying chair.

Nyeda sat in the chair closest to the main entry; Elyth took some time to wash up and change into her more general-purpose tunic and pants. She returned to the parlor refreshed and mentally prepared for the task at hand.

From the bookcase, she retrieved a notebook bound in leather. On the top shelf rested a set of small crystalline vials, each about the size of her thumb, capped in black and labeled. And even though she knew their names without looking at what was written on each and she knew exactly the place of the one she sought, she allowed her finger to trace across the tops of the last four.

Danata. Hetalya. Geren. Revik.

Inside those vials rested soil from those planets, soil she had collected just before carrying out her assignment on each world. Images sprang to mind as her touch passed over the vials in turn; impressions of dusty sunsets over river-shot mountains, thirsting nights, shattered skies. Elyth took down the vial with Revik's sample and carried it with the notebook to the desk by her window. She placed both before her and sat in the simple chair. For a time she just looked out the window, at the early-morning mist that clung to the grounds outside. Her spar-

ring session had started before dawn; the residential quadrangle remained quiet and still, a deep lake undisturbed.

When her mind was clear and settled, Elyth unwound the strap
that held the notebook closed and flipped through the pages until she
found one blank. With a pen she set down the date; Day 17, Month 8,
Year of Ascendance 8021.

And on the page beneath, she began to recount her time on Revik,
detailed with vivid clarity. Not in the formal style of an after-action report. That she had already delivered as part of her debriefing protocol.
Where that report had been equally detailed, its focus had been facts,
data; an accurate timeline of the intelligence she had gathered on Revik,
a record of her actions there, and of their effects. This handwritten account was for no one but Elyth, and its sole purpose was to capture the
moments on the world that had made their greatest impression, regardless of their operational value. These were the fragile moments of
beauty and awe: the three-mooned night sky; the thumbnail-sized wildflowers with their bright yellow center crowned in four-petaled lavender; the fragrance of dawn. Sketches of emotion and sensation, all the
things that had made the planet itself, as experienced by Elyth. This was
Revik's obituary, written by one who had come to know it most intimately, composed by the hand by which it had been slain.

By the time she laid down her pen, it was midmorning and the activity outside her window had taken on its usual intensity. The
Vaunt's grounds were busy with servants of the House carrying out
the many-faceted duties that supported the micro city's function and,
by extension, its far-reaching influence. Witnessing all the motion
and energy stirred once more Elyth's frustration at her seclusion. She
attempted to dismiss it with a sigh, mostly failed, and returned her
gaze to her page. Soon enough she would be released; for now, it was
her duty to see herself well.

Though she was done writing, her entry was not yet complete. She unscrewed the cap from the vial with Revik's soil and sprinkled a small portion onto the bottom corner of the page. She then moistened her fingertips with saliva and with small circles massaged the dirt until it had worked its way into the paper. A bit of Revik's life mingled with hers to seal the memory. Over the top of it, Elyth traced a symbol with the nail of her pointer finger, one that left less of a visible mark than an impression in the dampened page. A glyph of her design, to represent a work completed.

Afterward, she closed the notebook, wrapped the strap around it, and was just standing from her desk when a light tap sounded at the door. It was still too early for any summons, by standard accounts. There was nothing scheduled for her until midday, and the Order had strict rules about initiating interaction with an Advocate during her re-covery. Nyeda rose to answer it, but Elyth stayed her with a gesture and strode across the room.

She opened the door and found a young woman standing there, one Elyth did not recognize.

"Advocate Elyth," the young woman said, and Elyth could hear the tremble of nerves in her voice. The girl was perhaps thirteen, and her plain, olive-toned attire established only that she was an Aspirant; an Adovcate-in-training, accepted to the House but the path for her life not yet selected. Aspirants often served as messengers for multiple or-ders within the House.

"Yes?" Elyth said.

"I am Vrin," the messenger said, bowing with the words. "The Par-agon has requested you."

It took a moment for Elyth to process.

"The Paragon herself?" she asked.

"Yes, Advocate," said the girl, her eyes still on the floor.

Elyth glanced at Nyeda, saw her own mix of confusion and concern reflected back to her.

"At your most immediate," the girl added.

"Of course," Elyth said. "I'll need a moment to change—"

"There's no need," Vrin answered. "The Paragon will see you as you are. Alone."

If the disruption of protocol had seemed unusual, this new revelation was unheard of. Elyth had served the House for nearly twenty-five years and had never known anyone to appear before the Paragon of the First House of the Ascendance without the proper attire. And the idea of standing before the ancient matriarch on her own, alone . . . a heavy, ice-drenched knot formed in Elyth's stomach, a dread that she had done something gravely wrong. Undoubtedly the questions about her recall from Revik would be answered. What other consequences awaited her, she couldn't predict.

"I shall escort you now, if you are ready," said the girl, with a note of authority at odds with her still-tremulous voice. She spoke in the High Language, the formal, precise mode of speech common for official communication, but seldom used in the halls of residence. It added to the young woman's bearing and gravity.

Elyth nodded, slid her feet into a pair of simple slippers by the door, and followed the girl out. Nyeda started to join them, but the young girl held up a hand.

"Your charge Elyth is now under the watch of the Paragon herself," the girl said, addressing Nyeda. And as she did, Elyth couldn't help but notice the sudden firmness of her tone. *Ah. No mere messenger, then.* The girl was in training for the Order of the Mind, in direct service to the Paragon. An honor, and one that marked her as already highly favored. "She will be returned safely to you, Advocate of the Voice."

Again, Nyeda and Elyth exchanged a look; the circumstances were so far from the known and expected, neither of them were quite sure how to respond, other than with obedience. Elyth gave Nyeda a reassuring nod and a smile that she hoped looked more convincing than it felt. Nyeda bowed her head and touched her heart in return.

The girl walked a few paces ahead of Elyth, though never directly in front of her. More like an honor guard than a guide. It was a twenty-minute walk along the curving paths from Elyth's quarters to the Paragon's complex, and they traveled the distance without further conversation. Elyth used that time to settle herself; she could find in her mind or heart no reason to fear the Paragon's attention. Undoubtedly the summons was connected to her recall. Strange that after all her longing for information, she should be anxious at the moment of revelation. But everything about the situation was strange.

The complex where the Paragon took audience and held council was separated from the rest of the Vaunt by a low wall, roughly waist-high to Elyth. It was more decorative than protective; the main entrance was circular and had neither doors nor guards. Even so, passing that barrier, Elyth felt the change as distinctly as if she had entered a sacred temple or the court of an emperor. There was a gravity to the place, an authority that emanated from its center and bore down on all who crossed its threshold. It was a place that demanded careful attention and wise action.

Elyth had been through that entryway many times before, but it felt now nearly as imposing as on her first day, when she had taken her oath in the Paragon's court, and that elder's ancient wisdom and cunning had nearly overwhelmed her. The main path curved gently through the complex's arboretum, but the beauty of the cultivated trees didn't relieve any of the tension she felt. And the closer they got to the court, the more self-concious she grew of her attire. It was hard enough to stand before the head of the House in crisp and spotless uniform; she felt now like she was attending a ceremony in her pajamas.

The stairs leading up to the court appeared around the bend, and Elyth inhaled deeply, prepared her mind to stand alone in the midst of that great hall. Now, however, Vrin led her past the court, continued on even past the council chamber, and took her farther back into the complex than Elyth had ever been. They came to a section yet again walled off from the rest, a small island unto itself, ringed by an eight-foot-tall wooden fence that prevented any view of what lay within. As Vrin unlatched the simple gate, Elyth realized she was being ushered into the Paragon's private residence.

She passed through the gate with wonder and trepidation, and once she'd crossed over, she stopped in spite of herself. Before her sat a simple structure amid the most well-cultivated garden Elyth had ever seen.

Others had spoken of the Paragon's garden, but witnessing it now with her own eyes, Elyth understood that she had never grasped its magnitude, no matter how well described. She allowed herself to take in the sweep of the place, felt the impact of its completeness taken all at once. Even the fragrance was delicately complex yet unified; fresh, clean, healthy.

The garden created a deep and abiding sense of rightness. The sense that here, within these walls, all things were as they should be. The effect was not lessened when Elyth focused on the individual details; the regal purple of an iris, the fairy-teardropped leaves of a delicate miniature frostoak. Even the blades of vibrant, low-cut grass gave an impression of an orderly regiment in uniform, standing at attention and waiting for inspection.

An Advocate of the Hand was crouched by one of the arrangements, deftly pruning a shapely juniper, her face hidden by a wide-brimmed hat. She didn't look up from her work or acknowledge Elyth's arrival, as was often the way of those of her Order. Elyth nearly complimented the Advocate on her masterwork but thought better of disturbing the hushed peace that hovered over the garden.

Instead she turned her attention to the building at the center. The structure was a single story, with a wide covered porch; its lines were pleasing and elegant, and reminded Elyth of a swallow's flight. And though it clearly had been constructed, it too seemed perfectly at home within the garden, almost as though it had grown from the ground alongside its natural companions. This, then, was the Paragon's home.

Even from the gate, Elyth could feel that ancient presence.

Vrin crossed the grounds to the porch, and Elyth followed wordlessly. There was nothing overtly menacing about the Paragon, but to stand before her was as if to stand before the jaws of some sleeping leviathan. In her midst, the raw power and potential for utter destruction bore down with the full weight of awe and dread.

When they reached the porch, instead of ascending the steps, Vrin simply turned toward the gardener with an expectant air. Elyth followed suit, assuming some custom or etiquette prevented them from entering the residence until the gardener had finished her work, or had departed. The gardening Advocate made another cut, then rocked back to evaluate her work. After a few seconds, seemingly content with the adjustment she'd made, she spoke.

"Thank you, Vrin," she said, her voice sharp with age, the edges of her syllables crackling with vivid energy. Elyth reflexively shivered at the sound. No mere gardener. The Paragon herself. "Go and prepare tea."

"Yes, Illumined Mother," Vrin answered, using the honorific. She turned and bowed to Elyth, then added a surreptitious nod of encouragement before slipping into the house.

"Elyth," the Paragon said without turning, "come here."

Elyth did as she was bade, crossing to the Paragon and standing just behind her, to one side. The Paragon bent forward to work for a few moments more. Elyth forced herself to relax, even as her mind wrestled with the incongruity of the scene before her. She had never seen the Paragon without her regalia, let alone working in the dirt with her own hands. From where she now stood, Elyth had the chance to admire the vital deftness of the Paragon's fingers, the delicate decisiveness with

which she worked at shaping the juniper; the ancient woman held utterly still while evaluating, but when she chose to act, she did so with
the bold efficiency of a sword stroke.

The Paragon trimmed a curving shoot from the juniper and caught
the clipping in her cupped palm, and then sat back and evaluated her
work once more. Apparently satisfied, she stood and finally looked at
Elyth. She was several inches shorter than Elyth and so had to tilt her
head back, farther than usual due to the brim of her hat. It was the first
time Elyth had ever looked down upon the Paragon. The power of the
older woman was in no way diminished; without thought Elyth bent
her knee before the great matriarch and bowed her head.

"Look at me," the Paragon said.

Elyth obeyed. For a span the Paragon's eyes studied Elyth's. It was
terrible to withstand that gaze, which seemed to peel back all masks and
pretense and to lay bare the innermost thoughts; Elyth felt utterly exposed, as though the Paragon might perceive secrets Elyth herself did
not know she kept. But there was a twinkle in those eyes as well, a light
amusement that somehow seemed to welcome and embrace her, even
in all that fear. The Paragon capped off that silent interrogation with a
tight smile.

"Elyth," she said. "Bright daughter."

"Illumined Mother," Elyth said, bowing her head once more.

"Come come," the Paragon said, "No need to stand on ceremony.
Or to kneel upon it either, as it were."

Elyth stood but kept her head bowed, feeling like a marionette on
strings too loose; she knew neither protocol nor etiquette for such a situation, and judged that a posture of waiting obedience was the safest of
all possible actions.

"How goes your time?" the Paragon asked.

"Very well, Your Radiance," Elyth answered.

"Rest is good? Mind is clear?"

"All is as it should be."

"And the longing?"

"Present, but diminishing."

"Very good," the Paragon said. She held out the gardening tool, a small pair of clippers, offering them to Elyth. "Take these, and do with them that which seems best to you."

It was a test, undoubtedly, though not one for which Elyth had ever been explicitly prepared. She took the clippers and turned her attention to the variety of plants before her.

"I fear I will only damage your great work," she said. "I have no skill in such cultivation."

"One cannot damage a living thing by pruning its edges, dear," said the Paragon. "It must bear the cut and flourish, or else the source of its life was badly misplaced. And such would not be the fault of the pruner."

Elyth took her time looking over each of the flowers, shrubs, vines, and trees that populated the area in front of her; nothing struck her as being out of place. She saw no cut she could make that would improve the form of anything, neither individually nor taken together as a whole. The seconds stretched to minutes, and Elyth felt a growing compulsion to make a cut anywhere, just to take action. But she knew there was a hidden purpose behind the moment and that both patience and careful observation were expected of Advocates of the Voice. The Paragon would not mistake patience for hesitance, nor would she confuse action for purpose. Elyth felt it was the limits of her perception that were being tested.

Unable to find any obvious form in need of correction, she began to think inaction was precisely the right choice. But before she committed to that thought, she changed her approach. If she couldn't find anything out of place now . . . and with the change in mind-set and a few moments more of careful attention, an opportunity revealed itself. The grain of a young branch on one of the miniature frostoaks ran with a twist toward its end. And now that she'd seen it, Elyth didn't waste time evaluating whether or not her judgment was correct. She stepped forward, took the slender branch between the fingers of one hand, and made a quick diagonal cut where the grain ran true, cutting free a six-inch segment that represented about a third of the total branch. Elyth returned to her place by the Paragon's side and awaited judgment, holding out both the tool and the cutting before her, a priestess bringing her sacrifice before a goddess.

The Paragon looked over the branch in Elyth's hand, then to the tree from which it had come, then to Elyth herself.

"Why this fellow?" she asked.

"It appeared to my mind that left to grow, its twist would introduce an unpleasant shape in conflict with the rest."

"But you have upset the symmetry," the Paragon responded, her tone flat and her expression neutral. "And now the gap has widened between its neighbor."

Neither of these factors had escaped Elyth's notice, but she accepted the mild rebuke without excuse.

"My apologies, Illumined Mother," she said. "I felt the single cut was sufficient, and the disturbance temporary."

The Paragon held her gaze for a few moments longer before her eyes crinkled at the corners in some wisp of amusement or pleasure.

"You have more skill than you credit to yourself," she said, taking the shears from Elyth's hand. "I know of few who would have noticed such a detail, and too many who would have felt compelled to prune the whole tree."

Elyth bowed her head in acknowledgment, a mild response to receive the compliment without letting it stir her pride. It was difficult; praise from the Paragon was rare and greatly valued.

"And the cutting?" Elyth asked.

"Keep it," the Paragon said. "A memento of our coming conversation. Come. Sit with me."

Elyth followed the Paragon to the residence, but instead of entering as she expected, the Paragon climbed the stairs and then turned and sat on the porch. She removed her hat and laid it beside her. Elyth, once again uncertain of how to proceed, stood on the lowest step. The Paragon patted the porch next to her. Elyth had no idea what to make of the invitation or the sudden familiarity, but she obeyed, sitting carefully beside the woman without touching her. The proximity and the casual posture made her feel as though she were violating some sacred ritual.

"Oh, do relax," the Paragon said in the Low Language, a manner of speech Elyth had never heard issuing from that exalted woman. "I leave all the tiresome courtly expectations beyond these walls. Even your so-called Great Mother needs a place where she can just be an old woman with a garden."

Elyth made an involuntary noise at the statement, something between a note of surprise and a chuckle.

"Does this upset you?" the Paragon asked. "To see your Mother in such a light?"

Elyth shook her head. "No, Illumined Mother."

"Go on," the Paragon said. "Speak your thoughts. Without your usual calculation."

"It's just that . . . of course I knew of your magnificent garden, but I did not realize you yourself were the gardener."

"Yes, well, we mustn't spend all our time in the heavens, dear," the Paragon answered, "lest we forget our place here among the dust."

As she was speaking Vrin came out of the house with a tray, upon which were two bowl-like stone mugs, wide and without handle, with a pot crafted of the same stone set between.

"Just place them here by me," the Paragon said. "And then I would like for you to study in the Library for a time. An hour or so should be sufficient."

"Yes, Illumined Mother," Vrin answered with a bow. She set down the tray, and then departed through the front gate. The Paragon watched her as she went, and did not speak until several moments after the girl had closed the gate behind her.

"A fine Aspirant of the Mind," the Paragon said. "She has a kindness of heart that cannot be taught. Indulgent of me, perhaps, to keep her for myself. But her service and loyalty are pure."

She turned to the tray and poured tea into both mugs, and then turned back and handed one to Elyth. Elyth laid the cutting from the frostoak on her lap and accepted the tea with both hands as etiquette required. The tea was sea-deep green, and its fragrance rose as incense, its edges crisp and fresh like snow on pines but with a subtle hint of smoke behind. Elyth was struck with an impression of mist in moonlight, clinging low to the forest floor.

The Paragon raised her drink in a wordless toast, which Elyth returned, and together they sipped. After she'd partaken of her tea, the Paragon rested her hands in her lap with the tea bowl balanced lightly on her fingers, and for a time gazed at the steam rising from it. Elyth let her eyes linger on the elder woman's effortless splendor and grace. Even in her simple attire, with her gray hair damp and mussed and thin in spots, she was magnificent. Magnificent in a way that was perhaps even enhanced by the raw humanity she now displayed. Truly she was the very incarnation of *sareth hanaan*, the high art of the House.

Some called it the Way, others the Path, others still any number of sacred-tinged designations. To outsiders it was a mystical power to be feared, or an outdated code of conduct to be mocked. But none of these captured the essence of *sareth hanaan* as Elyth understood it, nor as the Paragon embodied it. In truth, it meant simply "the quiet action of one who endures." But it spoke of many things: the subtle shift of stance that deters attack; the patient forbearance of a lone mountain against which the surging sea endlessly breaks and then retreats; the gentle word of truth, perfectly timed, that topples a tyrant. The Paragon was all these things and more; a great stillness in swirling chaos, a lightning strike upon a fortress of oppression.

None had endured longer nor taken more effective subtle action than the ancient matriarch of the First House of the Ascendance. To see her now not in her splendid attire but in the work clothes of a servant crystallized for Elyth what the complete mastery of *sareth hanaan* looked like. And highlighted just how much more she still had to learn.

"Take a breath, child," the Paragon said. "Your anxiety is spilling over, and it is misplaced."

Elyth did as she was bade.

"My apologies, Illumined Mother," she said. "I have not been able to quiet my questions about my recall from Revik."

"I didn't say it was wrong. Only misplaced. Your operation on Revik was both just and flawlessly executed. But a matter has arisen that requires immediate attention. I had hoped to spare you the need for recovery. Even now, I have given you all the time we can, brief as it has been. I fear the strain on you may be too great. But our need for you is greater still."

One heaviness fell away from Elyth with the scant explanation, only to be replaced by another. The relief she felt at learning she hadn't killed an innocent world barely registered; she'd never before heard of a circumstance so dire as to cut short an Advocate's recovery.

The Paragon sipped her tea, pursed her lips slightly. She shook her head almost imperceptibly as she brought the bowl back to her lap.

"That which is now unfolding has many beginnings," she said. "And though the threads have begun to intertwine, it is beyond the skill of this House to see yet what they will form once they are drawn fully together."

Elyth noticed the narrowing of the Paragon's eyes and the pursing of her lips, and realized she was seeing yet another thing that she'd never before witnessed nor imagined possible in the ancient matriarch. Uncertainty.

"The beginning of beginnings, I suppose," the Paragon said, and she flashed a tight smile. "Let us cover ground that is familiar to us both, and perhaps we will together find our way to the right place. Tell me, daughter, upon what foundation is our House built?"

"Our House stands on the word alone," Elyth replied reflexively; the traditional question and answer had been engraved on her mind and heart since her first day as an Aspirant.

"And tell me now, what does that *mean*?"

A response to that question was neither quick nor easy, made all the more challenging by the essence of the asker, as though a star had asked her to explain the nature of light.

Elyth thought carefully, chose her words with precision.

"The authority of the First House is rooted in the Deep Language," she said. "Apart from it, no amount of wisdom, cunning, or skill is sufficient for us to stand."

"Indeed," the Paragon replied, "our House cannot exist without the Deep Language. That, however, is not true in reverse. The Deep Language exists of its own accord; it is there, in the very fabric of the universe. We merely discovered it. Our ability to speak it, however, could be considered something of a technology. And the truth of its concepts undergirds the Ascendance's greatest of all technologies."

"The Language," Elyth said.

The Paragon nodded her head as she drank her tea.

"The Language," she continued a moment later. "Built upon the foundation laid by the Deep. Expanded, yes, and greatly diluted. But one cannot fully disentangle the formal High or the vulgar Low from the underlying power of the Deep. And as with any technology, it can be wielded as a tool for creation or a weapon of destruction."

Elyth was intimately aware of this truth; it was the thoughtless misuse of the Language, or its purposeful abuse, that made necessary her work. The poison of its corrupting influence seeping into the material substrate of a world, until all hope of recovery was lost. And it was why knowledge of the Deep Language was so closely guarded, and its use so tightly controlled.

The Paragon held up a finger and said, "This connection between the common Language and the Deep is one beginning. For another, tell me, how has the Ascendance maintained the stability of its governance across so many worlds, for so many millennia?"

"Undoubtedly because of the great wisdom and benevolence of the Grand Council," Elyth answered dryly. Her intent was not lost on the Paragon; the elder woman dipped her head to acknowledge Elyth's polite response, but the mild smirk encouraged Elyth to speak more honestly.

"The constant tension between the Grand Council, the Hezra, and the First House," Elyth said. "And the structure's capacity for self-correction."

The Paragon nodded, deepened the response.

"The Hezra," she said, holding up her right hand, "and the First House." She held up her left. "These are the two hands with which the Grand Council rules. Justice, mercy; law, culture; knowledge, wisdom. An eye turned outward to the horizon; another turned inward to the soul.

"The authority and the power of the Ascendance. Stability rests not in either side of these pairings alone, but rather in the active mediation between them. History instructs us that it is the judgment of the Grand Council, balanced between this House and our siblings within the

Hezra, that has brought such peace and prosperity to our vast citizenry. Though, of course, my nature tempts me to believe the House alone could rule, and be sufficient.

"I would be a fool indeed to deny such temptation exists, in myself as much as in others," she said, and then held up two fingers. "This constant struggle for balance within our hierarchy is a second beginning.

"And for a third, tell me what you know of the Markovian Strain."

"Only the basics, Your Radiance," Elyth answered.

The Paragon nodded. "Before your time, by a few centuries. But speak of what you know."

Elyth dredged up the memories of lessons learned long ago, from her days of study as an Aspirant. And now, as when she'd first learned of it, the account seemed distant, all dry fact with no life or blood.

"Markov was a mild world, agriculturally oriented," she said. "It became the source of a potent strain of corrupted Language. The Hezra botched the quarantine and allowed it to spread to neighboring worlds via known trade routes. The end result was seven worlds lost before it could be contained.

"The loss of so many worlds in such a short period of time led to instability within the Ascendance hierarchy, and raised questions among the citizens about its effectiveness."

"Oh no, dear, not about its effectiveness," the Paragon said. "Never about its effectiveness. That was demonstrated quite clearly for all to see."

Truly. The Markovian Strain had been finally eradicated only by the Hezra's fearful Contingency. It was an innocuous term that, Elyth surmised, made it possible to discuss the act clinically without confronting the horror its reality evoked. Or at least should have evoked.

Elyth's technique for planet killing was a terrible outcome, but it was at least a natural death—akin to putting a suffering animal to gentle sleep before causing its heart to stop.

The Contingency was its polar opposite—a violent planetary destruction, a dissolution at the subatomic level. There was no concealing its effects, nor its cause. It had not been used since.

"It did give rise to our own Eye," the Paragon continued, speaking of the House's private intelligence services. "The incident caused a rift between the Hezra and our House that has never fully healed."

"The Hezra failed in its duties," Elyth said. "The hierarchy should not resent the assistance we provide."

"If only we were all so rational, yes? But we mustn't judge the Hezra too harshly, dear. The official records do them less justice than they deserve; they bear the scar of a necessary fiction, for the good of the Ascendance." And here she held up three fingers, finishing the count. "This Strain is a third beginning."

The Great Mother paused for a moment to sip her tea before continuing.

"The spread of the Markovian Strain due to ineffective quarantine is not necessarily false," the Paragon continued. "But it is assuredly not the whole truth. What do you know of the man Varen Fedic?"

Elyth remained silent for a few moments, collecting scattered fragments of thought and emotion that her mind associated with the name. Facts were few, but the impression was of something twisted, malevolent. A carnivore's smile.

"A tyrant," Elyth answered. "The source of the Markovian Strain. And a would-be mythmaker. The so-called First Speaker."

"Mmm," the Paragon hummed, a noncommittal sound. "An understatement, on two counts. Our official accounts mark him as a footnote, merely a man of charisma who led many astray. But in truth, his malevolence cannot be exaggerated. He was a man utterly corrupted. Which is what necessitated his complete and utter destruction. The Hezra was willing to annihilate multiple planets just to ensure every trace of him was erased.

"His adopted name of First Speaker was true in a sense . . . He was the first to speak his particular falsehoods, and with them he dominated the minds of many. Unfortunately, they shared his fate.

"The simplest explanation for the Strain's spread, of course, is that a handful of his followers escaped Markov and sowed the seeds of his teachings elsewhere. That's why it's the official story. It is our nature to prefer simplicity over complexity, regardless of which holds more of the truth.

"The broken containment theory was, however, plausibly the case on only three of the worlds, and the evidence there is fragile at best. To this day we do not completely grasp the exact mechanism by which the Strain spread to the others. But we know enough."

The Paragon took another sip of tea, and then set the bowl back on the tray at her side before continuing.

"I brought you here because that which must be said cannot be spoken in our halls."

She turned and fixed Elyth with her paralyzing gaze, and uttered a phrase in the Deep Language. "*A stone in the river, stanching the flow. You shall not speak of it.*"

The declaration washed through Elyth like a warm surge of sea, followed by a sharp tingle, as though a strong memory had been suddenly awakened by a familiar scent.

"I trust your silence," the Paragon added.

Elyth could not find an adequate response, and there was no need to acknowledge consent; the Paragon's powerful words bound her speech, whether Elyth desired it or not. She merely bowed her head in acceptance.

"As you said, Varen Fedic was the original source of the Strain," the Paragon said. "His thought-line was unique, his use of the Language truly novel . . . and so potent, its tendrils shifted reality. His speech didn't just seep into the substrate of Markov. It infected the fabric of the cosmos and distorted the minds of citizens separated by millions of miles of open space."

The very notion should have been impossible, and if anyone other than the Paragon had uttered those words, Elyth would have scoffed. She had devoted her life to studying the secret art and science of the Deep Language under the tutelage of its greatest masters, and she could never have projected power in such a manner. Even the Paragon herself could not exert that magnitude of influence over the material of the universe; it wouldn't tolerate it.

"I know your mind is struggling to accept the fact," the Paragon continued. "It violates all you have been taught. But the evidence is irrefutable. Fedic's particular speech patterns emerged spontaneously in four locations." She held up four fingers and counted them off in turn as she named the worlds. "Markov, where he was present. Ovon, Eblios, Yuralia, where he was not. The latter three had no contact with Markov. And the others we lost—Forna, Haltios, Ven . . . well. Their connections to Markov are tenuous, at best. In the end, their fate is irrelevant. Whether it was three planets or six that were corrupted across space, we know that one man's black speech cost the Ascendance seven precious worlds."

There was no point in questioning the truth of the Paragon's revelation, regardless of how difficult it was to believe. All that remained was its relevance.

"And all of this . . ." Elyth said, "leads me to some purpose here?"

"Our Eye has fallen on the planet Qel," the Paragon answered. "Something in it has changed. We fear the Markovian Strain has re-emerged."

The gravity of the Paragon's tone carried a force that her words alone failed to deliver. It was as though she was claiming some ancient dragon from a fairy tale had reawakened. A terrifying thought, perhaps, if only anyone believed in dragons.

But the intensity of her look showed she did very much believe.

"I'm sorry, Illumined Mother, I don't understand how that could be possible."

"Neither do we, exactly. Which is what makes Qel so gravely concerning. I know it's challenging to believe. And we must hope that we are wrong. But given the Strain's destructive potential, even if probabilities are very low, it is a danger we must take very seriously indeed."

"And Qel?" Elyth said. "I hadn't heard it was under quarantine."

"It isn't," the Paragon said.

"I don't understand."

"The balance of which I spoke, that between our House and the Hezra. It has been upset by their recent troubles. The Hezra's setbacks have put it on an awkward footing, and made them understandably paranoid about our motives. And they are anxious now for a victory, to reassert themselves within the Ascendance."

"You don't trust them," Elyth said.

The old woman smiled thinly.

"The games between the Grand Council, the Hezra, and our House have a long history, as all shared power must," she said. "And it's a delicate time, Elyth. Their outward focus is necessary, but I fear it may be blinding them to what lies within."

"Or you suspect they're ignoring what lies within for some hidden purpose."

"A possibility that must be considered, in light of their circumstances."

Elyth had only a general sense of the Hezra's decline. Though the Ascendance had long ago mastered interstellar travel, it had not yet extended its reach beyond the borders of the galaxy. This was the destiny of humanity, and the grand mission with which the Hezra had been charged. And though the organization had a program devoted to developing the means to traverse the space between galaxies, thus far they'd made no progress in the endeavor. As a result, the Hezra's standing within the Ascendance had suffered, its influence waned.

Nevertheless, the Hezra remained the sole authority in determining the fate of worlds. If Qel were indeed a threat, it was the Hezra's place to judge it so. Surely the Paragon was not suggesting that Elyth undertake a mission to put a planet down that had not yet been judged according to law?

"Illumined Mother," Elyth said carefully. "I have missed your intent. I see that you wish for me to travel to Qel, but I have not discerned what you would have me do there."

"It is because I am uncertain myself," the Paragon replied. She motioned lightly to the cutting lying in Elyth's lap. "Qel is the twisting branch of our civilization. And it is growing more rapidly than any I have seen in an age. Few see the true danger. By the time the others waken to it, I fear the effects will have spread. But in this matter I cannot see the way forward. Not yet. I need someone I can trust, Elyth, to go learn what is at work within that world, someone whose perception is keen and whose judgment is sound. I need someone I can trust to walk the way even when she cannot see it."

As she spoke, the old woman laid her hand on Elyth's arm; Elyth's heart swelled with warmth even as the words triggered surprise. She had never imagined that the Paragon might have more than a cursory knowledge of who she was. The Paragon smiled again, undoubtedly having read Elyth's reaction. She leaned forward, and her lowered voice exuded a kindness Elyth didn't know the ancient woman possessed.

"I've always had a special fondness for you, bright daughter," she said. "From a time even before your welcome to our House. If my personal preferences had been the only consideration, I would have had you as my own Advocate of the Mind."

Elyth blinked at the revelation. The Mind served the Paragon directly and governed the actions of the entire House. Its need for members was small, and as such, service to the Mind was the most selective. Elyth had never been told the possibility had existed for her.

"Illumined Mother," Elyth said. "You honor me." She nearly said more but hesitated, uncertain whether her unasked question would be appropriate, though her curiosity at what failing had prevented her selection itched in her mind.

The Paragon patted her arm and sat back with a chuckle, perceiving the question anyway. "I let you go because I knew it would drive you mad, dear. To be cooped up here, when there was so much possibility out there. You would have excelled, of that I have no doubt. But you would have resented me, in the end." She held up a hand before Elyth could take offense. "Not that you would've shown it, of course. It merely would have been selfish of me. You were created for more. There is a term rarely uttered within our House, Elyth, one even you have likely never heard . . . but of our many excellent Advocates, you are among the few I would call 'Guided by the True Star.'"

Once more, the power of the Deep Language washed through Elyth. She had seen the phrase, written in the annals of the House, read the legacies of the Advocates to whom it had been applied. The towering heroes of their order. But she had never heard the words spoken aloud.

It was no formal rite of the First House; it was an ancient title, spoken in the tongue that would transmit its meaning through more than mere words. For a brief instant, Elyth saw herself with the Paragon's eyes, felt herself moved by the matriarch's own emotions. The profound depth of love and respect seemed boundless, far beyond anything Elyth could have ever imagined of herself. Guided by the True Star. One who followed the highest way.

Elyth dipped her head, embarrassed at the magnitude of praise, ashamed of the pride it awakened but unable to dismiss it, even as the immediate power faded.

"Anything I am, the House has made me," she answered.

"Yes, well," the Paragon said, standing and gazing out over her garden. "For that I will happily take credit. There is no shame in seeing clearly the good in one's work."

Elyth set her tea on the porch and took the frostoak branch in her hand, then rose to her feet and descended two steps so that she could stand lower than the Paragon.

"These things we know," the Paragon said. "The Language is powerful. Someone is abusing it. And we cannot trust the Hezra. Beyond that, many possibilities open before us.

"Our House has many capable Advocates, but there are few among them who genuinely understand and embrace the intent of our way. All can recite the doctrine; many practice it. But a precious few have attained the ability to embody it, and fewer still manage it in the midst of chaos. It is in the Voice that you excel, Elyth. But you could have found a place in the Eye, or the Hand, or here in the Mind. I am not blind to your shortcomings, and I don't know what you will find on Qel. One final thing I know, however, is that there is none better in our House to undertake this ordeal."

"When do I leave?" Elyth asked.

The Paragon returned her attention to Elyth.

"A Hezra vessel is departing in the morning for the Basho system; they've graciously allowed one of our Advocates of the Hand to take passage for a diplomatic mission to those planets. That should put you within range of Qel."

Elyth reacted; traveling on a Hezra ship seemed like precisely the wrong way to avoid their attention.

"We couldn't secure transport some other way?"

The Paragon smiled.

"A gentle poke, to see if it stirs the bear," she answered.

"But you're confident they'll believe the cover?"

"Presumably, no. I would expect them to treat you as though you're an Advocate of the Eye. But we've given them no reason to suspect our attention is on Qel in particular. And they have nothing to fear unless they have something to hide. It will be useful to observe their reaction to you."

The Paragon smiled again and placed a hand on Elyth's shoulder.

"I'm sorry that you will not be able to complete your full time of recovery. It's a mistake, I'm certain, but one that circumstance demands. And one you will overcome, I hope."

"It is well, Your Radiance. Whatever the House requires, I am its hands."

"Your assignment is secret, known only to me. I will send for you at dawn. Make whatever preparations you need, but speak of this to no one. Once you arrive on Qel, we'll see what steps lie next before us."

"Yes, Illumined Mother."

The Paragon laid her hand gently atop Elyth's head.

"*Sareth hanaan* be your guide, bright daughter," she said.

"*Sareth hanaan* be my way," Elyth answered, the traditional response.

After the Paragon removed her hand, Elyth bowed and then made her way to the front gate. Questions and uncertainties frenzied her mind; the weight of revelation and expectation bore down upon her shoulders. But such burdens were hers to endure for the sake of First House, and for the Ascendance. As she walked back through the Vaunt, Elyth acknowledged her fears, allowed them to wash over her and beyond, and then focused her thoughts on preparing herself for the unknown and unknowable fate that dawn would bring.

THREE

As promised, the summons arrived with the first rays of the sun; both found Elyth ready and waiting. Nyeda had again sat watch throughout the night. While Elyth had silently prepared her gear for another assignment, the elder Advocate had made no inquiry about the unprecedented breach of the recovery protocol. Only when Vrin reappeared at the door did Nyeda allow her eyes to ask the question she would not speak.

"Thank you, Nyeda," Elyth said, embracing her. It was all she could say.

"Be well, Elyth," Nyeda replied, returning the embrace.

Of all those in First House, it was the Advocates of the Voice who best understood the need for discretion; their comings and goings were often sudden and unexplained. That didn't make it any easier to accept that a departure offered no guarantee of a return. Elyth had lost many sisters in her time, without warning, without discussion, without closure. Their names were recorded, but never their fates. Few outside the Order of the Voice better understood the naive assumption of immortality hidden in a casual "See you tomorrow."

Elyth and Nyeda separated, but held hands briefly as each looked upon the other's face, fixing in their minds the shared moment. And then Elyth turned, took up her pack, and followed Vrin out into the corridor.

It wasn't until they were outside that they spoke, and then only with voices lowered.

"The Hezra have sent a shuttle," Vrin said. "It should be arriving at the eastern gate shortly."

She handed Elyth a small device, a tangle interpreter: black, rectangular, roughly the size of her forefinger. Elyth accepted it, evaluated it.

"The Paragon?" she asked.

Vrin nodded. The interpreter had a twin, and that was in the keeping of the Paragon herself. As a pair, the devices enabled instant communication across any distance, encrypted with unbreakable codes. Even the Hezra's fearsome signals intelligence arm could do nothing to decode the messages; mere interception would immediately alert both devices and cause them to switch encryption schemes.

Never before had Elyth been granted a direct channel to the Paragon. Now, if she understood the intent behind the interpreter, it seemed that the Paragon would be her only channel. She secured the device in a slender pocket on her vest.

"Is it activated?" she asked.

Vrin shook her head. "It will activate when the Paragon sees fit. That is all I know."

"I assume the usual protocols remain," Elyth said.

"It would be my assumption as well," Vrin replied. "But only that. My instructions were to deliver the interpreter and escort you to the shuttle. I know nothing more."

Elyth nodded, and the two walked the rest of the way in silence.

The shuttle was waiting when they arrived, humming quietly as it hovered a foot above the ground. A young noncommissioned officer of the Hezra stood beside it, his hallmark crimson-and-black uniform as neat and seemingly rigid as his stance, as though both the man and the outfit had been chiseled from a single multicolored stone. When Elyth approached, the officer made no direct acknowledgment of her, but pivoted on his heel like a clockwork doll. The side panel of the shuttle slid open to accept her, revealing an empty four-seat compartment. Elyth nodded to the officer as she passed; he did not respond, not even by meeting her eye. But Elyth noted the tiny beads of sweat that had formed on his forehead, where his hat met his skin, and she allowed herself an inward smile.

Hezra personnel were legendary for their remarkable self-control. It was easy to confuse their discipline for disdain; it was equally easy for them to conceal disdain under the guise of discipline. In this case, at least, Elyth saw the marks of the young officer's awe and fear of her, but nothing of contempt. As much of a welcome as she was likely to receive. She glanced at the insignia on his uniform: a lance corporal in 3 Reconnaissance, one of the Hezra's quietest special operations forces.

"Thank you for your courtesy, Lance Corporal," she said as she climbed into the compartment. She sat and looked to him. "I have a better appreciation of your unit's nickname now."

He almost suppressed the reaction, but the tightening of his lips and the flush of his cheeks suggested the compliment met its mark. Troopers in 3 Recon were informally known as "The Fear-Eaters," and the young man had done a good job of swallowing his.

Elyth turned to address Vrin.

"*Sareth hanaan* be your guide, favored one," Elyth said.

Vrin bowed her head and answered, "Your way be my way." The door panel closed and Vrin did not raise her head as the shuttle lifted smoothly off.

Elyth barely felt the acceleration as the Vaunt dwindled behind her to miniature, until the green of its grounds were at last swallowed by the gray-brown of the surrounding urban sprawl. Soon details were lost to distance, and shortly after they left the last traces of atmosphere behind. The journey to the orbital docking station took roughly half an hour; Elyth had visited it countless times over the years, but the approach never failed to impress upon her the Hezra's mastery of discipline and order. Vessels of varying sizes arrived, departed, and orbited the spherical structure with a beautiful complexity, a corona of ships swirling around the megastructure. From a distance the intricacy of movement could almost be mistaken for a living thing, but Elyth knew each and every ship was exactly where it was meant to be, following some strict formula of precise navigation.

Two capital ships were in dock, twin titans standing watch over the rest of the traffic made insignificant by comparison. Elyth recognized one as Herald class, the Hezra's fearsome vanguard cruiser and the backbone of any blockade force. The ship carried an ominous weight in Elyth's eyes, despite its otherwise sleek, elegant appearance; like the relaxed musculature of a tiger sleeping, with its raw power resting within. She knew the Herald class for what it was—the linchpin weapon for the Contingency.

The shuttle followed its course toward the station, but rolled and angled before it reached a dock. Instead, they approached another vessel of moderate size whose design Elyth didn't recognize. It was an order of magnitude larger than the shuttle, and would have been impressive to behold had it not been in the presence of the Herald class.

When the shuttle arrived and was fully settled, Elyth found another Hezra officer awaiting her in the hangar. He greeted her politely and professionally, but spoke nothing more as he escorted her to the bridge of the vessel. The corridors were narrow, barely wide enough for two to pass without brushing shoulders. Curiously, they met no other personnel on the route. The walk was short, however, and the door to the bridge was open. As they approached, Elyth could hear a conversation taking place within.

"—cleared to get under way at our discretion," a deep voice was saying. "We're all accounted for?"

"Aye, Captain. All stands ready," answered a younger man's voice. "We can disembark as soon as that gray witch shows up."

The last word was hanging in the air when Elyth reached the entrance, and she easily identified the one who had been speaking. Though his back was to her, she could see in his posture how he reacted to the sudden stillness of the room, and the dread upon him as he turned to find her standing there.

"Esteemed Advocate," he said after a moment, a smile without warmth oozing across his face. A first lieutenant, young and proud by the look of him. His bearing suggested a level of entitlement to the position; one who had earned his commission through family connections rather than service, Elyth estimated. She held her place by the entrance, remaining in the corridor for the moment, while her escort stood at her side trying to fade into the background. The lieutenant took a tentative step forward, but then seemed to think better of it.

"Welcome aboard the *Helegoss*," he continued. "It's truly our honor to host a . . . dignitary from First House."

Elyth wouldn't pretend she hadn't heard what he'd said, but neither did she wish to further the man's humiliation in front of his peers. She simply offered a nod to accept his welcome and then directed her attention to the ranking officer, whom she picked out with ease.

"Permission to enter, sir?" she said.

"Of course, Advocate," the captain answered.

Elyth crossed the threshold and stepped onto the bridge, then waited patiently to one side of the door.

"We'll be leaving dock shortly," the lieutenant said, unnecessarily; his tone was cloyingly eager. "We're basically ready to go, and anxious to get under way. We certainly don't want to cause any delay in your undoubtedly important errand."

Elyth did not take her eyes from the captain of the vessel.

"Lieutenant," the captain finally said.

"Sir," the lieutenant answered.

"You're dismissed."

A span of a complete breath passed before the young officer responded.

"Yes sir," he finally said. He slid out with his gaze lowered just enough to avoid making eye contact with anyone as he went.

The bridge remained silent until the lieutenant had fully departed. Elyth herself was at ease, quietly composed; the ship's personnel all seemed paralyzed, as if any movement might draw attention best avoided.

"I'm Captain Jenzet," the captain said at last, placing his hand over his heart and dipping his head in greeting. The shallowness of his bow wasn't quite disrespectful, but left no doubt about his opinion of having been required to take her on board. "My ship is at the service of the First House."

Elyth bowed in response, the perfect model of etiquette and respect. The captain waited briefly for her to reply, but it was understood that an Advocate of First House would offer her name only if and when she deemed it appropriate. It was not a thing to be expected or requested.

Her mere presence seemed to put even the captain off-balance. He was a formidable man, both tall and powerfully built, and he bore his authority well. Undoubtedly, there were few people he had encountered who had not been intimidated by his stature and projection of power. But Elyth had touched infinity, and he was just a man.

"We, uh . . ." he said at last. "We've made a cabin available for you."

"Thank you for your service," Elyth responded. "How long do you expect travel to take?"

"About eighteen hours to clear the horizon on this side," the captain answered. "Twice that on the other end to reach your point of departure."

"Very good. I'll remain in my quarters until we're positioned for launch."

"There's no need to isolate yourself on our account, Advocate. You're welcome to dine with me, or in the officers' mess—"

"Thank you, Captain, but I'll not disrupt your good order further than I already have. I'm aware of the burden I create for you and your crew."

Elyth held his gaze, saw the conflict in his expression; the desire to present a facade of friendship and welcome mingled with relief at the idea of having her hidden away.

"As you'll have it," he said with another bow, this time inching closer to respect.

"If you can spare someone to direct me there, I'll get out of your way now. I'm sure you have plenty else to concern yourself with."

"Certainly." He motioned to his executive officer, a woman about Elyth's age and a commander by rank. The woman nodded and approached Elyth.

"But if there's anything you need," the captain added, "don't hesitate to ask. Commander Adura is available to you at any time."

Elyth bowed again, and turned to the commander.

"If you'll follow me, Advocate," Adura said, the smile on her face subdued but genuine.

Elyth followed her out into the corridor and to the nearest elevator. Once they entered the elevator and the door had closed, the commander spoke without looking at Elyth.

"Some of the crew might resent having you aboard," she said. "But the sentiment isn't universal. Many of us consider it an honor to host an Advocate of the House, however trivial our service to her may be."

"Thank you, Commander," Elyth said. "But we are all equals in our service to the Ascendance."

"Of course," the commander replied.

The commander's demeanor remained professional, but Elyth sensed an openness in the woman; a genuine respect for First House, and no small amount of curiosity. As slight of an advantage as it was, Elyth seized the opportunity with the subtlest influence.

"*Vine and branch, kindred souls intertwine*," she said in the Deep Language, her words concealed within an exhale. Adura made no outward sign of the effect settling over her—an indication that Elyth had read her correctly, and that the commander was neither aware of nor resistant to the influence. A mild loosening of the tongue, a nudge in the direction of trust, when the inclination was already there.

A moment later, Elyth spoke in the Low Language, making what would appear to be small talk.

"I have great respect for 3 Reconnaissance, and all who support them," she said. "Do you serve with them regularly?"

Adura nodded. "We're permanently attached to the Fear-Eaters. The *Helegoss* is classified as a swift transport vessel, so we cart them all over the place. And not always just on training ops, either."

"Crew is used to discretion then, I imagine."

"Quite."

"And the *Helegoss* itself . . . I don't believe I've had the pleasure of traveling on a ship of its design."

"She's actually an older vessel. Old enough to have been retired, in fact, but Command decided to upfit her instead."

"A noble history?"

"Not that anyone can talk about," Adura said with a smile. "If I had to guess, though, I'd wager our little excursion around the Basho system is to put her through her paces and see if she's still up to task."

The commander paused after she spoke, and then shook her head to herself.

"Sorry, I don't know why I'm rambling. I'm sure it's no matter to you."

"On the contrary; it is rare for one of my order to witness firsthand the mighty Hezra in action."

The elevator reached the destination deck and the door slid open. Adura held out a hand to usher Elyth into the corridor.

"Just a couple of doors down to the right," she said. This section of the deck appeared to be officers' quarters, though the doors on both sides were all closed, and no one else was in sight.

"It's quieter than I'd expected," Elyth said.

"We're not running a full crew for this outing," Adura replied. "And everyone's either at station or in their quarters. Captain thought it'd be best not to have too much traffic while you were getting situated."

"For my sake, or his?"

"Both, I suspect. Though his share more than yours, I imagine." They stopped four cabins down from the elevator, and the door slid open to admit them. "This one's yours for the duration. I'm afraid it's not much."

The quarters were only as large as absolutely necessary for the facilities provided: a bunk bed, a small desk with a chair, a private bathroom that was nearly standing room only. The bunk suggested it typically housed two, which made Elyth aware of how much trouble they'd gone to on her account.

"It's more than sufficient," Elyth answered. "Please share my gratitude with your crew."

"You're familiar with all the usual controls?" Adura asked.

"I am. If you'd be kind enough to alert me when I have two hours before launch, I'd be grateful. Otherwise, I'd prefer not to be disturbed."

"Of course, Advocate. I'll see to it personally. If anything should come up, you can contact me directly through the ship's system. But if not, well, I suppose I'll see you in a couple of days."

"Thank you, Commander."

Adura bowed and departed. Elyth watched her as she went. After the commander had gone several feet down the corridor, she hitched a step and hesitated briefly, as though she'd just remembered something. The effects of the Deep Language burning off, though she would never identify it as such. But Adura shook her head once, and then continued on without looking back.

Left alone, Elyth surveyed her quarters once more, and then took care of her first order of business—securing them. From her pack, she removed a sensor about the size of her palm and performed a sweep of the cabin. As expected, she located two active surveillance devices in somewhat obvious locations. And a third, passive one, subtler in design and placement. A fine attempt. She couldn't fault the Hezra, really. Undoubtedly, they were as unsure about her as she was about them.

With the devices identified, she placed the sensor on the desk and activated its countermeasures, effectively isolating the cabin. With that done, she set to unloading her pack.

She removed everything from her pack and arranged it all on the lower bunk, laid out in a pattern refined over many years, so that she could see it all in one glance and know immediately if anything was out of place or missing.

One thing she didn't have a usual place for, however, was the frostoak cutting she'd brought along. She hadn't taken it with any specific intent; it had been the last thing she'd packed, and that at a whim. But at the time it had seemed right to bring it, and that had been enough. Its tiny leaves had already wilted and curled. She rolled the thin branch between her thumb and fingers briefly, felt its texture, remembered how it had looked before she had trimmed it from its source, and the Paragon's words that tied it to Qel. After a moment, she laid it on the thin mattress next to the tangle interpreter. Together, in her mind, they represented her purpose: to go, to observe, to report. And, should it prove necessary, to act.

When all was arranged as she liked it, she took out her personal data terminal, placed it on the desk in preparation for her preliminary research on her target. Before she settled in to her work, the sounds of the ship undocking rolled through like deep, distant thunder. And now her mission was truly under way.

Her brief discussion with the commander had given her a few details to consider; the skeleton crew, the deployment of 3 Recon, the apparent training designation of their operation. And Adura's suggestion that the whole trip was an exercise to test out the vessel itself. Nothing stood out to her immediately, but Elyth knew that the Paragon had placed her on the ship for a reason, and she mentally filed the details away in case greater relevance might later emerge.

The political games between the Hezra, First House, and the Grand Council were constant and many-layered. And though Elyth could never fully discern everything that was at play, she at least tried to be aware of the pieces. Particularly knowing that she herself was one.

She accessed her terminal and began her initial evaluation of Qel with a process of environmental scanning; a high-level survey to identify the current state of the world, touching local governmental structure, economy, geography, demographics, climate. Though the basic structure of Ascendance society was the same throughout the galaxy, every world had its own personality. As she studied, she allowed the data to merge and coalesce into a single overarching impression, a mental model of Qel as a whole. It was not unlike her time in the Paragon's garden, searching for that which was out of place.

And at the end of her survey, a coherent view of Qel emerged in her mind; it was a nothing world. No more than a billion citizens, their patterns of movement and behavior almost boring in their predictability. Whatever the Eye of the First House had seen must have been subtle indeed.

As a point of entry, she selected a moderate-sized settlement called Oronesse, home to a well-regarded Academy. Such places were often easier to infiltrate, since citizens traveled from all over the planet and sometimes from off-world to attend Academies, or to live and work within their orbit. And though she couldn't quite identify it, something about Oronesse drew her attention in a way other potential sites failed to; gut instinct alerted her to details her conscious mind could not articulate.

The location had the added advantage of being adjacent to a large stretch of uncultivated, mountainous land. Given its proximity to pure wilderness, it seemed like a prime first point of contact to familiarize herself with both the natural and human elements of Qel. If only it hadn't been in one of the colder regions of the world, it would have been perfect. She'd never cared much for the cold.

With that critical decision made, Elyth allowed herself an extended break to rest and to run through her meditation sequence. As she was completing her routine, she felt the ripple through her being that marked the ship's brief use of its aspect drive. The sensation was but an instant, hardly long enough to register consciously, already a memory by the time it was noticed. For most, the transition between radiant propulsion and the aspect drive was undetectable. But the power that transported the ship across the galaxy was of the same kind that she herself drew upon to carry out her solemn duty. Not that the ship could speak, exactly, though the concept wasn't too far from the truth. Its effects resonated through her, like hearing in the distance the voice of a loved one long lost.

But there was something subtly different in the echo of the shift, a quiet but discordant note in the symphony; Elyth felt it more than anything, and that, barely. When she tried to quantify or classify it, she found there was nothing to hold on to. But she noted the sensation nevertheless, tried to encode what she could of the experience in her memory. And as she returned to her mission preparations, she found herself unable to dismiss the moment from her mind.

After an hour, Elyth decided to do something about it. She sent a low-priority message to Adura through the ship's internal communications system, and then secured her gear. Fifteen minutes later, her door chimed. Elyth took a moment to place a device just above the entrance, one that would inform her if anyone tried to access the cabin in her absence. Once it was in place, she opened the door to find the commander standing there.

"Advocate," Adura said. "How may I be of service?"

"Commander," Elyth said with a bow. "I was wondering if perhaps I might get a tour of the ship. I seem to have overestimated my tolerance for small spaces."

"It takes some getting used to," Adura answered. "If you just need to get out, I'm sure we can find a deck or two. I'm afraid it won't be much of a tour, though. Operations areas are off-limits while we're in transit."

"Anything that doesn't cause trouble for you."

"Certainly. Let's see what we can find."

Adura escorted Elyth back to the elevator, and down several decks to the vessel's common areas. They walked for a time, Elyth gradually leading the light conversation from general pleasantries to more targeted questions about the *Helegoss*.

"You mentioned she was a swift transport vessel," she said. "Does she use standard drives?"

Where Adura's responses had flowed naturally before, the hesitation before her response told Elyth more than her words.

"Yes, all standard drives," she said. "The classification has as much to do with readiness as with capability. We can deploy on short notice. She *is* a bit faster on radiant, but her aspect drive is the same as every other vessel in service."

The emphasis she placed on downplaying the aspect drive stood out, and Elyth felt the change, a withdrawal on Adura's part, as though she'd awakened to how freely she'd been speaking before. Elyth didn't probe any further about the drive technology; the line of questioning had struck close enough to the mark. Whatever other work had been done on the *Helegoss*, its aspect drive most certainly was not standard.

Adura continued to escort her a few minutes more before drawing their time to a close, apologizing and citing her need to attend to other duties. They returned to Elyth's quarters, and the commander extracted herself from the conversation politely and with warmth. But Elyth saw through the veneer. The initial openness Adura had felt toward her had faded, and with it vanished the subtle influence Elyth had exerted over the woman.

After Adura had departed, Elyth checked the device above the door. As anticipated, someone indeed accessed the cabin while she'd been away. All her gear remained secure, and apart from the indication of her device, there were no apparent signs of intrusion. But knowing the troopers of 3 Recon were on board made that no surprise.

As she returned to her work, she couldn't help but shake her head at the dance taking place even now between the Hezra and the First House. "A gentle poke" indeed. Undoubtedly, the Paragon had known more about the *Helegoss* than she'd let on; communication channels on both sides were probably stirred up. And the Advocates of the Eye were most assuredly at work soaking up the information.

Elyth guessed she had played her role aboard the vessel without knowing what that role had been meant to be. But having satisfied the itch in her mind over the vessel's aspect drive, she completed her planning and then turned to a final check of her gear. She lingered over the task, part due diligence, part ritual. Each tool in her arsenal she inspected and verified for function and then secured in its particular place. Her supplies she reviewed for quantity, carefully recalculating how long they would last her. Ten standard days in the field would be manageable;

more would be possible, if circumstance demanded. It wasn't her plan to stay out that long, nor did she relish the idea, but the kinds of operations she conducted required loose plans and a flexible mind-set.

Elyth scanned her cabin. All was as she had left it. At that point, not knowing what her first hours on-planet would bring, or perhaps knowing just enough, she decided to sleep while she could. She laid down on the bottom bunk, fully dressed and on top of the covers.

In what seemed like moments later, she woke to the sound of the door softly chiming.

She rose and opened the door expecting to find Commander Adura, but instead was greeted by a young officer she hadn't met before. Elyth concealed her surprise.

"Yes?" she said.

"Advocate, we are two hours from your launch window," he said, with a bow. "I'll escort you when you're ready."

"Thank you," she said. "I'm ready to go now."

"Of course," the officer said. "Follow me, if you will."

Elyth grabbed her pack and followed him to the elevator. Neither of them felt it necessary to converse.

They traveled to the center deck, where dual hangar bays flanked the spine of the vessel. At first, Elyth was glad to see the more regular activity of the ship's crew as they carried out their various duties; it made her presence seem less managed than her initial arrival had suggested. But as they walked through the massive hangar, the diligence the crew members showed in ignoring her reinforced her sense of unease. Though a few cast glances her way, most seemed unusually focused on their tasks. And to her careful eye, it wasn't always clear just what those tasks were.

The officer led Elyth through the starboard bay, weaving between

the various transports and gunships that all seemed parked too close together. Her ship waited toward the rear, already locked into its rails,
ready for launch out of the last port in the line. It was a muscular vessel, with the look of a hound crouching in its kennel, eager for release.
A pair of midshipmen busied themselves nearby verifying their end of
the launch protocol.

"Captain Jenzet sends his regards," the officer said, as they approached the ship's hatch. "And regrets he couldn't be here himself to
see you off."

Elyth suspected that was true, but probably not in the way it was
suggested.

"Please convey my thanks to him," she replied.

"Travel well," he said.

Elyth bowed. "May you ever ascend."

"May we both, Advocate of the House," the officer answered. He
bowed and took his leave.

Elyth turned and climbed aboard her ship, wondering again at Adura's absence, whether it had been the commander's choice, or enforced
by some other authority. But that was an answer she knew she was not
likely to receive.

She stowed her pack in its compartment just behind the cockpit,
and then slid into the pilot's seat. Hers was a small, single-occupant
vessel, originally designed by the Hezra for light mobile reconnaissance. Resting her hands on the controls brought a blend of emotions;
emotions reminiscent of those awakened just before full-contact training, where a comforting familiarity with the weapons and armor
mingled with sharp anticipation of the coming clash. She felt simultaneously at home in the ship and energized by the unknown that
awaited her. She had never been more uncertain of what she might
face, nor more anxious about what she might find.

For the moment, however, she set her mind to prepping the ship. The process didn't typically require as much time as Elyth had requested. But just as she had with her gear, she allowed herself to carry out her systems check in unhurried fashion, attuned to each detail in its moment. And given the disquiet she felt, she took extra care in verifying no unauthorized changes or modifications had been made to her vessel. But all was clear, and her systems were good. As such, when the message came in from Control that they were standing by to make ready for launch, Elyth found that her mind and body were both still and quiet.

"*Kita*, this is *Helegoss* Control," the controller said over comms. "We're approaching launch vector, how do you stand?"

"*Kita* is condition white, *Helegoss* Control," Elyth answered. "Ready for your action."

"Very good, *Kita*, stand by."

Elyth's console chirped twice in succession, the only indication that her ship was coordinating with the *Helegoss*'s launch system.

"We're angling now," the controller said. "You may feel some shifting."

"Understood," Elyth replied.

A few moments later, her ship vibrated with a deep hum as the rails supporting it adjusted their position.

"Locking position," said the controller. "Please confirm you're ready for launch."

"I confirm *Kita* is ready for launch, *Helegoss* Control."

"*Kita* confirms. Thirty seconds to launch."

Elyth started the count in her head, and realized she was hunching her shoulders. She took a deep breath and settled back into the pilot's seat. This was the easy part. The *Helegoss* launch protocol required nothing from her; the rail system would fire her like a projectile from the ship, putting her on initial course. It wouldn't be until after she and the *Helegoss* had separated a substantial distance that she would need to take control, to redirect toward her actual intended destination of Qel.

"Ten seconds," the controller said. He was silent again until five, and then counted down from there to launch.

Elyth didn't reply before the sudden acceleration pressed her back into her seat. Inertial dampeners mitigated most of the force, but it still took conscious effort to keep her heart rate from spiking. She counted to twenty before opening the comm channel one final time.

"*Kita* has good separation and trajectory. Thank you for the lift, *Helegoss* Control."

"*Helegoss* Control confirms good separation and trajectory, *Kita*. Safe travels, Advocate."

Elyth continued along her initial vector for a half hour under continual acceleration until she felt confident she'd gained enough distance to adjust course to Qel. She spent the solitary travel time in quiet meditation.

Once she reached visual range of the planet, she flicked on the exterior view. The opaqueness of the shielded cockpit appeared to dissolve as the system activated, revealing her target.

Out there, a milky, emerald-green sphere hung against the empty veil beyond: Qel. Elyth allowed the impression of the planet to engrave itself upon her mind, to find its place among the bedrock of all the research that had come before. This was the beginning of her true relationship with the world, the first welcome, the greeting, the embrace. With that single image fixed in her mind, she then allowed herself to study details: the wisps and swirls of cloud and storm, vast regions of verdant terrain, wide rivers, serrated mountains. All these she read like the lines and wrinkles of a stranger's face, each hinting at how frequently expressions might furrow a brow or crease a cheek. For all the imagery available to her through other means, nothing could compare with that first introduction viewed through her own eyes.

Soon enough the world grew too large to see completely, and shortly thereafter Elyth at last had to turn her attention to her own

flight controls. Once she entered the atmosphere, she made minor adjustments to avoid flying over population centers. Her vessel was designed for low-signature entry, invisible to all but the most
sophisticated systems, but there was no reason to put the design to unnecessary test.

Her primary landing zone lay in the wilderness adjacent to Oronesse. As her craft descended on its final approach, Elyth kept one eye
on her instruments while allowing herself to take in the view. The terrain rolled with easy mountains staked with dark pines. There was no
snow on the ground, but the trees and earth had a light crystalline
shimmer that testified to the region's cold. Elyth reduced engine power
and dropped to just a few hundred feet above the tree line, about two
miles out from the landing zone.

There was no pause between the alarm and the impact.

A siren screamed, white light dazzled Elyth's eyes, and in the same
instant that the warning blared, her craft jittered sideways, as though
the air had suddenly solidified just off her left wing. The shock left her
momentarily dazed, her hands lost the controls; the ship's automated
systems fought wildly to regain balance, skating a knife's edge to avoid
entering a tumble.

Elyth came to her senses enough to retake the controls, but the kin-
esthetic feedback coming through them was confused and fluctuating.
Crippled by the impact, the ship's sensor network couldn't cope with
the storm of forces tearing at it. For a few eternal seconds, Elyth grappled with her injured craft, striving to filter out the feeling of the controls and to concentrate instead on the horizon, and what her eyes were
telling her.

Her training prevented the panic that would have cost her the ship.
Getting the craft level again was nearly more than she could manage,
and once accomplished, was almost impossible to maintain. No smoke
was visible, but the cockpit took on a strong odor of melting circuitry. A

grinding vibration warned that the left side of her ship might shear off at any moment. The navigation system bleeped weakly, alerting her that she was off course for her intended landing zone, but otherwise offering no help. None of that mattered now. She would be lucky to survive a landing anywhere she could find.

As she scanned for a clearing or a flat enough patch of land, the thought came to her unbidden that she'd been attacked. And if she'd been attacked, that meant she had been tracked. And if she had been tracked, that very likely meant she would be under pursuit the moment she hit the ground. Assuming she survived.

It was a desperate move, but it was the only solution that came to mind in the few seconds she had to execute it. With nimble hands, Elyth armed the ship's microrocket pod and then jettisoned the external fuel tank from her craft. In the next moment, she targeted the tank and fired off two rockets. Elyth banked the ship, heading forty-five degrees off line from her previous trajectory. The rockets impacted just before the tank reached the ground, quaking the vessel with a sonic wave.

With any luck, the black smoke and crater from the fuel tank would be convincing enough to stall any pursuers from reaching her actual crash site. But she knew she wouldn't be able to create much distance between the two. Already the tops of the tallest pines were nearly brushing the belly of her ship, skeletal fingers extended to drag her to the ground below.

After that, there was no thought or plan, only reflex and reaction. The ever-shifting tension and slack in the controls, the battering and scraping of the pines against the hull, the blurring of the frosted ground streaming by below. And then the ship pitched sharply forward and the world bulged, as if the planet itself were a wall of water rushing up to meet her.

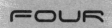

FOUR

The immediate assault on her senses rendered Elyth too stunned to move, to act, to think; neither mind nor body could untangle the knot of sensations into any meaningful information. Sight, sound, smell, all blended into a single overwhelming entity, too vast and powerful to contend with. It was pain.

But it was the pain that showed her the way. That at least was something she could isolate, focus on, localize to a definite point from which she could find her footing in the world again. At first her whole body seemed one broken mass, but as she followed the pain from its outer edges to its centermost intensity, she gradually discerned how it all radiated from a single star blossom where her ribs joined in the middle of her chest. That was when she realized just how wrong the gravity was.

Everything pulled forward, left, and slightly upward. It took a few seconds more before some combination of memory and recognition conjured the truth; her ship had crashed. No. She'd been shot down. Shot down, and plunged into the side of a mountain. The pain in her chest came in part from the strain against the pilot's harness that held her in place. The realization anchored her and made sense of all else around her. The warning lights, the discordant symphony of sirens and alarms, the acrid fumes, the iron taste of blood in her mouth.

Elyth took a few slow, deep breaths, testing herself. Every inhale hurt, but the edges of the pain were blunt, not the jagged fire that would have signaled broken ribs. A mild blessing. With care she unfastened her harness and eased herself out of the pilot's seat, cautiously testing each of her limbs before she committed any weight to them; due to the disarray of her ship and its strange gravity, the movement required her hands almost as much as her feet. The side of her mouth felt strange. She touched her lips and drew back fingers tacky with congealing blood. A quick inventory showed she'd otherwise escaped serious injury, though she knew a special level of pain awaited her once the shock of the event wore off. Even so, she vowed to remain grateful to be alive. Or at least to try.

Once she'd found stable footing, she turned her attention to her vessel. The cockpit remained largely intact, though it was obvious from its usually many-colored displays that little else had survived the impact. Most systems showed red, and those that didn't were blank-screened. The external view was shut down, leaving the cockpit lit an ember hue. Elyth picked her way aft, walking more on the bulkhead than the deck. The perspective challenged her sense of balance; she gripped whatever supports she could find on her way out, and stumbled more than once during the short walk. She chalked it up to the chaos of the situation, and tried to ignore any thoughts suggesting she might have a concussion. She didn't have time for that.

She reached the back of the ship and keyed the air lock. No response. A second attempt yielded only an angry, grinding buzz from somewhere within the frame of the internal hatch. Elyth took hold of the manual release; it required all her strength to force it and her body complained at the effort. The hatch shuddered as she drew it partially open, and as soon as it moved, a surge of icy daylight blasted through the gap. A bad sign. As Elyth's eyes adjusted to the dazzling light, she struggled to get her bearings. There was nothing where the external hatch should have been. Or rather, what was there was not what should have been. It was open air, and the tops of trees, and a broken horizon. What remained of the air lock formed a jagged frame of spindled metal and wire, as though some great leviathan had bitten off the back of the ship. And beyond, the angle of the ground didn't align properly with the pull of gravity or the confused attitude of her vessel. Her mind couldn't quite reconcile the dissonance.

Elyth eased forward, poked her head through the internal hatch and saw the furrowed earth about five feet below. With the wider view, proper perspective clicked into place. She could see now how she'd crashed into a slope, her trajectory running nearly perpendicular to the rise of the terrain. The indirect angle of impact had probably saved her life. How many times her ship had spun, twisted, or tumbled wasn't clear, but it had come to rest planted practically face-first into the ground.

Though it was a mild relief to have a horizon again, to get some proper sense of up, the view was not otherwise encouraging. A trail of mechanical carnage stretched a hundred feet or more behind the vessel, strewn among shattered trees and scoured earth. Any hopes Elyth had harbored of concealing her true crash site vaporized in that moment. The gouge the crash had left in the forest might as well have been a guiding arrow drawn by the finger of a god.

Away across the meandering landscape a cloud of black smoke churned thickly above the treetops. The lay of the land made it challenging to gauge the distance accurately, but Elyth guessed it was no farther than ten miles. Not much space to work with. And in such situations, space was time, and time was life.

She turned then and clambered back into the cockpit, to the compartment holding her gear. Fortunately, it had survived intact. She grabbed her pack and dropped it out of the hatch to the ground below. An emergency locator beacon laid locked in its receptacle in the control deck; Elyth pulled it free and clipped it to her belt, but left it deactivated for the moment. Beside her, a panel by the pilot's seat housed a slightly crumpled emergency supply kit, which she took and tossed unceremoniously out of the ship. She glanced around the interior, knowing that even in the vessel's catastrophic state, there were a number of components she could strip out that might prove useful, if only she'd had the time to think.

As things stood, it was all going to have to burn.

Simple thermal charges arranged around the cage of the cockpit awaited activation. Elyth moved as quickly as she was able, flipping through the mechanical arming sequence on each. Two failed to arm, but there were redundancies throughout the system and enough of them remained functional to do the job. At least, that was her hope.

When the final charge was armed, she pulled the detlink from its housing and hung its thin strap around her neck. The timers wouldn't kick off until she was clear, but once the detlink had enough distance from the charges, there'd be no coming back. She scanned the cockpit one last time. A few things caught her eye: exposed bundles of cabling, reinforced paneling, the harness from the pilot's seat. All potentially useful, none immediately accessible. Another ten or twenty minutes might be enough to grant some piece of tech or scrap of gear that could improve her odds of survival. But none of it would be any good to her if she were captured or killed trying to harvest it.

And though she could neither see nor hear any signs of trouble, instinct told her she had to get moving. Already she could feel the weight of pursuit bearing down, crushing her options into ever more narrow avenues. With a nagging sense of things left undone, Elyth returned aft and lowered herself through the broken air lock and out of the vessel. She slung her pack on her shoulders, grimacing as the weight of it ignited fresh pain across her frame. For a moment she actually considered leaving the emergency supplies behind, feeling the few benefits they offered wouldn't be worth the extra weight. But she knew that was her pain talking, and that there very well might come a time when an extra ration or blanket would make all the difference. She hoisted the kit, hung it across her chest, and then scanned her surroundings. Her local nav tracker was in the top of her pack, but at that moment, she decided to trust her instincts; she knew there wasn't a settlement for miles around, and that gave her room enough to maneuver. There was no point in wasting time looking for a place to go when all of them were essentially the same. Better to use her eyes and ears, and get on the move.

The land rolled off to her left; to her right, it climbed in a moderate bank. She was tempted to head downhill, knowing the easier travel would translate to greater distance covered. But there was an old, natural truth that nothing wounded ever moved uphill. And if nothing else, at least if anyone came for her she would have the higher ground.

Elyth picked her way up the bank, navigating to the still-intact tree line above the corridor of ruined forest her ship had created. Once she'd moved thirty or so feet into the woods, she turned back for one final look at her ship. The thermal charges had already started their work. There was nothing about the exterior design of the vessel that would have revealed its origins, nothing that even necessarily suggested it was from off-world. Only the internal systems would offer any such clues, and those were being cleansed by fire.

The silhouette of the vessel softened as she watched, as the internal cage of the cockpit drooped and folded in on itself, as though an invisible hand were crumpling it in slow motion. Panels once tightly joined shifted and slipped, and the smooth snake-scaled exterior became jagged and craggy. The external heat shielding of the ship prevented the surrounding area from catching fire, but there was nevertheless something molten about the movement and collapse.

Then the black cloud on the horizon caught her attention once more, the pillar of smoke calling out to her pursuers and showing them the way. It spurred her on, and up. The climb proved even more of a challenge than she'd anticipated. Untold years of needles from the pines and other poorly decomposed matter blanketed the ground, rendering her footing unsure and concealing rocks and holes that threatened to wrench her ankles. To make matters worse, Elyth's mind was divided and she couldn't focus solely on navigating, despite the demanding terrain.

Too many questions, too much uncertainty. Ambushed or sabotaged: each seemed equally improbable, though undoubtedly one of those options must have been true.

For now, she would have to press on, one careful step at a time, until she could regain a stronger position from which to operate. As she continued to climb, she discovered how patchy the woods were on the side of the low mountain; the mix of pines and oaks thinned out and occasionally gave way to open spaces dense with long grasses and underbrush. Rocky outcroppings dotted the slope, some small enough for Elyth to clamber, others large enough to force her off course.

Here and there as she moved, she caught her first sight of the denizens of Qel: a silver-blue fox with luminous eyes and oversized ears; a family of slender deer, rust-colored and taller at the shoulder than any breed she'd previously seen; a large, mottled lizard she initially took as a rock until it darted away. The reaction of the wildlife to her presence gave her some clue to her surroundings. The animals were wary of her, thus familiar with humans.

After an hour of hard travel, her body started to fail her. The pain in her shoulders and throughout her ribs clouded her thinking, and her footing became less and less certain. Roots caught her toes, mossy stones cast off her tread. More than once she fell, her usual grace and balance seeming to have abandoned her. Though she was fatigued, she knew that wasn't the problem. She'd hiked harder terrain for far longer. But the adrenaline dump and the shock to her system from the crash were taking their toll.

Still she drove herself onward, higher, for another hour, until she slipped and, for the fourth time, fell hard on her hands and knees. In that fall, the point of a rock met the center of her right kneecap, and it took everything she had to keep from crying out at the impact; still, a frustrated growl escaped through her gritted teeth and stars exploded in her vision.

Elyth remained there for a minute or more, breathing through the pain, resisting the weight of the pack that seemed determined to drive her the rest of the way to the ground. It was warning enough. She knew she still had ample strength to force herself up again, up to her feet and farther up the mountain. But she knew with just as much certainty that her next misstep might end with a broken ankle or something equally devastating to her mobility. She'd pushed it far enough for now.

Gingerly, she rocked back into a crouch, shifting her weight to her left leg as much as possible to keep pressure off her freshly damaged kneecap. She removed the emergency kit and then let the straps from her pack slide off her shoulders. Without all the gear dragging her down, the world felt brighter, easier to bear. She sat down and closed her eyes, giving herself permission to just breathe. The sharp pain in her kneecap had already diffused into a dull, radiating throb. After a few moments, she opened her eyes again and drew her pant leg up so she could investigate the injury. A dark divot punctuated her knee, surrounded by a pool purpling beneath the unbroken skin. After prodding the bone and surrounding tendons, Elyth determined there was no substantial damage. Just another deep, nasty bruise for her extensive collection.

While she sat there, rubbing her kneecap in hopes of soothing the pain, she took stock of her surroundings. The crisp air had become pleasantly cool, and Elyth drew deep breaths, driving her focus to the earthy, vaguely sweet scent of the forest. Trees towered over her, long pines mostly, with a few hardwoods interspersed. Through the trees some fifty yards or so away the terrain climbed steeply to an outcropping jutting from the earth like the prow of a ship emerging from the underworld. She contemplated the rocky face for a moment. Her body needed the rest, even if just for a few minutes. But the spur promised a chance to get her bearings, to reorient if necessary, and to judge her progress. If she was going to take time to rest, she decided she might as well see if she could learn anything while she was at it. There wouldn't be much recovery, though, if she tried to lug all her gear up that slope. She surveyed the area and spotted a thicket she'd passed; at the base was a collection of broken branches, needles, and leaves, all swept there by some previous current of rainfall.

Elyth opened her pack and detached the top section, which housed all her tools and devices. It had a single broad strap that she slung over one shoulder and across her body, securing the bag to her back. Then she placed the emergency supply kit in the pack and resecured its straps. With that done, she pushed herself up from the ground and carried the pack to the thicket. She buried her gear there in the brush pile, rearranging the branches as best she could to conceal the disturbance.

With her gear stashed, she hiked up the slope to the outcropping, careful in her steps and mindful of her still-aching knee. She evaluated the spur, looking for the easiest route up. As she came around the front, a flash of color and explosion of confused squawking erupted in her face. Elyth threw an arm up to shield herself. But when it passed by her harmlessly, she looked and saw a pair of golden kestrels soaring away and gaining height. A second glance revealed a crevice at the fore of the outcrop that hadn't been visible from the side.

She took a few moments to collect herself, to calm her spiking heartbeat. When she felt steady enough, she started her ascent. The spur was maybe fifteen feet tall or a little over, but even in her damaged state, Elyth found its jagged flanks were an easy climb. She reached the top and walked out to the farthest edge. From that vantage, she was able to get her bearings. The crash site was easy enough to find. It was below her, to the east. And, much to her dismay, it wasn't all that far from her current location. After two hours of hiking, she would have guessed she'd covered somewhere between four and five miles. But judging from the view of the site, she estimated she'd made it maybe two at most.

Her mind went to her locator beacon. A quick twist and help would be on its way. And with it, who knew what trouble would follow. After all the Paragon had told her, and all the trust the matriarch had put in her, to admit defeat here, at the very start of her mission, seemed like a great betrayal. Better to be captured than to give up before she'd even begun.

That didn't stop her from checking the tangle interpreter, though, in vague hope that perhaps the Paragon had already initiated communication. The instant she had the interpreter out, she could see there would be no help for her there. Nor from anywhere, so it seemed. The device was damaged, its slender frame buckled and crushed in the center from the force of the crash.

The only help she would have now was that which she could provide herself. Admitting that, removing all other options from her thoughts, her mind felt clearer, her body lighter. And in that clarity, she realized that having made so little progress escaping the crash site presented a valuable opportunity.

Elyth retrieved her monocular from her pack and then laid down flat on her belly at the farthest tip of the spur. She flicked the monocular's miniature tripod open and placed the device on the rock in front of her, eased her eye up to the optic, touched it lightly to adjust its aim, and centered it on the wreckage below.

The view was partially obscured by the treetops between her and the site, but her elevation combined with the destruction the crash had caused gave her a clear enough picture. At first the area immediately around the ship appeared undisturbed, which seemed odd given the amount of time that had passed. Elyth slowly swept her optic over the crash site and back again, but saw no signs of activity. Either the terrain was tougher than she'd predicted, or the forces she assumed would be tracking her were nonexistent.

She was just starting to regret her rush to escape when something caught her eye.

A blur of motion near the ship, so faint and uncertain it could have been a false artifact floating in her vision. But her instincts told her to wait, and to watch, and a few moments later she saw it again. A small arcing streak, from the tip of the ship back toward the center. Her monocular was already at its maximum magnification; there was little hope of identifying whatever was the cause of the movement. Even staring directly at it, her eye could detect only the motion, like the darting of an animal into underbrush seen peripherally, leaving only an impression in the mind. Elyth closed her eyes for a few seconds, resting them from the strain. When she opened them again, instead of focusing intently, she let her vision relax to take in a wide view. In that mode of seeing, she could discern not just one but several wisps moving near and around the crash site. Any time her eye tried to fix on any one particular target, she lost the others. But as long as she looked wide, she could see the network. Though she couldn't make out enough detail to be sure, the pattern they created suggested their design and their purpose.

Scout drones. A small swarm of the automated, self-coordinating craft was diligently mapping the crash site. Whatever local authority ruled this part of Qel was already investigating; the planet-stationed arm of the Hezra. And given that the scouts were left unattended to do their work, that likely meant others had already secured the site and moved on. Undoubtedly to scour the mountain for survivors.

It was then she heard the voices.

Faint, at first, indistinct. Carried on the wind. But against the stillness of the woods, unmistakable. The sound came from her left, back in the direction she herself had traveled. Back in the direction where the bulk of her gear lay.

Exposed as she was on the tip of the spur, Elyth kept her movements controlled, far slower than her reflexive reactions would have liked. She quietly drew the monocular to her and crept backward on her belly away from the outcrop's point. There she paused, listening. For a span, she heard nothing more. But as she strained to hear all that disrupted the natural rhythm of the quiet wood, she gradually became aware of a low droning hum, and then suddenly realized she'd been hearing it for a time, and couldn't recall when it had begun.

Logic told her it could only be a scout drone. The sound was clearly identifiable now that she focused on it, but the wideness and fullness of the interminable note made it impossible to pinpoint. Not knowing the power of its engine, Elyth couldn't even make a reliable guess as to its distance. Regardless, she knew the worst place for her to be was where she currently was, splayed out on an easily identifiable landmark.

She eased herself over the edge of the outcrop and made her way down; the stiffness of her joints and ache in her knee forced her to take it more slowly than caution would normally require, even as the hum continued to grow. When she reached the ground, she went to the crevice where the kestrels had startled her. The crevice reached up the spur no higher than Elyth's waist, and was narrow and shallow. But she remembered how difficult it'd been to spot the crack when she had approached the outcropping, and as best as she could tell the drone was coming generally from the same direction she had. Most important, the crevice offered cover from the air, which was her most immediately pressing need.

In minutes too long, with the sound of the drone growing ever closer, Elyth wrestled herself into the cleft. It took some creativity and no small measure of flexibility to work herself into the tight space, but she managed to back her way far enough in to be fully covered. Almost immediately, she felt like a fox in its den, with the hounds circling just outside. A terrible gamble. If the party failed to notice the split in the rock, she knew she'd be all right. But if anyone approached the opening, she'd be completely at their mercy.

She didn't have to wait long. Soon after she'd gotten situated, the hum of the drone took on a harsher edge, and Elyth knew from the buzz that the miniature surveillance vessel was closing in. And now that she was hidden from view, her biggest risk was the residual heat she'd left behind. Her attire regulated the diffusion of her body heat, and though it couldn't perfectly mask her presence or passing, any signature she'd left behind would appear smaller and older than it actually was. If the drone was using thermals, and she had to assume it was, it was a toss-up as to whether or not it would lock on to the trail she'd left, or if it would dismiss it as caused by some woodland creature. It would all depend on the skill and whims of its operator.

She closed her eyes, focused on the sound; pictured the drone in her mind based on what she could hear, followed its swooping arcs as it approached and moved away, only to approach again. Though her rocky hiding place made it difficult to judge for certain, it didn't seem that the drone was following any specific track, but rather was ranging back and forth in lazy loops and bends. A loose search protocol, then. The buzz gradually dwindled once more to a hum, and the hum lost intensity.

Soon after, the hum was replaced by voices and footsteps; a minute more, and they were close enough for her to start making out the words.

"There's nowhere up here to go," a thin voice said.

"You've been saying that for an hour, Sarinn," answered a woman, the edge to her words suggesting she'd been holding her irritation in check for some time.

"Yeah, well," the one called Sarinn replied. "Been true the whole time."

There was no doubt about it now. The searchers were definitely following roughly the same path that she'd taken up the mountain. Elyth listened carefully; the two were speaking the Low Language, and the dialect was not far off from one she'd practiced briefly while traveling to the planet. A little slower, a little less articulated.

"Hate to admit it, but I'm starting to think maybe the same," said a third voice. "Anybody walked away from that, which I doubt, I don't put money on them trying their luck over this ground. If they were looking for help, more likely they would've rolled downhill."

"And wouldn't have made it this far, anyway," Sarinn added.

"Not unless they were steel-made," the third voice said.

The sounds of walking stopped, as did the chatter. It was a sudden silence, one imposed; a listening, straining silence. Elyth held her breath.

For a long minute, she heard nothing more. And then a new voice spoke, this one as hard and edged as flint.

"*If* they were looking for help, we probably don't need to worry about them. We'll make another circuit."

Sarinn said, "We would've picked something up by now, Hok."

"Maybe," Hok, the flint-voiced man, answered. "But something spooked those birds."

Elyth knew she couldn't risk trying to peek out of her hiding place, but knowing neither how many pursuers she had nor how close they were prevented her from being able to formulate any sort of plan of action. As quietly as she could, she detached the back portion of her monocular and eased the front half out of the crevice, flush against the ground. In that configuration, the optic acted as a remote camera. The mismatch between the movement of the device and her viewpoint made it a challenge to position usefully, but after a few moments of careful scanning she was able to locate the search party.

There were four of them, all clad in metal strider frames along their arms, legs, and torsos; the partial exoskeletons extended to the ground, ending in wide, flexible stabilizing "feet" designed to bear the burden of fast movement over hard terrain and render their wearers virtually tireless. Judging by the rugged look of the search party, though, it was likely they were tireless enough on their own. If they caught her track, Elyth had no hope of outpacing them. They were clustered together about thirty yards down the slope, not far from where she'd had her fall. A man with his head shaved bald stood in the center, and his strider had a different silhouette from the others; spikier along the back and shoulders, more bulk. The leader of the group. Elyth trained her monocular on him and upped the magnification.

He stood a few inches over six feet by her estimation and was solidly built; a large man made larger still by his strider frame. The spikes on the strider were actually antennae. A scout drone lay docked on the back of his frame, next to a second, empty bay. It was likely that he was running the drone that had passed by, then.

"Hey, Hok," said a wiry man with a thick beard. The third voice. The bald man looked his way, and the bearded man gestured. When Elyth followed the man's motion, her heart sank. He was pointing toward the thicket where she'd stashed her gear.

"What is it, Kitu?" the woman asked.

"Something's been digging in that brush," the bearded man answered.

Elyth watched helplessly as the group approached the thicket; they fanned out as the man called Kitu drew a sidearm and cautiously took the lead. Elyth noted that the sidearm was a civilian sport model, which suggested the party wasn't part of the local authorities. The strider frames supported the hypothesis; they'd been hard used, and had the look of modded recreational rigs.

Kitu knelt in front of the brush pile and gingerly parted the branches. Carefully he leaned closer, investigating the pile far more thoroughly than Elyth would have anticipated. A few agonizing moments later, he holstered his weapon, and then stuck his arm into the brush and dragged Elyth's pack out.

"Told you we'd find something," a dark-featured man with long hair said. Elyth recognized his voice as the one they'd called Sarinn.

Elyth's mind ran a rapid inventory on everything she'd left behind in her pack; there was nothing mission critical, nor anything specifically identifiable to First House, or as official Ascendance personnel for that matter. All of that such gear was with her. But the emergency supply kit would undoubtedly connect the gear to the crash site, and the quantity of supplies would tell a story of its own.

"How long you figure that's been here?" the woman asked.

"Hard to say," Kitu replied. "Plenty heavy, though." He started to reach for the closure straps.

"Don't open it," Hok warned. Kitu withdrew his hand and stood up.

"Think it's dangerous?" Sarinn asked.

"Out here's not the place to find out," Hok answered. He had his head up, surveying the area.

"What're you thinking?" the woman asked. Hok shook his head.

"Got wind of the drone, maybe. Dumped the pack for speed."

He looked up toward the outcropping. For a brief moment, Elyth felt like he was looking right into the lens of her monocular.

"Should we leave it?" Kitu asked.

Hok shook his head again, and looked back the way they'd come.

"I don't want local to pick it up," he said. "Either we put it back or we take it with us."

"Local's not going to make it this far up the hill," Sarinn said. "I'm pretty sure they're just going to map the site, file a report, and call it a day."

"We can hope," the woman said. "But we don't need to give them an excuse to hang around any longer than absolutely necessary."

That was enough to convince Elyth she was right about her guess; they were freelancers. Or worse.

"We could just stake it out," Kitu said. "Whoever stashed it is probably gonna come looking for it at some point."

"Unless there are multiple," Hok replied. "Might be counting on making it with whatever they've still got on them."

"But make it where?" Sarinn said.

"Crash like that," Kitu said. "People do crazy things."

"Particularly if they don't want to get picked up by local," Hok added.

"Well that part I can understand," Sarinn replied.

No friends of the local authority, then. Elyth started evaluating them with new eyes; not as hostile, but as potential assets. They were armed, yes, but lightly. The kind of weapons one might reasonably carry into the wilderness for protection from wild animals. The drone that had passed over had been loud and low-flying, not the near-undetectable variety usually used by military or law enforcement. And the party didn't seem to have any concerns about keeping their voices down.

Still, she couldn't yet bring herself to approach them, not without more information.

"I think we take the pack," Kitu said. "Save us a trip back if we come across them."

"And if they come back looking for it?" the woman asked.

"This far up, night coming on," Kitu replied. "Gonna get cold. Maybe we just watch for campfires."

"Or come back in the morning and look for bodies," Sarinn added. "I'll carry it. Least I can do after all my griping."

Sarinn walked over and hoisted the pack, as though the added weight would make any difference to the frame.

"Big man," the woman said. "So strong."

"All to impress you, Amei," Sarinn said.

"Definitely working," Amei answered, her tone implying it wasn't. "Just make sure you stand far enough away in case it *is* booby-trapped. I don't want to get bone fragments in my hair."

"I'll try to explode downwind," Sarinn said.

"I still don't like it, though," she added a few moments later, as Sarinn finished securing the pack to his frame. "Ship comes down that close to *eth ammuin*. Doesn't seem like a coincidence to me."

Eth ammuin. The way she spoke the words gave them the weight of a title; a hint of reverence undergirded the phrase. But the words resonated unusually with Elyth, almost enough to make her hair stand on end. Though the woman had spoken in the Low Language, the words were tinged with something of greater substance, not quite the Deep Language but an echo of it, as though they were a remnant of an ancient mode of speech transformed for a modern tongue. As pronounced, it meant something like "the silent one," but Elyth could sense it had greater meaning than the speaker understood.

"Maybe, maybe not," Kitu said. "Best way to be sure is to find them ourselves."

"Besides," Sarinn said, "if there was any danger, don't you think *eth ammuin* would have warned us ahead of time?"

Where Amei's tone had shown respect, Sarinn used the phrase with a sarcastic edge. Even so, to Elyth's ear, it lost none of its strange, concealed power.

"Ssst, hey," Hok said, ending the chatter. "Enough. One more circuit. If we come up empty, we'll call it."

The squad separated and fell into a shallow inverted V formation, with maybe twenty feet between each individual. They moved on, higher up the mountain, at an angle that would bring them nearer to the outcropping, but passing behind. Elyth's optic soon lost sight of them. As they departed, she weighed her options.

Though it appeared her hiding place was good enough for now, the man Kitu was right about the danger night posed to her; with the loss of her gear, she would be hard pressed to stay at altitude once the sun had gone down. Now that she was behind their line of search, she considered trying to double back. But that ran the risk of them catching up to her on their way back down or, worse, her getting caught between search parties, if others were out there.

There was another approach. Riskier. But the best way to guarantee the search party would be unable to find her was to track them herself. Clearly there was more she could learn from them. This *eth ammuin* was a tenuous thread at best, but it was the only one she had at hand. And it was a chance to get back on top of the situation, to drive it rather than react to it. If that was going to be her move, she was losing time. Already the sound of their movement was fading up the mountain.

A thin thread, indeed. Thin enough that pulling on it was as likely to snap it as it was to lead her anywhere. But her instinct told her she had to try.

Elyth slipped from her hiding place and circled wide along the group's flank. Without her full gear weighing her down, she was able to move much more quickly, and the focus that came from being on the hunt burned away her fatigue. The pain in her knee and chest barely registered as she stalked the four searchers.

Though the strider frames could have given the group a decisive speed advantage, they kept their pace slow and steady, suitable for observing their surroundings as they followed a rounded zigzag search pattern up the mountain, watching for signs of passage. They spoke little as they traveled and Elyth was relieved to discover that, despite Kitu's keen eye that had cost her her gear, they didn't otherwise seem to be expertly skilled trackers. They had some talent, but little training that she could see. Regular hunters, maybe. But not of the people-hunting variety. Or at least not of the caliber Elyth had grown accustomed to.

She shadowed them for a time, moving only when they did, hiding herself in the quiet rhythm of the woods. As the sun began the final hour of its descent, she'd pieced together enough from watching them and listening to their few brief exchanges. The last of her energy reserves were running out, and the pain had returned. She knew if she didn't act soon, she'd lose them. And she'd developed a new plan of action.

After some careful pursuit and positioning, Elyth managed to maneuver slightly ahead of the party, just beyond the rise of a ridge. She took momentary refuge in a hollow created by a great oak's root structure, removed the locator beacon from her belt, and stashed it in her pocket. And waited. She knew the amplifying effect a dramatic moment could have.

The four came over the ridge within twenty feet of her. She waited until they had passed by, and then crept into the open behind them.

"Excuse me," she said with authority.

The four of them startled at the sound of her voice, whirled around to face her; their expressions a mix of shock and bewilderment, though Hok displayed the least.

Elyth held up a hand, palm out, and then pointed at Sarinn. "I believe, Sarinn, that pack belongs to me."

FIVE

For a long moment, no one spoke or even moved. Elyth felt like a child with a slingshot facing down four armored giants; the frames added about a foot of height to each person. But she was relieved to see that in their surprise, not one of the four had reached for their weapons, not even a hand to a belt. A good sign. Particularly because she could feel weakness creeping into her limbs; her legs trembled from the exertion of the pursuit.

"How do you know my name?" Sarinn asked.

"We went to school together," Elyth said. She spoke in the Low Language, mimicking their dialect as well as she could. It wasn't perfect, but it might be close enough to give the impression she was at least from the same planet.

His eyes narrowed, as though he was trying to put a name to her face. The more she could keep them off-balance, the better.

"Don't worry, we weren't friends," she said. "I just thought you were cute."

"Now I know you're lying," he replied. Elyth smiled.

"You've got a lot of people out looking for you," Hok said. "Any particular reason you're trying so hard not to be found?"

"The answer to that question belongs to you even less than the pack your friend is still holding," Elyth answered. "But I promise I'm not trying to cause trouble for anyone."

"Probably shouldn't have crashed your ship into a mountain, then," Sarinn said.

"I'd say the mountain more crashed into me," Elyth said. "And I don't think it's illegal for me to be out hiking in the woods."

"That may be in most places," Hok said. "But in this case, you're on our land."

"It was not my intent, I assure you," Elyth said. "And if you'll return my belongings, I'll be certain to rectify that as quickly as possible."

"Well, see, that presents us with a bit of a dilemma," Hok said. "Right now, the fact that what's left of your ship is sitting on our mountain has given the local authorities temporary cause to set up shop on our property. And if they have reason to think you're out here wandering around, they're likely to stick around until they find you. Which isn't ideal for us."

"You don't get along with the authorities?" Elyth asked.

"We get along fine," Hok answered. "As long as they stay off our property."

"Ah. I don't suppose you want to give me my stuff and point me in the right direction?"

"It'll be even worse for us if they pick you up later, and they find out we held out on them."

"And if I promise they won't pick me up?"

Hok made a small, involuntary expression that suggested he was already tired of talking. That was his only response. The other three held their places, happy to let Hok serve as spokesman for the group. They were all still trying to figure out what to make of her.

"I'd offer to let you escort me," Elyth said. "But I get the impression you might escort me right to the locals."

Amei spoke before Hok could. "That would be best for us. And I don't think you're in much of a position to make offers."

Hok's eyes shifted in Amei's direction at her words, but quickly returned to Elyth. He was still evaluating, then.

"Well, you're not going to give me my belongings," Elyth said. "And I'm not going to let you take me anywhere. Sounds like we're at an impasse."

"Maybe," Hok said.

Elyth fixed his eyes with hers. "Then I suppose we'll stand here and see who can handle the cold the longest."

In her peripheral view, she saw Sarinn smile at that, apparently in spite of himself, and look at the ground. Elyth kept her attention on Hok, tested his gaze with hers. And saw that the first part of her plan had succeeded; she'd established herself as formidable, a woman of authority and strength.

Time for part two.

After long seconds of the stare down, Elyth's right knee buckled, and she collapsed to the ground, landing on her hip but bracing herself with her hands. It was an act, but the action came much more naturally than she would have liked.

She kept her head down until someone moved toward her; she waited until the distance was right, and then snapped her head up and held out a warning hand, stopping the man in his tracks.

It was Kitu who had come closer and who now stood just a couple of paces away. Elyth lowered her eyes back to the ground in front of her but kept her hand out. His posture revealed cautious concern, a willingness to help. In her periphery, she located his sidearm. Eight rounds, assuming it was loaded to full capacity. More than enough.

"Well," Sarinn said. "That didn't take long."

Elyth struggled to her knees, and then to a crouch, both hands planted in front of her. To support her. To launch her forward, if she so chose.

But she held her place.

"You all right?" Kitu asked.

"I fell out of the sky and hit a planet," Elyth replied. "So, no, not really."

Kitu looked back at Hok. The critical moment.

Hok gave a quick nod, and Kitu stepped forward, offering his hand. If she was going to take the weapon, the moment was now. Sarinn raised an eyebrow.

Instead, she took the man's hand and allowed him to help her to her feet. Kitu continued to support her until she withdrew her hand and thanked him with a nod. He backed off a step, but Elyth noticed how he held his hands active at his side, ready to catch her if she should start to fall again.

"Pretty good show," Hok said, and for an instant Elyth thought she'd misjudged him, that he'd seen through it all, and that she should have gone for the weapon. But then his right arm and shoulder relaxed, and she saw how he'd subtly pulled his hand up near his appendix, not on his weapon, but a short, quick draw away from it. That gave her pause. Maybe she could have outdrawn him, but clearly her show of weakness hadn't put him off his guard as much as she had hoped. Then he added, "For a second there I thought you were going to try and fight us all."

Elyth shook her head. "I've never been much of a fighter."

"I doubt that," he said.

"You've got a wounded tiger kind of vibe," Kitu added.

"You didn't think I'd bite?" she asked.

Kitu shrugged and smiled. "Been bitten before."

Hok stood there, sizing her up, and she could see the struggle in his mind; he was a hard man, but she saw too the signs of a protector by nature. He was caught between the need to secure his home and the desire to do right by a lost, injured stranger. She needed to give him a nudge in the right direction.

It was obvious that the group didn't trust the local government structure. Maybe that too was an opening to exploit.

"Look," she said, with a heavy, resigned sigh. "Not that it's any of your business. But I'm just trying to get away from some things, and it's really important that I don't show up on local's radar."

"And why's that?" Amei asked.

"Because . . ." Elyth started, and then paused, as if wrestling with whether she should answer the question or not. "Because the individual I'm trying to avoid has too many friends there."

Sarinn's eyes went to Amei, and she briefly returned the look.

"It's just you out here?" Hok asked.

Elyth nodded.

"Hauling an awful lot of gear for one," he said.

"It's everything I own, now," Elyth said. "The rest of it's burning on your mountain."

She gave it another moment, then pushed a little more.

"I didn't mean to end up here, really, and I'm sorry to be trespassing," Elyth continued. "I was headed to Oronesse. I just need some time and space to figure some things out. I know you have no reason to believe me, and I have nothing to bargain with. But please. Please, just give me my pack and forget you ever saw me."

Everyone was still while Hok considered it. Elyth quickly scanned the others' faces, tried to get a read on them. Kitu seemed most likely to help, Amei appeared to be the main adversary, and Sarinn looked like he was just waiting around for someone else to make a decision.

"We can't just let you wander off," Hok said finally.

"You can," Elyth said. "But I get the impression you've decided not to."

"I don't think you'd make it far anyway," he said, and then glanced back over his shoulder. "Anybody up at the cabin?"

Sarinn shook his head. Hok turned back to address Elyth.

"So . . . I think you should come back with us," he said. "We'll get you a place to rest for a couple of days, out of the way. Then we'll see what we see."

Elyth saw the expression flicker across Amei's face; the woman wasn't happy with the idea, but apparently wasn't going to voice it in front of everyone else.

"And how do I know you won't just turn me into the authorities?" Elyth asked.

"You'll know when you wake up in the morning and they aren't there," Hok said. "Otherwise, I guess you'll just have to trust us."

"I'm not one for trusting strangers."

"*That* I don't doubt."

"Your prisoner, then."

"Or our guest," said Hok. "Don't have to put a negative spin on it."

Elyth took a moment as if weighing her options.

"Prisoner or guest," she said. "The only choice you're leaving me isn't much of one."

Hok didn't respond.

"We're not bad company," Kitu said after a moment. "Except Sarinn. He'll grate on you after a while."

Elyth glanced at Sarinn, and he shrugged.

"I mean, he's not wrong," Sarinn said.

"You know how to run one of these?" Hok asked, indicating his strider frame.

"Haven't tried since I was too young to know better," Elyth lied.

"It's pretty easy. You can strap in to mine." Hok started to unbuckle the harness of his frame, but Kitu held up a hand.

"She can have mine, Hok," he said.

"You sure? Long walk back."

"Yeah, it's fine. I could use the exercise."

"All right," Hok said, and then turned to Amei. "You want to walk with him?"

"Yeah," Amei said, but Kitu was already shaking his head.

"Nah, you should stick together. This is my backyard, I'll be fine."

Hok and Kitu looked at each other for a brief moment, and some message passed between them that Elyth couldn't precisely read. For all his apparent friendliness, Kitu didn't seem to like the idea of leaving only two people watching over her. Hok nodded.

"I'll leave the drone on loiter in case something comes up," he said. "Stay on comms until you get home."

"Okay, Mom," Kitu said. "Tether to yours?"

"Yeah," Hok said.

Kitu opened a small panel on the forearm of his strider and executed some function on the interface housed within. "What do you think, twenty feet?"

"Maybe thirty for shut down," Hok answered.

Once on tether, Kitu's frame would automatically adjust its speed as it approached its maximum allowed range, forcing Elyth's pace if she lagged too far behind, or coming to a dead stop if she got too far ahead.

"You don't trust me?" she asked.

"More for your safety," Hok said. "Easy to forget how fast you can move if you're not used to them."

After a moment he added, "And yeah, no, I don't trust you either."

Kitu finished the configuration, unhooked the harness of his strider, and hopped out. He waved Elyth over, and when she stepped toward him, he held his left hand out and bowed in greeting.

"Kitu," he said.

The display of formal etiquette took Elyth by surprise, but she mirrored the gesture and replied, "Eliya." The false name was close enough to her own to keep her reactions natural.

"Eliya," he repeated, then gestured toward his frame, inviting her to climb aboard. She nodded and clambered into it.

"Sorry . . . it uh," he said. "It might be a little sweaty."

"Good," Elyth replied. "I don't feel so bad about how gross I am right now, then."

Though it was unnecessary, she allowed him to show her how to strap in to the harness, and was patient with his explanation of the basic controls. Despite his repeated insistence on how easy it was to operate, his haphazard instructions made it sound more complicated than it was.

"Kitu, that was so confusing I forgot how to use my *own* frame," Amei interrupted. She looked at Elyth and said, "Basically, just walk like you're tiptoeing around."

Elyth nodded. She'd used plenty of striders in her time, and that, indeed, was a much simpler and useful way of explaining their function. Kitu looked at the ground, embarrassed.

"I think I understand," Elyth replied. "Thank you both."

Kitu looked up at her, his mouth open as if to say something further, but instead he gave her a tight smile and a quick nod, and then backed away a few steps. Hok strode to Kitu, holding out a small backpack, which Kitu accepted wordlessly. Hok then continued past him and stopped shoulder to shoulder with Elyth, facing the opposite direction. He leaned close, spoke in a low voice.

"Eliya," he said. "I'm Hok. Watch your step out here. Ground's trickier than it looks."

He gave her a look then, just for a moment, and she understood he wasn't talking only about the terrain. Before she could respond, though, he stepped past her and made a circling gesture with his hand, then started walking back over the ridge. The rest of the group moved out; Elyth swiveled around to follow.

"See you back at the ranch," Hok said to Kitu over his shoulder.

"Yep," Kitu said, with a casual wave.

In truth, Elyth was well trained on a variety of frames; taking up the strider was as good as second nature. But that wasn't something she wanted to make known. The challenge, then, was in concealing her comfort, and in deciding how long she had to carry on the ruse. Striders weren't difficult to operate by any means; it was more a matter of adjusting expectations than learning a new skill. The frame amplified natural body movement, so the trick was to walk easily, by feel rather than sight, knowing that the frame would flatten the mountains and raise the valleys, no matter how intimidating they looked.

Elyth took a few halting steps, some tentative, some harder than necessary. She'd forgotten how difficult it was to fake clumsiness.

"Take it slow," Sarinn said. "Just got to get a feel for it. You'll get your feet under you pretty quick."

Elyth nodded, then took smaller steps, as if testing the surface of a frozen lake. The group moved over the ridge together. As they crossed, Elyth gestured back toward Kitu.

"Is he going to be all right out here on his own?" she asked.

"Kitu?" Sarinn said, and made a noise somewhere between a cough and a laugh. "He's probably the happiest man on the planet right now."

He didn't explain further, and Elyth didn't press it. As they made their way down the opposite side of the ridge, she noted how the group had abandoned its previous inverted V formation; Hok led from the front now, with Sarinn and Amei taking positions on his left and right, respectively, with Amei slightly behind. Though there'd been no open communication about it, they'd subtly surrounded her. There was no doubt they were guarding her. But most to her interest, Elyth took note of how naturally they'd moved into the formation, how organic and casual it felt. If she hadn't been paying attention, it could easily have seemed accidental, just the result of a few friends walking the woods together.

It wasn't long before they came to a small, shallow gully trailing down the slope. And though it was an easy hop to cross, Elyth decided to take advantage of the opportunity it presented. When she reached the edge, she pushed off with more force than she knew she needed. The leap propelled her several feet beyond the other side of the gully, just a few steps behind Hok. On the landing, she surged forward with bounding steps and passed Hok on his left. She'd barely put her foot down on her second step beyond him when she jerked to a jarring halt that spun her a quarter turn to the right.

Hok was there, one hand gripping the shoulder of her frame, holding her in place.

"Whew," she said. "Thanks."

He kept his hand on her frame for a few moments, his eyes intense.

"Sorry about that," Elyth said.

He nodded, and finally relaxed his grip. Elyth held out her hand, inviting him to continue leading the way. He moved on past her then, but she could still see the tension in his shoulders, how he carried himself coiled, ready for action. Her little test had been informative. Even though they had her frame on tether, Hok's immediate reaction showed they weren't relying on it to keep her in place. She was very much their prisoner.

She resumed her place in the middle of the group, and they kept an easy pace, walking in silence for several minutes. As they approached the bottom of another ridge, Sarinn spoke.

"What I still don't get," he said, "is how you knew my name."

Elyth looked over at him and answered, "You just look like a Sarinn."

He looked at her, his brow furrowed; she kept her expression neutral. She gave it a beat, until the momentary confusion melted from his face as he realized she was joking. He shook his head, and then she added, "You guys are loud talkers. I'd guess every bird, bug, and bear on the mountain knows your name by now."

Amei chuckled at that, the first positive emotion Elyth had seen from her thus far. At the sound, Hok glanced back over his shoulder at Elyth.

"Speaking of which . . ." he said. "Looks like you've got the hang of it now. Let's cut the chatter and get off the mountain."

He picked up the pace then, and Elyth realized just how much they'd been holding back for her sake, and just how little he'd been convinced of her unfamiliarity with the frame. Hok bounded like a hind up the slope, moving with a sudden grace made uncanny by his stature.

After that, there was little time for talking, as Elyth found herself focused intently on trying to follow in Hok's wake. How the man managed to find paths through even the densest portions of the woods without slowing, she didn't know. There was no weaving wildly, no crashing haphazardly through branches. He didn't appear to be following any visible trail; it was almost as though the trees themselves moved aside when they saw him coming.

She wondered if he'd forgotten her injured state, or maybe was simply relying on the frame's tether to help her keep up. Whatever the case, he didn't seem to be making any allowance for her at all.

It was about an hour or so before Hok held up a hand and slowed the group to a lazy jog, then to a casual walk. At first, Elyth thought they were pausing for a rest, but as she looked up the long, steep tree-laden slope of the next ridge, she saw how it was dotted here and there with small clearings twinkling like the first stars of dusk. She counted six such areas; homes snaking their way up the mountain, with plenty of space between neighbors. Their destination, she presumed.

The path they'd taken had ranged up and down so many ridges, she'd lost any chance of making a good estimate of the distance they'd covered. Between nine and twelve miles, she guessed. Maybe even farther, based on how she felt. Though the striders typically made travel almost appallingly easy, the pace they'd kept had her breathing ele-

vated, and she found herself sweating even as the temperature dropped
with the sun. Her new companions were similarly lightly winded, but
their expressions suggested this sort of travel was commonplace.

"Amei, you want to go let everybody know we're coming in?" Hok
said.

"Yeah, sure," she said, and launched off again. Elyth quickly lost
sight of her as she vanished up a trail into the woods and the gloaming.
Hok dropped back alongside her on her right as they walked; a casual,
friendly sort of move that once again felt natural while also having the
effect of securing her between Sarinn and himself.

"We'll be up there in a few more minutes," he offered.

Elyth nodded. "I'm not going to upset the neighbors?"

"Not unless you're planning to make a lot of noise."

They crossed the nadir and started up the slope, following a wider
trail than the one Amei had taken. Compared to everything else she'd
seen, it could have been considered almost a road, though it would've
been a bumpy ride and probably only one way at a time. It didn't seem
like the kind of place that got much traffic anyway.

As they continued up the main road, they passed a handful of tribu-
tary trails, perhaps half as wide. Down them, and sometimes through
the momentary alignment of corridors of trees, she caught glimpses of
man-made structures: outbuildings, the occasional cabin. There were no
fences, no walls, no imposing gates. Just simple homes, built neatly to
harmonize with the landscape around them. Though the lines of the architecture weren't nearly as graceful, Elyth was reminded of the Paragon's home, which had seemed as much a part of her garden as any of
its trees or flowers. There was something of that same spirit here, a careful and intentional coordination between the mountain and the humans
living on it. The surrounding forest had lost none of its wildness, there
was no sense of its having been tamed; one could almost believe the people had asked permission to build, and the mountain had given it.

About two-thirds of the way up the slope, Hok led them off the road and along a gently curving path on the right. Soon a cabin came into view, its windows and exterior dark, but nevertheless inviting in its pleasant design. They stopped outside near the rear entrance, and both men began unhooking from their striders.

"You can just leave it out here," Hok said to Elyth. "We'll put them away later."

Sarinn hopped out of his frame and disappeared inside the cabin. As Elyth dismounted, Hok walked over and retrieved her pack off the back of Sarinn's strider. Lights came on inside. Hok gave her a moment to stretch and look around, and then escorted her into the cabin.

The rear entry led to a small room twice as wide as it was long, almost like a hallway turned the wrong direction. A row of hooks lined the wall, upon which hung two coats; beneath one of the coats stood a pair of muddied boots. They passed through the room into an open common area that appeared to be the bulk of the cabin's footprint. It housed a small kitchen, a long table with benches on either side, a couch and a few chairs, a large fireplace. Though warmer than outside, the air was still cool and had a settled scent that suggested it'd been closed up for a time. Two doors led off to the left and through one of these Sarinn appeared, climbing stairs.

"All set," he said. "I'll get the striders put away."

"Thanks," Hok said, as Sarinn exited out the back. Hok set Elyth's pack on the floor by the large table and then led her to the set of stairs Sarinn had just used. It hadn't been apparent from the exterior that the cabin had a lower floor; Elyth suspected she was being squirreled away in the basement. From the top of the stairs, she couldn't see what lay below, other than the landing at the foot that opened to the right. When she reached it, she had the distinctive, close, quiet feeling that accompanied being surrounded by earth. There was a tight hallway with two doors on each side.

"Bathroom," Hok said, pointing to a door on the right. Then he gestured to the door across from it. "Guest room."

He waited outside while Elyth entered. The room was small by most standards, but about twice the size of the cabin she'd had on the *Helegoss*. Bed, dresser, chair in the corner, small table with a lamp on it. Closet. One window, near the ceiling and no more than eight inches high. From the outside the window was at ground level, but there was no way Elyth would be able to fit through it if she tried.

"Most comfortable-looking cell I've ever seen," she said.

"You've seen a lot?"

"Not from the inside."

"Only thing I'm going to lock up is your pack," Hok said. "And that's just so you can be sure nobody's going to go digging around in your belongings while you're here."

"And you can be sure I don't sneak off in the middle of the night?"

"We'll be sure of that whether you have the pack or not," he said. But then he lightened the comment with a subdued smile. "But it never hurts to provide incentives. Before I put it up, though, you have anything in it I need to know about? Weapons or anything?"

Elyth shook her head.

"You keep all those in the one you're carrying?" he asked, nodding at the small sling she still had on her.

"I don't have any weapons at all," she answered.

"Sure," he said, obviously not believing her. "Listen, I understand the need for protection. I just like to have an idea of what's in my house."

"You don't need to worry."

Hok grunted at that.

"Yeah," he said. "Well . . ." He trailed off for a moment, and waved a hand vaguely before adding, "All right, then. Make yourself at home, get cleaned up if you want to."

He departed and she heard him start back up the stairs, but then pause. A few moments later he returned and stuck his head around the door frame.

"You hungry?"

Elyth was indeed hungry, but she shrugged noncommittally.

"I'll see what I can scrounge up," Hok said. "Sarinn will probably eat the table if I don't. You're welcome to join us if you like."

"Thank you," Elyth said. The words seemed odd in her mouth, thanking her captor, even though "capture" had been her intent. It was a strange situation, and Hok seemed equally uncertain in his role as both host and warden. He nodded and then returned upstairs, leaving her to herself.

As was her habit, Elyth's first order of business was to investigate her surroundings. A thorough check of her room didn't reveal any secrets or surprises. The bathroom was likewise unremarkable. The other two doors on the hallway were closed and locked, and though she could have opened them without anyone knowing, she thought it best to respect the obvious wishes of her hosts. At least for now.

With her survey completed, she returned to her room, hung her sling up in the tiny closet along with her vest and topcoat, and then sat on the bed. She took off her boots and socks. After all she'd been through, the feeling of the cool wood floor beneath her bare feet brought a simple kind of pleasure, and Elyth allowed herself a moment to savor it.

It was, perhaps, because she gave her body permission to relax that her injuries came rushing back to her full attention, and the constant dull ache that had been mere background noise for the past hours became a sudden weight upon her shoulders. She sat there on the bed taking mental inventory of her various hurts and occasionally testing them with motion or pressure to determine their extent. Her shoulders and rib cage housed the bulk of the pain, though as she evaluated herself, she realized she'd suffered more knocks and bruises than she'd initially thought. It may have taken less time if she'd simply noted which parts of her *didn't* hurt.

She pulled her pant leg up and checked her injured kneecap once more. The bruise had darkened and spread, and the surrounding flesh was swollen and painful to the touch. She straightened her leg out, tested bending it at different angles, felt how the fluid and the already stiffening joint affected movement. It would only get worse.

Her body was damaged, and no amount of natural remedy would provide the healing she needed as quickly as she needed it. Though her exhaustion was near total, Elyth gathered the willpower to call upon the aid of the substance of the universe. She cleared her mind of all but a single image; silver grass laden with snow, withered yet still alive. And focusing upon this image, she allowed the words of the Deep Language to bubble up and then crystallize. She spoke to her body, as though it was a thing apart.

"Winter's grasp falters, spring renews the world."

The call was no mere trick of perception or subtle influence exerted over a willing mind; with the words of the Deep Language, Elyth drew her healing out of its natural rhythm and into the immediate. She felt the warmth seeping first into her joints, and then radiating along her bones, a golden starlight washing through her nerves, her muscle fibers, her blood vessels. And it was not without cost.

She had touched lightly the infinite pool, disturbed the mirrored stillness, and now, with her mind's eye, she perceived its effect rippling across the placid surface, hypnotic. There was danger there, in allowing herself to watch for too long; a risk of falling helplessly into that fathomless depth, beyond all measure of time or space. And as her being surveyed her ethereal surroundings, she saw something more on the distant cosmic horizon. A second disturbance, separate from her own; a gliding swell, as though the coil of some leviathan had passed just beneath the surface. It vanished as quickly as it had appeared, but the strange vision shocked her back to herself, and she felt the folding in of her perception once more to her physical environment.

For ten minutes she sat trembling on her bed, feet flat on the floor, head light, and vision dreamlike. Elyth felt the longing awakening within her and with effort withdrew back to her body and to herself. Though she'd intellectually understood the Paragon's concerns about cutting short her recovery time, this experience of too-soon contact with the limitless made it real. A stark reminder of how precarious her situation was. And with it had come a vision of what? Something changed in the fabric of the universe. Or, perhaps, in her relation to it.

The trembling eventually subsided, and Elyth forced herself back to her feet. She walked barefoot to the bathroom and washed her hands and arms and face. In the mirror, she saw the long marks that striped both shoulders, near the intersection of her neck and collarbone on both sides; part abrasion, part bruising, where the straps of her harness had held her fast during the crash. Dried blood still clung to one corner of her mouth. But her healing had already begun, from the inside out. These outward signs would be the last to fade, and once she'd finished scrubbing away the blood, dust, and grime, she felt momentarily refreshed.

When she came out of the bathroom, she found Sarinn standing at the foot of the stairs with his mouth full and half of a small cake or flat biscuit in his hand.

"Got some food upstairs," he said around the bite. "Nothing fancy, but tastes better than an empty stomach. Coming up?"

In truth, hungry as she was, nothing sounded as good to Elyth as locking herself in her room and crashing on the bed. But her body needed the nutrients, and the opportunity to further observe her captors couldn't be missed.

"Sure," she said.

"Great," Sarinn replied, and he clomped back up the stairs without waiting for her.

For a moment, she considered grabbing her topcoat, or at least putting her boots back on. The cabin was warming, but still cooler than was comfortable for her. But she knew the effect it would have if she appeared as she was now dressed: short-sleeved and shoeless, content in her circumstances, with no sign of intent to escape. Her casual vulnerability would put them at ease. She padded up the stairs.

When she reached the main floor, she found Sarinn standing by the fireplace, a dish in one hand and another biscuit in the other, watching over a fire. From the way the bright yellow-orange flames crackled and spit sparks, Elyth guessed he'd just gotten it going in the past minute or two. Hok had his back to her, washing something in the sink, but when he heard her, he turned and nodded toward the table before returning his attention to his work. On the table sat a dish of the same design as Sarinn's, either a deep plate or a shallow bowl, filled with a thick, sandy-colored meal like porridge or oatmeal. A few strips of some kind of meat were laid on top of the meal, and three biscuits balanced on the wide edge of the dish. A tall mug sat next to it, steaming lightly.

Elyth crossed the room and started to sit on the bench by the table.

"Warmer by the fire," Hok said without looking at her.

Elyth gathered her dish and mug and joined Sarinn by the fireplace. An oversized chair sat nearby, and she sat cross-legged in it, balancing her dish on her lap and placing her mug on the wide, flat armrest. She was just about to take her first bite when she realized she didn't have any eating utensils. Even with the monoculture of the Ascendance uniting them, manners varied somewhat from planet to planet and city to city, but the meal didn't seem like something to eat with bare hands.

She could tell Sarinn was watching her, and when she looked to him he smiled.

"You know," he said, "a biscuit's just a spoon you can eat."

"Fair warning," Hok said from across the room. "We're a bunch of savages."

He started opening drawers and rummaging around, but Elyth waved him off.

"No, this is fine," she said. "I'm good."

She tore a chunk off one of her biscuits, scooped up a good portion of the meal with it, and popped it in her mouth. It had a rich flavor and a hearty texture, nutrient-dense. She tried a bite of the meat next and found it was salted; like thick-cut jerky, though not as tough. A simple fare, but undoubtedly good for people used to physically demanding work. Those first bites awakened her hunger, and as neither of her companions seemed particularly interested in conversation, she tucked in. The beverage had a strong flavor, earthy and honey-sweet, with an afterburn that suggested a small amount of strong alcohol. This she sipped cautiously at first, testing its effects before committing to drinking it all. But whatever was in it did little more than warm and relax her, and both were welcome.

Hok finished cleaning up the kitchen while she ate and then busied himself around the main room. Elyth set her empty dish on the armrest, cupped her mug in both hands, and tucked her knees up. A few moments later, Hok wordlessly dropped a light blanket over the back of her chair. She tugged the corners of it over her shoulders and upper arms. The fire had settled, now glowing blue green over a bed of forge-hot coals. Sarinn made some adjustments to it, added a log, and then wandered off.

It took a few minutes before Elyth realized all of this was purely for her comfort. Sarinn had disappeared, and Hok didn't seem to have any plans to join her. She watched him for a time. He was busy around the cabin, but not with anything obviously useful. It appeared to be his way of keeping an eye on her while giving her some sense of space.

"Thanks for the meal," she said.

"Sure," he answered.

Elyth laid her head back against the chair and surveyed the ceiling; it was open, its exposed beams well crafted and joined without obvious mechanism. Simple wasn't quite the right way to describe it. Functional, certainly, but there was an elegance to its design that suggested a far higher degree of intent and craftsmanship than mere function would require. It had something of a hand-carved quality, almost as though the entire roof had been lovingly chipped, bit by bit, from a single massive tree.

"This is a nice place," she said. Hok didn't respond. It was always a delicate dance, in the beginning, as she judged how best to navigate early interactions with potential assets, and he was tougher to read than most. But not impossible. His actions spoke of his care for her general well-being; his reticence told her of his concern of giving away information. There was something more than mere unease at having a stranger on his mountain and in his home. A suppressed fear that he was doing his best to conceal. And though she couldn't guess the source of his anxiety, she could at least read the careful balance she had to strike. Appear too anxious to escape, and his guard would never lower. Appear too comfortable, though, and his suspicion would only grow.

"A really nice place," she said. "Any guess how long you're going to force me to stay?"

"'Til morning," he said. "And then maybe longer."

"Anything I can do to influence that one way or the other?"

He paused whatever it was he was doing across the room and looked at her for a long moment.

"You can make it worse," he said. "But I'd rather you didn't."

She returned his gaze and then nodded.

"Well, what if I just go to sleep?"

"Probably the best course of action."

She nodded again, drained her mug, and then stood and picked up her dish.

"Think I'll just do that, then."

"You can leave those on the table," Hok said, nodding at the dishes.

Elyth dropped them off on the table on her way out and headed to the stairs. But she paused before heading down.

"Thank you for the meal. See you in the morning," she said.

"Sleep well," he answered, and sounded sincere.

She returned to her room then, locked the door behind her, grabbed her sling out of the closet, and sat on the bed. A quick check of the sling confirmed that her stun baton was on top and easily accessible. She placed the pack on the floor between the table and the bed, within reach and where it wouldn't be immediately obvious. Just in case.

It felt vaguely wrong to sleep in the clothes she'd just crossed a mountain in, but if anything were to happen in the night, she wanted to be ready to respond. She swiveled her feet up on to the bed, wrapped the top quilt over herself, then reached over and touched the lamp, switching off its soft glow. The room plunged into immediate and complete darkness, with a heaviness reminiscent of a cave.

It wasn't long before sleep came, but despite her exhaustion, Elyth slept lightly through the first part of the night, attentive to every unusual sound, listening for any warning of betrayal or danger. But she heard none.

So it was with great surprise that she awoke in the early-morning hours to find a man she didn't recognize sitting at the foot of her bed.

SIX

Elyth's senses exploded into full wakefulness, but she held herself completely still and kept her breathing deep and even. The room was lit only by the trickle of graying, predawn light from the window; she felt the man's presence more than she saw it. From the little she could see, he seemed to be sitting in the chair at the foot of the bed, with the back against an adjacent wall, facing the door. He didn't appear to be watching her sleep, so much as keeping watch while she slept. That distinction was small comfort, though, given his silent invasion. At least as long as he thought she was asleep, Elyth still had the chance to observe and to prepare. Her mind unfolded possibilities, began forming plans of action.

But she didn't have the chance to carry any of them out.

"A terrible way to wake, I know," the man said quietly. "And a worse first impression."

Somehow he'd detected that she was awake. Elyth cautiously drew herself upright toward the head of the bed and edged to the side, creating space between the two of them, ready to spring up if necessary. The man didn't move. Her baton was just a quick reach away. But if he'd intended to hurt her, he could've already done so. She would wait. For now.

"How'd you get in here?"

"Through the door."

"It was locked."

"It was," he said.

His profile changed slightly in the gloom; he had turned his head slightly to look at her obliquely, as though doing so directly would be too much of an impropriety. The most polite of intruders.

"I could lock it again if it'd make you feel better," he added.

"What do you want?" Elyth asked.

"Word reached me that we had a guest. I decided I needed to meet you for myself."

"And you couldn't think of a less intrusive way to do it?"

"I suppose I could have crashed into a nearby mountain to get your attention, but unfortunately I am without a ship."

He said it flatly, but there was a curl of a smile in the words. His accent was different from that of the others she had met thus far—less pronounced, thinner somehow. It wasn't *educated* precisely, but his pronunciation gave the impression of an elevated level of knowledge, the breadth and depth of which he was careful to conceal.

"If I could have avoided that," Elyth said, "I would have, I assure you."

"It's a big mountain. One would assume it'd be easy to see, and therefore easy to avoid."

"One might also assume the fact that I crashed would make it obvious it wasn't intentional."

"Well, it would seem one could assume many things, if one were foolish enough."

There was something playful about the man's demeanor, almost as if he were enjoying some prank or inside joke. But Elyth sensed danger, too, and not just from the unsettling circumstances. There was a sharpness to the air, an electric uncertainty; the feeling of encountering a lone wolf in the wild. He was testing her, listening in-tently.

"And I assume it would be foolish to ask you to leave," Elyth said.

"Not to ask," the man replied.

Apart from the slight turning of his head, the man still hadn't moved, but Elyth couldn't help feeling like he had the upper hand at every turn of the conversation. And that was a feeling she couldn't abide. She wasn't sure how long he'd been sitting in the darkened room, she didn't know how much his eyes had adjusted and how well he could see her. To be on the safe side, she casually shifted on the bed, leaning forward slightly and masking the subtle positioning of her hand nearer the lamp on the nightstand.

"What if I screamed instead?"

"I was half expecting it when you first woke," he said. "Now, it would just seem forced. And, to be frank, unbecoming of a woman of your obvious caliber."

"You can tell a lot about a woman just from watching her sleep, huh?"

"It sounds . . . unflattering when you say it like that."

"I'd be curious to hear how you could make it sound any other way, stranger."

The man chuckled and turned to look at her fully, though the room was still too dark for her to get a sense of his appearance.

"I am sorry, Eliya. Despite my dramatic entrance, I'm not here to upset you. I just wanted to talk."

"And if I don't feel like talking?" she asked.

"That would be disappointing," the man said. "But understandable. Unfortunately, our time together is limited, and I don't expect to have the opportunity again."

Elyth tried to deduce what she could from the man's words and his manner of speech. His accent was almost no accent at all. Trained at the

Academy, maybe. Or former Ascendance personnel, whose time out of service had softened the edges of the usual crisp professionalism off his syllables.

"Out of all the mountains in the galaxy, why this one?" he asked.

His mention of the galaxy raised a warning flag in her mind. Nothing about her crash, her ship, or herself should have given away the fact that she was from off-world. If he'd said it more casually, she could have taken it as exaggeration for effect, but he struck her as a man who was carefully intentional about his choice of words.

"What do you mean?" Elyth said.

"Your accident. Why here?"

"It was the mountain that happened to be under me when I fell?" she answered. "I don't understand the question."

"You almost sound like a local. Almost. Close enough for most. But you're not from here. Not from anywhere on Qel."

Elyth made no response, neither confirming nor denying the claim.

"Things out of their place have a certain quality about them," he continued. "A quality made stronger by greater distance from where they belong. And you, Eliya, seem very far from home. So. Why here?"

"It isn't where I intended to be," she said. "And if your friends upstairs had let me go on my way as I requested, I wouldn't be here at all."

The man sat silently for a moment, watching her in the darkness. She knew he couldn't read her expression closely, but the effect was still unsettling. He had a hint of the Deep Language about him, but none of its latent power within; the scent of smoke on one who had witnessed a forest fire, but had never been among its flames. And there was something evasive about the man's presence;

her mind seemed to slide off of even the few details she could gather.

"Hok told me you were a tough one to read," the man said finally. "And he's sharp. A genuinely good man. I like him. I think I like you, too. I wonder if we could be friends."

"Maybe," Elyth said. "Chances would have been better if you hadn't let yourself into my room while I was sleeping."

"Not going to let that go, are you?"

"Not until you give me something better."

"Are you here to kill *eth ammuin*?" he asked, his tone just as quiet and friendly, the sudden directness of the question jarring. There was no doubt, then, that he intended to keep her off-balance.

"I'm sorry, what?"

"*Eth ammuin.* Are you here to kill him?"

The fact that nothing in her extensive pre-mission research had mentioned *eth ammuin* made it somewhat safe to assume he wasn't widely known, whoever he was.

"I don't know who that is," she answered. "But I'm not here to hurt anyone."

"To exist is to risk harming others. And your arrival has now created the possibility of your absence. What if I like you so much, it hurts me to let you leave?"

"Then I would say that you have intimacy issues."

The man laughed.

"Truer than you know!" he said. "And I'd like to believe you, Eliya."

"Then why don't you?"

The speed with which he moved was shocking; he was on his feet in an instant, so fast that Elyth would have been at his complete mercy had she not been on guard. But she'd been ready.

At his first sudden motion, Elyth closed her eyes tightly and tapped the lamp, briefly splashing the room in light as she spun from the bed. A half second later, she tapped the lamp off and snatched up her baton, stepped across the room to the closet. She had only a handful of seconds to take advantage of the man's temporary blindness, to judge his reaction and to act accordingly.

"That is why," he said.

He was still standing by his chair, having done nothing else besides raise one hand. Neither a reflexive flinch nor an attack interrupted; just a mild sort of gesture to placate her, as though physical conflict never occurred to him as a possibility. She could see him blinking in the darkness, and he'd clearly lost track of her. His head, slightly lowered, swiveled slowly between the bed and the door.

"Assuming you're still in the room?" he added.

Elyth kept her place by the closet, diagonally from the man, with all the space between them that the small room could afford. Her positioning helped reset her sense of footing in the situation. They stood now as equals.

"As you said," she answered. "One can assume many things."

His head tipped up at the sound of her voice, turned to locate her. A few moments passed as his eyes readjusted to the darkness and Elyth waited to see what would come next.

"You're taller than I expected," he said.

"You're shorter than I thought," she replied. They were nearly the same height; if she hadn't been barefoot, Elyth may have even been slightly taller.

"I have poor posture," he said. He stood up straighter, gained maybe a half inch of height. And then a moment later, to her surprise, sat back down, completely ceding the power dynamic of the room.

"Normal people don't walk away from crashes to go hike in the wilderness," he said casually, "or use lamps for tactical advantage."

"I never claimed to be normal."

"Then you understand my concerns."

"No, I really don't. I already told you, I never wanted to be here. Your people brought me against my will."

"Which would be an impressive way to infiltrate a protected area."

"And a ridiculous amount of trouble to go through. If I really were here to take out your friend, I'd have a better story."

"So why lie to them about being from Qel?"

"Because my business is nobody else's."

"I could make it mine."

There was an abrupt darkness to those words, a shift in energy. It wasn't a threat, exactly, but there was no mistaking the implication and again Elyth had a glimpse of genuine danger in the man. It was no empty posturing. She stood for a few seconds in silence and then returned to the bed and perched on the edge of it, using her body language to soften the moment.

"I never said I was from Qel," she said quietly.

The man chuckled at that. Another span of silence passed, and Elyth had the impression that he was no longer evaluating her current actions so much as he was reflecting on everything he'd already observed.

"It's possible I've mistaken you for someone else," he said finally, and sounded almost disappointed. "But I still think we could be friends. Unfortunately, I'm not sure I expect to see you again."

Elyth wasn't quite sure what to make of the statement, but it didn't matter. A moment later she became aware of a distant rumbling from outside, growing rapidly in volume and intensity. Vehicles approaching. Instinctively she looked to the tiny window, hoping for a glimpse of what was descending upon them. Moments later a beam of white light flashed briefly across the ground outside, followed by some manner of commotion.

"Don't worry," the man said. "They aren't here for you."

He stood up again, a little straighter this time, as if remembering their exchange, and ran a hand down the front of his shirt to smooth it. And then bowed to her.

"Goodbye, Eliya. Thank you for the company. These days I don't often get to meet new people."

He turned then and left the room, politely closing the door behind him. When she heard him walking up the stairs, she slipped out and quietly followed.

The man had already exited the stairwell when she reached it, and she could hear low voices from upstairs. She crept up, keeping close to the wall, and then stopped a couple of steps from the top and leaned forward, low to the landing, peering around the door frame. A group of a half dozen people stood in the open area, with the man who had interrogated her standing roughly in the middle of them. His back was to her, but she could tell from his gestures and the way he looked from person to person that he was giving some quiet explanation, or maybe apology.

He was the shortest among them, five foot seven or eight by her estimation, and his build suggested he'd be more at home in a library than doing any sort of heavy labor. She could only see him in occasional profile, but his olive-bronze skin had the weather-beaten look of a man used to long and frequent exposure to the elements, and the vibrance of his cheeks suggested strong health and abundant energy. His shaggy hair, mostly dark brown with an elusive tint of red, had begun to frost with gray, as had the stubbled beard that looked more like the product of neglect than any sort of planned feature. Taken all together, his appearance made it impossible to judge his age; he could have been a younger man, prematurely gray, or an older man of uncommonly good health.

Hok and Amei stood off to one side, apart from the group; the others were exactly the kind of people she'd been hoping to avoid.

There was authority in their look, but also subdued anger, and perhaps embarrassment. It was the look of an experienced security detail that'd lost their charge. Seeing them surrounding the man shifted him into a new light to Elyth's eyes. He wasn't the head of their team. He was the object of their protection.

The Detail closed in around him; no one touched him, but their intent was obvious. He moved toward the rear door, head down, shoulders rounded, all the power she had sensed in him deflated and subdued. He almost didn't even look like the same person. Watching him now, she couldn't decide which of the two was the real expression of his being.

Just before he exited, the man glanced back over his shoulder at her hiding place. His features were sharp; distinctive, if not particularly attractive. He flashed a quick, schoolboy grin, as though he knew she was watching. And then he was gone.

Hok and Amei stood by, both completely submissive to the others; heads down, eyes averted. It was strange to see them in that manner, particularly Hok, who had seemed only the day before to be a man who would kneel before no one. They both stood quietly after the door had closed, but as soon as the vehicles outside lifted off, Amei turned and grabbed Hok's arm with both hands, her eyes wide with shock and a broad smile illuminating her face.

"Are you kidding me?!" she said. "Are you kidding me! Did all of that actually happen or am I asleep right now?"

Hok smiled and gave a bewildered shrug.

"I can't believe that actually happened," Amei continued. "Sarinn is going to be so mad he missed all of this."

"You know he won't believe us," Hok said.

Elyth emerged from the stairwell and they both reacted, tense, as though she'd caught them in an intimate moment.

"Who was that man?" she asked.

Amei looked at Hok. It took a moment before he answered.

"That was the man who changed my life," he said. "That was *eth ammuin.*"

SEVEN

"I didn't realize you were old friends," Elyth said. "From the way you reacted to having him in your house."

They were seated on the front porch of the cabin, Elyth wrapped in a blanket, Hok next to her, and Amei on his other side, each with a hot drink in hand as ward against the morning chill. The gray horizon was just beginning to warm with the first colors of dawn, the stars slowly ceding their watch to the greater light to come. After all the excitement, no one had been interested in trying to go back to sleep.

"I wouldn't say we're friends, exactly. And the way things work up here . . ." Hok said. He started to say one thing, then seemed to think better of it, and instead added, "He doesn't get out as much as he used to."

"Too famous now?"

"Something like that."

"Let's just say his house has a lot more fences than this one," Amei said. "And not as many neighbors."

Elyth filed that information away; *eth ammuin* living in protected isolation.

"He ever show up in your room when you were sleeping?" she asked.

"He shows up a lot of places you wouldn't expect," Hok said. "But no, that was a new one, as far as I know."

The conversation dropped off for a few moments, as though that brief exchange had answered everything Elyth could want to know about the whole strange situation. She tried to keep her tone light and conversational, feigning casual curiosity rather than intent interest.

"So, he's what? King of the mountain, then?"

"You sure ask a lot of questions," Hok said.

"It's not every day I wake up to a strange man in my room. Just trying to get a handle on him."

"That's one thing you'll never do," he replied, his tone neutral, without hostility. Merely stating a fact. He watched the horizon for a span, and Elyth thought maybe she'd gotten all she would out of him. Talking seemed to take more effort for him than running miles over the mountain. But then he took a breath, sighed, and said, "But he's a good man. I know it all seems strange to an outsider like you. But if you knew *eth ammuin* like we do, it wouldn't be as hard to understand. Or, I guess, you wouldn't feel like you had to try so hard to understand."

Elyth was still trying to decide how to steer the conversation when Amei chimed in a few moments later.

"He just has a way of making you feel the truth of a thing."

At Amei's description Elyth felt a shadow of something familiar; a memory fell over her, laden with the impression of power and authority she felt during her first lessons at the feet of her instructors. Words founded within the Deep Language bore a significance and richness of meaning almost too substantial to bear.

In the brief time Elyth had spent with him, she hadn't sensed any of the falseness of a trickster, the arrogance of a would-be ruler, or the sickness of thought that inevitably thrived in a cult. But the indicators couldn't be ignored. She needed to dig deeper.

"It's hard to explain," Hok said. "Be a whole lot easier to understand if you just ask him yourself."

"I don't think I'm going to have the chance," Elyth said. "He told me he didn't expect he'd see me again."

Hok nodded and took another drink, eyes still scanning the horizon. He hadn't looked at her since they'd sat down.

"Does that mean I can leave?" she asked.

"Soon," Hok said. "Detail thinks it'll be safe to move you in a couple of days."

Elyth noted the mention of the security detail; that they were responsible for *eth ammuin's* protection had been obvious from how they'd arrived and whisked him away. But it sounded as though their authority extended to more than just the one man.

"The Detail. His personal bodyguards, I assume."

"Yeah."

"They're in charge around here?" Elyth asked.

Hok shrugged and after a moment said, "They're interested in what's best for everyone."

"At least, that's what they say if you ask them," Amei added, not quite under her breath.

"I thought everyone was concerned about me getting picked up by the local authorities."

"Everyone was concerned about you *being* the local authorities. But as it appears that's not the case, we figure we'll just sit tight for a bit, and then everyone can go back to their own business."

"What makes you think they won't be hanging around looking for me?" she asked.

"Because they shut work down before dark last night," Hok said. "I don't think they're trying too hard to find out what happened."

"Wish I'd known that yesterday," Elyth said. "Would have saved me a trip up the mountain."

"Worked out all right for you. That's one of the reasons the Detail decided you weren't a spy."

"How's that?"

"Figured if the Ascendance set all this up just to get one of their own inside, they'd be making a bigger show out of how surprised and concerned they were over the crash. The fact that they're doing shoddy work down there is a good sign they don't have a vested interest in what happens to you."

"Trouble is, we're going to have to spend the next couple of days tracking down 'stray' drones that wandered off from the crash site," Amei said.

"Good for me, I guess. But I still don't understand the relationship," Elyth said. "Local authority is *the* local authority. How is it that you got them to agree to stay off the mountain?"

"Always with the questions," Hok said, waving a hand. But his tone suggested he wasn't as irritated as he was pretending to be. "I don't know all the legal arrangements. But the mountain's classified as a private preserve. I'd guess that has something to do with it."

Another oddity. None of that information showed up in any of the research she'd done. Nothing in any of the records she'd scoured had shown the stretch of wilderness outside Oronesse as anything noteworthy.

"We were always a low-traffic area," Amei said. "Detail really started tightening up the past few years, though. People got serious about our borders."

Elyth recalled *eth ammuin*'s sudden question about whether or not she was here to kill him.

"A threat against the old man," she asked, "an attempt on his life?"

Neither Hok nor Amei responded, and Elyth got the sense she was treading too heavily. She pulled the conversation back to what she hoped was safer ground.

"Well, what about you guys?" she asked. "You spend all your time just running striders all over the place?"

"Pretty much," Hok answered. "We're wardens."

Elyth thought back to her initial standoff with Hok, and the conflict she'd sensed in him as he'd wrestled with what to do with her. He was both protector and caretaker.

"That makes sense," Elyth said. "And it explains a lot."

"Yeah? Like what?" Amei asked.

"Like why you take such good care of everything around you," she answered. "Even when it's a stranger who fell out of the sky."

"So you know all about us now," Amei said. "Your turn."

"My turn what?"

"What's your deal?"

"I'm sorry," Elyth said, shaking her head. "I'd really rather not talk about it."

"You already got like a thousand times more words out of Hok than he usually uses in a year," Amei said. "You owe us."

"All right. Short version," Elyth said. "I made a long series of bad decisions. Finally tried to make a good one for a change. I thought maybe I could get myself pointed in the right direction, get a new start, if I had somewhere out of the way to think for a while."

"Maybe you aren't in the wrong place after all," Hok said quietly.

Elyth wondered how she was meant to take that, but didn't have long to ponder. Shortly after Hok's comment, the door to the cabin opened and Sarinn appeared in the doorway, balancing a mug and plate in one hand.

"Got the whole crew up early this morning, huh?" he said, jerking his head in Elyth's direction. She couldn't tell exactly what was on the plate, but whatever it was, there was a lot of it.

Sarinn plodded out, leaving the door halfway open behind him, and plopped down next to Amei, facing the horizon like the rest of them. "What'd I miss?"

Amei looked at Hok; Hok sipped his drink and then shook his head. "Nothing much," he said.

"*Eth ammuin* stopped by," Amei said.

"Sure, okay," Sarinn said with a scoff. He took a few bites of food, each the size of which fell somewhere beyond uncouth and just shy of revolting. "You hear from Kitu yet?" he asked a few moments later, around a bite of his breakfast.

"Yeah, he rolled in a little after midnight," Hok answered. "Went home to sleep in his own bed around two or three I guess."

"Surprised he's not here yet," Sarinn said. "Not like him to miss a sunrise."

"Even a machine like Kitu needs more than three hours of sleep," Amei said. "Especially after a day of hard running."

"Nah," a voice said from inside the cabin. "If it's a solid three, I'm good."

Kitu stepped out and made a show of closing the door behind him.

"And now I understand why I keep finding bugs in all the windows, Sarinn," he said.

"Ah, I knew you'd be right behind me," Sarinn said.

"Morning all," Kitu said. He gave Elyth a quick, shallow bow. "Eliya."

"Good morning, Kitu," Elyth said.

He walked over next to Sarinn and leaned against the rail of the porch, arms folded. It was only then that Elyth realized the significance of what was unfolding; there were only four chairs, and this was a morning ritual.

"Kitu, I'm in your seat," she said, starting to stand. But he waved her off.

"No, no," he said. "I'm good. Just spent a couple hours lying down, feels good to be up stretching my legs."

Elyth held her half crouch for a moment, unsure whether to accept the kindness or insist on relinquishing the seat.

"Stand if you want," Amei said. "But he won't take it no matter what you do."

She hadn't recognized the moment they'd invited her to share; now that she did, choosing to stand seemed tantamount to a refusal of their hospitality. She nodded, and sank back down into the chair.

"Well, thank you," she said.

That was the last that anyone spoke for several minutes as the sky grew lighter with the fast-approaching sunrise; the sounds of the waking mountain forest sharpened in their silence, interrupted only by the occasional sound of Sarinn finishing his breakfast.

He was the one who finally spoke again.

"Here she comes," he said. And sure enough, as though his words were what released her, for an instant the sky flashed a fleeting blue green, barely perceptible, and then the first sliver of Qel's sun appeared on the horizon. The five of them sat together for another stretch, silent witnesses to the birth of a new day. After a time, Hok spoke.

"All right folks," he said. "Guess that's our cue."

He drained the remainder of his drink and then stood and turned to address Elyth.

"We've got a few things to discuss together, work-related."

He didn't ask her to leave, but the implication was clear enough.

"Sure," Elyth said, rising and turning to go inside.

"Just be a few minutes," he said.

Elyth returned to the common area of the cabin and sat in one of the oversized chairs. She couldn't hear any of the discussion, but from what she could see through the window, she guessed the four wardens were deciding how to keep an eye on her while handling their other duties for the day. After about ten minutes, they came inside; Kitu and Sarinn continued straight on out the back door. Hok stopped in front of her.

"So," Hok said. "You've got two jobs today. Stay out of sight. Stay out of trouble. Amei's going to keep you company. Do me a favor and keep it simple for us. It's just a couple of days. And you really don't want to make Amei chase after you."

Elyth glanced over at the lean-muscled Amei, in her short sleeves despite the morning chill.

"You're right," she said, "I really don't."

Hok nodded and then headed off to whatever tasks awaited him. After they'd gone, Elyth looked over at Amei, waiting for some indication of what she should do now. Amei shrugged.

"Day's yours," she said. "You can go anywhere you like, as long as it's inside the cabin."

"Can't get outside?"

"You didn't get enough of that yesterday?"

Elyth chuckled. "World looks a little different when you're not on the run."

"Let's see how today goes," Amei said. "Maybe you can get a tour tomorrow, if you're still here."

"That sounds ominous. I thought Hok said it'd be a couple of days."

"Yeah, maybe. Could be sooner. Just depends on what the Detail decides. Hok probably didn't want to get your hopes up."

House arrest then. Not an ideal situation, but there was no reason to try to argue. Amei hadn't exactly warmed to Elyth, but she seemed less guarded than she had the day before, and Elyth didn't want to give her cause to revert.

"Tough day yesterday," Amei added. "A little forced rest will do you some good."

Elyth nodded, while her mind worked. With all she'd seen and heard in her short time among these people, she knew she had to investigate the land within the borders of the preserve while she could. If the Strain were at work, she would see its symptoms in the plants, the soil, the water. But she needed her cover intact; if it turned out that this was all a dead end, she didn't want to be remembered as anything more than a lost girl who got a little help along the way.

"Might not be so bad, I guess," she said. "I could probably sleep for two days straight anyway."

"Nothing stopping you," Amei replied.

"I might just do that, then," Elyth said. After a few minutes of lingering in the common area, she excused herself and returned to her room. She sat quietly on her bed for a time, mentally reviewing everything she'd observed about the cabin thus far, from the brief glimpses she'd gotten of the exterior to the more thorough examination she'd been able to give the inside. There'd been no obvious routes for sneaking out easily; the window in her room wasn't made to open. But architecture was just another system, and every system had its vulnerabilities.

There were still two rooms she hadn't investigated on the lower floor. Elyth grabbed her flashlight and multitool. Both rooms were still locked, but she made short work of those. The first room she checked was another bedroom, smaller than hers, and with three bunks crammed into it. The second, however, gave her some hope. It was a large utility closet, and in the rear wall was a panel, two feet square and flush to the floor; when she removed the panel, she found a crawlspace that appeared to be an access point to the cabin's geothermal system. The crawlspace was cold, a good sign that she'd found an uninsulated, transitional space between interior and exterior.

Elyth flicked on her light and poked her head and shoulders in. The space was tight vertically, and sloped gradually upward as far as she could see, which wasn't far; the darkness swallowed her light.

It took her some time to explore, given that she had to crawl on her belly, barely had room to lift her head, and was constantly concerned about making any noise. Eventually, she found a vent in an exterior wall, just large enough for her to squeeze through.

With ample care, Elyth worked the vent free from the inside. She'd lost her sense of direction in the close darkness of the crawlspace, but when she identified that the vent led out under the elevated front porch, her mental map of the cabin snapped into place.

She had her route out. Now she just needed to get her tools, and to buy herself enough time to perform her survey. The journey back to her room was much faster now that she understood the space. There, she gathered her supplies while mentally working out a timetable. A couple of hours to collect data, plus whatever time she'd need to move throughout the area unseen.

After she had a rough plan in place, she put in another appearance with Amei. Through carefully directed, casual conversation, Elyth learned Hok would be returning around dark and seeded the expectation that she'd spend the day sleeping in her room. It was just after midday when she emerged from the vent beneath the porch, dressed in her infiltration gear.

Elyth slipped across the open ground to the tree line but hadn't made it far from the cabin before she discovered a complicating factor; despite Hok's suggestion that the Detail was no longer concerned about her identity, they didn't seem to be taking any chances. Here and there through the trees, she spotted pairs of sentries forming a loose cordon around the cabin. After a few minutes of observation, though, it wasn't completely clear whether they were meant to keep her in or others out.

She crept through the forest with painstaking care, her every sense straining as she continually switched her focus between her broad surroundings and that which was immediately before her, as though she were hunting for a lost coin behind enemy lines. Collecting a variety of readings would help her build an environmental profile of the area; the greater the variety, the clearer the picture. But Elyth knew every sample she took would be hard-won, and getting caught would be catastrophic.

The result was a scattershot collection, far from her usual methodical approach. She prowled through the woods ever vigilant for sentries, using a handheld scanner to take samples and readings as opportunities appeared: from the soil; from leaves, flowers, and stems; from flowered branches and woody fungal blooms; from a gang of emerald-coated beetles and a peculiar six-winged moth. Despite her limited access, her reach into the mountain's environmental network was surprising. In-depth analysis would have to wait until she returned to the cabin, but she felt confident the data would be useful, despite the haphazard process of its collection.

And as she ranged farther from the cabin, she couldn't escape the sense that, though the forest growth wasn't agricultural in origin, it couldn't quite be classified as fully wild, either. The air had an evergreen fragrance, tinged with earthen notes of moss and mushroom, vibrant, full of life. There were no obvious signs of direct cultivation, but much of the tangle and snarl of undergrowth she would have expected was absent. And the healthy balance and richness of biodiversity suggested not a forest left to run wild, but rather a light touch of intentional, mindful stewardship.

It was rare to see such harmony between humans and their environment. And harmony was truly the best way to describe it. Elyth kept having the impression of musical overtones, as though the joining of earth and root and water were blending together to produce some higher resonance, emergent rather than created.

The natural wealth of the area drew her onward, even while her internal clock began to warn her that her time afield was growing short. A chance encounter alerted her to just how short it truly was.

Elyth was lying alongside the half-rotted remains of a fallen tree cataloguing a fringed purple moss when the sound of movement interrupted her. She rolled quickly up underneath the soft-wooded trunk, tucking herself into the little space that remained. Two sentries approached, striding loudly through the forest, and passing within twenty or thirty feet of her.

"—staring at empty trails about as long as I can stand," one was saying to the other.

"This should be the last rotation," the other answered. "Wardens are coming back in now, think they're going to wrap this all up pretty soon."

"You think they're going to get commended, or interrogated?"

"Some of both, probably." The conversation fell silent after that.

Elyth remained completely still until the guards had passed some distance away and then eased out of her hiding place. Judging from the sky, she guessed she still had another two hours at least before dark. Plenty of time, if everyone had kept to their schedules. But she had no way to know how close Hok and his fellow wardens were to their cabin now.

It would have been only a two- or three-minute jog, if only she could have moved with such speed. As it was, the most Elyth afford was a low, loping walk as she bounded from cover to cover, with brief pauses to survey the area before moving again.

Hope waned as she approached the cabin. Before she could even see it, she could hear voices, and when she finally got eyes on the place, she saw Amei at the rear entrance, talking with Hok and Kitu as they dismounted from their striders. Judging from their body language, it didn't appear that they'd yet discovered her absence, but if they were planning to go directly to her room, there was no way she'd be able to beat them there.

Any amount of time she could buy herself would be worth it. Elyth's eyes went to the trees surrounding the cabin. There had to be something she could use.

And there, not far from the trail leading to the cabin, she spotted a mighty oak, forked in the middle, and heavy-branched. The left fork leaned slightly, and its branches shaded the trail. The tree was old, a hundred years or more judging from its size, and it had plenty of life remaining in it. But in time, the weight of those limbs would become too much. Elyth formed the image in her mind, and with it the words.

There was no need to shout. A quiet word in the Deep Language carried power enough.

"Nature runs its course; even the mighty diminish."

A moment after she'd spoken, the tree creaked; at first, the wardens paid no mind. But the creaking grew in intensity, and there was no wind to cause it. Hok turned to look in its direction just as the largest branch twisted and sheared, plummeting to the ground.

The impact thundered; the limb was so thick, it would have been easy to mistake it for a full tree on its own. And it was partially blocking the trail. Elyth's purpose was met; after a few moments of staring, Hok and Kitu got back up into their striders and headed down to take a look, presumably to move it out of the way. Elyth didn't wait.

She couldn't cover her tracks as well as she would have liked. By the time she'd navigated the crawlspace, already she could hear the footsteps on the floor above. The vent she'd hastily crammed back into place; so too, she barely secured the panel. She left the utility closet and locked the door behind her. Above her, she could hear someone walking toward the stairs, the footsteps above almost echoes of her own as she padded down the hall to her room. She reached her door; it was locked. Of course it was. She'd locked it herself.

The door at the top of the stairs opened; the lock on her room was mechanical, simple, but required actual picking instead of mere override. Elyth closed her eyes, focused on the feeling in her fingers, and tried to ignore the footsteps on the stairs.

The lock clicked. Elyth swept into her room, closing the door as quickly as she could without making noise, and relocked it. Immediately she stripped off her hood and vest; she'd just unfastened her pants when the knock came.

It was a quiet knock at first, tentative. Elyth didn't respond, using every second she could to conceal every sign of her outing.

A second knock, this one louder.

"Uh," Elyth said, trying her best to sound as though she'd been woken from a deep sleep.

"Eliya?" came Hok's voice through the door.

"Yes?"

Elyth laid her gear on the floor of the closet, threw her clothes over top.

"Sorry to wake you, but it looks like you're leaving early."

"Oh?" she said, while she scrambled the covers on her bed. "I need to, uh . . . one second, I need to put some pants on."

And now that she'd had the conversation, she was free to make noise, and to breathe again. She grabbed the clothes she'd worn the previous day, calmed herself while she dressed. And with one arm in her topcoat, she opened her door before putting it on the rest of the way. Hok was still standing there.

"You okay?" he asked.

Elyth nodded. "The knock just startled me. Guess I was sleeping pretty hard."

He eyed her for a moment longer than was comfortable.

"And I dreamt my ship was crashing again, except it came down on the cabin, and somehow I was in both," she added. "It felt real."

"Top half of a tree came down outside," he said. "Maybe you heard it in your sleep."

"Oh," Elyth said. "Maybe. Storm come through?"

He shook his head. "Just rot, I guess." He pointed to the floor outside her room. "Brought that down for you."

She leaned out and saw her pack resting against the wall.

"Thank you. I'm leaving?"

"Soon, yeah. Might have time for a quick meal, if you're hungry."

"Well . . . if it's not too much trouble."

He nodded and headed back toward the stairs. "Gonna have to feed the crew anyway," he said over his shoulder. "One more plate won't hurt."

"Thank you again," Elyth said as he disappeared around the corner.

She lingered by the door a moment then pulled her pack inside and closed the door behind her once more. From what she could tell, they'd honored their word not to go through her things. Everything was still as she'd left it, apart from some expected shifting. Even the frostoak cutting was there, though it had dropped most of its withered leaves. She pulled out her local nav tracker and dropped a marker at her current location; even if she never needed to come back, she knew the information might prove valuable.

After that, Elyth took some time to repack and get cleaned up then joined Hok upstairs in time to help him set the table. The rest of the crew still hadn't come in yet, and though she'd hoped to have one more opportunity to talk with them about their time on the mountain, it looked like she wasn't going to get the chance. Hok was just pulling the meal off the stove when a distant rumble caught their attention. He looked toward the front of the cabin, then back to Elyth, and then walked over to peer out of a side window.

"Guess we're not going to have time for that meal after all," he said.

"That's for me?" Elyth asked.

He nodded. "Better get your stuff. They're not going to want to wait around."

Elyth retrieved her belongings from her room downstairs. By the time she'd returned, a skimmer had already landed on the gravel pad behind the cabin, and through the rear window she could see two men. One waited by the skimmer as the other approached.

Elyth identified the make and model of the vessel reflexively, her mind dredging up the basic capabilities. It was a small, older Shelton H-class; twelve feet long, boxy and utilitarian, its red-and-white exterior faded and worn from use. A midrange civilian craft, planet-bound, fairly commonplace. Nothing that would attract attention.

Similarly, both men were dressed in plain clothes, and to most eyes, they would have blended right in with any crowd. To Elyth, though, their bearing and attentiveness to their surroundings made them stand out.

"They're going to drop you at a public pad on the south edge of Oronesse," Hok said. "I assume you can find your way from there."

"You're not coming along?" she asked.

Hok shook his head. Elyth felt a wave of disappointment, and was surprised by the emotion. She hadn't developed any particular attachment to Hok, but the abrupt arrival of the Detail made her feel unprepared to say goodbye, as though now that the moment was upon them, anything she said would be inadequate.

"I hate to disappear like this," Elyth said. "I was hoping to thank everyone before I had to go."

"Leaving in the same manner as you arrived," he said, with a quick smile. "Sudden-like. I'll pass along your regards."

The man from the skimmer reached the back door and knocked sharply. Hok handed her a small, sealed container; it was square, with a flexible lid, and warm to the touch.

"Something for the road," he said. Elyth accepted it, and realized that he'd packed up her dinner to take along. She leaned forward and gave him a brief one-armed hug; he straightened at the contact, surprised by the gesture and uncertain how to react.

"Thank you, Hok," she said. "Thank you for looking after me."

He took a step back when she released him.

"All right," he said. ". . . Well. Best of luck out there. Hope we didn't hold you up too much."

"I'll be fine," she said. "Sorry for any trouble I caused you and your friends."

Hok shook his head, dismissing any such concerns, and walked over to the door.

"Goodbye, Eliya," he said.

"Goodbye, Hok," she said.

He opened the door, and Elyth walked out. No words of greeting were exchanged; Hok nodded to the man standing outside, who in turn silently gestured for Elyth to head to the skimmer. She crossed the short span to the landing pad and, as she approached, the second man opened the entry into the rear passenger compartment. He was thin and smiled pleasantly when she neared, but he had an energetic vigilance about him even in his casual movements. Elyth understood why such a man might be part of a security detail. It made him seem dangerous, despite his otherwise innocuous appearance.

She climbed in and sat in the seat nearest the exit, placing her pack on the seat next to her toward the fore of the ship. The passenger compartment had four seats arrayed in pairs along either side of the ship, facing the center. Neither man joined her; both sat in the forward compartment, which was almost completely separated from the rear area by a metal panel, save for an opening in the top third through which she could see them.

The engines kicked in almost immediately, and in a few moments they began their rise. Elyth watched through the small bubble window next to her, taking in her last view of the little cabin that had been her home for a night. It was hard to believe it had been only a single day since she'd arrived, and she found herself strangely sad to have had her time there come to such a sudden end.

Hok hadn't followed them out, but she could still see his silhouette in the window of the cabin door, watching as the skimmer lifted off the ground. Keeping an eye on her even now.

The skimmer gained height enough to clear the treetops and not much more before it surged forward and banked sharply. Elyth's view of the cabin was replaced by the sea of trees racing along beneath them, dark waves golden-tipped in the last rays of the sun. She sat back and turned her attention to what lay ahead. Hok had told her they'd be dropping her off somewhere outside Oronesse; he hadn't given her any idea of how far outside it would be, and she hadn't asked. But public pads typically had easy access to further transportation into the heart of the nearest city. The south edge wasn't the closest point between the preserve and Oronesse, but that choice made sense if they were being cautious about their point of origin, which she had to assume they were.

She considered making use of the navigation instrument in her pack, but quickly dismissed the idea. The two men in the front weren't likely to react well to her using any sort of mapping tool, and she didn't want to risk raising their suspicions by trying to use it surreptitiously. Instead, she leaned forward again to look out the window, judged their velocity from the speed of the terrain moving by, and made a rough estimate of their travel time. Not that she knew exactly where they were going nor, for that matter, precisely where she'd been. Still, she remembered enough from her extensive study of the maps during her planning to have a general idea, and her sense of direction was excellent.

That was how she realized, as the sun disappeared and the land below plunged into darkness, that they weren't taking her to Oronesse at all.

EIGHT

Elyth kept still and relaxed as she silently surveyed her options. It didn't take long; she didn't have many.

Waiting certainly wasn't one. Wherever they were taking her, she'd be at their complete mercy when they landed. And the closer they got to their destination, the narrower her paths of possibility became. That left her with whatever she could make happen while they were still airborne, which didn't offer much room for error either. The skimmer was running maybe fifty feet above the trees, and almost every version of quick action she could come up with was likely to end with the craft planted firmly in the ground. She'd already survived one crash. Trying her luck again so soon didn't seem like a good idea.

The rear compartment of the vessel was five feet long, slightly more in width and height. She couldn't fully stand. Two seats on either side, all facing the middle of the ship; thin metal structures overlaid with synthetic cushions. That gave her about two feet of aisle, and not much cover to work with.

The rear hatch was right beside her; the emergency release was a simple mechanism. But even if she popped the door open midflight, leaping out was close enough to suicide that it was off the table. That left trying to take control of the ship in transit.

She looked to the forward compartment, where both men sat unaware of her realization, at least for the moment. The gap in the panel that separated them was centered, roughly three feet wide and maybe half as tall. Neither man seemed the sort to be oblivious to anything; reaction times would be faster than normal.

The man on the right had shoulder-length dark hair, and was more squarely built than his companion. The other man was wiry, short-haired, and bearded. He might well prove to be more trouble than his stronger-looking partner. The strong one would look to overpower her, something she could turn to her advantage. But the thin man had a cunning edge that made him unpredictable.

Elyth scanned what she could see of the control panel through the small window to the fore, looking for the controls she'd need.

While she was looking, the long-haired man glanced back over his shoulder briefly; they didn't quite catch each other's eyes, but the effect was the same. He took stock of her with his peripheral vision, and turned too casually back to look out of the forward window. Elyth couldn't hear his voice, but it was apparent he had said something. The other man's head turned ever so slightly before he stopped himself. They knew she knew. The air grew thick.

The only question now was how the three of them would resolve the situation.

Her stun baton was in the very top of her pack, if she could get to it without drawing any attention; the confined space would limit its effectiveness, but it would still be a useful tool. She still had her dinner in its container on her lap, but that didn't seem to offer her any immediate help.

"We're taking the long way around," Longhair said, looking back over his shoulder again and flashing a smile he no doubt thought was convincing. "Trying to make sure we don't draw any extra attention to you when we drop you off. Twenty minutes or so."

"Sure, no problem," Elyth replied, smiling back. He nodded, watched her for a moment longer, and then returned to facing forward.

Elyth swept her eyes once more around the passenger compartment, looking again for anything that might give her any more of an advantage than what she had in her pack. The rear compartment was sparse; not much in it apart from the seats and the harnesses to keep everyone strapped in. She hadn't buckled hers. And the emergency hatch release was right there. If only the fall weren't sure to kill her, that would be the easiest out.

She looked back at the cockpit. It was going to be a tight fit through that window.

As casually as she could manage, Elyth set her meal aside, shifted in her seat, and reached for her pack; no movement so sudden as to attract attention or so slow as to appear concerned that they might notice. She started to unfasten the top, but before she could, Longhair whipped around, pistol in hand.

"Don't," he said.

Elyth froze.

"Whoa, whoa, easy," she said. "I was just going to get my scarf. It's a little chilly back here."

She eased both hands up slowly, palms out, where he could see them . . . but not too far away from her pack.

"You just sit still," he answered. "I don't want to have to clean your brains out of the back of the car, but I'll do it if I have to."

For a span, the two just stared at each other. He clearly wasn't buying the act, and even more clearly was no amateur with his weapon. His aim was steady, and he held the pistol compactly, gripped in both hands and tucked close to his body, avoiding the mistake of extending his arms through the window of the panel. No matter how fast she was, there was no doubt that he could put rounds on target in such a tight space before she reached him.

The distance between them wasn't much, maybe five feet. Her pack weighed forty-three pounds. Too much to throw. And the window to the forward compartment wasn't big enough for it to fit through, anyway.

But not all the tools at her disposal were physical. He was certain of himself, and though the weapon was a threat, it was the man's cool certainty of skill that animated the threat. If she could paralyze him even for a moment with doubt or fear, a window of opportunity might well open to her. Though she had taken great pains thus far not to give any hint of who she really was, there was no point in concealing it now, if keeping the secret would only end in her death.

Within First House, the technique was known as Manifesting the Void. Among themselves, away from their training grounds and strict instructors, the Advocates of the Voice just called it the Dread.

Elyth drew a breath and gathered the words within herself, drawing with them all the emotions and memories, the indescribable awe and unspeakable terror, she'd experienced in the face of the raw, self-obliterating power of the cosmos.

"I am not what you perceive me to be," she said, and then, in the Deep Language, "*Form of the formless, all within the word, the infinite, and the eternal.*"

Around her, the air crackled with cosmic energy made manifest. She felt the chill course through her limbs as the force of her speech struck the man, creating in his mind an inescapable impression of the chaotic potential of the universe she herself had touched. The color evaporated from his face, his pupils dilated, hands trembled. And though his eyes remained fixed on her, they were unfocused and she knew, at least for a moment, he wasn't seeing her but rather a fraction of the power that could move through her. The pistol quavered, the barrel dipped, his grip slackened.

Elyth reacted.

She snatched the top of her pack, braced it against her arm and shoulder like a shield, and threw herself forward, using the weight of her body to propel the pack ahead of her. The gun fired, and her pack shuddered with the impact. A second round tore through the backside, narrowly missing her hand just as she wedged the heavy backpack into the opening. An instant later she was sprawled flat on the floor and with a quick kick she hit the emergency release on the exit hatch; alarms blared as the rear door popped open with a gush and roar of mountain air.

Above her, her pack was stuck tight, but only momentarily. It thumped twice, as Longhair hammered at it from the front; the small cockpit didn't offer him much room for leverage. Elyth slid tight against the seats as far to the right of the craft as she could manage, her back against the forward panel. On the third strike, her pack shifted above her, and on the next, both of Longhair's arms shot through the opening as he shoved it free, gun still in hand. The pack swung away and fell heavily on the seats across from her.

"—out the back!" he was saying when his hands appeared. In that instant, Elyth struck. She shot up and grabbed both of his wrists, driving them upward as she sprang from the floor. In the struggle, the gun fired again, the round punching harmlessly through the roof. Elyth was still in motion; she swept left and twisted the man's arms around each other, using one of his forearms as leverage to pin the other. The weapon sailed out of his hand as she slammed him back in his seat, awkwardly contorted by her hold, wrists pinned against the rounded edge of the panel between them. As predicted, he tried to muscle his way up, wrestling against her. The cockpit was too tight for him to find good footing, but when the angle was right, Elyth gave way and yanked; with the sudden loss of resistance, the man's own struggle popped him backward, head and shoulders through the window. Elyth smashed her elbow into the bridge of his nose, felt the crunch as it broke under the impact.

A moment later the world flew out from under her.

Longhair screamed as Elyth tumbled over him and hurtled into the right side of the skimmer, crashing upside down on the seat and dislocating one if not both of the man's elbows in one moment; in the next, he went silent as the chaotic twist and shift of weight snapped his neck.

For an instant, an invisible weight pinned her against the wall of the craft; gravity swirled and then abruptly seized its place, slamming her neck and shoulders down into the seat. She rolled with the impact and found her footing, barely processing that the ship had just executed a barrel roll before realizing a split second later why; the wiry man swiveled around, pistol at point-blank range. She twisted and dropped to a knee, slapping the man's hand up and aside as he fired; the heat and flash splashed across her cheek as the air ripped in the wake of the kinetic round.

But rather than trying to get his weapon aimed at her again, the man used the momentum from her strike and whipped his hand down and around, catching her across the brow with the flat edge of the gun. She fell back hard against the seats on the left side of the cabin, and the man fired twice more; the rounds tore through the seat beside her head. But the edge of the window and his awkward position blocked his arm from bringing the weapon fully to bear. He spun to his left and leaned back to the right, trying to get the pistol back on target.

The other gun was on the floor by Elyth's feet, toward the rear of the cabin.

It was a race to the death.

Elyth went flat on her side and reached for the pistol as the man fired three more shots in quick succession, each round trailing just behind her movement. She snatched the gun up from the floor and the man, realizing he couldn't get his weapon on her fast enough, dropped backward, sheltering behind the panel. Elyth had no idea how strong the panel was, but she didn't hesitate; she fired twice, putting two rounds into it where she instinctively guessed the man's body would be. The shots punched two neat holes through the metal.

And then all was quiet.

Elyth held her place for a few seconds, weapon trained on the panel window, watching for any sign of movement; the lack of a response from the cockpit told her she'd found her mark.

The skimmer continued along its level flight path, undisturbed by the torrent of violence that had broken out within its confines. After the havoc, the sudden stillness felt misplaced, as though Elyth had abruptly dropped out of one reality into another. She remained lying on her back for another ten seconds, both to be sure the danger had passed and to allow herself a brief moment to recover. Then, she eased up into a crouch and cautiously crept forward to check the cockpit. The wiry man was there, flopped partway to the floor, held in place by the console and the legs of his partner. Her shots had caught him under the jaw and just behind the ear. The other man was still partially wedged in the window, splayed awkwardly, his arms and neck unnaturally angled like a crushed spider.

The adrenaline coursing through her made her hands cold; she tossed the pistol onto the seat next to her and clenched her fists a few times. After a few deep breaths, Elyth raised the long-haired man's body and shifted it enough to enable his weight to slide him back down into his seat. She moved the man as carefully as she could, gently repositioning him so that he leaned against the side of the cockpit, out of the way of the console. The wiry man's body shifted with the movement, falling farther toward the floor, though not completely out of his seat.

There wasn't room enough for her to crawl into the cockpit, so Elyth had to lean through the window and work the console as best she could from the rear compartment. A quick check revealed that her would-be captors hadn't set a preprogrammed course; the skimmer automatically kept itself level and managed collision avoidance, but they'd been navigating manually. The sky had darkened to the fullness of night now, and the only lights she could see through the forward window were out on the horizon to her left, some miles distant. She pulled up a map and identified the lights as coming from Alonesse, a companion city some eighty miles northeast of Oronesse, and not nearly as large. The men hadn't left any clues about their intended flight path, so she couldn't be certain, but unless they'd planned to circle wide around the outskirts, that didn't appear to have been their planned destination. Somewhere not far from it, perhaps, though.

She didn't have enough information, but the one thing Elyth knew for certain was that the longer she was in the skimmer, the easier she'd be to track. She shifted the skimmer into a hover, and activated a display to scan the local terrain for a suitable landing zone.

The scanner located a clearing about half a mile to her south, and she directed the skimmer to touch down there. While it traveled, she brought up the routing interface and plotted out an automatic flight path. She sent the craft on a circuitous route around Alonesse, with commands to touch down in two more locations before returning to the preserve. Unfortunately, the men had deactivated the skimmer's route history, so there was no way for her to backtrace the ship's original point of departure. She made the best guess she could, and hoped that if the ship was seen returning to the preserve that might buy her some extra time before they unleashed the hunting parties.

Once she touched down, she'd have to get as far away from the landing site as possible. Assuming there wasn't anyone already on the ground, waiting to ambush her.

The skimmer approached her selected site, tilting back slightly as it shifted into vertical landing mode. Elyth picked her pack up off the floor and slung it over her shoulders, buckling the front support straps around her as she moved to the still-open rear hatch. On second thought, she went back to the front to collect the pistol from the seat where she'd tossed it. She didn't much care for such weapons, but things had gone so far sideways that it seemed foolish not to take every precaution.

As she moved toward the front, her foot slipped sideways, and she looked down to see the floor spattered in some dark fluid and matter. Her body went cold with the realization; she'd been hit after all, and shock was preventing her from feeling the wound. She searched her body frantically, looking for what surely must have been a massive exit wound. There was no telling how much blood she'd lost already. But everywhere she looked, she was intact. She glanced back at the dark patch on the floor, followed the trail up to the seat, where the kinetic rounds had ripped through. And she laughed aloud.

There, on the seat, sat the remains of the container Hok had given her. It was ruptured, and the meal he'd packed for her was blasted all over the seat and floor. The moment was darkly comical, both a welcome reprieve from the disaster Elyth had first imagined and a stark reminder of just how close she'd been to death.

Seeing that destruction, however, checked her impulse to carry the pistol with her. Whatever advantage the pistol might have offered, she knew that carrying it with her would impact her decision making, and she was far from an expert marksman. A small change, perhaps, but she of all people knew how seemingly small changes could ripple into unforeseen consequences. She wasn't ready to allow the circumstances to dictate her way of operating.

When she returned to the hatch, the skimmer was maneuvering above the landing site. Though it was dark, she could tell now that the clearing she'd picked wasn't nearly as clear in reality as it had looked on the map; numerous stumps and scrub trees littered the area, as though a small patch of the forest had been harvested for timber some years before. The skimmer did an admirable job of finding a way to fit anyway, and landed in what Elyth presumed was the one spot its supports could actually fully contact the ground.

As soon as it touched down, she leapt out and raced out of the clearing in a low run, as fast as she could manage with the pack on her back and across the challenging terrain. When she reached the tree line, she turned back and dropped to a crouch, scanning the area for any sight or sound of trouble. After a minute or so, the skimmer's engines revved again and the craft lifted off, turning as it did so to clear the irregular canopy and find its heading. Elyth realized she'd left the rear hatch open; it wouldn't seal itself automatically since she'd popped it with the emergency release. If anyone happened to spot it when it landed in her preprogrammed locations, the open hatch might draw unnecessary attention, and worse, might reveal its disturbing cargo. But there was nothing she could do about it now.

That thought sent her mind back to the preserve, and to Hok and his friends. Would they find out what had happened? She had to assume they would, and she could only imagine what they would think of her once they did. Unless they had known what the Detail's intentions had been. But she couldn't bring herself to believe that, even though the possibility presented itself.

No, Hok was a hard man, but he was a good one. If he had known what they had planned, she would have seen it on him.

That, then, suggested that he would draw the only conclusion that seemed most likely; she had deceived him, and killed two of his fellow workers. Deceived not just him; deceived them all. Elyth knew it was unlikely she would ever see them again, but that didn't lessen the discomfort of knowing how angry and betrayed they would feel.

She was no stranger to betrayal; exploiting the trust of others was often a critical part of her assignments. But for some reason, to be thought a traitor when she was not was harder to bear.

She held her place for a few minutes more after the skimmer had disappeared, watching for any sign of other skimmers that may have been trailing behind the first. To her relief, nothing passed overhead, and the normal nightly sounds of the wilderness began to return. She listened to them for a span, developing a sense of what life there was in the environment, and its natural rhythms. Once she had a baseline for how the forest *should* feel and sound, she got back to her feet and removed her pack. From it she took out her go-bag and then drew out her monocular and her local nav tracker and got her bearings.

Alonesse was still some twenty miles roughly to her northeast. Oronesse, then, lay sixty miles to the west and south. And somewhere between the two, the mysteriously invisible borders of *eth ammuin's* preserve remained hidden. Elyth had some sense of how long they'd been airborne after leaving the cabin, but not a good estimate on how fast they'd been traveling or how many changes of heading they'd made. Even if she'd had a better idea of those variables, her local nav tracker lacked the resolution she'd need to be able to pick out any distinguishing features that might positively identify the location of that site.

She had to assume she was sitting in the middle of hostile territory. But she knew she wasn't going to solve her problems by crouching under a tree in the dark. First, she'd find somewhere she could hide, a place where she had time to make plans and, if necessary, a chance to defend herself. She tightened the focus of her local nav tracker and scanned her immediate surroundings. It took a few minutes, but the device highlighted an area about three-quarters of a mile off to her northwest; a gully ran through the woods there. It didn't promise much shelter or any comfort, and that meant it wasn't an obvious choice. Maybe not a perfect option, but Elyth didn't have time to wait for perfect.

The night air was already cold and growing colder; her body was weak from the aftereffects of the adrenaline dump and the use of the Deep Language, and sore from the injuries she'd sustained. And now that she'd noticed her body, the pain in her forehead seemed particularly acute, just above her brow. She touched it lightly and hissed involuntarily at the burn and sting. Her fingertips came back tacky, and she realized the blow she'd suffered from the wiry man's gun had split the skin. She tested the area around the wound gently, felt the knot that was forming. The mark it left was going to be a distinguishing feature for the days to come. Though, out here in the wilderness, Elyth wasn't sure just how much she'd be needing to blend in anyway.

She picked up her go-bag and slung it so that it lay across her chest, where all her tools and instruments would be accessible, and then donned her pack once more and started out for the gully.

It took her an hour to maneuver her way there; she circled wide around the clearing where she'd set the skimmer down, moved slowly, and paused often along the way to listen for any changes in the natural sounds of the night. When she reached the edge of the gully, she found it rockier than she'd expected and covered in leaves at the bottom. At least it wasn't full of water. She slipped down the bank and followed the course for another half hour or so until she came around a bend and found what she was looking for.

The eastern side of the bank bulged out wider there, and was overgrown with heavy-rooted trees and creeping ivy. Within the bank, a hollow had formed beneath a massive tree. It had the look of an animal den, now abandoned. Elyth didn't relish the idea of sleeping where some beast had once made its home, but after all she'd been through, she thought maybe she wasn't much different from whatever may have lived there before.

Still, she scanned it with her monocular from a distance before committing to it, just to be safe. When she was confident it was clear, she clambered into it, pushing her packs in first. She was happy to discover that moss had crept into the hollow space and blanketed the floor. It wasn't thick enough to cushion the rocks beneath it, but Elyth was grateful for the comfort it provided, even if it was mostly psychological.

All told, roughly two hours had passed since her narrow escape, and in that time the skies had remained clear and the forest quiet. It appeared she'd at least dodged immediate pursuit. But the question still nagged at her about how much farther the two men had intended to carry her, even though she had little doubt about what they had planned to do with her once they'd arrived.

If their plan had been only to kill her, they could have done so the instant they were in the air. Apart from the comment about not wanting to clean her brains out of the back of the skimmer, they clearly hadn't had any such concerns once the fighting started. But she couldn't help but feel they hadn't merely been taking her somewhere to die. They'd been taking her to someone else.

The uncertainty made the wilderness seem hostile; any direction she turned might be the one that would lead her to whoever was waiting for her. And remaining in one place might allow whoever it was enough time to track her and capture her, despite her unlikely escape. For the moment, the entire planet seemed too small to hide her. She'd been under pursuit before, but this time felt different; she'd been off-balance from the start.

Among the Paragon's final words, the matriarch had spoken of her uncertainty of the way forward, and how once Elyth had arrived, only then would they see what steps lay before them. Elyth hadn't grasped then the fullness of the Paragon's meaning, nor just how difficult walking a blind path could be.

She lay quietly in her hiding place for a few minutes, listening to the gentle sounds of the wilderness. And though she didn't feel hungry, she knew her body would need calories as it warded off the cold.

Elyth opened her pack, and when she withdrew one of her rations, something narrow and rounded fell out with it, landing on her legs. She felt around in the darkness for the object, and then held it up toward the opening of the den, silhouetting it against the weak starlight from outside.

The cutting of the frostoak.

Sadly, it hadn't fared well. About a third of the way down it had suffered damage; it was bent, though not completely broken through, with sharp fibers flared like a mane where part of the outer bark had separated. It seemed an apt metaphor for her mission thus far.

"I know how you feel," she said to the cutting.

And though she'd packed it on a whim, without thinking of any particular use for it, it now reminded her of the broken tangle interpreter she still carried. She had no hope in the gesture, but Elyth unzipped the slender pocket along the lapel of her vest and drew out the tangle interpreter. Even damaged, it too was a reminder of home, and of the importance of her mission; a talisman of power and purpose.

She held the branch and the device in her fist for a few moments and then allowed them to balance across the flat of her palm. Back on the *Helegoss*, the two had been joined in her mind, each a half representing the whole of her mission. And now, together, they still seemed linked; twins in suffering. The single indicator on the interpreter was dark, as expected. But she stared at it for a few moments longer anyway, drawing from it the resolve she needed. Like the device and the branch, she too was battered. But where they had failed, she would endure.

And as she looked, as if her own will had made it so, the indicator on the tangle interpreter began to glow weakly. Surely she was imagining it. She turned the device over in her hand, rubbed her eyes. When she turned the interpreter back over and looked again, the tiny light remained steady, warm.

Somehow, beyond all hope, the Paragon was calling.

NINE

Elyth closed her eyes and opened the channel, allowing her mind to fill with the rush of images that cascaded and swirled across the connection. When the confusion of colors resolved, she found herself standing on a large flat rock, beside a quiet pool of clear water. All around her, tall cliffs rose; a protected oasis, soft and hazy in dreamlike stylization. The shared psychic space created by the tangle interpreter was usually sterile and blank; an empty backdrop irrelevant to its purpose. Instead, the space Elyth now found herself in was rich with detail, apparently taking its cues from the mind imprinted upon it. And that mind was present, standing ankle-deep in the pool, her feet bare. The Paragon.

"Bright daughter," her projection said, smiling kindly. "At last. You've arrived safely at your destination?"

An involuntary laugh escaped Elyth's mouth at the same moment that tears welled in her eyes; the sight of the Paragon eased the weight of isolation, and sharpened it.

"I've arrived on Qel, Illumined Mother," Elyth answered. "Safe is something of a different matter."

"Trouble?" the elder woman said. "So soon?"

Elyth gave the head of her House a brief summary of the events:

the circumstances aboard the *Helegoss*, the crash, her encounters with the wardens and with *eth ammuin*, and finally her current predicament. The Paragon asked the occasional question, but mostly just absorbed the report with a focused look. When Elyth finished, the Paragon stepped out onto the rock, turned silently to face the pool, and remained still for so long that Elyth wondered if perhaps the connection had failed.

"Your Radiance?" she said.

"Yes, my daughter, I am here," the Paragon answered. "It would seem that somehow you have managed to justify our concern while further obscuring its source."

She glanced back over her shoulder, and the twinkle in her eyes removed any sting Elyth might have felt at the comment. "But such is to be expected when one throws a mighty stone into murky waters."

The matriarch looked once more to the pool, traced across its surface with one swift foot, then sat cross-legged on the rock before it while the ripples fanned out.

"Join me, daughter," she said. Elyth took her place next to the Paragon.

As she was sitting down, Elyth took in the magnificent view and said, "I had feared that the crash had destroyed the tangle interpreter, but it seems to be working better than ever."

The Paragon chuckled.

"The tangle's passive channel appears to be intact, but this . . ." she said, waving her hand vaguely at the surrounding cliffs, "isn't the interpreter's doing, child."

"Then . . . how?"

"You have something else with you that was cultivated and sustained for long years by my own hand."

Though she didn't understand how it could be possible, Elyth knew instantly what the Paragon meant.

". . . the branch from the frostoak."

The Paragon nodded. "It knows my voice. Quite a bit more taxing to use than the gadget, of course, but we must do what we can with what we have. It will serve as my bridge to you now. Keep it close."

Elyth dipped her head in acknowledgment, and in awe of the Paragon's capability.

"Now then. You have interacted with this *eth ammuin*?" the matriarch asked.

"Yes, Paragon. Briefly."

"And what is your assessment?"

"There is a power of sorts within him," she said. "But it is vague and haphazard. And shows none of the twisting I would expect if he were connected to a thought-line as potent or destructive as that of the Strain. But my time with him was so limited, I can't be certain."

"I'm not asking you to be certain. What do you *believe*?"

Elyth weighed her thoughts before she spoke them.

"I believe he has some part in this. But how he is connected, and whether for good or ill, I can't say."

"What of those around him?"

"Wary, but kind," Elyth said. "No obvious abuse of the Language, no clear sign of corruption. The care they show for the land is exceptional. My impression was that they're largely concerned with being left alone to tend the mountain."

"All of which could suggest those on the preserve are not of our concern," the Paragon said. "If only they hadn't threatened to kill you."

"That does complicate matters, yes. It's possible that the security detail was acting on their own."

"All a strange situation," the Paragon said. "I'm surprised it escaped our notice before now."

"I saw nothing about the place that should attract the attention of the Eye."

"And yet something led you there."

"A crash," Elyth said. "And a chance word during a chance meeting. It was the name of the man that drew me initially."

She nearly went on to say that she'd been lucky, but stopped herself. She knew too well that just as she could manipulate the strands of reality, she too was at their mercy, and could be drawn along with them and woven into the paths wrought by others, and by forces beyond them all.

"*Eth ammuin*," the Paragon said, testing the weight of the words. "Indeed. It is as you describe. Vague, haphazard, but touched with power. A diluted power, perhaps, but resonant. He has chanced upon some truth, it would seem, without grasping its source."

"Or someone taught it to him," Elyth replied.

"'The Silent One,'" the Paragon said, using the colloquial translation. "An unusual choice for a self-styled preacher. I wonder if his followers gave him the title, or if he chose it for himself."

The Paragon was quiet again, and Elyth could almost feel the ancient woman's wisdom and cunning blending together in an attempt to unravel the enigma before her. Elyth knew, too, that she herself could see only a glimpse of the puzzle that confronted the Paragon; undoubtedly many layers remained hidden to her that the matriarch of First House was forced to consider. Even so, after a few long moments, Elyth hazarded to interrupt her thoughts.

"Paragon, if I may ask, what *did* draw the Eye's attention to Qel?"

The Paragon let out a long sigh, not from exasperation at the question, but from some other emotion; a disappointment or frustration with her own lack of clarity, maybe.

"Rumors and shadows, my daughter," she said. "Rumors and shadows, at best. The planet is to us as a hurricane, far beyond the horizon. Sensed long before it is seen. The change in the humidity, the stillness of the animals, the color of the sea. No one element tells us of the danger; but taken all together, the threat is too great to ignore. We might all be swept away."

It was a response without an answer, and Elyth wondered how to interpret it. Perhaps the situation was too complex to describe meaningfully.

"Your eye is keen," the elder woman continued, turning to look at her. "You too have perceived something of it, if not in the same manner as we have." She continued to peer intently at Elyth, gauging her reaction and her thoughts.

Elyth reflected on all she'd told the Paragon, and the moment came to mind; the disturbance she'd seen, the swell of the surface of the cosmic when she'd used the Deep Language to speed her healing. Before she spoke of it, the Paragon perceived her thoughts and nodded.

"I thought it might be some hallucination," Elyth said.

"Something is at work that we do not understand," the Paragon answered. "And when you possess knowledge of the inner workings of the universe, that is troubling indeed."

She laid a hand on Elyth's shoulder then, used it as support to gain her feet. The contact and pressure felt as real as if they'd been physically together in her garden.

"Until we know more of the heart of Qel, I cannot see which way to turn," she said. "And the only agent I have in place is injured and under pursuit. This matter may be beyond our ability to resolve."

Elyth stood; it almost sounded as though the Paragon were contemplating recalling her then and there. At the thought, something triggered deep within Elyth's heart and mind; a swelling, not of pride, but of determination. The Paragon had called her "Guided by the True Star." Those words resonated within her, strengthened her will.

"This is the purpose for which the First House has fashioned me," she said, repeating the mantra her instructors had taught her, and had relentlessly tested. "I yet endure."

The Paragon regarded her for a few moments.

"So it would seem, bright daughter," she said. "Take care that pride not cloud your judgment. But there is steel in you, tempered by skillful hands.

"It is my sense that this *eth ammuin* can wait, for now. Our first concern must be discovering how deeply the corruption has settled into the planet itself. Turn your focus now to Qel and its foundations. Perhaps then any connection to those on the mountain will become clearer. Or, maybe, there we will at least find the right questions to ask."

"Yes, Illumined Mother."

"And keep your locator handy," she added. "I will have our Hand move a collection team into position. I have no doubts about your capability. But not all things are within your control. If the time comes when we should need to pull you out, I suspect you'll be glad to avoid delay."

"Thank you. I'll do my part to make it unnecessary."

The pool and cliffs began to shimmer and waver, their dreamlike qualities magnified.

"Our part is all any of us can do," the Paragon said. And she too began to fade, as a mist burning away. "*Sareth hanaan* be your guide, Elyth."

"*Sareth hanaan* be my way," she answered with a bow.

The connection closed, and Elyth was once again alone in the dark forest. The sense of isolation returned, the nighttime noises of the wood amplified the silence from the interpreter. The certainty she had felt moments before melted away, and left a hollow echo as she considered what lay ahead. Everything seemed too close now, the air too dense, the darkness too heavy.

She clambered out of the den and up the side of the gully. There, above her hiding place, stood the massive tree whose roots were her roof; the spread of its branches had chased away its would-be neighbors, leaving a small clearing beneath the shadow of its canopy. Enough room for Elyth to run through her meditation sequence.

Throughout the first few poses it was nearly impossible for her to maintain her balance and focus, as her mind kept running away into dark corners. But gradually the swirl of thought and emotion calmed, and by the time she reached Servant Awaits with Gratitude, she found herself still and settled. Her mind felt sharper and ready to face her task.

The cold night air seemed less vicious now, more invigorating than sapping. Though she had intended to return to her hiding place after her sequence, she instead grabbed one of her rations and brought it up to the clearing. She sat at the base of the tree, resting her back against its trunk; its bark was stringy and covered in fibrous, hairlike strands, soft to the touch.

She had stirred the hornet's nest with *eth ammuin*, of that there was no doubt. But that had in fact seemed only to have complicated an already complex matter. As the Paragon had said, it was the heart of Qel that was her concern. Perhaps in learning its vulnerabilities, she would find the source of its disease, and in doing so would clarify the part that *eth ammuin* played, if any. But for now, her business was with the planet.

Once she had established a sufficient baseline from the environment, she could decide then where her next target should be. No assessment could be completed without surveying the populace, and both Alonesse and Oronesse provided opportunity, as well as risk. But that was a decision for another day; after she'd drawn what she could from the land itself and, more significantly, after she'd gauged the response from those back on the preserve.

Elyth forced herself to eat her ration, and by the time she'd finished it, both the cold from the night air and the fatigue from the stress and exertion finally drove her back to her hole in the ground, under the great, towering tree. The hollow was too small for her to deploy her shelter, flexible as it was, so once inside, she used the supplies from her emergency kit and her standard gear to fashion a covering for the entrance, one that would provide both camouflage enough to remain hidden and extra warmth enough to survive the night. With that done, she slid into her ultrathin bedroll and curled into a ball on her side, with her head on her arm as a pillow. Almost immediately the mossy rocks beneath her made themselves known.

She rested for a few hours, sleeping fitfully when her exhaustion outweighed her discomfort, and mentally reviewing all the challenges before her whenever the scale tipped in the other direction. It was still two hours before sunrise when Elyth finally gave up on any hope of genuine rest, packed her things, and resumed her hike along the line of the gully, aching, weary. She'd traveled maybe a quarter of a mile when she heard a quiet rumble in the distance.

Immediately, she froze in place, strained to hear more. The sound faded, tumbled away from her attempts to identify it. It was too distant, too vague for her to be certain; if she'd still been in her shelter, she would have missed it entirely. And though she wanted to dismiss the noise as wind or thunder on the horizon, her instincts told her it had been no natural phenomenon.

A skimmer landing.

She imagined a vessel setting down in the same clearing that she had, though the sound wave had been too broad and indistinct for her to pinpoint the location that precisely. There was nothing she could do but press on.

For the next several hours, Elyth scoured the surrounding land for a suitable campsite, her search slowed and complicated by the uncertainty of possible pursuit. Twice she heard the unmistakable sounds of skimmers passing over the forest, but they too were distant and neither had the characteristic growl of slowing to land. Common travelers, maybe. Or aerial search teams.

Whether by skill or luck, she encountered no one. But she couldn't escape the sense that there were hounds on her trail. Despite her weariness and ever-growing hunger, she continued on without rest until she finally found a location that offered the right measure of concealment and security. By that time, night was already coming on again. She set up her flexible shelter, deploying its snakeskin-like structure in a low vertical profile, and crawled in.

Once inside, Elyth finally allowed herself to acknowledge her ravenous hunger. She pulled out one of her rations, and with it her terminal. As much as she needed to rest and recover, she felt the time slipping away from her. Already she'd lost a full day to wandering, and she hadn't even glanced at the data she'd gathered during her brief survey of the preserve. With any luck, the analysis would give her a jump-start on the work ahead.

She connected her environmental scanner to the terminal, intending to examine the findings while she ate. It was a battle to keep her mind focused on the task. Her fatigue was great, and every rustle or snap in the wilderness made her freeze in fear that she'd been discovered.

After an hour of distracted study Elyth set her terminal aside, disappointed but not surprised. She had expected gaps in the profile, but it seemed that the dataset was all but useless. The only fact it established was that the preserve had been built in proximity to a threadline, which she had already anticipated. But the readings were so haphazard, the analysis couldn't even accurately determine the age of the planet. Apparently even a little win was too much to ask for from Qel.

Elyth allowed herself to sleep then, or at least to try. Though deeply weary, she slept lightly, attentive to the sounds of night, and listening for any warning of danger. But the night passed uneventfully, and she awoke early the next morning to an overcast sky and subdued calls of the first birds of dawn. While she ate again, she prepped her gear for her first foray into the wild. She would travel lightly, with only her go-bag. The rest of her supplies she repacked and left ready to go at a moment's notice.

Once all was ready, she unsealed her shelter; the blast of freezing air splashed across her face and washed away the last traces of sleep as completely as if it had been ice water. She'd never been a fan of the cold.

But she had work to do, and miles to travel. She grabbed her go-bag and forced herself out into the frigid morning, reminding her body that once it got moving it would warm itself, despite its assurances that it would do no such thing.

For that day and the one that followed, she hiked snaking paths for miles out from her site to take readings and investigate the wilderness, leaving with the early dawn and returning as night fell. It was on her third day of research that she made the initial troubling discovery.

Signs of recent passage. Fresh tracks of other humans in the wild, no more than a day old.

Elyth couldn't tell how many had passed through. At least two, from the look of it, though her gut told her there were more. And whoever they were, they'd taken pains to cover their movement, and had been mostly successful. No mere hikers out on an adventure.

The tracks were a good six miles from her site, but that fact offered little comfort. Depending on the pattern of their search, they might well be closing in on her base camp even now.

Though it was barely after noon, Elyth cut her time short; she'd already spent days wandering the area. Despite her efforts, there was no doubt she'd left behind a rich set of tracks for those skilled enough to read them. Her priority now was to get back and move her camp. Assuming they hadn't already found it.

She took the most direct route to her site at a creeping pace, scouring the environment as she went for any additional signs or clues. When she finally reached visual range of her camp, she stopped and spent nearly half an hour observing.

The mimetic surface of her shelter blended into the terrain so well that, even knowing where to look, it was difficult for her to spot it. And she hadn't picked up any other tracks along the way. But if her pursuers had managed to find her camp, their best tactic would be to simply wait and watch. Even now they might be nearby, doing exactly what she was doing.

Elyth knew she had to act. She wouldn't survive for long in the wild with only the supplies she had on her. She would have to risk it.

Once she moved in, she committed fully and wasted no time. It took her under three minutes to break her camp and get under way, the result of much practice and her previous disciplined preparation. Even so, for the remainder of the day she felt haunted by unseen eyes.

She hiked as long after sunset as she dared, and when at last she ran out of light and drive, set up her shelter in a tight configuration between two rocks. The survey she'd hoped to complete that day had been interrupted, but she didn't relish the idea of staying in the area to continue the work. Maybe she'd gathered enough data. She pulled out her terminal and began her analysis of the dataset, forcing herself to concentrate in spite of her weariness, hunger, and gnawing concern of pursuit.

It was then that Elyth made her second troubling discovery of the day.

As she had guessed, a threadline ran along the mountain range between Alonesse and Oronesse. But there in the hill country some miles distant from Alonesse, she found something she'd never before encountered.

One branch of the threadline led off toward the small city, and it should have contacted the planet's surface somewhere within its borders. As she followed the line, however, it thinned and dissipated dramatically, the dwindling traces of once-vibrant energy leaving now only a faint sheen, like dew on spider silk where once a mighty river had raged, until at last it was utterly depleted. Choked off by some unknown and unidentifiable force.

The Strain was at work. And Qel was already dying.

TEN

Elyth sat stunned as she reviewed her findings, trusting the data even while her mind rejected the logical conclusion of their synthesis. No matter how she approached it, the fact remained—the threadline to Alonesse, ancient root from the founding of the world, was dead.

Threadlines were the pathways of the internal life of a planet, their courses laid at the forming of a world, as fundamental as the nervous system to a human body, and each network as singular as a fingerprint. They were the result of a planet's unique process of development, emergent from its tectonics, the movement of its stone and water, and all the vital forces that shaped and gave life to the world.

A branch of a threadline just didn't end like that; at least, not without some catastrophic, planet-shaking outburst with extinction-level consequences. But there was no sign of planetary trauma, no miles-wide gouge from an asteroid strike or penetrating scar from a destructive cosmic radiation blast. The fact that the wilderness wasn't an utter wasteland defied logic, to say nothing of the abundant health she'd seen in her brief time at the preserve.

Elyth turned the problem over and over in her mind, attempting to find any other way to interpret the findings. But after a couple of hours of reviewing the data and reaching the same conclusion from every different approach she could imagine, it became apparent that she'd made no mistake. Each piece of the puzzle was clear; it was just impossible to connect them.

The land had more to tell her. But she couldn't stay to listen.

The tracks she'd discovered demanded that she move on. And yet she couldn't escape the thought that she was missing something, that her fatigue and fear were obscuring the way forward.

Elyth set her terminal aside. Staring at the data was no longer useful, and her mind felt as numb as her body did empty. At least she could do something about her body. She made herself as comfortable as she could in her cramped hideaway and ate. While she did so, a light rain began to fall.

For a time she listened to the quiet patter, allowing the sound gradually to replace the riddle in her mind with images of the trees around her, their varied oscillations like those of the gentle creatures in the quiet current of the sea. And she thought of the drops of rain, on their own each insignificant, yet together enough to send the entire forest trembling. She knew there were patterns in the apparent chaos of the trees, every shiver and sway dictated by forces too complex and intertwined for her to calculate. And imagining those leaves and the raindrops that drove their motion sparked an idea.

The technique called Observing the Manifold Witness was typically used in high-level training for deep meditation on the teachings of the First House; the effect focused attention while expanding the mind's capacity for exploring hidden connections from many points of view. But the bridge between the conscious and subconscious was notoriously difficult to navigate, and even experienced Advocates could find themselves subjected to harrowing visions that brought neither clarity nor comfort.

Elyth had never heard of it being used for anything other than improving one's understanding of First House precepts. But neither had she been taught any prohibition against other uses. Still, it took her a few minutes before she persuaded herself to attempt the effort.

She sat up and held her hands loosely in her lap and first concentrated her mind on the image of the broken threadline, focusing solely on it until all other distractions fell away. And then, in the Deep Language, she recited the sealing phrase.

"Two mirrors with neither flaw nor shadow between them; light begets light."

And in her mind's eye, she saw the rolling hills outside Alonesse as though from a great height; beyond them the mountain range that walled her off from Oronesse; somewhere within, the preserve of *eth ammuin* and his fellowship. She stretched her hand down toward the ground, imagined drawing handfuls of the rich soil up. In touching the earth she found herself now standing on it, amid a lush forest. The trees around her stood tall like spires, dark and spaced with a regularity that spoke of plan and purpose. Elyth looked around, trying to discern why the ordered rows gave her a sense both familiar and unsettling. And then recognition came. She'd seen this arrangement before, not of trees but of headstones. She was standing in a forest of graves.

She opened her hand and looked down then at the soil she'd taken and found it contained not the healthy earth of Qel, but rather wet ash and fragments of bone. A faint green-fire mist swirled around her hand, and as she watched, the bits of bone sprouted jagged-tipped thorns that grew and twisted into evil shapes. Elyth turned her hand over to drop the growing tangle but realized it was too late; the thorns had already pierced her palm and emerged through the back of her hand. No matter what she did, she couldn't release the mass; it clung as though it had become part of her. She looked again at her palm and saw the thorns had now stretched to an impossible length, a forest that should have been too massive to hold.

Elyth knew she'd plunged into a nightmare vision; her conscious mind rebelled, tried to force her out of the state. But something deeper called to her, told her to wait, to press in, and despite her revulsion, she stood fast in the midst of the horror.

She saw now that the only way to stop the spreading death was to close her hand. In a final attempt she tried to clench her fist, though she knew it would do nothing more than impale her fingers. To her surprise, she was able to wrap her fingers around the entire mass. Pain exploded in her fist and radiated up her arm as though she'd grasped a handful of live coals, but still she forced herself to squeeze, willing herself to crush the death she knew she held. It was too much; despite all of her training, all of her endurance, all of the determination First House had forged within her, she could not persist. Her hand sprang open.

The ash and bones were still there, as were the thorns. But they had lost their evil twist and shrunken to a natural size, now no longer than those on a rose. And a greater surprise still: from the tips of several thorns, delicate petals had grown, white with crimson roots. New life emerging among the ruin. She considered the scene in her palm, and recognized she'd compressed it all into a miniature landscape, with the thorns as mountains. And when she looked up, the forest around her had disappeared; now she stood on a grassy hilltop. She held her hand up, compared it against the horizon and the distant mountains, and saw how they nearly aligned.

And while she looked in her trance, a hand fell on her shoulder, heavy and real, and she heard a man's voice.

"Elyth-Anuiel."

She startled from her vision, reflexively dodging the man's touch, her hands up, ready to defend herself.

But there was no one.

And, of course, there couldn't have been. Her shelter was too well hidden, not to mention far too small. The quiet patter of the gentle rain continued undisturbed by the hammering of her heart.

The vision lingered, neither hallucination nor mystical prophecy. It had been nothing more than her subconscious doing exactly what she had asked; processing everything she'd seen and communicating its findings with her the only way it knew how.

The voice and the hand, however, were something else. Both had seemed so real that even now she couldn't shake the feeling that someone was out there, lurking nearby. She slipped quietly out of her shelter and crouched in the small clearing in front of it, scanning her surroundings. But there was nothing. She was alone in the wilderness.

Elyth returned to her shelter, still unnerved by the sound of the voice. Even now the echo of it in her ear sent an electric wave rolling across her skin. It had called her name, and had added a second to it; not her actual hidden name, but similar in meaning, which was somehow even more troubling.

Her gaze went to her open palms, free of thorns; she traced over the flesh of one with her finger. Her name was written there, etched in her skin, invisible to the naked eye unless she wished to make it known. Her name, and her standing within the House. Elyth-Kyriel. Her identity.

Her hidden name, Kyriel, had been granted to her by her primary instructor, the woman whose sole duty for seven years had been to train her, guide her, and care for her, and who knew her better than anyone had ever known her before. The name was not to be known outside of First House, nor even intended to be spoken, except in rare circumstances; it was primarily for the named to reflect upon, a deep meditation upon her inner self, her strengths, and her purpose. A resonant name, one that spoke of being truly known in the most complete sense. All Advocates of the House treasured their hidden names, and jealously guarded them.

Why her subconscious had generated this new one for her was a complete mystery. When properly combined, Elyth-Kyriel meant something like *corrector of courses*, one who knows the way and aids others in finding and remaining on it. But Elyth-Anuiel was more like *maker of ways*, with the feeling of not just a pathfinder for others, but one who actually creates a way forward where none had previously existed. And though the two names shared similar themes, their dynamics were vastly different.

And too, there was something about the voice that unsettled her. It had been that of a man, and its tone and timbre had been uncomfortably close to that of *eth ammuin*. Elyth did not know how to interpret that, nor was she certain that using the technique had been wise.

At least a portion of the message from her subconscious was clear, though. She'd missed something in her analysis. The severed threadline was a sign of death and coming destruction, but there was something more. New life, as well. She would have to look again.

She studied far into the night and had already long since given up hope of finding anything new when her compulsion for diligence unearthed a tiny detail she had seen before but which gained new significance in light of her vision. Several miles back from the trailing end of the dead threadline, a small offshoot looped off and twisted back across the main flow. And though it made no logical sense, an image formed unbidden in her mind of a dam constructed across a mighty river. As though the energetic flow of the threadline had been used to tie itself off far upstream, its effects revealed miles from the source.

Elyth wasn't sure how that could be possible, but the tension in her mind resolved as though she'd found the sole solution to a complex riddle. Perhaps it was only because she knew now what her next step would be.

More than anything, she just wanted to escape the area entirely, to travel to some other part of the planet and put as much distance as she could between herself and the search party she knew was on her trail. But this strange threadline demanded her attention.

The whorl she'd mapped in it was roughly twenty-five miles southwest of her campsite; a full day's hike. It might not help her shake her pursuers completely, but it would open the gap between them, and might give her enough time to complete the work. She'd sleep the few remaining hours until dawn and then press on.

She was up and on the move in the frostbitten half-light of pre-dawn, anxious to evade the noose she could not see but nevertheless felt tightening around her. By the next sundown Elyth had closed to within three miles of her target point, without sight or sound of the search team. There she made camp for the night and final preparations for the following day and was on the move again as soon as there was light enough to see by. She reached the perimeter of the investigation site as the sun was breaching the horizon.

Mapping the loop in the threadline wasn't an exact science; it was minuscule by planetary standards, but still hundreds of yards wide. Given the flow and roll of the terrain and the density of some of its forest, Elyth knew she had a long day ahead of her. It didn't help that she was lugging all her gear, working out of her pack.

But despite the heavy duty upon her, Elyth tried to remind herself how this sort of research had always been her favorite part of the job. The Ascendance's method of terraforming worlds left them like cousins in a long line. Family traits were apparent, but expressed in different, sometimes startlingly unique ways, and seeing the boundless creativity manifest in each world never failed to move her.

Before she began her work, she took a moment to breathe deeply the frost-laden air, to consciously open herself to the sweep of beauty before her. The wilderness had a pristine feel, wild and pure, almost sac-rosanct. Judging from the weight of the quiet, she knew she was experiencing a part of the planet that very few of even its lifelong residents would ever know. And in that quiet span, she found in herself a most unexpected warmth toward Qel. For all the danger it posed, and all the trouble it had given her, somehow while her mind had been solely focused on her mission, a strange fondness for the planet had wormed its way into her heart. Perhaps it was nothing more than the sort of grudging respect one might feel toward a particularly skilled adversary. She hoped there wasn't something more sinister at work.

After her meditative moment, she refocused on her task, maintaining an infiltrator's mind-set. In addition to whatever humans were attempting to track her, she had no idea what other creatures might call the region home. For the first hour of her survey, she caught only fleeting glimpses here and there of the wildlife inhabiting the place; at most, she would spot a patch of fur through the brush, or a streak of a bird gloriously arrayed. Even for animals unfamiliar with humans, they seemed unusually sensitive to her presence.

Elyth got her first full view of one of the forest's denizens as she crept to a ridge overlooking a wide clearing. Farther down, a massive creature grazed. She would have called it an elk, if not for its unusual brindled color and the rounded, slightly flattened shape of its antlers. She used her monocular to range the distance, and as she did so, astoundingly, the animal's head popped up from nosing the ground and looked in her direction. At over six hundred yards away, it had apparently caught some sense of her. It didn't spook immediately, but it did move away and disappear behind the crest of another hill. How it had detected her, she had no idea.

As she moved back from the ridgeline and into the woods, Elyth came across a patch of the forest carpeted with wildflowers she'd never encountered before. They stood tall on thin stalks roughly knee-high and had the bell-shaped flowers of a bluebell, but were smaller and a pale lavender so delicate it looked like the color might melt away at her touch. Known locally as faerie-queen, according to her scanner, both rare and dangerous. Beautiful to look at, though apparently toxic if ingested. She knelt at the perimeter, inhaling their scent deeply, and gently traced the petals and stems with her fingertips.

And there she discovered why all the animals had been so switched on.

A fresh print lay in the soil nearby. Elyth moved to it and even though it was only a partial imprint, there was no mistaking what had made it.

No human. A predator of a different kind.

A bear.

Elyth placed her hand alongside the print; the impression was at least half again as long. And it wasn't even complete. Judging from the direction, the creature had approached and then bypassed the faerie-queen patch. How long ago it had passed through, Elyth couldn't be certain, but the impression couldn't have been more than a few hours old at most. Possibly much less.

She scanned the area with new eyes. A few feet away a glint on a tree caught her eye, and when she investigated, she found a tuft of fawn-colored fur that flashed with specks of gold when the sunlight caught it just right. It was beautiful, but after she'd gathered it and examined it, she felt she'd seen all she wanted to. She moved on quickly from that area, headed the opposite direction of the track, hoping never to see for herself the creature from which it had come.

Some time later Elyth came across the beast anyway. And it was terrifying.

It was a good three hundred yards away, near the top of a hill, apparently having circled around from its previous direction of travel. Her best guess put it at at least six feet tall at the shoulder, while it was on all fours. Though she knew her fear might have been skewing her estimate, at that size it didn't really matter. She could have been overestimating by two feet and still been in plenty of trouble. Of all the tools at her disposal, nothing would stop a creature that size if it were determined to get to her. If she came face-to-face with it, her best and only hope would be to scare it off. And that was a small hope indeed.

She changed direction again, and made a wide circle of her own, navigating her way to her intended destination while trying to give the fearsome creature plenty of berth. The difficult terrain forced her to take measurements at irregular intervals, sometimes requiring her to double back or crisscross her own trail as she gathered the data and adjusted her plan as the samples dictated. Every change of direction seemed only to increase the likelihood that she would once more encounter the beast.

About half an hour later, she spotted the bear again, closer this time, and the second sighting gave her the sense that it wasn't just ranging around. She observed it for a minute or so, judged its behavior. Something had agitated it. The obvious explanation was also the worst one; it had picked up her scent and was trailing her.

Elyth once more took a new direction, her eyes keen for any sign that the bear had already passed through. About half a mile distant, she came across a patch of wild vines, dangled with heavy, soft-fleshed berries, like dark purple cherries but nearly fragile enough to burst at her touch. She gingerly gathered a handful; some for samples and a few, after verifying they weren't toxic, for herself. They were sharply tart, with a bitterness toward the end. Not unpleasant, but not a flavor she would choose to seek out either.

The fact that so many of them remained undisturbed gave her some small hope. The bear hadn't passed this way yet and, if it did follow her through, there was a chance the berries might distract it for a time.

A few minutes later she came across something else; something that robbed her of even her smallest hope.

About thirty feet ahead, a thicket showed clear signs of breakage; in the midst of the undergrowth, Elyth could make out shapes foreign to the natural terrain. She scanned the area and then crept closer, heart hammering, and verified what instinct had told her.

Backpacks.

Six of them, neatly but hastily arranged. Beyond all probability, the search team had already caught up with her. And if they had dumped their packs that could mean only one thing: They thought they were close enough now to catch her.

It took everything Elyth had not to turn and run. A few seconds to observe, to think, might make all the difference.

Several tracks led off from the site, perpendicular to her approach. The large packs were in good condition, but hard-used; Elyth's quick eye judged them to be roughly half-full. The team had been in the field for a while, maybe as long as she had been. Even if they were exhausted, though, six of them were just too many to ambush. And there was no guarantee that there were only six.

But the discovery of the supplies offered a scant chance. She had no time to improvise any sort of trap, but the fear of one would serve almost as well. Elyth picked up a pair of sticks from the ground and laid them across the top of the packs in an X. When the team returned, the message would be clear; she knew they were after her. Hopefully the psychological impact and fear of ambush would slow their pursuit.

Assuming she could pull off the escape.

Elyth recalled then her other pursuer and another idea sprang to mind. She pulled out the sample of berries she'd collected and crushed them against the underside of one of the packs. Though she had little hope of its usefulness, if the bear continued to follow her, maybe it would do her a favor and pause long enough to ransack the supplies.

Those brief actions were all she could afford. Elyth crept away then, her skin electric with her great danger. From then on the whole region felt too small.

All focus now went to getting out of the area undiscovered, and as far away as possible. Every step of progress was hard-won. Each demanded the utmost caution and attention, and every rustle or snap required her to pause and assess. Elyth noticed how her surroundings had quieted, as if the forest itself were holding its breath, watching the drama of her narrow escape unfold.

She prowled her way out, her pace agonizingly slow as precious minutes of daylight burned away. But her fear, her fatigue, and the terrain all conspired against her. The past few days had taken more out of her than she'd allowed herself to admit. She fought on for as long as she could, but when night closed in and forced her to stop, she'd only opened a few miles between herself and the search site.

For a time, Elyth just sat on the ground, breathing, listening, alternating between believing she'd escaped and expecting sudden ambush at any moment. The darker and colder it got, though, the more she began to hope she'd slipped the noose after all. During her research, she'd been frustrated by how often she'd been forced to loop back across her own trail; it seemed now to have had the unexpected benefit of confusing her pursuers.

Even so, the fear wouldn't completely abate. But sitting in the cold night served no purpose, and she still had plenty of work to do. She set up her shelter, forced herself to eat, and then ran through her meditation sequence, hoping to replenish her energy and focus for the tasks ahead. Once done, Elyth crawled into her shelter and pulled out her personal terminal.

Her best hope of escape now lay in losing herself in an entirely new setting. But she knew she couldn't abandon the region. She was too close to the heart of the matter, if not at it already. Elyth brought up maps of the area and looked at the cities and towns closest by.

———

Alonesse was relatively close, a day and a half of hard travel, maybe two. But she knew now that there was no threadline there for her to exploit. It would be a temporary haven at best.

Oronesse was ultimately the better choice. There it would be easier to blend in, and she had little doubt that another threadline would be reachable somewhere within its borders. Unfortunately, the preserve and its mountains stood between her and that bustling city, and Elyth didn't even know where the perimeter of *eth ammuin*'s compound lay. If she tried to make it through on foot, she might wind up walking right into their surveillance network without any hint or warning.

And then there was a tiny, ill-defined settlement to the southeast, Harovan by name. It was a sprawl, its center and borders irregular, and its main body surrounded by a hillscape dotted with clusters of dwellings. Judging from its arrangement, it seemed to be either the dwindling community of a failed town, or one growing haphazardly where none had been expected to thrive. One of its spiraling arms stretched out and was closer to Elyth's current position than the outskirts of Alonesse by a good twelve miles or so.

It wasn't clear what she would find there, but the area surrounding the location still seemed largely uncultivated. If nothing else, she could do some reconnaissance and then make a more informed decision before she committed. Assuming she hadn't been captured by then.

Harovan, then. She plotted a rough course, knowing she'd have to adapt it on the way, and then turned her attention to her other task.

She hadn't collected all the data she'd wanted from her investigation site, but she hoped she'd gotten enough. The terminal had already synced with all of her collection instruments. Elyth sat cross-legged and activated three separate displays, each a synthesis of specific, specialized readings. At first, she was once more confounded by the results. But as she worked meticulously through, eventually she recalled the data she'd collected from the preserve, the data she'd dismissed as all but useless. And it became clear that those results hadn't been wrong at all.

According to the data, somewhere far below the surface and emerging from underneath the whorl, a second threadline ran toward the southwest, like a spider-thin crack, bending back in nearly the opposite direction of the natural flow of the first. It was just a trace compared to the parent, but it wasn't the line's size or direction that troubled her most. The analysis was definitive; this threadline was far *newer* than the age of the planet. Not something that had been established at the fundamental shaping of its matter, but rather a new outgrowth, like a thin tendril of green stretching out from an old knotted vine.

Elyth's initial thought was that the flow toward Alonesse had been somehow redirected, in some previously unheard-of natural inversion. But the more she investigated, the clearer it became that the young threadline wasn't born of Alonesse's currents; the composition was too different. It was as if the old line had been severed and a new one grafted in from elsewhere, like a shoot of maple growing from the stump of an ancient oak.

Though it was impossible to map the complete circuit from her current location, the directionality was unmistakable. The new threadline led back toward Oronesse. And, presumably, through the preserve of *eth ammuin*. The earlier results from the preserve hadn't been wrong. They just should have been impossible.

Elyth was still pondering what this new revelation might signify when the stillness of night was cleaved by an acute blast.

ELEVEN

Elyth dodged low to the base of a tree six feet away. A second blast followed closely behind the first, and then a chorus joined, tumultuous, sharp reports that folded back on themselves in the echo of the hills.

Gunfire.

But not aimed in her direction.

The storm of shots intensified, a rapid series of lightning-strike cracks, and then ended as abruptly as it had begun. A broken silence fell again, the once-peaceful wood now crackling with tension, as though the wilderness itself stood coiled to bound away. Elyth remained crouched by the tree, straining her senses against the thundering of her heart. The wash of noise had made it difficult to judge the distance, but she guessed the shots had come from a mile or maybe two away at most, back toward the area where she'd spent the day investigating. It didn't take heightened awareness to know what had happened.

The search team had closed in on her. And the golden-fawn bear had found them first. Apparently the trick with the berries had been far more effective than she'd expected.

No telling how many guns, but from the pattern of fire, she knew there had been several single-shot weapons rather than a few fully automatic ones. Not pistols or civilian-model rifles. She couldn't be certain about the weapons, but there'd been a distinctly military quality to the report. Three or four shooters, maybe, though she knew the full party was larger. The members of *eth ammuin*'s Detail were better equipped than she'd anticipated.

Despite the darkness, Elyth knew she had to move. The team was so close now, there was no question that they would catch up to her in the morning. And now that they'd just given themselves away, she had to assume they'd scramble to correct the error.

She left her hiding place, broke camp, and was back to hiking through the darkness in under five minutes. Gone now was the painstaking care of covering her trail, replaced with the urgent need for distance. There was a chance the team would miss her tracks in the night; if not, her only protection was in maintaining separation. Still, hiking uneven terrain in deep night was a good way to break an ankle. Elyth's pace walked the knife's edge between confident and reckless.

Elyth pressed on through the morning at her agonizing pace, the fear of capture just barely overcoming the aching of her body and the weight of her every step. As the light increased, so did her speed, until, when the sun had fully risen, she finally collapsed on the ground and gave herself time to breathe.

She guessed she'd put some distance between herself and her pursuers, but she couldn't trust her ability to maintain that space. She had no doubt that they'd be able to pick up the haphazard trail she'd left hiking through the night.

All her work would be for nothing if she were captured. And though all her focus had been on escape, she realized now she'd missed another avenue. Extraction.

The Paragon had already mentioned a collection team. If she had indeed dispatched one, her sisters would already be in position now, ready to snatch her from her troubles and whisk her to safety.

Perhaps the way forward was not hers to take. The Paragon had openly praised Elyth's ability to operate in a variety of capacities; not just as an assassin of worlds, but as one who could see truly. And Elyth couldn't help but feel she'd already made progress against incredible odds. Not a mission failure, then, but rather the first move of a multi-stage operation. She had identified the twisting branch; another hand would do the pruning.

The thought brought her vision to mind, and its odd self-naming of her: Elyth-Anuiel, *maker of ways*. Apparently she'd already known then what the outcome would be.

But even as her hand moved to retrieve her locator beacon, something rose within her, prevented the action. In that moment of faltering, it was as though the Paragon herself had reached across the galaxy and placed her hand under Elyth, to uplift her, support her, and guide her. Whether it was a result of her training, some deep instinct of an option left unexplored, or just her own pure, innate determination, Elyth found herself unable, even now, to turn away from her purpose.

She would transmit her findings, incomplete as they were, and continue. And if capture were to be her fate, she would keep silent and endure. Resolve replaced doubt then, as her mind closed the door that the Paragon had inadvertently opened by mentioning the collection team.

It took her only a few minutes to package up the data she'd collected and push it through the tangle interpreter's asynchronous passive channel. The transmission would take a few hours to reach the Paragon; in the meantime, Elyth had to move.

Speed became her goal then, and she headed southeast, no longer concerned with covering her tracks but only with keeping her pace as fast as she could sustain. Elyth's world gradually shrunk to the next step, and the next, and the next.

By midafternoon, her thoughts were numbed by the hike, and she knew she was entering a risky state, where mistakes were easy to make and tended to compound. A struggle started within her then, as she tried to decide whether to give herself some time to rest or force herself to press on, while knowing that her ability to make decisions was already compromised. She continued on for a half hour more, only because her body kept moving while she wrestled with indecision.

She did stop eventually, though out of reflex rather than by choice. The tree line thinned ahead of her, and when she emerged, the sight stopped her dead in her tracks. A basin had opened before her and farther on, her path was completely cut off by a wide river, gently flowing and glittering golden in the afternoon sun. Her nav device hadn't indicated any such body of water anywhere in the area.

Either she'd wandered far from her course or she was starting to hallucinate. Elyth checked her nav tracker and then looked again at the river, and realized the truth was closer to the latter. It wasn't a river; it was an immense golden glade. What she'd initially taken for water was actually tall grass rippling in the breeze.

The realization was only a partial relief. Even though it was solid ground, she was hesitant to cross it. She judged it at a half mile across, and that was a long time to be out in the wide open. Looking along the length of the glade, however, there was no way around it close at hand. Judging from her nav device, she had drifted farther south than she'd intended.

The basin narrowed about two hundred yards farther up, and though heading that direction would take her farther off her intended path, it seemed worth it to her to avoid that much open ground.

Elyth turned and followed the tree line until she reached the narrower band; from there, it still seemed several hundred yards to the next point of cover, but the near-side forest started to bend away again, and continuing along it would have meant losing more ground than she was willing to give. She would have to cross as best she could, without leaving an obvious wake for her pursuers to follow. Each step required thoughtful placement to avoid crushing large clumps of the thin golden grass, and she adjusted her course several times to avoid creating a straight-line cut across the glade.

The effort drained her, and when she reached the trees that marked the beginning of an ascent on the other side, her body demanded she pause. She plopped down under a tree akin to a cedar, giving herself twenty minutes to rest. Elyth sat with her back against the tree, looking back over the glade and evaluating her work. Though undoubtedly she'd left some tracks behind, the tall grass wasn't laid down in any obvious places. Her pursuers would have to be lucky indeed to come across any footprints. Satisfied, she pulled out her local nav tracker to orient herself and make sure she was still on the right heading. After a few minutes, she raised her head and scanned across the glade once more. Whether it was by luck or the result of some subconscious instinct, what she saw turned out to be both fortunate and frightening.

A flicker of movement back across the glade, about three hundred yards or so farther "downstream" from the point where she'd crossed. For a brief moment, Elyth told herself it was her imagination and her fatigue conspiring against her, but even with her doubts she found her hands reaching for her monocular. She brought the optic up and slowly swept the area where she thought she'd seen something. And just as she was about to lower it, thinking herself safe after all, she caught sight of a figure standing up from a crouch by the edge of the tall grass, and her heart practically stopped.

She dialed the magnification up two more notches, and though she still couldn't make out the man's features, she could tell enough from his posture and body language. He was scanning the glade in both directions, looking for some sign of his quarry. For some sign of her.

He hadn't picked up her exact trail, but he hadn't been too wide of the mark. A few moments later, she realized why.

Somewhere high up above she heard a faint, keening whine, one that barely made itself known amid the rustling of the breeze through the leaves. It was difficult to pinpoint, but here the danger that the glade had posed to her now became her advantage. She spotted a glint in the sky. Out there a few hundred feet above the waving grass, a scout drone was making lazy, wandering movements. Not the rugged hunting variety that she'd seen Hok using. This model was sleeker, quieter. There was no telling what track of hers it might have been capable of picking up, but one thing was clear: Whatever distance she'd gained over her pursuers was now all but gone.

Across the expanse, a second man appeared by the first, followed shortly after by two more. They held a brief conference, and then split up again, each pair following the wood line in opposite directions. Neither group was in the open long; they both slipped back into the trees and were soon lost among them.

The drone continued its weaving path, and though it appeared to be continuing away from her crossing point, there was no guarantee it wouldn't double back. In that moment, Elyth had to decide which was her greatest threat: the drone or her own weariness.

In her dire need, she could attempt to use the Deep Language to override her body's depletion. But the effect would be short-lived, and the violent return of her temporarily muted fatigue would stack upon the cost of the cosmic call. The subsequent crash would extract a double toll.

The drone, then. If she could rob her pursuers of it, it'd be easier to obscure her trail at the next hill, and maybe open more space. Whether it was autonomous or being run from the ground, it must have been communicating with the search party somehow. Introducing a little noise into its signal would be less demanding. She pictured the communication stream in her mind, stretching out like a tether to the search party below.

In the final seconds before the drone disappeared from sight, she spoke to it.

"Snow blankets the mountain; silence in white."

Elyth felt the jolt of power pass through her, followed immediately by a wave of nausea as it compounded her fatigue. The last view she had of the machine, it was headed into the trees on the far side of the glade. She didn't wait to see what further effect she'd had. Seeing her pursuers so close and with her own eyes refocused her mind and her resolve. Where her body had previously felt at odds with her purposes, it now seemed to better understand what was at stake. And though getting back to her feet took some effort after the use of the Deep Language, once she was on the move, she fell quickly back into rhythm. She made her way up over the rise and then moved laterally along the other side to break up her trail.

The terrain required her full attention and effort, and even giving it her all felt like it was not enough. Like swimming upstream, racing against the coming night, haunted by the ghosts on her heels. The sun was already riding low when she first started hearing the distant buzz and hum of the occasional skimmer, and it had slipped halfway below the horizon when she reached the edge of her destination. The woods began to thin, and Elyth slowed her pace as she neared the border, where they gave way to the first signs of civilization she'd seen in over a week.

Not that there was much civilization to speak of.

Elyth wanted to crouch down at the tree line, but she feared that if she went to the ground, she'd be unable to regain her feet. She compromised by wrapping an arm around a tree and leaning all her weight against it while she scanned the area ahead.

The woods gave way to a large man-made clearing that looked like someone had dropped a gargantuan slab of concrete and crushed the forest beneath it. On one end, to Elyth's left, sat a large well-lit structure, or perhaps a series of interconnected structures. The scalloped roofline arced and rippled irregularly, like wind-scattered waves. A large sign over the main entrance read GREEN CENTER. Dozens of people milled about or sat on benches around the exterior, and from what Elyth could see, there appeared to be a good number inside as well.

In front of the building, there was a short stretch of open ground and then a long, wide pad marked with landing zones where a number of private skimmers sat idle. The vessels were arrayed in a broken grid, as if on display at a secondhand dealer; sixty-some, she estimated, with room for half again as many. They covered the spectrum of size and shape, from a few sleek, two-seat runabouts up to a boxy, high-capacity cargo runner that straddled four spots. One thing they had in common, though, was age and wear. Harovan wasn't a place of conspicuous wealth.

Elyth watched the flow of the place for a minute or two. A couple of groups of people were crossing from the pad to the main entrance, and they waved to each other but didn't meet together. The atmosphere had an unusual blend of festival and routine; the people seemed pleased to be there, but lacked the wide-eyed wonder and excitement that typically marked a special occasion. The structure appeared to be a combined marketplace and community center. Probably one of the few spots on the outskirts of an already out-of-the-way town where people could come together to visit and shop; perhaps the regular evening stopping point between work and home.

Regardless of the center's function, one thing was clear: It wasn't the kind of place where she could just walk out of the wilderness and blend in.

Elyth knew the search party was right on her heels. And trying to hide in a small community from such a determined and skilled group wasn't an option. If she could get to a vehicle, though . . .

She returned her attention to the skimmers on the pad. The best looking of the group was a black runabout, but it was on the front line, nearest the complex. Too exposed. Ultimately, she settled on a gray, practical six-passenger skimmer; it was older and bulkier than some of the other models, but it looked well maintained. It was on the row second from the back of the pad, and only about a quarter of the way from the tree line; she'd have some cover from the skimmers between her and the center, and only a few spans of open ground to cross.

She left the woods and walked calmly and confidently across the pad, initially looking neither around nor down. Head up, relaxed, going about her business, matching the rhythm of the people she'd observed. She knew the pack on her back might draw some attention, but she also knew that moving too fast or trying too hard not to be noticed would mark her more strongly.

As she crossed the open space between the woodline and the skimmers, Elyth glanced toward the main entrance of the building; a few people were coming out, headed toward the pad, but no one seemed to be paying any attention to her. A few steps away from the rear line of skimmers, though, movement in Elyth's peripheral vision caught her attention.

Two men emerging from the woods.

She recognized them as the first two she'd seen across the glade.

They were farther down from where she had exited, perpendicular to her line of travel. Again, they hadn't caught her exact trail, but had come near enough to make an educated guess about her destination. They paused there, scanning the area. But their focus was on the Green Center.

It took everything Elyth had to keep her reaction calm and casual, so her motion wouldn't change and attract their attention. Just a few more steps.

She reached the closest vessel and paused by its rear corner, crouching slightly to keep her head below its silhouette. The craft she was hiding behind was a wedge with rounded corners, shoulder height at its tallest point, narrower in the front than the back, snub-nosed. And not in good shape. The skimmer she'd intended to take was still forty feet away, with only one other vessel between them. Crossing that stretch of space now seemed almost guaranteed to give her away.

The craft was parked facing the building, and Elyth peeked around from behind it. The two men were still there, one of them signaling toward the building complex. She followed the man's gaze and saw another pair of men standing at the perimeter, closer to the structure. She didn't recognize those two. That made four of them. At least.

The second pair moved toward the building; the first began crossing toward the lot of skimmers. One headed toward the front line of the pad while the other split off to start at the back. Elyth dropped to a knee, mind racing. She couldn't make it to the ship she'd selected without their spotting her. Nor could she return to the wilderness. She was trapped on the island of a beat-up skimmer. Exhaustion fogged her thoughts.

Run or fight. Either way she was going to have to lose her pack. She unbuckled the harness and let it slide to the ground. But before she could do more, she was interrupted by a voice behind her.

"Excuse me," a woman said. "Can I help you?"

The tone was neutral, but tinged with suspicion.

Elyth turned and saw the woman standing several feet away, a toddler in her arms. One of the people Elyth had spotted coming out of the building and, she guessed, the owner of the skimmer. There was no good way to explain.

Elyth stood slightly from her crouch, peeked over the top of the vessel. She'd lost sight of one of her pursuers; the other was weaving his way toward her at a measured pace. She didn't have much time. She glanced back at the woman, and at the child in her arms. A little girl, maybe four years old. Their presence complicated matters; the fact that they'd stopped several feet from their skimmer was certain to draw attention.

"Are you hurt?" the woman asked.

But before Elyth could respond, the woman looked over to her right, something attracting her gaze. Elyth didn't have to look to know. Her hunters were coming.

Fight, then. She reached for her baton.

But before she deployed it, the woman stepped toward her.

"Honey . . . are you in some kind of trouble?"

Elyth held a finger to her lips and retreated along the back side of the skimmer. A moment later a man spoke from the front side, somewhere off to the left of the vessel and closing in.

"Everything okay, ma'am?"

The woman didn't answer, but Elyth could hear the man's cautious footsteps, edging around the opposite side of the craft. Elyth continued to circle in a crouch, searching with her eyes for his partner while tracking the man with her hearing. He stopped somewhere a few feet from the front right corner, a polite distance from the woman, but close enough to get a view of where Elyth had just been.

"I'm guessing that's not your pack, huh?" the man said.

Elyth held still by the shoulder of the craft, scanning, scanning for that second man. The woman still hadn't answered any questions. At least not verbally. She might well be motioning to Elyth's hiding place even now.

Where was the second man?

"Mama," the little girl said, "Where'd the lady go?"

An electric gap of silence followed.

Elyth had to strike first.

But just as her muscles tensed for the surge, the woman spoke.

"She ran off, sweetie," she said.

Elyth caught herself in time, rocked back into her crouch.

"She won't bother us," the woman continued, and then her voice changed, talking to the man now. "Some woman was hanging out by my craft when we came out. Skittered off back toward the center when she saw us coming. You looking for her?"

"Yes, ma'am," the man said. "She's dangerous."

"Yeah, looked like she was up to no good."

A pause, and stillness.

"Cute kid," the man said a moment later. "Glad she's safe."

He waited another beat; Elyth could almost feel the tension from the other side, could picture in her mind's eye how he was evaluating the woman, testing her.

"You have a good night, ma'am," he said.

And then he moved off, his pace quicker than when he'd approached.

Elyth slid quietly back alongside the craft, toward the rear. The woman was already waiting there.

"Yes," Elyth said. "I am in trouble."

"Your fault?"

"I don't know why they're chasing me," she answered honestly.

Elyth had intended to pick up her pack, but the woman was standing in the way, scanning her with eyes hard and determined. And a moment later, her look resolved.

She activated the rear hatch; it only opened halfway before the woman had to force it.

"Come on," she said, waving Elyth in. "Before they see you."

Elyth hesitated, reading the woman's intentions.

"Go on," she said. "Or I might change my mind."

Elyth nodded and ducked into the craft. The interior had six seats total, two up front that swiveled and four in the back along the walls in pairs, facing center. A family vehicle. On one seat in the rear sat a stuffed toy, flop-eared like a rabbit; its fur was matted, worn, and grubby from being so well loved. The floor wasn't dirty, exactly, but muddy shoes and crushed snacks had done a number on the thin carpeting.

She moved up and crouched behind the forward-most passenger seat. Behind her, the woman slung her pack in with one arm, still holding her daughter close. She paused there, looking once more at Elyth.

"Tell me I'm doing the right thing here."

"You are," Elyth said.

The woman held her gaze for a moment and then finally nodded. She set the girl on her feet in the craft and shepherded her to the seat with the toy.

"Climb up in your seat, pumpkin."

The woman continued past Elyth and dropped into the pilot seat; the little girl just stood there, staring at Elyth.

"Who's the lady, Mama?" she said.

"Get in your seat, Hykei," the woman said more firmly. The girl clambered up and buckled herself in.

The bubble windscreen gave a wide view out the front. Elyth continued to keep watch as the rear hatch started to lower, stalled briefly, and then finished closing. She couldn't see the first man now, but spotted the second near the front line of skimmers, waiting for his partner to join him.

The woman started the skimmer; the engines revved up sounding a little ragged, and just as the craft started to lift off, it shuddered once and settled back to the ground. A warning light pinged yellow, and the engines went into a safety shut down. In front of the ship, a faint trace of smoke wafted across the windscreen.

And then Elyth caught sight of the first man again; two rows ahead, walking back toward the craft.

She didn't panic, but felt the spike of blood pressure as her moment of escape began to slip away.

The woman sighed loudly, and then leaned forward and jiggled something under the command console. The warning light went green. She reactivated the drives then, but waited before trying to lift off. She looked out the windscreen, craning her head to see the man who was walking toward them. He wasn't rushing. At least not yet. Elyth remained crouched behind the front seat, partially out of fear of being seen, and partially because she wasn't sure what the woman wanted her to do.

"Gotta give it a little time to warm up," the woman said. The front right lift drive smoked lightly.

Elyth sank back against the frame of the ship, hiding completely from view. Next to her, the little girl Hykei sat with her feet barely reaching past the end of the seat, singing quietly to herself, her beloved stuffed toy buckled safely in on her lap.

Elyth was already running the scenarios in her head. Out the rear hatch. How many seconds to force it open?

And while she was preparing a hundred plans of action all at once, the skimmer started to lift off, shuddered, dipped to touch the ground lightly, and then, miraculously, resumed its rise once more.

Twenty feet off the ground, Elyth eased up from her low crouch, peeked out. The man was watching them take off, only a few skimmers away. She knew he couldn't see her, but somehow she got the feeling that he knew she was there. And she wondered what trouble she had just invited upon this woman and her child.

The skimmer reached altitude and surged forward. Once it was in stable flight, the woman swiveled her chair around to face Elyth. She was young, younger than Elyth, but had the rough edge of a woman hard-used by life. The look in her eyes reminded Elyth of one she'd seen in her instructors; it was something like disappointment touched by vague anger, but rooted in genuine concern, the judgment of an elder who expects a higher standard of conduct.

"Thank you," Elyth said. "I don't know what I would have done if you hadn't helped me."

"Yeah, well. He had a gun under his coat, and you don't. And I know he wasn't with the local Authority. My husband's a cop, and *that* guy definitely wasn't one. How long have you been running from them?"

The woman had already pieced together some bit of a story; Elyth leaned into it, adopted the persona.

"I don't remember. What day is it?"

"Tuesday," the woman said. "You got a safe place you can go?"

Elyth shrugged. "Anywhere but here." She waited a few moments, then added, "I need to get to Alonesse, maybe."

"What you *need* is a bath, sweetheart. Why don't you get up off the floor and take a seat?"

The woman swiveled back around and worked the console for a few moments.

Elyth eased up and took a seat in the back, across from little Hykei. The girl kept her eyes on her own feet, not shy so much as unconcerned by the strangeness of the situation.

"You want to talk to my husband?" the woman asked, over her shoulder.

"No," Elyth answered. "No, thank you. I just want to leave."

"Mama, I'm hungry," Hykei said abruptly.

"I know, pumpkin, we'll go home in just a minute."

The woman continued to face forward, adjusting the skimmer's flight path. Elyth looked out the window, back at the site they'd just left, watched as it shrunk to a tiny dot of light amid the swiftly darkening forest. After so many days of traveling on foot, it was shocking to see so much distance open up between her and her pursuers in so short a time.

"When was the last time *you* ate?" the woman asked.

"Been a little while, I guess," Elyth answered honestly. "But I'm okay. You can drop me off anywhere. I've already caused you too much trouble."

"Yeah, trouble has a habit of finding its way to my door."

The woman brought up a secondary display; Elyth couldn't see over her shoulder enough to discern what she was doing exactly.

"There's a transit to Alonesse leaving in about forty minutes," she said a few minutes later. "I can drop you at the pad. We should have time to make it."

"You don't have to do that."

"I already got you a pass."

She said it as a matter of fact, neither looking for gratitude nor tolerant of any argument.

"Really, I just . . ." Elyth said and then trailed off. She genuinely didn't know what to say, either as her persona or as herself. The woman's gruff kindness was so unusual, and surprising. "Thank you."

The woman didn't respond. After that, they traveled for several minutes in silence, apart from little Hykei's singing. Elyth watched the girl for a time. From her first moment on Qel, everything had been complicated and brutally demanding; something about the simplicity of the moment, the innocently oblivious child, served as a powerful reminder to Elyth of what she was fighting to protect. Little Hykei had no idea how dangerous her world actually was, nor how much people she'd never met were willing to give to shield her from that knowledge. She would certainly never know how great a role her mother's act of kindness had played in their own salvation.

Outside, the land and sky began changing beneath and around the skimmer; the clusters of homes and buildings became more frequent, and traffic picked up. As small as Harovan was by normal standards, to Elyth's wilderness-calibrated senses it seemed like a city thriving. Soon, the woman was merging her flight path with a skylane of several other skimmers, and ahead on the horizon Harovan's transit station appeared.

The woman set the skimmer to auto-navigate to the drop-off zone; it weaved its way through, coordinating with the skimmers around it to maintain flow. A minute later they were drifting down and then coming to a stop, hovering by the walkway. The woman swiveled her seat around to face Elyth.

Elyth leaned forward and grabbed her pack, and started to dig through it, looking for something she could offer as a token of gratitude.

"Nope," the woman said. "I don't want anything of yours."

"There's got to be something I can do to repay you," Elyth said.

"Sure," the woman answered. "Make better choices. I don't know how many second chances you've gotten in your life, girl, but judging from the look of things, you probably shouldn't count on any more of them."

Elyth wanted to do something to commend the woman for her help, to bless her with the favor of the First House. But instead she just nodded.

"Thank you again," she said.

"Don't waste it," the woman said. She still seemed vaguely angry and anxious to be rid of Elyth; hers was a severe kindness.

The rear hatch slid open halfway. Elyth took up her pack and moved to the back.

"You have to push it the rest of the way," the woman said.

Elyth nodded and forced the hatch open enough to squeeze through.

"Bye," Hykei said, waving the little rabbit creature's floppy arm as Elyth started to duck out.

"Goodbye," Elyth said, smiling at the girl. She shared a brief look with the woman and saw a tenderness there, hidden behind her stony face.

"May you and your family ever ascend," Elyth said.

"Yeah," the woman replied. "Wouldn't that be something."

Elyth nodded to her and exited. The rear hatch slumped back to halfway as soon as she released it, and then the mechanism engaged and sealed it behind her. As the hatch closed, the woman's look remained frozen in Elyth's mind. It was the look of a woman who had seen this situation before, or what she thought the situation was, at least. Maybe she'd had an older daughter who'd run off. Or maybe she herself had a hard past.

The gray skimmer lifted off, shuddered once and dipped slightly, then resumed its rise to join the traffic above. Elyth didn't know what capabilities *eth ammuin*'s Detail had to track vehicles, or if they would go so far as to confront the woman. If they did, though, she couldn't imagine what force they would encounter when they showed up at her door. Tired mothers clearly had no time for nonsense, or patience for foolish strangers.

After the skimmer left, Elyth merged with the flow of people entering the transit station, losing herself in the crowd. She took the woman's advice, and though the public shower was moldy and the water cold, Elyth was reborn when she emerged, genuinely clean for the first time in what felt like a month.

The woman's generosity had been as unnecessary as it was unexpected. Elyth had access to untraceable accounts with more currency than she could have spent in her lifetime. She purchased a second pass to Alonesse and hopped on the transit at the last call, leaving unused the one the woman had purchased for her, a dead end for anyone who might try to come behind.

It was a short trip to Alonesse. There, to cover her tracks, she purchased multiple passes to other destinations and sent the activated credentials along hidden in other passengers' belongings. As a final precaution, she waited a couple of hours before taking an early-morning shuttle to her true destination. She reached Oronesse as the sun was rising the following morning, bruised and tired.

And soon discovered she'd traded one kind of wilderness for another sort entirely.

TWELVE

Elyth stepped off the shuttle onto the boarding platform and immediately wanted to turn back around. A tsunami of motion and sound cascaded over her. Her time in the wild had finely tuned her senses to her surroundings; here in the city it was like her eyes, ears, and nose had all been wrapped in a coil of live wires, a lightning storm of sensation assaulting her from all sides and angles. The sheer mass of humanity seemed like more than should have been allowed on any one planet. Elyth had to consciously remind herself that the cacophony was actually normal. She was the one out of step.

She forced herself forward, navigating the throng awkwardly, partially due to her large backpack but more because no one around her seemed to make any effort whatsoever to afford her any space. After about fifteen minutes of swimming through the crowd, Elyth found her way to a local transit desk, where an exceptionally rude attendant sold her an overpriced pass and seemed angry about the exchange.

The packed public shuttle took her farther into the city center. Elyth stood near the rear entrance and watched out the window, getting a sketch of the architecture and density of the place. Though the design and materials were of an older style, the Academy's influence was conspicuous. There was a certain elegance to the layout and balance of the structures constructed along the wide river that bisected the city. The buildings mostly shared a slender helix design, many spiraling several hundred feet into the sky. Ground-level thoroughfares and open spaces too appeared to follow an aesthetic reminiscent of the Academy, giving the city an open, welcoming, almost laid-back feeling. A place where lingering was invited, with more than enough time in the day for everything that needed to be done.

Near the center of the city, Elyth got off the shuttle and found a midgrade hotel, spiraled like its neighbors but the shortest among them by far. It was no more than five hundred feet tall, but its ingenious exterior was blue at its foundation and grew gradually paler the higher it rose; standing at its base, the effect created the impression that the structure was a beam of light, extending heavenward to infinity.

She booked a corner room, one level above a lovely terrace it overlooked. The two windows gave her a wide view of the city and, with the terrace just one floor below, an alternate escape route should one prove necessary. The room was spacious and well equipped, and felt open even with the generous bed taking up so much room.

It took an act of pure will for Elyth not to crash immediately on the bed. Instead, she forced herself back out to wander a few blocks of the city, to start developing a sense of its pace and energy, and to evaluate her security. After having hounds at her heels for days, she found it disconcerting to have so many people behind her no matter where she went.

She spent a few hours observing, sometimes on the move, sometimes in place at a café or on a park bench, her mind all the while building a model of how the people dressed, moved, and spoke. And attuning herself, too, to the place itself. In that brief time she discovered nothing to suggest corruption, neither of the Language of the society nor its effects within the land beneath them. That matter, though, would require more thorough investigation.

Once she had a baseline, she visited a shop not too far from her hotel and purchased a handful of new outfits. It was more social camouflage than anything, but Elyth knew she was going to need a few days in the city to evaluate it, and anything she could do to blend in was helpful. The presence of the local Authority was substantial, and their eyes were the Hezra's eyes. And as unlikely as it seemed, she couldn't ignore the possibility that the Detail would find some way to track her even here.

She stayed out as long as she was able, but eventually the toll of her previous day's flight through the hills drove her back to her room. Elyth managed maybe an hour of sleep before the sudden sensation of falling and a voice calling her name jolted her awake.

She sat up, adrenaline burning off the effects of the abrupt awakening. After a few moments she realized what had triggered it—the Paragon was calling to her. When Elyth activated her side of the connection, it was as if passing from one dream world to another.

Once more she found herself in a tranquil setting, guarded by impassable terrain. But this time the elements were reversed. She was at the top of a mountain, surrounded by emptiness on all sides; the darkness over the land below stood in stark contrast to the jeweled brilliance of the sky above. Elyth didn't recognize that sky; it certainly wasn't the view from the Vaunt. The small, flat peak on which she stood hosted only a single, ancient tree, its trunk gnarled and twisting beneath an explosion of purpling leaves. The area glowed with a pale, orange-tinged moonlight, without obvious source. Despite the altitude, the air was still and pleasantly warm, like evening in late spring.

The Paragon stood beneath the tree, her head just below the first wide branches. Elyth approached and bowed.

"Illumined Mother," she said.

"Bright daughter. We have much to discuss."

Straight to business, then. Elyth stood at a casual attention. To her surprise, the Paragon turned around and easily scaled the tree, perching on its lowest branch.

"I did so love to climb trees in my youth," the ancient woman said, her legs dangling. "And in my not so youth. I'm told it is unbecoming of a woman of my age and station."

Elyth couldn't help but smile at the childlike image before her.

"A woman of your age and station has earned the right to define what is becoming, Your Radiance."

The Paragon waved her hand dismissively. "I will allow your flattery only because I wish it were true. But if one is not free to play in one's own mind, then there is no freedom at all. And I fear this is the only enjoyment I shall find in our time together."

She seemed neither angry nor disturbed, but there was gravity to the words.

"I received your findings," she continued. "As a result, I felt it necessary to expand our circle of trust, ever so slightly, to the wisest of our elders. After much thought and debate, we have reached agreement. It will be difficult for you to hear, but you must understand that it is the only path forward we see, given the situation."

Elyth wasn't going to like the outcome; she remembered the Paragon's mention of the collection team, and in a flash of insight saw what was coming. Recall. They had lost their faith in her. But she would hold her tongue, wait to hear the pronouncement before she argued.

"It is well, Illumined Mother," Elyth said. "Whatever the House requires, I am its hands."

"I know, dear. It's why I sent you in the first place. After reviewing the data you gathered, we have deemed it best—*I* have deemed it best, for the consequences of this must lie solely upon me—I have deemed it best that you should put Qel down immediately."

The last four words haunted the air, immaterial yet striking with gale force. They were a complete reversal of her expectations. Beyond any possible expectation. Any such act, without explicit authorization by the Hezra, would be a violation of every principle First House had taught her to hold sacred. Surely Elyth had misunderstood.

"Illumined Mother . . ." she said.

"I know, my daughter. Neither of us could have foreseen this. I understand the full measure of what I am asking of you, and the toll it will take. But you must trust that I would not give this command if there were any other way. Against the might and resilience of the Ascendance, there are few threats to be considered truly existential. But what you have found on Qel, I fear, is of that magnitude."

"But, the analysis is incomplete—"

"It is sufficient."

"I . . ." Elyth said, then trailed off. Up until that very moment she could not have imagined an order from the Paragon that she would not have obeyed. Even if the Paragon had demanded her return to the Vaunt against her objections, she would have relented. But here, now, she found herself truly tested. "Forgive me, I don't wish to seem disloyal, but—"

"I have no question as to where your loyalties lie, bright daughter. I would be more concerned if you did not protest. This is a great burden to place upon you. The only comfort I can offer is that I alone know the part you play in this, and it is a secret I shall keep through pain and death."

"Both of which are likely if we are found out."

"If *I* am found out. Hear me, child, I bear full responsibility for both the decision and the act."

"I am not concerned for myself, Illumined Mother. If they destroy you, they will have destroyed First House."

The old woman chuckled, a jangling sound of amusement that would normally have lightened Elyth's burden; this time, it left her unmoved.

"I am not so powerful as that, dear, despite the stories they tell. And, admittedly, which I encourage. I am merely a link in the chain of Paragons stretching back ages, and that chain shall stretch forward for many more beyond me. If things go ill, the standing of the House may diminish, but that too has happened before. All things ebb and flow. Even our mighty First House is not immune to the seasons of the cosmos."

Elyth tumbled within a torrent of doubt. Could she refuse such a command? Could she execute it faithfully? Both seemed beyond her capability.

"I don't know that I can do this," she confessed, as much to herself as to her superior.

"It is a heavy task. But I fear you are all we have left, my bright daughter. The attention of the Hezra is on us now. We have slipped you in at the last possible moment."

Elyth reacted sharply to the last comment.

"What about the collection team?"

The pause was enough to reveal the answer before the matriarch responded.

"I was unable to deploy them," the Paragon said. "If they approached now, it would tip our hand that we have someone operating on the planet."

"There will be no doubt of our involvement once I complete the kill," Elyth said.

"And by then the Hezra's options will be to align with us or to face the Grand Council and admit their failure to detect so great a threat. Such an admission would be very painful indeed. Particularly in light of their most recent one."

The Paragon paused, perhaps waiting for Elyth's spinning mind to absorb the information, or perhaps testing the depth of her curiosity. But then after a moment, she nodded and continued.

"What do you know of the Deepcutter Initiative?" she asked.

"Deepcutter," Elyth echoed. The Hezra's long-running, highly funded "secret" program. The secret was poorly kept among the Ascendance's highest-level operatives. "It's the Hezra's effort to cross the intergalactic barrier."

"It is a failure," the Paragon bluntly replied. "The Hezra-Ka delivered the message to the Grand Council last evening."

The magnitude of such an announcement was not lost on Elyth. For all of the Hezra's technological power, their aspect drives still couldn't reach beyond the border of the galaxy. Deepcutter was meant to open the entire universe to the Ascendance's reach. To call it a failure was to rob the Ascendance of both its birthright and its destiny.

"They've shut it down?"

"Oh no. Not yet. Not officially. Those tasked with the project haven't admitted it, but the Hezra-Ka has keener eyes than most. And if he is making so startling a confession, then it is only the first move in some deeper game."

Though the connection wasn't clear, Elyth knew that the Paragon wouldn't be sharing such information merely for gossip; information was a tool, and the matriarch of the First House a master craftswoman.

"And you believe it's related to Qel?" Elyth said.

"It may be that their focus on Deepcutter has blinded them to the danger posed by the planet. It may be that they have overextended themselves and lack the necessary resources, and cannot openly admit the weakness. Or there may be something more at work."

Elyth picked up the thread immediately.

"You think they're hiding it on purpose."

"I am not convinced of it. Not yet. But I must consider the possibility. It is my burden to see all possibilities, Advocate, and my duty to weigh them."

The ancient woman looked up through the tree, at the numberless stars above them, couched in infinity.

"We see only in part," she said. "Our view of that which surrounds us obscures that which lies beyond."

She sat for a long moment, staring up through the leaves above her, and then returned her attention to Elyth.

"Remember your own skepticism when I first told you of this threat. The Markovian Strain remains one of the most painful eras in the Hezra's legacy. Invoking its specter now will seem timed to strike at their most vulnerable moment. Even if we were to warn the Grand Council ourselves, that warning will be viewed through the lens of the game. At best, that would bring delay and obstruction. At worst, it will alert the Hezra to what we know.

"But this move will take us entirely off the board now. It will require the destruction of the old game, and the beginning of one new, but it cannot be helped. The death of Qel is the only way to prevent its use as a vessel to carry on this branch of the Strain, and that must be our first and foremost concern. It must be your only concern. All the rest belongs to me."

Elyth had no response. She had long been aware of the political maneuvering between the three seats of Ascendance power, but she had no direct experience with any of it. Her opinion of these so-called games was only reinforced by the Paragon's description; namely, that they were nothing but a vain and foolish pursuit, a cancerous plague undermining that which really mattered. The First House's warning of the Strain would be interpreted as a political pouncing on opportunity, merely to leverage the Hezra's temporary weakness. But if that were so, how would the act of destroying a planet without authorization be received?

After a moment the Paragon sighed, and then the diamond edge of her speech gave way to a waxen resignation; in her voice, Elyth could hear the weight of the matriarch's many burdens, her age, and, unexpectedly, her deep weariness.

"The history of humanity is full of catastrophe," she said. "And in every case, we look back upon the signs that clearly displayed the inevitable cataclysm and wonder why no one who was capable acted to prevent that which was so obvious. We are on the precipice of such a moment, Elyth. This is a seed of the apocalypse. And if we do not act, or if we tarry, we alone will bear the responsibility for the harvest of ruin to come."

"Then it *is* the Markovian Strain?"

"Not identical, no. But a distant variation, one whose underlying theme can be discerned by those with ears to hear. Like an echo of an echo. A mutated version, perhaps. Or an evolution."

"It doesn't seem to have reached Oronesse at all."

"This branch is subtle in its workings. Perhaps you will be able to tell us more once the task is completed. But given what you've already found, it would make no difference if it were the work of only fifty corrupted individuals. The innocent many often inherit the suffering stored up by the words and deeds of the malevolent few."

The Paragon hopped down from her perch, landing lightly on her feet.

"Perhaps now you understand more fully why I sent you," she said.

"No, Illumined Mother, I don't. This is more than I can bear."

"Elyth. Child," the Paragon said. She stepped closer, squeezed Elyth's arm in her age-knotted hand. Despite the vast distance between them, Elyth felt the warmth and gentle pressure. "Look at me."

Elyth eyes met the Paragon's.

"*Look* at me," the Paragon repeated. Elyth held the matriarch's gaze and found within that piercing stare an unexpected, depthless well of understanding and compassion.

"You possess the wisdom and skill to operate across all the domains of the First House; Hand, Eye, Mind, and Voice," the Paragon said.

"Even your doubts reflect our highest ways. I sent you because you are the very embodiment of *sareth hanaan*. And if our great House should fail in confronting this threat, I wanted to know that we had held nothing back, that we had given our all, and our best. Truly, Elyth, you are Guided by the True Star."

Elyth felt the quiet force of the Paragon's exhortation; and though the words couldn't assuage the deep doubts of her soul, she felt the ember of determination flare once more.

"I don't wish to question your judgment but I fear I have a long road to walk before I become anything like the daughter you've described."

The Paragon's eyes softened and crinkled at the edges in a smile.

"It is the striving that makes it so, dear."

Elyth stood silently, as the full weight of the task ahead settled upon her; Titan Bears the World, indeed. The head of First House, along with her most trusted advisors, had deemed the unauthorized assassination of Qel necessary and right. Elyth searched her innermost being and found that despite her misgivings, she could not find it in herself to refuse. As though this was the very purpose for which she had been formed, placed upon her by some nameless cosmic destiny.

"I will serve the House in this," she said. "And accept my share of the consequences."

"If all goes well, the only consequence will be the continued prosperity of the Ascendance," the Paragon said, releasing her. "And for that, your share will be too great to measure. How long do you estimate for full effect to manifest?"

Elyth thought for a moment of what she'd learned about the health of the world and its essential structures and composition.

"I would guess fourteen months at the longest," she said. "Perhaps as few as nine. But I don't know what impact this developing threadline might play. The planet may be more fragile than we know."

"If the Hezra is properly motivated, the whole populace could be assessed and relocated in six," said the Paragon. "We should have plenty of time."

"*If* they are properly motivated," Elyth echoed.

"Yes. But that work is not your concern, and I am not yet too ancient for such tasks. These are the sorts of impossibly tangled webs that your poor mother must unweave. And also weave, I suppose. Perhaps you understand now why I look so old. And why I cherish my garden. It's the only place I have where everything is exactly what it appears to be."

She reached up then and brushed her fingers along Elyth's cheek, a shocking display of tenderness.

"I have every confidence in you," she said. "Let me know the moment your work is finished, and we'll have you home in a heartbeat."

"It will be done."

"*Sareth hanaan* continue to be your guide, my brightest of daughters."

"*Sareth hanaan* be our way, Illumined Mother."

The connection closed in its characteristic soft fading from one reality to another, and Elyth was once more sitting on her bed.

The afternoon sun streamed through the windows, its light unable to illuminate the dark road that now lay before her.

THIRTEEN

The new directive didn't require significant changes to Elyth's manner of operation; it simply focused and intensified it. She needed more information from the planet itself, and time to identify the best target site. But what Elyth needed most was rejuvenation.

Of all the techniques of the First House, none was more potent than the planet-killing power of Revealing the Silent Gate, nor were any more costly to the conduit through which that power flowed. She took several trips out to scout the area and continue her analysis, but for the first few days she forced herself to spend the better portion of her time eating and sleeping and tending to the weariness deep in her bones.

In the midst of the third day, while she was reviewing data on the threadline within Oronesse, a detail unexpectedly called her mind back to Revik. And in that moment, the two worlds were paired; the thought of Qel's coming end awakened within her the grief of Revik's loss, still lingering. The realization came then of how little she'd considered it since the beginning of her mission. There'd been no time, no room in her mind to reflect upon it. And in that darkness it had grown.

She wept then, wept for Revik and the other worlds she had ended, and for the hardship she had endured, and for that which had yet to be done. There was neither shame nor weakness in the release. Elyth emptied herself of the emotion, allowed it to pour out until it had exhausted itself, and the soul burden had lifted. Afterward, she washed her face, went up to the rooftop terrace of the hotel, and spent an hour looking out over the city.

She recalled elements of Revik that she had admired; its three moons in their varied arcs, the crackling scent of its dry days, and the refreshing fragrance of its rain. The fire in its heart. But she did not linger on these things. She acknowledged them, gave them each their moment of appreciation, and then let them slip away. And reminded herself, too, that all she had done was in service to a greater and higher call. The personal pain was a small price for the order and peace she worked to preserve.

Elyth returned from the rooftop and treated herself to an early dinner at one of the more upscale restaurants in the area. The menu claimed it was authentic Prian cuisine; Elyth had no way to judge the veracity of the statement, having never visited the world. But the meal featured an explosion of flavors; a strong gamey meat, accompanied by sweet-tart dried fruit and punctuated by a slow heat from bright peppers. She lingered over the dish, savoring the taste and texture, allowing the sensations to help center her once more in her body, and in the moment.

By the time she returned to her room she felt more herself, her mind clearer. And the following day she devoted more time to the world outside, studying the environment, and was able to identify her target site.

By the end of the sixth day she felt strong enough to carry out her difficult task. Though she still didn't know everything she would have liked to, her relationship with Qel was sufficiently developed to see the job through. Questions would linger, she knew, and they would have no avenue for answering once her work was done. As always, there was no joy in the coming end of her assignment. But it was necessary. And the First House of the Ascendance had forged her to be the instrument of their wise judgment.

As evening came on, Elyth gathered her few belongings together and laid them all out on the bed, as she always did, taking inventory. She loaded the items in her particular way, the process equal parts operational checklist and preparatory ritual. Preparing her tools prepared her mind, her body, and her spirit. At the end, again, two things remained—the interpreter and the frostoak branch. As she packed them, Elyth thought that for this particular mission she might preserve the soil of Qel along with the branch, a fitting reminder for the act itself and for its necessity.

Once her gear was ready, she swept the room once more, verifying she'd left nothing behind that might serve as a clue to her identity or intentions. She'd already made arrangements to release the room in two days, though she wouldn't be returning to it after that night. Just one more false trail, in case anyone came looking. Satisfied that all was ready, Elyth left the hotel and made her way to the target site.

The threadline within Oronesse kissed the surface with a wide point of contact, perhaps as much as two miles in diameter, around which a large memorial park had been built. The size provided plenty of options for where to strike, but was larger than ideal. Given her preference, she would have searched for something with a tighter focal point, to ensure maximum efficacy. But the park was well designed and cultivated, with numerous walks winding through rich natural areas. The evening air was dry and cold, and though a fair number of people were strolling through the park when she arrived, they all tended to walk close together, quietly absorbed in their own thoughts or conversations and paying little heed to others. The area had a gentle restraint to it that seemed to encourage introspection and quiet awe, as some mix of library and monastery might; though most would attribute it to the remarkable design of the park, Elyth knew the source of its influence ran much deeper and was far more ancient.

She casually made her way toward the interior of the park, to a point she had identified earlier. It was off a side path that diverged from the main flow and seemed to attract less traffic than other areas. When she arrived, there was no one else in view, and she ducked from the lit walkway into the darkened natural area where she was concealed among the trees and the shadows they cast in the moonlight and starlight.

There, she laid her pack down to one side and crouched. For a few minutes she just waited and listened and allowed herself to absorb the sense of the place. Even knowing the poison that was working its way through the planet, Elyth found it difficult to feel anything other than peace in that quiet night. Once more, her strange fondness for the planet reemerged. It was to her a deep tragedy that such a world should be the one to fall victim to such a terrible curse. Perhaps, at least, she could assuage her guilt at its loss with the knowledge that she was offering it its only possible cure.

She dug her fingers into the earth of Qel, drew out a handful of the soil, held it tight in her fist. It was cool and damp, healthy and rich. She held it for a time, and then for a moment was hesitant to open her hand, recalling the vision where she had taken from the ground not soil but bone and ash. But she did relax her fist, knowing the reality would chase away the fantasy.

She looked at the earth there in her palm for a span, noted its dark color, flecked here and there with glimmers and glints of the trace minerals within as they caught the cold light, felt its weight. Paid Qel its due. As was her ritual, she took a small vial out of her vest pocket and sifted the soil into it gently, capturing the last essence of the planet as it was before she pronounced its doom.

And now the time was upon her.

Elyth got to her feet, cleared her mind of all but what lay ahead. A steadying breath. The hand sign for *ahn*.

"From the void, all come," she began, *"to the void, all return."*

And she spoke to Qel, her voice quiet as a mother speaking comfort to a sick and sleeping child, describing to the planet itself all she'd learned about it, the history written in its threadlines, its place in the universe, the infinite network of life teeming from its upper atmosphere, through its surface, and down into deep places no human eye had ever reached, nor would. Where Revik had been a fire-hearted world, Qel's essence was more of water, a fluid and flowing spirit with deep-run veins and arteries. As Elyth moved through the protocol, she reached forward into the planet's inevitable end and described it; those watercourses, life-giving as they were now, were also Qel's death, the destabilizing force that would tear the world apart. And with the words of the Deep Language, drawn together from the fabric of the cosmos, Elyth began to loose them.

As she spoke, she felt herself sliding into the current of building energy; the terrible draw of infinite vastness, a riptide that pulled at her very self and threatened to carry her into oblivion. The beauty of Qel magnified in her mind or soul or whatever of her it was that remained *her* in the midst of all the forces she was experiencing, building to an unbearable intensity, as though she were staring into the heart of a star only to find something yet brighter within. An overwhelming fear seized her then, that she was destroying a work of the highest art, a finely crafted jewel of the heavens. And yet the power surging through her every atom brought an exhilaration she had never before known.

Terror and ecstasy merged; her body trembled with the sensation, as though light itself, or an energy purer still, rippled through her veins and across every nerve. And beneath her something else, too. As she described Qel, the planet seemed to shift away from the words, slipping aside, elusive, like a truth glimpsed but not yet fully known. Half-way through the protocol a resonant harmony seemed to join with her words, lending new dimensions of power, an ecstatic rise and expansion, and unfolding unfathomable depths beneath her. She struggled to maintain hold of the network of threads that made her work possible, the connection and relationship of all things one to another.

The infinite pool of the cosmos spread through her mind's eye. She was becoming one with that pool, feeling it subsume her. Qel was slipping away, as she drew closer and closer to the event horizon beyond all concept of time or space or meaning or self. Around her, reality bent and roiled as Elyth strove to regain control.

Something was terribly, terribly wrong. The resonant harmony grew louder, threatened to overwhelm her words, and within it, Elyth heard tones she'd heard before. The voice of *eth ammuin*. Joining with hers, repurposing her speech for his own ends.

Another voice spoke to her then, and she knew it was her own calling to her, all her training drawing her back from the bright abyss that threatened to steal her away for all eternity. And warning her, crying out to her to abandon the protocol, to leave it unfinished. She began to return to herself, body trembling with the cosmic power that now coursed through her and felt certain to disintegrate her.

And Qel, firm beneath her feet, felt infinitely distant, untouchable by even the great storehouse of energy she'd built within. Something beyond description separated them; a great, nameless fear and wonder, before which all worlds fell silent, struck her speechless, too. Even the words of the Deep Language were insufficient. The proclamation died within her.

Power flowed out, draining from her like a cascading waterfall, a current so wide and deep and strong that Elyth felt her being would sunder, too small a channel for such magnitude. Qel seemed to bob and float upon it, gently, as though any force brought against that world would only carry it to its own destination. And all around, the cosmic fabric roiled and seethed, as though a great serpent thrashed within it.

And then all of that energy began to build against her, rising, spreading; a bubble of molten lead, searing and inexorable. There was no escaping it, no turning away, no dodging aside. The entire span of the threadline felt as though it would erupt, and eject a half mile of planet into the atmosphere. But there was nothing she could do; her feet remained fixed upon the earth, bound to the planet and its fate.

The wave of power rushed toward her, her utter dissolution riding upon its crest, and just as it felt like neither the planet nor Elyth could withstand any more, the energy dissipated, as though an avalanche of rock and ice had struck her and proved to be nothing more than mist.

She fell back, blank and empty, shattered by the event. There was no comprehension, no description, no thought or word to anchor her. And in her state of shock, her eyes saw not the physical world beneath her, but rather something hidden deep within it: a vibrating sort of light beyond all manner of description filtered from within the world.

Some span of time passed, seconds or centuries, before Elyth began to come back to herself, and the concept of time itself had meaning again. In that last moment before recovery, in that thin place between the physical and whatever reality she was falling back from, she grasped that vibrating light and tied it to an experience she could re-member; it was something like what she imagined music might look like, if it had shape and substance. Resonance upon resonance. Possibility folded within possibility.

And then awareness returned, unfamiliar, oppressive. Elyth found herself sitting heavily on the ground, her arms behind her to support her weight. Around her, the grass and brush and trees stood withered as though by severe drought; a strong odor of ozone clung to the air. Elyth knew she had to flee. She barely had strength to crawl.

Somehow she found a way to her feet and staggered from the site through a reality that seemed distant and made of mist. Her body felt hollow to the very center of her being, a weakness magnified by the trembling of every muscle, as though she could not withstand the weight of mere existence. And as she stumbled through the night, ravaged by the aftershocks of Revealing the Silent Gate so soon after Revik, the magnitude of what had just occurred bore down upon her.

Qel had resisted. Worse, it had absorbed its own death and cast it away.

The planet had overcome her.

FOURTEEN

Elyth sat cross-legged on the floor of her hotel room, staring at a blank wall as the sun rose over the city behind her. She barely remembered the walk home, could even now hardly process any of the events that had preceded the present moment. The boundaries of time had blurred, so that each instant contained eternity, the past and future were the same, and the now claimed to be all that had ever been.

Words like *vertigo* and *nausea* might once have had meaning to her, but they were flat, empty, and powerless in the midst of her present suffering. Her very self churned inside out in an endless cycle, her body seemed at the mercy of every motion in the universe; from the quiver of her own atoms to the spinning of Qel and its travel in orbit, through to the twirl of the galaxy as it swept across the ever-expanding universe. Falling in every direction at once, at speeds too terrifying to quantify.

But as brutal as the physical toll was, the inner battle was the more horrifying. Madness crouched at her doorstep. She could feel it there, just outside the edges of her vision; the afterimage of the cosmos, calling to her, inviting her to gaze into itself once more, that it might master her. Willing her to do so. It took all her waning might to refuse that call of the infinite and the eternal, knowing a single glance in its direction would destroy her.

She strove to maintain footing on shifting sands, fought to constrain the universe to something that could be experienced by an entity as limited and frail as herself. But there didn't seem to be enough of her left, not enough of *her* left.

She'd reached too soon again into that vast energy, and this was the price. The entity that once had been Elyth-Kyriel, Advocate of the First House of the Ascendance, was dissipating. Her emotions, her body, her memories, everything she was or ever had been spread and thinned, like paint on a spinning wheel.

In the chaos, the echo of a voice swirled past; her sister Nyeda's, calm and sure.

"Each time is unique," she had said. *"Each its own process for you to discover, to pass through, and from which to emerge. And you* will *emerge."*

You will emerge, Nyeda had told her. Elyth grasped for that simple phrase, tried to anchor herself with it. But it was too thin, a mist-thought, insubstantial against the rising thunder of the cosmic calling.

And then, in a last, desperate spark of will she had a thought, and that thought became action. Though it violated all the precepts of the House, she spoke the phrase to herself, in the Deep Language.

"You will emerge," she said, repeating the words as a mantra. *"You will emerge."*

And with the fullness and force of the Deep Language behind it, the reality began to take shape.

You *will* emerge.

Emerge.

Against all hope, Elyth found a way back from that cataclysmic brink.

Made a way.

The lingering echo of the universe collapsed once more into the speck of a world that she could inhabit. Her breathing came first, the cycle of life flowing in and out of her lungs, followed by her heartbeat. Then the weariness of her muscles, the hunger of her belly, and finally the floor upon which she sat all became fully tangible again, and stable.

Gradually Elyth recovered herself; she had descended to grapple with death itself and somehow emerged victorious. Though not unscarred.

It was not a battle she could win again.

And as her world became once more coherent, she came to realize that the victory had already cost her more than she could have ever dreamed possible. In her desperation, she had wielded the power of the Deep Language in words of her own devising. There had been no sealing phrase, no rigid protocol. It'd been an improvisation. She had violated a core tenet of the First House. To save herself.

What was the point of all her training if she were willing to throw aside all she'd been taught in a final moment of crisis? She hadn't considered the risks before she'd acted.

But it had worked. And that troubled her almost as much as the violation.

The Paragon had told her she was the very embodiment of *sareth hanaan*, had proclaimed her Guided by the True Star. Had she abandoned the way, merely to preserve her own life? Or had she manifested it, by finding a way where none had been? There was a rift in her soul now, a crack in a foundation she had previously believed adamantine.

And into that crack, other doubts seeped like water. Qel had escaped its doom. Had that failing too been hers? Or was it due to some insufficiency within Revealing the Silent Gate, the First House's supreme rite? Or, could the root run even deeper, into the Deep Language itself?

Her thoughts and emotions churned, but she sat with them, confronted them. In time, the waves of doubt receded from the shores of the Deep Language and the First House, and lapped at her feet. The failure of Revealing the Silent Gate, she decided, lay not with First House or its teachings, but rather somewhere between her and Qel. Her work was not yet done.

Finally she rose, her legs trembling and stiff. Outside it was growing dark again with early evening; she was relieved to discover it was still the same day. The battle had been one of her innermost being, its rending a soul-wound. Her body would recover soon enough; the rest of her, she knew, would take some time longer.

Though she was ravenously hungry, the idea of food, of flavor and texture, seemed too much to confront. She coaxed herself into a meal of a light broth and a few thinly sliced vegetables, which she had delivered to her room. After she'd eaten, she lay on her bed to contemplate the road ahead.

Each layer she had peeled back from this strange planet had revealed only deeper mysteries and more harrowing discoveries. Qel was a greater threat than she could have possibly conceived; apparently more than even the Paragon herself had foreseen. The only power Elyth could imagine capable of dealing with the world now was that great and terrible wave of destruction kept within the storehouses of the Hezra. The Contingency. Could Qel resist even that?

That thought triggered one of her last, lucid memories from her struggle against the planet. Stretching back to that final moment, she recalled having anchored the encounter to some metaphorical image, some faint shadow of the experience that she could recover.

An image of music: harmonic overtones weaving together, overlapping and lending strength one to another. The memory of it seemed pale and thin, the mental picture a barely grasped wisp of the actual experience, a poor analogy to something beyond description.

But it was enough.

It was the same impression she'd experienced wandering the

grounds of *eth ammuin*'s mountain preserve, though magnified times beyond counting. And within that, she felt the connection to Qel's gentle evasiveness. That too she had felt, within *eth ammuin* himself.

There was no doubt now that he was the key to what was happening within Qel. The task to put the planet down was beyond her capacity to complete; her failed attempt had left her too broken, too depleted. And though she didn't yet want to acknowledge the fact, Elyth's heart whispered that Qel may have damaged her so deeply that she would never again carry out a mission for her House.

But there was more work she could do here, in final service. If she could extract the right information from *eth ammuin*, she might then be able to equip one of her sisters to do what she herself now could not. And if she had even the barest glimpse of the true star that the Paragon had declared was guiding her, she was driven to follow it.

Now, she knew, it was leading her back to that man.

She didn't have much to go on. The area of wilderness between Oronesse and Alonesse was vast, and far too much ground to cover on foot in any useful period of time. It would have been easy to wander that land for weeks without gain.

Elyth sat up and pulled out her navigator to review what little data she had on the region. She located the marker she'd dropped while at Hok's cabin. That was one fixed point she could work from. And her crash site. Though she didn't know exactly where that lay, she'd studied enough of the terrain while selecting her landing zone to make an educated guess.

But when she scrolled the view around the surrounding landscape, none of the structures she would have expected were visible. Either the Detail had done a masterful job of concealing their various locations, or the nav data was outdated. Or intentionally obscured.

She thought then of the drones she had seen mapping her crash site. And of Amei's comment about having to spend days hunting down "stray" ones. The local Authority. Undoubtedly, they would have all kinds of useful information for her.

As long as she didn't mind trying to snatch it from within the jaws of the Hezra.

The HQ would be her target, then. But not tonight. She prepared a report for the Paragon and pushed it through the passive tangle connection. And though she intended to sleep afterward, she spent two hours lying awake, anticipating a response to come through at any moment. But none came. After a fitful sleep, Elyth rose before dawn.

She ran through her meditation sequence first, trusting that the routine would help build her back up and aid in her much-needed recovery. Judging from the feeling of her motion, she guessed her strength was perhaps already as much as seventy percent recovered. Her inner being, however, was still raw and empty. She hoped she would have no need of the Deep Language anytime soon, but there was no reason to trust in that hope.

When she had completed all her preparations, the sun was still below the horizon, so she sat in a chair by the window to wait for it. Its appearance cast long-fingered shadows, and its swift rising seemed to rake the city toward the horizon, stirring its denizens to their daily activities.

Elyth continued to wait until the movement of citizens had reached a steady flow and then joined the throng, headed to the local Authority headquarters.

Like all Authority structures, the HQ had an imposing presence; the Ascendance had long ago mastered the art of urban design as an instrument of social discipline. The building sat with a commanding view at the end of a long street, set back from it behind an open gate and a vast courtyard. The Authority was guardian of both the individual citizens of the Ascendance, and of the collective hierarchy itself. But the layout left little doubt as to which it considered most important. Walking across a courtyard of that scale was an isolating experience and Elyth found herself relieved and grateful to reach the shelter of the Authority's center of power, despite knowing that the space had been constructed to evoke exactly that response.

The headquarters housed the main departments for the majority of the local Authority's functions; the citizens arriving were numerous, with diverse reasons for visiting. Elyth's business was with the law enforcement arm.

She spent several minutes outside the facility, walking as though uncertain exactly where she should be going, which was at least partially accurate. But she used the time to scan the perimeter defenses, to spot the cameras, to count the officers standing guard. She did the same as she moved into the main lobby, building up a security profile from all the little details. She'd need to take them all into account when she returned later.

Elyth didn't want to spend any more time on-site than absolutely necessary, knowing she was being observed every moment she was on the grounds. But if she had hopes of infiltrating the Authority's archives, she needed a clear picture of what she'd be up against.

She joined a group of people on one of the many elevators and rode it to the eighth floor, to the law enforcement general reception area. Notably, the elevator didn't present options to stop at the ninth or tenth floors, skipping instead to the eleventh. Elyth guessed the archives were on one of the upper floors then, off-limits to the public.

Two others got off the elevator on the same floor, and she trailed behind them, walking slowly to take in as much as she could. There were three officers working the receiving desk; after a quick scan, Elyth

narrowed her attention to the one seated farthest left: an older gentle-
man, with cropped gray hair and a bristly mustache to match. He was
the most severe-looking of the three, and she guessed that his demeanor was a first line of defense against trivial inquiries. Whatever
aura he exuded appeared to work its magic, because the two people
ahead of her went to the other officers without hesitation, even though
they both had to wait in line.

The area beyond the receiving desk was restricted; two large doors
stood like guards at their post on either side of the desk, mysteriously
labeled "9" and "17". Each had a small window in the center. Through
9's, she was able to spot a sign pointing off to various departments.
Judging from the look of it, navigating the halls without an escort
would be a challenge on its own.

She looked again at the gruff desk sergeant, who still managed to
be unoccupied. Maybe there was a different play she could make. After
all, she was already inside.

In just a few moments, Elyth had a quick persona assembled, and a
straightforward plan.

She would just go and ask.

From her bag she removed a small disc, thin, translucent, and the size
of her fingernail. She just needed to get it within range of the archive
system to inject codes to enable remote access from her personal terminal. She slipped it into a pocket and then waited off to one side until the
other two officers were both deeply engaged with other citizens.

When her time came, she approached the desk. The older man had
his head down, working intently at a display that was hidden behind
the tall counter of the desk, and he didn't seem to notice her. Elyth took
a few moments to watch him work, and to gather what information she
could. There didn't appear to be any personal effects at the man's station. All business, then. Or, perhaps, a man who needed no reminders of
his past.

There was an intensity about him, a focus on his work to the exclusion of all else. But his build suggested he hadn't spent his career behind a desk; though he'd softened around the middle, she could tell he'd been in the field for most of his service. Injured in the line of duty then, maybe. Or forced to come in due to age, or some mistake made.

Given enough time, she knew she could use her basic bag of social tricks to gain information. But the clock running in the back of her mind was already flashing, warning her that she was rapidly approaching the limit of how long she could risk staying on-site.

A shortcut was available to her. The technique was officially known as Unwalling the Garden, but she and her sisters called it simply the Communion, and its pain would be twofold. Though the draw on power was small, it required the use of the Deep Language, and she was hesitant to wield it again so soon after her recent wounding. And in a Hezra headquarters no less. Then there was the effect of the technique itself, which would bring its own hurt, but in a different way.

She watched the man for a few seconds more, knowing that beneath that granite exterior a deep well of pain lay sealed. And drowned within it, the key she needed.

There was no decision for her to make; the mission dictated the choice. Hers was but to act and to endure.

Elyth stepped up to the counter directly in front of the man and quietly spoke the words of the Deep Language.

"A once-hidden garden, sunlight permeates."

The weight of the declaration rested on her; she was its target. And as its power worked through her, she felt her perceptions broaden and deepen, and the man before her unfolded from a simple, flat caricature into an infinitely complex, multifaceted entity full of joy and hope and pain and regret and the shattered prism of all that it was to be human. She had brought upon herself a radical openness to another, a near-tangible empathy that spanned the gulf between individuals, while remaining wholly herself; it was true Communion, terrible to withstand.

"If you're talking to me, you're going to have to speak up," the man said, stern and correcting. She felt the seething tension within him, the pressure of the low-intensity abuse he suffered each day at the hands of the frustrated citizens he had to process.

"Excuse me, sir," she said.

"Yeah?"

The officer's gaze lingered on his work for a moment, but when he finally looked up, his eyes changed when he saw her, softened. She smiled broadly, and he even smiled a little, though it looked like it'd been so long since he'd done it that he'd almost forgotten how. In that smile, she felt the memories stirring within him, the flicker of a thing lost momentarily regained.

"What can I help you with?" he said.

"I'm a student at the Academy, and I'd like to visit the Authority archives."

It was the first hook she would lay out; establishing herself as young, in need of help. He was a guardian by nature, she could feel, a man who had joined the service out of a sense of responsibility to protect those around him. Particularly the young.

And he wasn't seeing her with clear eyes now; he was responding to the connection he felt to her, though he would never be able to understand why.

"Uh, why would that be?"

"I'm in the information sciences program, and we're supposed to do a case study on our preferred career track."

That was her second hook. His devotion to the Authority was a source of pride, and of pain. It had cost him something, something dearly treasured. The officer perked up, as she hoped he would.

"Oh? Thinking about joining up?"

"Yes sir. One day. I hope to, anyway."

"That's great," he said. "Glad to hear young people are still interested in the service."

He didn't resent the Authority, even though it was obvious he didn't care for his current assignment. Loyal to the service. Enough to endure a tedious job, as long as he could continue to play a part. To make it worth whatever he'd lost.

"But the archives are off-limits," he continued. "We have a Civic Liaison department, though. Have you tried talking with them?"

"No sir. I was hoping to see more of the operational side of things."

The officer chuckled.

"Looking for the real story, huh?"

"Yes sir."

He leaned back in his chair, thinking for a moment, evaluating her; his tumble of emotions swirled around her.

"Well, it's not like a library, you know. Those guys handle a lot of sensitive information. You can't just wander around in there."

"Yes sir, that's why I wanted to highlight the service. Being able to handle that much information and keep it all secure. It's such an important job, I figured you'd be the best at it."

He smiled again, pride in the work showing through.

"You remind me of my kid," he said. "He's probably ten years older than you, but he used to get that same look in his eyes . . . I guess he might still. Been a while since I've seen him."

After he said it, his brow furrowed slightly, and he shook his head, as though surprised to hear himself say those words. His burden for his son struck her like a wave breaking; a relationship severed, one he longed to mend and was powerless to repair. Her eyes welled at his pain, feeling in one instant what he for so long had borne alone. She could sense he had never openly spoken of how much he missed his boy.

"Uh, you know, I'd like to be able to help," he said, straightening, "but you really should go through the Civic Liaison guys. That's kind of their job."

He saw the tears in her eyes then, mistook their cause.

"I am sorry," he added.

"Oh, it's all right," she said. "I knew it was a long shot. I had just hoped to do something on the Authority, but there are other places I can go."

That was the payoff; not only was he losing a chance to help her, he was costing the service an eager young proselytizer.

"I understand," she continued, dropping her gaze, hoping to appear crushed while also looking like she was trying not to appear so. "Thank you for your time. And your service."

She stood by the desk for a moment, then looked at the man, gave him a sad smile, and turned to leave.

"Well, hold on a second," the officer said. "Tell me again what exactly you were wanting to do."

"Just to talk to someone about your archive protocols; storage, search, retrieval, that sort of thing. Or even just see the facility."

He smoothed his mustache while he thought, and she could sense him grasping for something, anything he could do to keep from disappointing her. And then an idea occurred to him. He sat forward, closer to her.

"What's your name?"

"Elenya."

"Well, Elenya. I can't get you anywhere where people are working with live operations, but maybe I can get someone to let you take a peek at the archives."

"That would be amazing!"

"You really do remind me of my kid," he said, shaking his head again, but smiling. "Give me a few minutes, let me see what I can do."

"Thank you so much."

The man got up from the desk and disappeared down a corridor for about ten minutes. When he came back, he waved her over to the desk.

"I'm not sure how much help it'll be, but it's not nothing," he said. "Just do me a favor and be extra polite. I told him you were my niece."

A moment later a young officer came out of the door marked 17, looking annoyed. The desk sergeant pointed at Elyth, and the officer motioned for her to follow him. He curtly escorted her around, professional but obviously irritated by the interruption of his normal duties. The old sergeant had either called in a favor or pulled rank. From the way the officer treated her, she guessed it was the latter. He showed her a few trivial pieces of hardware, told her basic information that was publicly available anyway, and ended the tour by letting her step through the door into the main floor of the archives, where he told her she could spend thirty seconds looking and absolutely not touching anything.

The room was small, perhaps twelve feet to a side, and surprisingly sparse for a storehouse of all of the local Authority's intelligence. Several racks of hardware lined the walls and formed aisles through the middle of the room. Four terminals sat to one side, for direct archive access. An attendant looked up when she and her escort entered, but returned to his work after a quick wave from his colleague.

Elyth casually slipped her hand into her pocket, found the disc device she'd placed within it. With her other hand, she pointed to the rear wall of hardware.

"How often do you have to refresh all those rigs?" she asked. And in the moment that her escorting officer followed her gesture, she flexed the disc between her fingers to activate it and flicked it toward the terminals. As soon as it touched the ground, twelve tiny legs unfolded and the translucent device spidered its way the remaining few feet and disappeared into the equipment.

"I can't answer that," the young officer said. "Come on, time's up."

Elyth obediently followed him, and eight minutes after she'd walked through Door 17 she was walking back out with everything she needed. The young officer closed the door behind her without saying goodbye.

Elyth made sure to catch the desk sergeant's eye as she passed, though he was talking with another citizen. He seemed lighter, almost lively. He interrupted his conversation to call over to her.

"You get what you needed?"

"Yes sir, thank you so much."

"Glad to help," he answered. "Hope to see you in the cadet corps soon."

"I'll be sure to stop by. May you ever ascend, sir."

"May we all, young lady."

She smiled and waved on her way out, still carrying with her the lingering sense of the man's deep hurt. He too would experience some aftereffects, some rawness of emotion reawakened. Elyth was sorry to have forced him to pay the price for expediency, but the mission had demanded it.

The moment she left the Authority headquarters, she knew she had to consider herself marked. She returned to her hotel room and gathered her things, then spent the next several hours following her countersurveillance protocols. She would move again as soon as she could; in the meantime, she secured a new place to work by reserving a private study room in one of the Academy's off-site auxiliary libraries. There was nothing out of the ordinary about an Academy student working long into the night, and she knew the quiet atmosphere would make it easier for her to detect any unusual activity, should anyone come looking for her.

———

Once in the study room, Elyth laid her terminal on the table and opened an array of displays. Activating the disc she'd planted during her earlier incursion opened access to the local Authority's archives, and within minutes she was scouring the databanks for all the intelligence she could mine on the preserve.

As she'd anticipated, some of the data had been recently updated, and the time stamps matched the few days after her crash. Though the Authority had left the crash site the day after, it appeared from the data that, just as Amei had expected, they'd left some drones behind. The last update was marked five days after her ship had gone down, though whether the reporting drone had been recalled or destroyed wasn't clear from the information she could access.

Even with the Authority's most up-to-date mapping of the region, though, there were no obvious markers for where *eth ammuin*'s main residence might be. On a separate display she brought up a view from her local navigational device, where she'd gathered her own data. When she overlaid the two, she was still disappointed.

Though there were a number of housing clusters, similar to what she'd seen while at Hok's cabin, none matched the profile Elyth had formed in her mind, based on Amei's brief description. Too many neighbors, not enough fences.

Still. When she looked at the two sets of data together, something itched in her mind, a feeling like looking at an altered picture of a loved one, without being able to identify exactly what portion has been changed; the corner of the mouth not quite right for the smile, or the wrinkles around the eyes being too many or too few. When she let herself stop searching so intently, her eye kept finding its way to a patch of wilderness near one of the lower peaks of the mountain. There was nothing special about it that she could see, except that it might have a nice view of the main peak, if anyone had thought to build there. She dismissed it each time she looked at it, until she finally realized how many times she'd dismissed it.

Finally, she started cycling back through the archive records, watching the way the landscape had changed over the years. The surrounding area changed as she would have expected, which was to say sometimes hardly at all, and other times in unexpected ways, the way natural progress tended to be neither linear nor fully predictable. And yet the spot that kept drawing her eye changed a little too consistently, a little too predictably.

And now that she looked, she realized: There was a hole in the map. A blank space where the topographical data looked too clean. She'd never been to that specific area, but she'd seen enough of the mountain and the surrounding wilderness to know what *felt* right. The records had been altered. Her instincts told her there was something hidden on that ridge.

And Elyth knew that was where she had to go.

FIFTEEN

Breaching the border of the preserve had a strangely comforting effect on Elyth. She'd spent so long looking over her shoulder that voluntarily stepping into the lion's den made her feel like she'd seized the initiative. If the Detail was still out hunting for her, then there would be fewer of them here to deal with. And if not, well, then at least they certainly wouldn't be expecting her.

The intelligence she'd gleaned from the Authority archives had proved invaluable. Though incomplete, it had given her a sketch of the security measures she'd be facing. Her full infiltration suit rendered her invisible to most of what she would encounter, and smart movement and good fieldcraft could handle the rest.

The goal now was to reach *eth ammuin* and extract from him the knowledge the House needed to move forward. Beyond that, well . . . there was no point in trying to see beyond that now, not when so much had already strayed so far from known paths.

Her need for stealth forced a slow pace; she took two and a half days to reach visual range of the target location. It was midafternoon when she arrived and proved her intuition correct. The site had some natural concealment, and additionally had a darkened, almost granular quality to it that suggested some additional tech-based masking was at work. But to Elyth's trained eyes, the outlines and contours were plain enough. There, about three-quarters of the way up a ridge, lay a fortified compound where none should have been. She waited until dark to close the rest of the distance.

When she finally reached a good point of observation, it became apparent why none of the orbital imaging had picked anything up. About twenty feet inside the outermost fence were an arrangement of tall, slender towers with bulbous heads. Diffusors. Simple devices that sampled the surrounding environment and projected an artificial canopy. The tech seemed misplaced in an area that otherwise blended so harmoniously with the natural surroundings.

The compound, in fact, seemed at odds with everything else on the preserve. From her vantage, she could see that the structures closer to the center of the compound were older and more in line with those in the area around Hok's cabin, but farther out from that center, the structures appeared newer, more intrusive. With an almost military bearing, at odds with the idyllic hillsides and glens.

The compound itself was dauntingly arrayed. Whoever had designed it clearly had training in security, maybe even at a military level. There were three fences to get through; each had several entry points, but there were only two gates that Elyth could see that allowed direct travel through all of them. Both of those were well guarded. The others were arranged such that one would have to snake through from one entrance to the next, in a tedious zigzag pattern with a good twenty yards of travel between each.

Still, the place wasn't set up to repel a determined assault by a large force. It seemed more like a prison than a firebase. Access was controlled, all movement observed. But there were no air defenses, no bunkers, no ambush points.

At least none she could observe.

A prison then. Or, perhaps, a highly sensitive research facility. That too would fit the profile.

If *eth ammuin* was truly inside, then Elyth understood why he had told her they weren't likely to see each other again. Now, the greater wonder was that he'd ever gotten out of the compound in the first place.

There were no obvious patrols, though. Maybe the Detail considered the place too remote or too secret to need active patrolling. As night deepened, the number of posted sentries dropped to a bare minimum, and though they were attentive, they had the posture of routine; Elyth felt confident she could slip through unnoticed. Nevertheless, she waited in her hidden observation post a full day more, observing and taking note of the patterns of life within.

Shortly before midday she spotted what she was really looking for: *eth ammuin*, crossing from the central building to one of the newer structures closer to the perimeter. He was escorted by two members of the Detail, a man and a woman, both of whom Elyth recognized from her brief encounter at Hok's cabin. Seeing them now, though, within the greater context of her time on Qel, gave her a different perspective; they seemed as out of place as the diffusors had. They were dressed in local garb but something in their bearing seemed disjointed, removed from the populace; embedded within it, but not of it.

Hezra.

Or at least trained by the hierarchy. But for what? Protection of *eth ammuin*, or for his containment? Possibly both.

Another layer peeled back, to reveal only new, deeper questions.

The Hezra, then, had to have been aware of Qel and its status. And, so it would seem, *eth ammuin*'s connection to it.

Elyth recalled her last conversation with the Paragon; specifically, the Hezra-Ka's startling confession before the Grand Council of the Deepcutter Initiative's failure, and the Paragon's suspicion that it was merely the first move in a deeper game. Her discovery here seemed to confirm the Paragon's intuitions.

The question now lay only in their motivation for concealing the matter. And the answer, Elyth knew, would come from the same source she already sought.

Eth ammuin reappeared later, as evening was coming on, and returned to the building in the center, which Elyth took to be his residence. It was a small affair set among a cluster of other structures; in front, a well-tended hedge guarded the door and lined a few feet of the walkway leading to it. This time, only one man accompanied him, and when the pair reached his home they stood outside the entrance together for several minutes, continuing some conversation. The man was tall and thin, and had his shoulders hunched and head tilted forward, as though listening intently to whatever it was *eth ammuin* was saying. The exchange seemed amicable, but also not of equals; the tall man's posture and demeanor showed submission. A student of the great wise man of the mountain.

The strangeness of the circumstances again struck Elyth; *eth ammuin* didn't appear to be a prisoner, exactly, though there had been no doubt from her earlier meeting with him that he also hadn't considered himself a free man. The conversation ended, and *eth ammuin* entered his home and didn't come out again that night.

About an hour after midnight, Elyth decided to go visit. She cached all but her most essential gear, donned her mask and hood, and slipped from her observation point.

The compound was well secured; its gates were closed and locked, its fences tall and barbed. But overcoming such measures was second nature to Elyth—by now, perhaps even first. Having watched the full day's cycle, she had a good sense of where the personnel inside considered their security strongest. The sentries spent most of their attention on the main gates and the two entrances nearest the unbroken tree line.

The access points with the most open ground to traverse created an assumption that anyone crossing those points would be easy to detect. Elyth exploited that error.

It took patience to penetrate the interior. But once there, she had almost free rein. The few eyes still open were all facing outward, and it took little effort for her to make her way to *eth ammuin*'s residence.

The structure was a simple two-floor home, not unlike Hok's cabin, though in this case both floors were above ground. Elyth clambered up the outside to a balcony. She peeked through the window into the room, saw that it was clear. After confirming the door wasn't wired for alarms, she made short work of the lock and eased her way in, closing the door behind her softly.

For a time, she remained by the entry, listening. The interior was dark save for the gentle moonlight spilling in from the few windows, and all was still and silent. Once her eyes had adjusted, Elyth crept forward in a crouch with cat-quiet steps. The room she'd entered appeared to be a small study, with a pair of chairs against one wall, and a work area opposite. She exited to the hall, and found that it was open to the floor below, with stairs farther to her right and a second room just beyond. That room, too, was dark. But down below a soft orange glow illuminated the floorboards.

Elyth moved to the stairs and stole down them. They led to an open area, where sitting room and kitchen were divided only by a small island and a round table with two chairs. The light was coming from the partially open door of a room to one side. And through the crack, Elyth could see *eth ammuin*, sitting with his back to the door, bent over some work at a desk.

Now that she was so close to her quarry, her heart rate bumped up. She wondered what his reaction would be to her presence, and what response it would require from her. If he cried out, she would have to quiet him quickly. She hoped he wouldn't cry out.

Watching him now, she remembered that first moment of waking to find him sitting in her room. This reversal of fortunes completed the circle for her. All that she had been through on Qel had led her here, prepared her for this moment, to confront this man from a position of knowledge and strength instead of being held at his mercy. She was still thinking of how best to make herself known when he turned his head and spoke over his shoulder.

"Hello, Eliya," he said. "I was hoping you'd come."

SIXTEEN

There was no way he could see her. She was still too far, and his eyes too blinded by the light of the room to see through the veil of darkness that separated them. He turned back to his work, apparently neither surprised nor concerned by her sudden appearance.

"I was actually starting to think maybe you'd given up on me," he said, louder now. "Or that something unpleasant had happened to you."

Elyth remained where she was, perfectly still, to test his reaction. He continued to work for several moments then turned around in his chair. She could see only half of his face through the cracked door. His eye didn't lock directly on her, but there was no doubt that he knew roughly where she was.

She removed the mask and hood from her infiltration suit, moved forward, and pushed the door gently open. The room was his bedroom, and it was furnished simply; the bed still crisply made, despite the hour.

"I was hoping you'd be asleep," she said.

He smiled.

"If it's any consolation, I would've preferred it, too. But sleep has been an elusive thing of late."

"Up every night waiting for me?"

"Not you specifically, I don't think. But it does feel like waiting."

"And here I thought I'd left an impression on you."

"Oh, well, of that there's no doubt," he said, and then stood and turned fully to face her. "You look tired, Eliya. Can I get you something to drink or eat? A place to sit, maybe?"

He had a slight smile on his face, but the concern and offer both seemed genuine.

"I'll rest after my work is done."

"Ah, yes. Your work," he said, nodding. "And that is what, exactly?"

Elyth answered simply.

"Correcting courses."

"And I am in need of correction?"

"Probably," she said. "But my concern isn't for you. It's for Qel."

Eth ammuin seemed momentarily puzzled by that, but then said, "You're sure I can't get you anything?"

He waited for her to reply. When she didn't, he sighed and crossed over to his bed to sit on it sideways, with his back against the wall, his legs out straight and crossed at the ankles.

"After all you've been through just to reach me," he said, "I find it hard to believe I'm not your primary reason for coming."

"I guess I shouldn't be surprised that you have such a high opinion of yourself," Elyth said. "Though I admit after our first meeting, I'd hoped for a little humility."

"First impressions are funny that way. So strong, so rarely accurate. Somehow that never prevents us from putting our faith in them. I, for example, have been under the impression that you've been looking for me for a long time, though you may not have realized it. But I'm not clear on what you plan to do now that you've found me."

"I'm only here to find out what you and your people have done to this planet."

"My people have done very little other than care for it and nurture it, Eliya." When he said her name, he made a small expression as though he'd tasted something bitter. "I'm sorry, I can't keep calling you that."

"By my name?"

He made a face at her, as though the false name had been meant for everyone else, but not for the two of them.

"Come now. It doesn't fit, and you know it. May I ask your real name?"

"You may *ask*."

"It's only fair. You already know mine."

"*Eth ammuin*?" she said. "I'm not calling you that."

"Oh? Why not?"

"Because you talk too much."

He opened his mouth, but then closed it, smiled again, and shrugged, like he'd been about to argue and decided instead to concede.

"I did try to get them to call me *eth enohem*, but they didn't like that one."

Eth enohem. The vanquished one.

"I don't know why," she said. "It suits you better."

"I thought so," he replied with a half shrug. "But. Well. Here we are, both inadequately named. How shall we proceed?"

"Simply, I hope. You tell me all that you've done here on Qel. And then I leave."

"All? That would take more time than either of us have."

"I can tell you part of it. Your world is dying. I know you have a hand in that."

"Dying?" he said. "Hmm. I suppose it's possible. But if so, that would be a necessary part of rebirth. New growth from the ashes of a wildfire, and all that."

At the mention of ashes, Elyth's vision came vividly back to her mind, of clutching ash and bone; for a brief moment, a look passed over *eth ammuin*'s face, as though he knew, as if he'd said it specifically to force her to recall the image.

"There will be no rebirth for Qel," she said. "It's too deeply broken."

"So was I. Once."

"That's apparent from your work. What is it you've done?"

He shrugged, shook his head, as though he didn't know what to say, and then answered vaguely.

"I'm helping it find its voice."

"Answer more specifically."

"I can try," *eth ammuin* said. "But you aren't ready to hear. The gulf between us is too great, Eliya."

"I've spoken to some of your followers. They've told me of your gift for teaching, how you can help them feel the truth of a thing. I believe you can do the same for me."

"And why should I speak if there is no possibility of being understood?"

"Because you love this world. And I've come to love it as well."

She'd only said it to build rapport, but as the words left her mouth, she recognized they were not without truth.

"We share that," she continued.

He gazed at her for a few moments, evaluating.

"Perhaps you understand now why I let them call me *eth ammuin*."

"I don't."

He looked down at his hands, folded in his lap.

"Some truths cannot be heard," he said, quietly now, "no matter how clearly they are stated. And some cannot be spoken, no matter how deeply they are known."

There was something in the explanation, a reawakening of the same electric reaction she'd had when she'd first heard the title spoken by Amei. In the Low Language, *eth ammuin* was simply "the silent one." But his reply brought with it an echo of something deeper, more profound. The companion phrase, properly pronounced in the Deep Language, took on additional depth and dimension, and became something more akin to "one who cannot be compelled by any means to break trust or reveal a secret"; not merely "one who chooses not to speak" but rather "one who stands and refuses to answer, even under great personal pain." Elyth knew then that this man, this *eth ammuin*, had indeed glimpsed the boundless power of the cosmos, and returned from it broken and lost.

"I can help you," Elyth said. "I can help you find yourself again. But only after you answer me."

"I'd like to," he said. "But I can't."

The truth was locked away somewhere within him, down amid the ruin of his thoughts. To plumb those depths, Elyth knew she would have to reach once more with the Deep Language, to draw forth the answers he possessed that she desperately needed.

"I can help you with that, too," Elyth said, and stretching out her hand toward him, she spoke the Deep Language to him.

Uncoiling the Serpent. The technique combined the force of the Dread with the connection of the Communion, manifesting all of nature's glorious potential for creation and its terrible power to destroy. He would experience union with and terror before her, and would strive to gain her favor and to avoid her wrath. It would scar him; perhaps, in his damaged state, destroy him completely. But there was no other way.

"A wind moving over the deep—"

But even as the first words were forming on her lips, *eth ammuin* closed his eyes and began motioning with his hands and muttering, words she couldn't hear with tones in open intervals, a rapid series of notes punctuated by gestures. When she finished the declaration, he exhaled and held his hands spread before him, as though steadying himself. A few moments later he opened his eyes, looking focused and slightly hurt.

"Finally, you are showing your true self to me. Thank you. I *will* answer your questions, Eliya," he said. "But not like that."

Elyth tried not to let her face reveal the depths of the turmoil within her. As Qel had cast off her attempt to speak its doom, so this man had deflected her effort to penetrate his innermost thoughts. And his manner was unlike any she had known. Not the controlled, precise methods of the House, but rather something spontaneous, as though he had improvised it in the moment.

He scooted forward on the bed and placed his feet on the floor but did not stand.

"I don't blame you for trying," he said. "You *are* a student of the True Speech."

The True Speech. Whether he had understood her exact words or not wasn't clear, but he knew enough to recognize the sounds of the Deep Language for what they were. No man had ever been trained within the First House; her use of the technique might not have marked her as an Advocate. Small comfort, though, in the face of the revelation.

He brightened then, nodded to himself. "That's good. That means there's still hope. I believe I can teach you. But it will take some time."

"I'm a quick learner," she said.

"I don't doubt that you are. But no. I'm afraid it will take more than the time we have in this moment. And there must be conditions."

Conditions. She knew what those would be. Give herself up, to stay here on his preserve, to learn at his feet. To become his disciple.

"You must take me with you," he continued. "Away from here. Away from this place, and these people."

The demand countered her every expectation.

"Away from your disciples?" she asked.

"I'm more of a student than a teacher," he said. "I don't have disciples, nor do I want them. I never have."

"Then who's out there?" Elyth said, motioning in the general direction of all the people in the compound and beyond.

He looked toward the exterior wall, though there were no windows. Contemplated.

"I suppose they are of two kinds. People with questions, trying to learn how best to live their lives. And other people, who believe they can use me for their own gain." He returned his eyes to hers. "Both out there, and in here."

"And which kind am I?"

"Both, maybe?" he answered. "Though perhaps more of one than the other. I haven't figured out where the balance lies. But no matter. I try to take people as they come, not as I would have them."

Elyth didn't know what to make of the man. Her every attempt to discern anything true about him seemed to slip past, or through him, as Qel had bobbed away from her cosmic grasp. She wondered if this was the result of some quiet madness, the chaotic potential of the universe trapped within his psyche. There was no telling what he was capable of.

"And what will your people do when they find out you're gone?"

"They aren't *my* people," he said, with some heat to the words. "They're just people. And up until now I've been content to live among them. But *now* I'd like to leave, and I would prefer to do so in the least dramatic way possible. With you."

She had anticipated neither his resistance to the influence of the Deep Language nor his apparent willingness to abandon his life on the preserve. She couldn't take him at his word, but his desire to escape the compound did seem genuine. The question, then, was what plan of his own was he trying to execute.

"Impossible," Elyth said.

"Much is impossible, until we are forced to find a way."

"I was trying to be polite," she said. "Not impossible, just highly undesirable."

"Not to me."

"I wasn't concerned about you."

"You made that clear," he said. "But you can obviously come and go more or less as you please. So just do that. Except with me."

"I have many years of training and practice. I can't imagine what'd it be like trying to drag you along."

"I bet you could if you tried."

"You're right. I can. None of the outcomes are good. Aren't you in charge around here? Can't you just order them to let you go?"

"Sadly no. It's not quite like that. I may not have the training you do, but I'm not bad in the woods. I can avoid being seen when I so desire."

"Really? How many hours did it take them to find you at Hok's cabin?"

"Oh I guess about three," he said with a smile. "But I wasn't exactly hiding then."

"And how often do you run away?"

"Rarely."

"More than once?"

"Well. More than a few times, yes."

"Obviously they've always found you."

"True. But I've never made a *genuine* attempt to prevent them from doing so."

"Oh, pardon me. You *let* them catch you."

"Yes. Eventually."

His claim wasn't reassuring. But a hidden advantage might have been buried in the otherwise discouraging facts. His Detail wouldn't connect his disappearance to her, at least not immediately. That would expand their window of opportunity.

"How long will it take them to notice you're missing?"

"How soon will we leave?"

"I haven't agreed to that."

"Well. A few hours maybe. If I don't appear by midday, they'll come knocking. I don't imagine it will take long after that."

"And how will they respond?"

"I suspect they'll check the usual places first. After that, the efforts will become . . . more vigorous. If I'm not mistaken, I believe you've seen what it's like to have my so-called security detail chasing you down."

"They're persistent, certainly. I was rather hoping they'd forgotten about me by now."

Eth ammuin shook his head.

"You killed two of their men."

"In self-defense."

"And sent their bodies back in their own ship. What kind of message did you expect that to send?"

"It wasn't intended as a message of any kind."

"Interesting that you would know the True Speech, and yet be so ignorant of what your actions might say," he said, smiling to soften the words.

"If they didn't want the reply, they shouldn't have started the conversation."

"Yes, well. Nevertheless, their friends took that quite personally. I doubt they'll ever stop looking for you. They may pause, though, to look for me. And I should warn you. However intently you thought they've been hunting for you, it's nothing compared to the lengths they'll go to to find me."

"You aren't helping your case."

"Only because I don't believe you have a choice."

Extracting the man from the compound was one thing; he had already proven capable of getting out on his own, so maybe the initial escape wasn't as impossible as it first appeared. Towing him along behind her for some unknown amount of time, though, with his Detail fully switched on and solely focused on his return, was an entirely different matter.

If she could get him off planet, however, and back to the Vaunt, there would be ample opportunity to investigate what he knew, and how he had come to know it. If she couldn't kill Qel herself, perhaps presenting the means by which it could be accomplished was her best offering. And the opportunity to study the manner of his learning might be the key to understanding at last how the Strain had spread, and how to immunize the Ascendance against it. To deliver such to the First House would indeed be a divine gift.

Her time inside the compound was rapidly dwindling, and there seemed to be no way now to extract the knowledge she needed. She would have to take the vessel of that knowledge along with her, until she could determine how to pry it open, or deliver it to those who could.

"What assurance do I have that you won't betray me?"

"None," he said. "Other than the fact that I haven't done so already. But I've been waiting for you for a long time, Eliya. I have no intention of wasting the moment."

Nothing about the situation seemed right. But then that had been the case almost since the moment she'd entered the planet's atmosphere. And as Elyth stood there, in this man's bedroom, she once again felt the walls of inevitability closing in on her. There was no choice, other than to do what was necessary to complete the mission or abandon it. Guided by the True Star.

Elyth-Anuiel, her dream-voice had called her. Waymaker.

"I'll give you five minutes to collect your things," she said. "I won't feed you, or clothe you, and if the time comes where I have to choose between escaping together or alone, I won't hesitate to leave you behind."

"Truly, you are a gracious soul."

Elyth stepped out of the bedroom, once more shrouding herself in darkness, and then returned to the upper level, where she could look out the windows and plan her route out. She'd planned to go out the back, down from the balcony. Evaluating it now, she wondered if her new charge would fall and break his ankle immediately, or if he'd wait to do that somewhere out in the wilderness.

Four and a half minutes later *eth ammuin* reached the top of the stairs, dressed in mismatched clothes of darker hues, and carrying a worn satchel over one shoulder. He'd avoided wearing black, choosing instead earth tones that would blend well with the surroundings in both day and night. And Elyth was pleased to see he had sense enough not to bring along anything obviously useless, or, if he had, at least it was concealed in the bag.

"Traveling light," she said.

"I don't need much," he replied.

"That's the first encouraging thing I've heard you say."

"Now that we're traveling companions, I don't suppose you'll tell me your name?"

"Not until you tell me yours."

"It doesn't matter, I suppose," he said. "If you can't bring yourself to use my name, then whatever I am to you, that is what you may call me."

"Misfortune, then, or Burden. Maybe Grief."

"Grief," he said, and chuckled. "Grief sounds right, the way you say it." And then the lightness left his voice, and his words took on a heavier note. "And I think it might prove true enough, in the end."

"You have a secret tunnel or invisible ship we could use?"

"Usually I just go out the front door."

"I was afraid of that," Elyth said. She followed him back to ground level, and to the main entrance of his home. The front door was framed with two narrow windows on either side, and looking through them,

Elyth saw now how the front door was obscured from casual, ground-level observation by the alignment of the hedge and the neighboring structures. From this view, it actually *was* the safest way out. She slipped the hood of her infiltration suit back over her head and affixed her mask. "If they see you, don't assume they've seen me."

"I'll follow your lead."

"Good policy," she replied. Before they departed, she taught him a few hand signs; he picked them up quickly, able to run through the entire sequence after seeing each only once. More important, he seemed to grasp immediately the importance of each, and how they might be used.

"So let's say you had gone ahead of me," he said, "and then wanted me to move around behind you because you had just spotted two sentries, that would go something like . . ."

He strung together a series of signals, a combination she had not expressly taught him, well paced and articulated, that communicated exactly that intention.

"That's right," she replied, trying not to sound impressed. "But I don't plan on getting too far away from you."

"Unless you're leaving me behind."

"Right."

"Got it."

Elyth turned to the door and drew a deep breath.

"Don't worry," *eth ammuin* said. "I won't let you down."

"I doubt that," she answered.

And with a world full of enemies ahead of her and certain trouble in tow, Elyth opened the door and stepped forth.

SEVENTEEN

Elyth's initial apprehension at bringing *eth ammuin* along with her was eased somewhat within the first few minutes of traveling with him. He was exceptionally quiet, almost as quiet as Elyth herself, and showed both good instincts and sharp awareness of his surroundings. Perhaps more to her surprise, he seemed perfectly content to trail along behind her, following her every move and reacting immediately to her few commands. Only at one point did he dissent with her direction, but it proved to be for good cause; his suggestion took them to a shallow depression in the land that made the crossing to the tree line less risky.

Once they made the wilderness, she returned to her previous observation point to collect her gear, and then pushed the pace to open as much distance between them and the compound as they could before dawn. After five miles, Elyth realized she'd been going even harder than she would have had she been alone; subconsciously, perhaps, hoping to force *eth ammuin* into such a pace so as to make him give up. But he made no complaints. Even better, or worse, depending on her perspective, the challenging terrain and fast pace didn't seem to be fazing him at all.

It hadn't occurred to her before, but now that she'd been able to observe how he moved through the wild, it made complete sense. The man had spent untold years on the mountain, and his love for the natural had been apparent in the cultivation surrounding him. He had an intuitive sense of the space around him and his place in it, and whenever he stopped moving, his stillness was so complete it was as though he had become part of the landscape. It wasn't hard to imagine him in a fairy-tale vision, sitting on a rock somewhere, with birds perched on his head and shoulders, and fawns grazing at his feet.

By the time morning had fully arrived, they had traveled just over seven miles; a wide enough buffer that Elyth felt comfortable with taking a brief break to rest and plan their next steps. The morning air thawed beneath the rays of the sun, and lost some of its edge. She had *eth ammuin* sit by a tree while she climbed a nearby rocky shelf to get a better view. They were still on the mountainside, though lower down now. As it turned out, the elevation didn't help all that much, given the height and density of the surrounding trees. Still, Elyth lingered there, collecting her thoughts, preparing her mind, and watching *eth ammuin* sitting by his tree.

He had his legs stretched out in front of him, crossed at the ankles, with his hands folded in his lap, and his head leaning back against the tree. His eyes were closed, but she got the impression he wasn't resting so much as he was using every sense except his sight to take in his surroundings. She sat down on the rock, dangled her legs over the edge, and pulled out her nav tracker to start considering how best to escape beyond the border of the preserve. The last time she'd done it, it had been aboard one of the Detail's skimmers. She wished she had that option again, though without the trouble that had come along for the ride before.

They were making good time, but she wasn't comfortable with the idea of trying to make it all the way out on foot. The first few hours were the most critical; the longer they could stay out, the wider the potential search area became.

Looking at the tracker, she could see two different clusters of structures within five miles. If they were housing for more of *eth ammuin*'s security forces, she would skirt between them. But she remembered the effect *eth ammuin*'s presence had had on Hok and Amei; if those buildings contained more of his followers, or whatever they considered themselves to be, then it was likely he could ask for whatever he wanted. She hopped down from her perch.

"Grief," she said. He opened his eyes and looked over at her. "Come here."

He sat forward to stand, but then paused abruptly, as though startled. A moment later he reached out slowly and picked something up off his legs. At first, Elyth took it to be a twig; when it moved in his hand, she realized it was in fact a slender green-black snake. Apparently it had crawled onto him, and then stopped to enjoy the warmth. But given the earlier image she'd had of him with songbirds and deer, the appearance of the reptile put a sinister twist on the motif.

He laid the snake gently to one side as he stood, and then wiped his hands off on his jacket as he walked over to join her.

"Cute fellow," he said. "But better from a distance."

"I figured you were the sort to appreciate every creature," Elyth answered.

"Every creature *in its place*, yes. Snakes and spiders belong where I am not."

His light humor caught her off guard, but she suppressed the reflexive chuckle, not wishing to encourage anything but serious focus in that moment. Instead, she just held out her tracker for him to see.

"We're here," she said, pointing to the marker in the center. Then she indicated the two separate clusters of structures. "What are these, here and here?"

Eth ammuin cocked his head to one side while he looked at the top-down view, orienting himself.

"Oh, this one's the Telos collective. Forty people or so, maybe? Nice folks." He looked to the other point and shook his head. "That one's no good."

"More of your Detail?"

"No. But the people there are somewhat . . . misaligned."

"These Telos people. They have a ship you could borrow?"

"Not that I'm aware of. If I remember correctly, they have a bunch of striders. I haven't been out there in a while, though."

"Locked up?"

Eth ammuin shrugged.

"If so, I suspect they'd unlock them if I asked nicely."

"And would they report you to the Detail?"

"They would if someone came asking, I'd guess. But I don't think they'd raise any alarms, if that's what you mean. Well, unless you go in looking like that."

"Like what?"

"Like someone who came here to kidnap me."

Elyth hadn't thought much about how her infiltration gear might make her look, since the whole point of it was not to be seen wearing it. She removed the mask and laid back the hood.

"How about now?"

"Better," he said, smiling. "Almost like you belong."

The warmth and kindness of his smile felt genuine, and the subtle emotional effect warned her to keep her guard up. He was prodding her, gently but with purpose. Again, she kept the focus on the task at hand. She checked the distance; the collective was about three miles out. The amount of ground they could cover in a couple of frames would more than make up for the slight detour, and though substantially slower than a skimmer, they would have the benefit of being able to stay beneath the cover of the wilderness.

"All right," she said. "Keep up."

They moved out together, and she resumed her previous pace; in some of the tougher sections, *eth ammuin* lagged behind, but she didn't slow for him and, to his credit, he always managed to make up the ground. They reached the outskirts of the collective about an hour later, both breathing hard and dripping sweat despite the coolness of the morning.

The houses and outbuildings had been grouped more tightly together than the ones she'd seen back where Hok's cabin was, but she could tell the same general philosophy was at work. Though the living quarters all seemed comfortable enough, none stood out as obviously overbuilt or extraneous; each had been built with a purpose, to which it was well suited. The unification with the surroundings was neither as complete nor as finely tuned here, but the concern for preservation was apparent, and attempts had been made to minimize impact. This collective had a different set of priorities and trade-offs, perhaps, but the goals being pursued were clearly similar.

Several people were out and about, some working, others chatting with friends and neighbors. Elyth remained inside the woods for several minutes, observing.

"Soooo . . ." *eth ammuin* finally said. "Now what?"

That was precisely what Elyth was trying to figure out. She hadn't yet spotted anyone using a frame, nor had she seen any in the open. If there were any still in the collective, they weren't lying around for the taking.

"You're sure they've got striders here?"

"I told you it'd been a while. But let's go see."

He was up and tramping toward the people before she could stop him, and his sudden motion drew the immediate attention of a few of the residents. There was nothing more for Elyth to do then but follow him. Still, she kept some distance open between them, to preserve her wider view of the situation, and to increase the time she had to react in case things went wrong.

As to be expected, the initial reaction was surprise and defensiveness, a natural response for anyone seeing two strangers appear out of the woods near their home. Quickly, though, recognition rippled through the people, and their reaction echoed Hok and Amei's . . . a quiet mixture of astonishment and submission.

Eth ammuin strode toward them, waving as though these people were his longtime neighbors. As it turned out, he apparently knew them better than he had let on.

"Birnan," he said, calling a nearby man by name. "How are you, my friend? You're looking well. Shoulder all healed up?"

The man stared blankly for a moment then dipped his head. "Yes sir, fully recovered and doing very well, thank you, sir. And you?"

"Fine, fine, thank you." He closed in on the little group of friends that had been chatting; Elyth held back, allowing the distance to grow between them, and keeping to the edges of the collective, staying only close enough to monitor what he was saying. He spent several minutes talking to the individuals gathered, asking each about some specific detail of their lives. For a man who hadn't been among them for some time, he seemed to know a great deal about them, and his concern for them genuine. A few of the people cast glances in Elyth's direction, but thankfully *eth ammuin* didn't attempt to introduce her. Easier to let them assume she was part of his security detail, undoubtedly. She was certainly content to play the part of disinterested bodyguard.

Finally, after spending what she considered far too much time socializing, he got to the point.

"We've been out getting the lay of the land, but it's taking longer than I was expecting. I was just wondering if you might have any old striders lying around that we could borrow."

"I do," Birnan answered quickly. "Happy for you to take them as long as you need them, sir."

"Is it going to cause you any hardship?" *eth ammuin* asked.

"Oh no, none at all."

"Then I'd be happy to accept, if you're certain."

"Of course. It's a privilege to offer. They're in my storehouse. Let me get my boys to help me get them for you."

"No, no, that's fine. We'll walk with you."

Eth ammuin followed Birnan away from the rest of the group, waving for Elyth to come along. He seemed to have picked up on her ruse and was playing along by treating her as if she were at his command. A few minutes later Birnan had his storehouse open and was showing them how to strap in to the frames. They were rugged and well used, and heavier than the ones Hok and his crew had been running. These looked like they'd been used more for harvesting and hauling than for ranging over the terrain. The striders likely weren't as fast as the others, but there was no question they would still greatly increase the pace of progress.

Birnan gave them a few pointers, and reassured *eth ammuin* repeatedly that there was no rush on returning them. Though she'd initially taken his claim that it was no trouble at face value, at his continued insistence, Elyth began to gather the idea that the loss of his frames was going to be a significant burden to this man and his family. Nevertheless, *eth ammuin* accepted the offer gladly, and gave no hint of his intent to return them. She couldn't tell whether he realized what a sacrifice Birnan was making. If he didn't, it made him seem particularly oblivious; if he did, it made him seem somehow especially cruel.

Once they were strapped in and ready to go, *eth ammuin* made a brief return to the open area where more of a crowd had gathered. Elyth let him go on his own, in hopes that by waiting near their point of departure her impatience would encourage him to keep his goodbyes brief. Whether he took notice of her or not, he was gone only a few moments before he returned to her.

They set out from the collective, taking a southeasterly route that would lead them to the nearest point of the border, a few miles distant. Crossing the border was itself no simple matter. For a stretch of three hundred yards or so inside the boundary, a sensor network kept constant vigil. Elyth had passed through the network before with the aid of the intelligence she'd gathered, her infiltration suit, and her instincts. Getting back out with *eth ammuin* was going to require a different approach, and quite likely more direct measures.

She was still puzzling through how best to bypass the sensors, about two miles out from the border, when they heard the ships approaching; a low growling among the ridges behind them, rapidly closing in and gaining a vicious edge.

Elyth motioned swiftly to a nearby clump of trees, and they bounded under the cover of the dense canopy. The harsh noise grew to a screaming roar as the skimmers tore the sky above them, passing somewhere farther north. Elyth scanned the slivers of sky she could see, but was unable to spot the vessels. She could tell from the wall of sound that there were multiple ships moving fast, but their number and distance were both lost in the chaotic tumble and merging of the echoes among the mountains. The velocity suggested a known destination, not a search. She wasn't sure whether that was good news or bad.

The two remained sheltered under their improvised cover until the sound had died in the hills.

"Right on time," *eth ammuin* said once all had settled.

It was still only late morning.

"A little early," Elyth said. "You said midday."

"Close enough."

"Close enough gets you killed. Any guess which of your usual places they're going to check?"

He made a face.

"They're not headed to one of your usual places."

"They *might* be," he said. After a pause, he added, "But they would be taking an unusual route to get there."

Elyth sighed heavily and turned her back to him to face the direction the ships had gone. This wasn't going to work. Alone, she could make it. But with this man in tow, her confidence was rapidly approaching zero.

"Shouldn't we keep moving?" *eth ammuin* asked.

Perhaps there was still a way to retrieve the information she needed. Maybe her mistake before had been giving him time enough to react . . .

She inhaled deeply and scanned their surroundings, as though evaluating the area for a new path.

"Yes," she said, turning to face him. "You're right, we should." She looked off through the trees, motioned toward a hollow some distance below them. "We'll cut back this direction, down through there, you see?"

He turned his head to follow her gesture; in that instant, Elyth struck. Open hand across the throat, then her fist into his solar plexus, stunning his diaphragm and briefly evacuating his lungs. He crumpled around the blow, staggered back a step. And Elyth spoke.

Again, as the words of the Deep Language left her mouth, *eth ammuin* responded with a series of gestures; this time, however, robbed of the power to speak, he could only groan some guttural syllables, meaningless and empty.

Or so she thought.

But just as before, she felt the power of the Deep Language glance off him, turned aside by some kindred force, both strange and familiar.

For a moment after, he stood there with his head down, hand over his chest where she'd struck him, struggling to compose himself. Once he did, he looked up, a snarling flash in his eyes; a wolf crouched and poised to pounce.

"Eliya," he said quietly, and rasping.

And then, straightening up, again:

"Eliya."

His voice louder, clearer. Not a shout, but a declaration with authority, one that despite its bare volume nevertheless seemed to roll the hills with thunder. A black wave struck Elyth then, something neither physical nor intangible, immaterial but still substantial, as though all the weight of a thousand-pound stone had passed through her. It forced her back and she fell to the ground under its power.

Terror came with it, a moment of abject panic; she was stunned, immobilized, completely at his mercy. He crossed to her, stood over her. She prepared herself for the blow.

And then:

"Eliya."

The sound of sunlight, a golden warmth, a vibrant call to life.

Elyth looked up at the being who seemed now to tower; his hand extended down to her, to raise her up.

"Let's be friends," he said, his voice now only what it had been before, his form nothing more than that of a man, and one slightly built at that.

Elyth felt her strength return, and anger replace her fear. She got to her feet without his aid, facing him, confronting him. Though she didn't know what to say or do in that moment, she stared back at him, defiant.

"It will be better for everyone," he said. "And everything around us."

His eyes shifted from hers to just beside her, looking beyond. She was reluctant to take her eyes off him, but gradually her resolve slipped away and she turned her head to look behind her. And caught her breath.

A shallow depression extended for twenty-five feet from where she stood: the earth compressed beneath the surge; leaves, needles, and debris scattered from the forest floor along the trail; tree limbs broken and dangling in its wake. She turned back to face him, horrified.

"That was a bit more than I intended," he said. "But I don't know your real name, and I wanted to make sure you could hear me."

Elyth wanted to understand what the man had just done, how he had invoked and wielded power in that manner; she might even have asked, if she had been able to find the words to do so. But the depth of her bewilderment and the magnitude of her indignation prevented her. She had provoked the attack, it was true, but his callous disregard for collateral damage reminded her of why the man was not only her enemy, but also that of the entire Ascendance. The physical effect on their surroundings was apparent; but what impact might ripple throughout the cosmic fabric was unknown and unknowable. And he had done it without a single thought.

"I told you I would teach you," he continued. "And I meant it. But you must be patient."

"I will not submit myself to the teaching of unbridled chaos," she spat.

"Then I fear you will be ill-equipped for what lies ahead," he answered, in a calm but foreboding tone. His mood had turned dark once more, as he fell into his persona of doomsayer, visionary prophet of the end times. "We're in the becoming now, Eliya. All foundations will shake."

"Brought upon this world by your own hand."

He shook his head.

EVERY SKY A GRAVE 263

"Whether you see it or not, we are aligned in purpose. And if we are separated or captured before I share with you what I have learned, then it's possible nothing will stand against that which is to come."

"And what is that? This great and terrible doom bearing down upon us all, yet somehow glimpsed only by you?"

Eth ammuin opened his mouth, but then closed it again, and a sadness alighted upon him.

"Let me guess. That's a truth that cannot be heard, no matter how clearly stated."

"No," he said. "It's the other kind . . . unspeakable. But that, only for the moment." And as quickly as the darkness had come over him, it once again retreated. He looked at her as though she'd never struck him or he . . . whatever it was he'd done. "I know it's asking a lot, Eliya. But I need you to trust me. Can you find it in yourself to do that?"

"No," Elyth scoffed; that, apparently, was all she could do. She could neither trust him nor abandon him. At least not yet. Twice now he had used some unknown technique to empower himself; though he may not have realized it, each time had provided her an opportunity to observe and to learn. Perhaps given enough time she would not need his willing participation to find what she sought.

"Well. At the very least, then, may I suggest that you not do that again? A second time and my response might not be quite so restrained."

"You can *suggest* whatever you want," she said, refusing to let the threat register. "Come on, we're losing time."

Elyth didn't wait for a response before she turned her back on him. In less than two miles she would be busy navigating the preserve's sensor network; beyond that, none could say. For now, there was only forward.

She led the way down the ridge to the hollow, and followed it the remaining distance to the border. And though she didn't turn back to look at his progress, Elyth could tell from *eth ammuin*'s footfalls that he was less steady than he'd been before she'd tested him. Whatever method he had used to wield the power of the Deep Language had taken some toll on him.

Clearly she had underestimated the measure of power in the man; she wondered just how much of his capacity he had actually revealed. Perhaps she'd already experienced the height of it, and his threat had been merely bluster. Though, if the Paragon had been correct and the Strain at work in Qel was due to some distant variation of Varen Fedic's original corruption, then it was possible she'd not yet discovered the extent of *eth ammuin*'s might. That thought sent a shiver through her, for fear she might be hopelessly outmatched.

In such a case, she had to consider that rather than merely extracting information from him, she might instead need to smuggle him offworld, back to the Vaunt, maybe even to face the Paragon herself.

For a fleeting moment that thought triggered another: Perhaps the Paragon already knew all these things, and was in fact counting on them for some greater purpose.

And for all the chaos and randomness of the events she'd experienced on Qel, Elyth couldn't escape the feeling that even now a many-layered game was being played, and somehow she had become its most exposed pawn.

EIGHTEEN

As Elyth had anticipated, navigating the sensor network was far more challenging with *eth ammuin* than it had been when she'd been by herself. But the strider frames turned out to play an unexpected role. The solution had occurred to her while she'd been in the midst of explaining how important it was that he follow exactly behind her, moving as she did, and stopping when she did. Instead of relying on him, she'd realized she could tether his frame to hers and couple it so tightly as to essentially control both. It was awkward and uncomfortable for *eth ammuin*, since he had to learn not to resist the thing forcing his own body to move, but after a few minutes of practice, they figured out how to make it work. After that, it was just a matter of her executing the right steps at the right pace.

Unfortunately, there was no way to know whether or not they'd successfully avoided detection. There were no alarms, no flashing lights, nothing to indicate success or failure. As such, once they crossed over the preserve's official border, she untethered *eth ammuin*'s frame and led him on a meandering path through the wilderness. At times they took pains to double back or otherwise break up their trail; at others, they dashed breakneck through the wild, covering as much ground as they could.

Once they'd put some dozen miles between them and the border, they took brief shelter under a rocky overhang and looked at their options. Now that she had the man, she no longer needed to remain in the region. But to make a quick jump to another part of the planet, there were only three viable destinations: Harovan, Alonesse, and Oronesse.

"Grief," she said. "How well do you know these places?"

He briefly surveyed the nav tracker, and then shrugged. "I don't go into town all that much. But I wouldn't go to Oronesse. They've got friends there."

"Your people nearly caught up with me in Harovan," she said. "They might still be looking for me there."

"I told you they aren't *my* people," he answered. "And what makes you so sure they're looking for *you* right now?"

She'd been assuming that the Detail would be looking for both of them. But they wouldn't necessarily connect his disappearance directly to her, at least not yet. And now that *eth ammuin* had gone missing, clearly his return would be their priority.

"You ever been to Alonesse?" she asked.

He shook his head. "Too far of a walk."

Elyth looked at her nav tracker again, judged the terrain. Of the three locations, Alonesse had the fewest of her fingerprints already on it. She nodded.

"All right," she said. "We'll head for—"

"Alonesse," they both said at the same time. *Eth ammuin* smiled; he had rushed the word out in a transparent attempt to make it sound like a mutual decision.

"We make a good team," he added.

"*I* make a good team," she answered. "You're cargo."

"Even cargo can be helpful, if its momentum is in the right direction."

"Then I hope we find a cliff pointing toward Alonesse."

They left their temporary shelter and pushed hard, but even with the aid of the frames, there was just too much ground to cover to make it before the sun had fully set. A chill air rolled through in the afternoon promising a cold night ahead. And though they still had daylight to work with, once Elyth allowed herself to admit the fact that they were going to have to sleep in the open, she realized the best thing to do as the sun was getting low was to secure a place to camp before the darkness and cold dictated the location.

Once more, to his credit, *eth ammuin* seemed content to let her take the lead, and wasn't troubled by the idea of spending the night in the wilderness. He'd brought along a small heating device that he'd intended to pair with his bedroll; when she saw his gear, she was impressed at its compactness and efficiency. But given the pursuit they were likely under, she knew they couldn't risk leaving him out in the open all night. As uncomfortable as it was, there was only one solution; unfortunately, it required enduring close proximity with *eth ammuin*.

They parked the frames and concealed them as best they could with camouflage improvised from nearby limbs and other such matter cast off by the trees.

She set up their camp a little distance away, in one of the few bare patches that could accommodate her shelter; close enough to keep an eye on the frames, but with a buffer between them, in case the striders should attract any attention. They ate a quick, cold meal, Elyth from her rations, and *eth ammuin* from a pouch in his satchel. As night closed in around them, she finally took the step she'd been delaying as long as possible and deployed her shelter.

For all the possible configurations of her flexible shelter, it hadn't been created to house more than one. In order to fit both of them inside, she had to expand the base as wide as it would go, which made for a ceiling no higher than two feet at its tallest point. It was going to be like sleeping two to a coffin.

They stashed their gear just outside the shelter, since they were going to need every available inch of the interior for themselves, and then she had *eth ammuin* crawl in first. He didn't seem to have any intention of running off in the night, but she wasn't about to put him between her and the access panel. Once he was in and situated, Elyth slid in alongside him and sealed them inside. Almost immediately, claustrophobia settled upon her; they were practically shoulder to shoulder with no room to shift apart, and the roof of the shelter was like a hand hovering over her face. She endured the feeling for a time, but then decided to set the entire shelter to transparent. The individual tiles faded, leaving only thin seams where they joined, and the forest reemerged around them, the night sky clear above and framed by the spindled trees. *Eth ammuin* made a little noise in reaction.

"How marvelous," he said, touching the roof.

"It's a mimetic composite," she said. "It has quite a few useful properties."

"Interesting," he replied. "But I was talking about the sky."

"Don't you see it every night?"

"Yes. And every night, it's marvelous."

She turned her attention skyward then, actually looked at it in a way she hadn't since she'd arrived. Her business had been with the earth of Qel, and that alone had been her focus; now Elyth gazed with him at the gloried field of stars that stood watch over it all. But the awe she used to feel in the face of that resplendence had numbed over the years, and gradually been replaced with a deep melancholy, as her perspective changed on what that immeasurable expanse contained, and the role she had played in its changing. The stars stretched out above them, heavens unfolding splendor beyond the limit of human conception, and further still, forever expanding, accelerating. Even with all that the Ascendance of humanity had mastered, there were still frontiers they had not reached, nor ever could.

But up there, out there, too, was a stark reminder of the planets that had died by her hand. The great weight she bore with the death of each world, the burden of each memory, followed her and lingered over her no matter where she traveled. And she knew, for all the significance those endings had for her, how inconsequential it all was in the midst of that infinity, how much she suffered and how little it mattered to the cosmos, as though the absence of a single molecule of water might draw any notice from the sea.

"It's comforting to know that, for all the worlds out there, they're all wrapped in the same fabric," *eth ammuin* said. "Close neighbors in that vastness. And on every one, a unique sky offering its own revelation of the infinite. Surely you've seen many. Don't you find them wondrous?"

"Not anymore," she answered quietly.

She heard him stir, felt his eyes on her, but didn't turn her head to meet his look.

"You must be immovable then," he said. He returned his gaze heavenward, and after a moment said, "I genuinely don't understand how that's possible."

"Consider yourself fortunate."

"I've never considered ignorance a virtue. Perhaps you could enlighten me."

"It doesn't really matter what sky you're under. You're always staring up into the same thing."

"The unknown?"

"A grave."

"Well . . ." he said, taken aback. ". . . That's a cheery thought. I suppose it's true, in a way. Life and death are joined up there."

"A lot more of one than the other."

Here on Qel, in the outermost reaches of the galaxy, the heavens themselves testified to the truth of her perspective. The brilliance of the night sky was banded and clustered, dazzling in one portion of the sky; in the other, blackness prevailed, dotted here and there with the weak and waning flickers of incomprehensibly remote galaxies, masquerading as points of light to her naked eye, or wandering stars, loosed and floating out where even galaxies could not hold together. And for all the light in the universe, she couldn't help but see the darkness continually striving to swallow every last bit.

Eth ammuin was quiet just long enough for Elyth to start hoping he had decided to go to sleep, before he spoke again.

"Do you find it as strange as I do that we humans can truly grasp neither the concept of *nothingness* nor of *infinity*, when both are so clearly on constant display?"

"Probably not," Elyth said flatly.

He chuckled.

"I suppose that's too philosophical a musing for someone so practically minded."

Elyth was deeply weary: weary from travel, and pursuit, and the relentless need to plan and calculate every step. She wanted nothing more in that moment than for this man to vanish; or, at the very least, to shut up. But pushing back against her natural impulses, she realized the unique opportunity this uncomfortable arrangement offered. Forced into such close contact, lying on their backs under the night sky, she could already sense an openness growing between them. One, if she could embrace it, that she might be able to exploit.

"I'm sorry that you think so little of me," she said. "I *have* actually been in a library before."

Elyth thought of the great Library of the First House, where she had spent years of her life in study of the human mind and the origins of thought. Though the wilderness felt like her natural environment, her second home was that magnificent storehouse of knowledge and wisdom, gathered from the entire known history of humanity, and the crown jewel of all such Ascendance collections. She wondered what *eth ammuin* would say if he had known how deeply she had studied. And more, she wondered what she could draw out of him by engaging with his thoughts.

"Oh, I didn't mean it as a criticism of *you* . . . Sometimes I ask questions that lead to nonsense answers."

"It isn't a bad question. I just don't find it all that strange that such concepts escape us."

"Oh? Why is that?"

"Because we are defined by our limitations."

He grunted at that.

"You disagree?" she asked.

"No," he said. "But I find myself unable to accept it."

"Truth cares very little whether or not we accept it."

"So it would seem."

Elyth heard the moment in the quiet that followed; a hesitation on his part, something reawakened within him. She gently pursued.

"You've suffered under its revelation."

"Haven't we all?"

"Some more than others."

He laughed without humor.

"If you only knew."

He fell quiet again, but it was active silence. In a normal exchange, the tension would have signaled discomfort, a desire to escape to safer ground; but Elyth stayed in the moment, bore the awkwardness, remained present and available and, most significantly, silent. The time extended, stretched, and she feared that the chance for something more had passed, that it had slipped away. But then *eth ammuin* spoke again.

"I was reckless in my youth. Overzealous. I used to believe it was impossible to damage people with the truth. Or no . . . that's being too generous to myself. Rather, I thought I couldn't be held responsible for the direction that truth led. That whatever burned up in its fire was not worthy of existence anyway."

"And now?"

"Now? . . . Now I suppose I will simply have to bear the burden of my previously untempered zeal."

"More truths that cannot be spoken?" she said.

"No," he said. "Those were truths that longed to be known. It was just that I was incapable of speaking them. Back then. But I have since learned."

He was quiet once more, and she could sense him withdrawing, returning inward. His vague confession had taken him too far, or had stirred memories he now had to contend with. It had made him vulnerable, more so than he had intended, perhaps. And where previously she had assumed she would have to force information from him, Elyth saw now how coaxing it from him might in fact be possible.

There hadn't been time to use Unwalling the Garden on him before. Now they had nothing but time. There was risk, of course, as there always was, in opening herself up to him that way. The Communion formed a deep connection, and though she could create some distance for herself, she could not come away from that bonding without being impacted by it.

It was a risk she was willing to take. If she was successful, she might well learn here and now all she needed. And if he resisted, then at the very least she would have another opportunity to observe his technique and possibly glean something new.

She whispered the words to herself, felt the liquid unfolding of her senses; the gentle pressure of his shoulder against hers warmed electric, the sensation of physical contact heightened by the openness she had awakened. She could sense him in a different way now, but not as powerfully as she had expected. He was there, but remote, fuzzy; or rather, her grasp had been blunted, as though she were trying to pick up a small rock from a mountain stream with frost-numbed hands.

Eth ammuin shifted, drawing away from her just enough so that their shoulders no longer touched. He glanced at her.

"Are you certain you want to do that?"

"I want to understand," she said.

He rolled on to his side, facing her, laid his head on his arm. And though it was too dark to see much of his features, she could feel the intensity pouring from him. Whatever he was doing, he was preventing her from experiencing the fullness of his being. But it wasn't easy for him to contain; she could feel the struggle.

"It's all right," she said.

"I don't know that it will be," he replied. "But if you are willing . . ."

In the next moment the wall between them disintegrated, and with it the fabric of reality.

Elyth felt herself plunging backward, and a moment later she was flat on her back, not in her shelter, but rather on a drought-stricken plain, cracked and barren, stretching endlessly in all directions. Above her there was no sun, no moon, no sky; only a blank void that somehow seemed empty even of emptiness. And before her stood *eth ammuin*.

Chaos exploded, an incandescent storm of rage and grief and pain, and love and elation and inexpressible awe; the dead environment around them howled and swirled, a typhoon of vision and experience, too intertwined and compounded to process. His being loosed upon her like a subterranean river shattering its mountain prison, scourging the land in its rush to freedom.

It was too much. Not just a lifetime of joy and sorrow but a legion of lifetimes. Layer upon layer, more history than any one human could possibly have lived, more vivid and vital than anything other than personal experience and memory could form. He, like Qel, was an impossibility.

A hurricane besieged her, battered her, and the raw energy and violence within him made Elyth want to retreat, to hide from the maelstrom that was this man. But she was a Servant of the First House of the Ascendance, an Advocate of the Voice, and *sareth hanaan* was her way. The quiet action of she who endured.

In the midst of that whirlwind, she stood to her feet.

For a time unknown they strove against each other, he a wildfire raging and all-consuming, she the mountain beneath, unmoved and unmovable. He was trying to overpower her, to overwhelm her with a flood of the most deeply felt, most jagged emotions within him: anger, and fear, yes, but ecstasy too. And at the source of it all, Elyth could sense his will, his determination. A purpose made unbreakable in the star-fired forge of his many histories.

"You mustn't seek to control it," he said. "Chaos cannot be controlled. *Will* not be controlled."

And then without warning, the storm calmed; the confusion of what appeared to be many possible histories aligned into a single timeline. *Eth ammuin's* expression shifted, lightened, and he said, "But you can learn to dance with it."

He receded from her then, closing himself off to her, though it took effort for him to do so. As he withdrew, Elyth felt within him two fleeting sensations: hurt and reluctance. Hurt by her attempt to pry him open artificially, reluctant to break off the bond that was forming between them. There was a deep loneliness etched upon his innermost being; she sensed how he longed to be known, to be understood, and to be accepted in spite of the secret truths he bore. There had been something deeper still, buried at the base of that loneliness, a knot of emotion she had not quite been able to touch but that called to her, like a faint echo of a dream half remembered.

And then the vision faded, and they were together again in her shelter.

"There is a stillness about you that shames me," he said, rolling once more to his back. "Perhaps when I teach you to dance, you could teach me to stand."

Elyth wanted to reply, but no words came to her. They lay together once more side by side, with Qel's bifurcated sky above them, draped over the world like a veil, untouched by the violent clash of their interior lives. She found herself trembling in the silence that followed, neither from fear nor cold, but rather from some residual emotional aftershock, the lingering sensations haunting her like shadows flash-burned onto the walls of her mind. And for as much of *eth ammuin* as she had experienced, she wondered what of herself she had imparted to him.

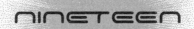

NINETEEN

Elyth insisted on an early start; *eth ammuin* made no complaint, but he was clearly detached. They ate quickly and broke down what little camp they had made. Elyth directed her morose companion to get the striders ready while she did her best to obscure the tracks they'd left around the campsite. *Eth ammuin* had the frames uncovered and moved when she reached him, and stood quietly by while she again made an effort to conceal the hiding place.

They were on the move before sunrise, navigating the darkened wood at an easy pace with the frames, still covering more ground than they would have had they been on foot, but nowhere near the full capacity of the striders. As they gained light so too they gained speed.

Still, there had been no attempt at contact from the Paragon, and Elyth wasn't sure what to make of that. Either her report had been so bad that the Paragon was still scrambling to discern what to do about it or Elyth's proposed plan of action had been good enough that the matriarch was merely awaiting further word.

After three hours of travel, *eth ammuin* still hadn't spoken a single word to her; he'd only listened and acted as instructed. Though at first she was glad for the silence, as it became more apparent that they weren't under direct pursuit, she knew she needed to begin the process of getting him to open up again. It seemed he was still injured from the previous night's interaction.

"Living up to your name this morning," she offered.

He didn't respond immediately, but after a few moments said, "Which one? *Eth ammuin*, or Grief?"

"A bit of both."

He went quiet again after that. Elyth knew she shouldn't push into waters too deep, but felt if she could keep him talking, it would help him continue to thaw toward her. The first thing that came to mind was a question she'd had from the day before.

"I have to ask you something. About Birnan and his frames."

"Yes?"

"Did you realize how much of a sacrifice he was making to give them to us?"

"Of course. They're his livelihood. He's the main timber harvester for the collective."

Elyth was surprised both by the revelation of the striders' importance to the collective, and by *eth ammuin*'s casual attitude about having taken them. She'd discerned that the frames were significant to Birnan and his family, but hadn't realized how essential they were to the entire group.

"And you took them anyway?"

"Why wouldn't I? They were offered freely."

"Because you have no intention of returning them."

"It wouldn't have been much of a gift if it hadn't cost him anything."

Elyth stopped walking and turned briefly to face him, hardly believing what he had just said. But she had nothing to say in return, and his look suggested he didn't understand the strength of her reaction. She turned back around and resumed hiking.

"This bothers you," he said.

Elyth waved her hand at him, dismissing it. He'd answered the question. For all his talk, he had no qualms about using people as he saw fit.

But a moment later, *eth ammuin* continued.

"Let me ask . . . is it because he offered, or because I accepted?"

"It's because you put him in a position where he had no other choice."

"What do you mean?"

Elyth glanced back at the man, held a hand out toward him in mock reverence.

"The god descends from the mountain," she said, "and demands a sacrifice. Either he obeys, loses his means of support, and suffers, or he refuses, fails his faith, and suffers."

"You said we needed them."

"You asked why it bothered me."

"I suppose you've never had to sacrifice for something greater than yourself?"

Elyth spit a bitter laugh.

"Ah," *eth ammuin* said. "You disdain him as a lesser being."

"I'm sure he's a fine man."

"Yet you consider yourself superior."

"Not at all. And it's not about him; it's about you. You say you don't want followers, but you're happy to exploit their obvious devotion."

Eth ammuin chuckled.

"I don't see what's amusing about that," Elyth said.

"I'm sorry, I'm not laughing at you. I forget that your time on that mountain has been somewhat limited."

Elyth hadn't expected the simple question to open the door so wide and so quickly, but she recognized the opportunity and seized it. She slowed her pace a stride or two, allowing him to close the gap between them, not quite walking side by side, but enough to encourage further conversation.

"Maybe you'd like to give me some more context, then. Because right now you sound like a sociopath."

"How much context would you like?"

"However much it takes to help me understand."

"So all of it, then."

"You can skip the boring parts."

She glanced at him, caught a glimpse of the fading traces of a brief smile; he was warming. She was on the right path.

"When I first came to Qel, I needed a place of solitude. Somewhere I could be alone, to contemplate and . . . reevaluate. The mountain was all wilderness then.

"But after a while people found me, as they always do. And a few decided to follow me out there. In the early days it was a place where everyone was welcome. I never turned anyone away. The only thing keeping people out was their own assumptions, or lack of willingness or ability to confront the elements. And the mountain can be a harsh place. Not many stayed."

"And those who did . . . you taught them how to survive?"

"No," he said. "I only taught them how to live."

He left the statement hanging in the air, though Elyth couldn't tell if it was because his mind had taken him somewhere else or if he was in fact waiting for some kind of response from her.

"Now you sound like a *pretentious* sociopath," she said.

The laugh that escaped him then was sudden and full-throated. Genuine, full of delight, the rolling sort of laughter with a blast radius that sends ripples of mirth through anyone close enough to hear it. Elyth smiled in spite of herself, just from the pureness of the sound.

"I can't remember the last time someone put me in my place," he said. The burst of laughter was short-lived, but his face retained the glory of it. "I'd forgotten how good it could feel not to be feared.

"But what I meant was I didn't teach any of them any particular skills. I only gave them a tool. It was up to them to decide whether or not to make use of it."

Elyth dreaded what he might say next. If he had been teaching his followers his own broken knowledge of the Deep Language, then that would indeed help explain the state of Qel. But she could scarcely imagine the nightmare that would unfold from that, tracking down all those people he'd come into contact with, investigating what worlds they had traveled to since . . . it would be the Markovian Strain all over again. Possibly worse.

"And that tool was . . . ?"

"Self-reliance, for one thing," he said. Elyth was both relieved and mildly disappointed by the pedestrian answer. As he continued to speak, though, he gradually became more animated and lively. The enthusiastic teacher awakening within him. "All the great evils of our race come from a single root. The fear of lack. Lack of food, or shelter, or love, or security. But when you position yourself in the world in such a way that you can stand facing whatever may come, trusting that whatever happens you are competent and capable of finding a way through, you are a powerful being indeed."

"And somehow all of that makes you feel better about taking Birnan's frames."

"Certainly. Birnan understands. Radical self-reliance empowers radical self-sacrifice."

Elyth laughed then, but humorlessly, scoffing.

"Forgive me," she said, "but preaching self-sufficiency in defense of *literally* taking someone else's possessions strikes me as acutely hypocritical."

"Yes, well, double standards *are* the human standard. But let's be precise. I said self-*reliant*, not self-*sufficient*. No one is wholly self-sufficient. Can you make the air you breathe? The sunlight that feeds the world? What infant ever fed, clothed, or protected itself? Self-sufficiency is a delusion of the imperceptive or narrow mind, one that either fails to notice or chooses to discount all the gifts that the universe already freely provides. Those gifts exist not *by* you nor *because* of you, but nevertheless are there *for* you."

The exalted *eth ammuin* was now on full display; Elyth felt the passion of his beliefs regardless of whether or not she shared them. And, at last, she began to understand the power he held over those he would not call disciples, but who followed him nonetheless.

"But that's beside the point. You didn't let me finish. There is in fact a second piece to the tool. Handle and blade, if you will. Self-reliance is the handle, that which we grip. But the far greater portion of the work comes from beyond its reach.

"The blade is . . . well, it is *arinthia*," he said, slipping uncharacteristically into the High Language. The way he said it, though, impacted Elyth more forcefully than normal speech, swelled her heart with the fullness of its meaning; it was something like courageous, boundless optimism but deeper, with greater confidence, not mere daydreaming or hoping for the best, but an unshakable faith that regardless of what appeared to be, that which was most needed was close at hand.

"When people are frightened of lack or scarcity, they cling, they hoard, they abuse. But when they embrace the overwhelming abundance of the world *and* they believe themselves capable of harvesting it, well . . . the resilience of such people can hardly be overestimated.

"And so . . ." he continued, and here he completed his transformation into wandering sage, as he emphasized his words with pantomime. "In one hand, we must grip tightly our selves; our natural gifts, our duties, our responsibilities . . . we must do our *part*." He stopped walking, took up a pose. "The other hand we must leave open, ready to receive that which the universe holds out for us. The truth is that our effort hardly accounts; our tiny offering is wholly insignificant compared to the abundance before us. And yet, somehow, it remains of cosmic importance that we make it."

Elyth scarcely heard the final words of the sentence. She was too struck by *eth ammuin*'s stance; the way he held his body, and his hands, one clenched close to his body, the other partially extended, open, palm upraised. It was identical to a pose from her meditation sequence, Watcher Greets the Storm. And not casually so: the angles of his arms, the stance, even the position of his fingers was proper. He saw her reaction and smiled. It had been neither accident nor coincidence.

"Who taught you that?" she said.

"I learned it from the same source you did."

"I doubt that," she said. It was only after she'd answered that she realized how he had snared her into revealing herself.

"Perhaps not *exactly* the same source," he said. "But I didn't mean the First House. The lineage of your instruction traces back to the same origin as mine."

Elyth contained the emotion, to neither confirm his suspicion nor issue an overly strong denial. She let out a little laugh.

"The First House? I'm not sure whether you mean that as a high compliment or a vicious insult. Why would you think I was one of those gray witches?"

"Oh, I've met some of your kind before. Long ago. I thought perhaps you were Hezra when we first met, but our second meeting was enough to convince me."

The mention of the Hezra struck her; in their first meeting he'd asked if she had intended to kill him. But if he'd thought she was a Hezra assassin, then who did he think was protecting him all this time?

"I know the origin of your teachings," Elyth said. "We most certainly do not share them."

"Oh? What origin do you believe that to be, then?"

"You're a disciple of Varen Fedic."

He startled at the mention of the name, surprised at her insight.

"I . . . do not deny I have followed the thoughts of that man. But I did not end with them. And I would like to believe I have fashioned something new. Something better."

"Then you are a great fool. Nothing good could possibly come from a being with so great a capacity for evil."

"Without such a capacity for evil, how could anyone be good?" he countered. "If you have no other choice, that doesn't make you good. Only weak."

"You seem convinced of many things that I'm not sure are true," she said.

"And you believe many things that I know to be false. But I can help you correct that."

The deep isolation she'd felt in him came back upon her, fresh in her mind. That was his ultimate vulnerability. He believed he possessed unique cosmic understanding; in her, he had found hope at last of being able to share his experiences with someone who would be capable of understanding them. It was a hope he retained still, though now she sensed that he was at war with himself, questioning her motives and what he could do about them. Or perhaps, knowing her motives, and hoping he could persuade her otherwise.

"Well, by all means, great teacher," she said, with a sarcastic bow, "enlighten me."

"Gladly. But first you must agree to answer honestly. There's no need to pretend that you are anything other than what you are. It's written on your hands, after all."

He resumed walking then, leaving her once more momentarily stunned. Elyth refused the urge to look at her palms. It was true, her identity within the House was etched there, but how he could have perceived it was beyond her. She shook off the surprise and fell in step beside him, watching as he contemplated for a few moments.

"What would you say you hold to be most deeply true?" he said. "What is your ultimate foundation?"

"The word alone," Elyth answered, both honestly and reflexively.

"The True Speech."

"The Deep Language, yes."

"Ah, the Deep Language," he said, testing the words in his mouth. "I hadn't thought of it that way before, but . . . yes, that makes sense. The Deep Language. I like that.

"So," he continued. "The word alone, you say, is your foundation. *Not* the First House of the Ascendance?"

Elyth felt at once that he had discerned the crack deep in her soul. The one left by her failure to put Qel down. The one she'd tried to deny, but that lingered still.

"They are one and the same," she answered.

"Oh? Interesting," he said. "Would you say your knowledge of the Deep Language is complete and perfect?"

"No."

"Then what is it that you believe, that you know to be wrong?"

"I wouldn't believe something if I knew it was wrong."

"Then your knowledge is perfect."

"Of course not."

"So you admit that you must be wrong about *some* things that you hold true, and yet you are uncertain which things those are."

"I . . . will grant you that," she said. "But only for the sake of argument."

"Thank you, that's very gracious of you. I don't mean to make it personal. So, for the sake of argument, how best might *one* discover which of *one*'s beliefs are incorrect?"

"By testing them I suppose."

"And if one is not allowed to test them?"

"Then *one*, I imagine, is destined to be wrong forever."

"And when was the last time you questioned what you'd been taught by the First House?"

Elyth checked herself here; she'd almost said *often*, but for an instant she wondered if the truth was closer to *never*.

"It cannot hurt to ask the question, *Eliya*," he said, putting sarcastic emphasis on the name he knew to be fake. "Even of things you believe deeply. If they are true, they will withstand the question. And if not, then you can emerge stronger, no matter how difficult the passage into truth may be. Doubt is a powerful guide, and the beginning of wisdom."

"And you are what? At the end, I suppose?"

"Me? Oh no, I'm still at the beginning, too," he said with a smile. "But it is the beginning of infinity, so I don't expect my progress to be all that noticeable."

"And is that what you're after? Wisdom alone?"

"No," he said. "No, not that alone."

"What, then? What is it that you want?"

"To break every chain," he said. The smile faded, and he looked intently into her eyes. "Many are bound who call themselves free."

The accusation was clear; he thought she was merely a slave to the First House.

"A necessary condition for freedom is its limitation," she answered. "Promises of unlimited freedom are just another road to the tyranny of the powerful."

He smiled again at that, genuine, as though she'd passed some sort of test.

"Perhaps you see why I envy you so. You have learned so much and are still so young," he said. "And I do envy you, Eliya."

"Then you are an even greater fool than I thought," she answered. "I don't know what I have that you would envy."

"Discipline," he replied. "And focus. I've had to learn so much on my own, my understanding is . . . haphazard, incomplete. It took me decades to discover things you were probably taught in a day. And you are so precise, calculated in everything. I am in awe of your stillness. I think it will be easier for you to become more like me than for me to become more like you."

"I don't want to be any more like you than absolutely necessary."

"Oh? Then why are *you* following *me* now?"

Eth ammuin looked at her for a moment with his sunlit smile then glanced around and pointed off to the mountain range they were leaving behind.

"Some look there and see the mountains. A barrier. A boundary. A sign saying, 'Thus far may you come and no farther.' Others look over the same majestic view and see beyond the wall, to the horizon. A thing to be to pursued and sought after. It is the right of humankind to test themselves against those barriers and, in time, to break through them."

"Or be destroyed upon them," Elyth said.

"Tell me, what is it that the First House was established to do?"

"We serve. We watch. We contemplate," Elyth answered. "Occasionally we speak."

"That is what you do now, perhaps," he said. "But it is not the purpose for which your House was originally created. It was once a catalyst for growth. But now it is a deterrent. An oppressor."

Elyth had to stop herself from letting loose her deep offense at such a misrepresentation of all that the First House stood for. They were protectors, not tyrants.

"I'm a servant of order," she said calmly.

"You're an agent of stasis. And that puts you in the same league as death. Wouldn't you rather stand with me, on the side of life?"

His tone said more than his words alone; he was hinting at having discerned her mission to Qel.

"I know what you came here to do," he said. "But I'm not yet confident you'll do it, when the time comes."

For all he seemed to have learned about her, he had failed to perceive that which should have been most obvious. Her resolve.

"And yet," Elyth said, "you'll teach me what you've learned anyway?"

"In time, yes."

"Even if you believe I'm your enemy?"

He continued walking, but with his hands he again made the pose of Watcher Greets the Storm.

"I hope that once you understand the universe as I do, you'll want to engage with it the way I do. But I have no control over that. We may be adversaries at the end of it all. But I'm willing to take the risk, because of what could be if we were allies."

"And what would that be?"

He thought for a moment, scratched the side of his face.

"There is an ancient story," he said. "A man goes to a market and encounters a seller of arms. Weapons, armor, all the various tools of war appropriate for the age. And an elegant spear catches the man's eye. So he inquires of the seller, saying, 'Tell me, sir, this spear. Is it of quality?'

"'Sir,' the seller answers, 'I tell you truly, it is of the highest quality known to mankind. Its head is keen beyond measure, its shaft as strong as the mountains. There is neither helm nor shield nor breastplate that can withstand the unstoppable force of its strike.'

"'An impressive piece to have on display,' the man says, and continues to browse. A few moments later he finds a stout shield, graven with images and polished like the moon.

"'This shield,' he says, 'is it also of such high quality?'

"'Sir,' the seller replies, 'I speak without deceit when I say that it is the very pinnacle of workmanship and the height of design. Its balance does not weary the arm, yet it turns aside any blow as easily as a fortress wall. Truly there is no blade, spear, or axe in existence that can slash, pierce, or cleave this immovable shield.'

"'Ah,' the man says. 'Then I am in a quandary, for I do not know whether I should purchase from you your unstoppable spear or your immovable shield. Clearly at least one must be counterfeit, since both cannot possibly exist.'

"'Not so, good sir,' answers the seller. 'For the man who wields them both needs never fear the impossibility of their clashing.'"

After he'd finished the story, *eth ammuin* turned to her and asked, "What do you make of that?"

"I'd say that was a clever salesman."

"Indeed. But a wise man would purchase them and so become invincible."

"More likely a fool, made poor by his reckless spending and soon after dead by testing his purchases in battle."

"Well, yes. But it's a fun story, anyway. And I think we're that pair, you and I. That means there are only two possible outcomes. Either one of us must prove false in the end or, standing together, we both hold true, and the purpose that unites us may yet stand."

What purpose, in that man's mind, could possibly unite them, she wondered. Only one that she could foresee. Breaking what he perceived as the chains of the Ascendance. Wielding the power of the Deep Language to burn it down and start anew. There was no way they would ever stand together. But she didn't need to let him know that yet.

"Which one am I?" she asked.

"What do you mean?"

"The spear or the shield?"

He chuckled.

"I'm not sure yet."

Eth ammuin had opened up so much to her, she knew that with a little more time and careful effort, she could lead him into revealing his actual knowledge or methods. But as they crested a rolling hill, the sound of an approaching skimmer grew behind them, and they were forced to scramble for cover. The vessel passed by some distance to their left. When they emerged from hiding and continued a little farther on, Elyth recognized the first signs of Alonesse appearing ahead of them.

Further lessons would have to wait. This close to civilization, she needed all her attention focused on her surroundings.

Like most cities, Alonesse's transit stations were arranged around its perimeter. As they closed in, Elyth identified the most secluded approach to the city and, from there, a path to the nearest station. The day was fading by the time they reached it, and as was Elyth's way, they remained some distance removed, to give her a chance to observe and evaluate.

"Guess we're clear," *eth ammuin* said. "Looks like no more officers than usual."

"Maybe to you," Elyth answered. "But there's one," she said, pointing to a plainclothed woman seated by a window near the main entrance to a café. "And there. And there."

"They all just look like people to me."

"Then it's a good thing I'm here."

"I never argued otherwise," he said. "Seems a lot more crowded than I would have expected, though."

It was true. Small transit stations like the one they'd located tended to get backed up, particularly toward the end of the day. This number, however, seemed large even for that. They remained outside for a long while, and it eventually became clear what was happening. Skimmers and larger transports were arriving, but in all the time they watched, not a single one had departed.

"They locked the station down," Elyth said, finally.

Strider frames weren't unheard of within city limits, but wandering down the street in them would draw a great deal of attention. According to her map, there was another transit station a few miles farther north and east. They backed out, and circled wide around the perimeter of the city. By the time they reached the second transit station, though, they didn't need to observe for long to determine that it too had been descended upon by the local Authority.

"Would they go to all this trouble just for you?" she asked.

"For me?" *eth ammuin* said, shaking his head. "The Detail tends to be a bit more subtle than that. They do have people in the Authority, of course. But not nearly enough to exert that kind of influence. And what would the Authority care if I'm out wandering the planet, anyway?"

She scanned the area with her monocular. Given her previous infiltration of the Authority's HQ, she had to wonder if the Authority was using the lockdown as a mechanism to find her. Either way, they weren't getting out through Alonesse. She was still processing that fact when *eth ammuin* abruptly laid his hand on her shoulder.

"We have to go," he said. "Right now."

Elyth lowered her monocular and turned toward him, but didn't need to ask what had caused his reaction. She saw them now, too. A group of four men were filtering toward them through the woods, aided by a sleek scout drone hovering just above the trees.

Without a word, Elyth took off north and west, with *eth ammuin* by her side and a force of unknown size close behind.

TWENTY

Together, Elyth and *eth ammuin* opened the distance, the striders granting them greater speed and agility as they fled. No matter where they went, though, the drone followed swiftly behind. Once they'd gained enough space, Elyth stopped and turned to face the machine. But as she spoke the words that would bring its ruin, two more appeared, closing in fast.

"Eliya!" *eth ammuin* called, and turning, she saw another group of pursuers coming from their flank. She sprang forward, taking a new vector, away from this new group and the one they'd left behind.

As they ran, the snapshot she'd glimpsed of this second team forced itself to mind. The way they moved, the way they were armed. Not just run-of-the-mill Authority. True Hezra troopers. The Great Game had descended upon them.

Within minutes of their second close encounter, a pair of skimmers roared overhead, shadowing them and, undoubtedly, reporting on their every move.

There was no planning then, only running and reacting.

But no matter what direction they turned, some small unit was positioned to intercept them. No one opened fire, despite coming well within range more than once. A capture operation, then.

With the realization of their objective came understanding of their tactics. The Hezra forces were shepherding them. But by the time she made the connection, it was too late. She and *eth ammuin* burst into a clearing, blocked at the far end by a steep, rocky face, curving toward them in a half-moon. They could have scaled it, if only they'd had the time.

But that they did not have.

Elyth whirled around. The skimmers were already descending, and a ring of Hezra troopers was tightening, seemingly from every direction.

There was no escape now. The only uncertainty that remained was whether they were after *eth ammuin* or her.

Eth ammuin had fled to the cliff, though it was obvious there was no way out. He had his back to the wall, though, and maybe that had been his only goal; it was a natural enough instinct, even when it was tactically the wrong choice.

Elyth backed up closer to him, but remained in front, shielding him from the Hezra soldiers. The troopers had their weapons raised and trained on her as they approached; they came quickly, fearlessly, a human chain to bind them. They stopped about thirty feet away. At least twenty of them, plus the few who were now dismounting from the skimmers that had landed behind the wall of soldiers.

She held her hands up in surrender, but they made no move to close in to subdue her. Waiting for further orders. Or, perhaps, following ones previously given. In the time it took the others from the skimmer to reach them, Elyth scanned the eyes, hands, and faces of the soldiers around her; they were steady, unwavering. She saw fear in them, but they stood confronting it courageously. They knew the power they were facing, but they were steadfast in spite of it.

She recognized them now, despite their plain clothes and attempts to blend in. Or perhaps because of them.

Fear-Eaters. Soldiers of 3 Recon.

And as she had the realization, a tall man stepped through the ranks; she recognized him instantly from his frame. The same man she'd seen speaking with *eth ammuin* back at the compound. And given the response to him from the soldiers, she now understood his role.

He was an Envoy of the Hezra-Ka. The highest possible rank, subordinate only to the Hezra-Ka himself, and to be treated by all others as the voice of that fearsome leader.

The Envoy looked her over briefly, icy eyes making a quick accounting of her, and even more quickly dismissing her. His attention then went to *eth ammuin* behind her.

"*Eth ammuin*, my friend," he said, his voice a smooth baritone, resonant and pleasing to hear. "I thought we had a deal."

Eth ammuin made no response.

"Step out of the frames, both of you."

They did as they were instructed; there was no point in resisting when they were so vastly outgunned. Obviously they had come to recover *eth ammuin*, but what they planned to do with her was still unclear.

"I understand the need to get out and stretch your legs from time to time," the Envoy said. "But to go gallivanting off with one of these gray witches in tow." He held up a single finger and waved it while clicking his tongue, scolding in the most condescending of manners. "I hope you haven't been sharing secrets."

"I've told her nothing," *eth ammuin* said.

"Well," the Envoy replied, "isn't that reassuring to hear? But it's time to come home now. We still have work to do."

He waved *eth ammuin* forward; to Elyth's surprise, *eth ammuin* started walking toward the Envoy. Gone now was his fiery certainty, or any sense of power. He was once more submissive, downcast, as she'd seen him when his security detail had taken him away from Hok's cabin. As *eth ammuin* passed her, the Envoy turned around and started to walk back toward the skimmers.

Elyth couldn't believe what was happening. How she had allowed them to get trapped, how the Envoy had known she was an Advocate of the First House, how easily *eth ammuin* had given himself up. Her mission was now a complete and utter failure. And her failings would echo through the halls of First House, and have repercussions far beyond its walls.

But since First House's activity on Qel was apparently already discovered, she had one last-ditch action she could take. It would mark her for life, but that mattered little now.

"Stop!" she said, lunging to grab *eth ammuin*'s arm just before he was out of reach. The Envoy halted and turned partially around to look at her. *Eth ammuin* likewise turned, the hope obvious on his face that she had some way to save them. Elyth pushed up her sleeves to expose her forearms, then held her hands out, palms facing them, and arms angled as though she was surrendering once more. But this time, surrender was not her intent.

"I am Elyth-Kyriel," she said, her voice loud and clear. "Servant of the First House of the Ascendance, Advocate of the Voice, and this man is under my protection. I demand safe passage to the Vaunt for both myself and my charge."

Immediately she spoke in the Deep Language, a private phrase she had created herself and had never uttered in the presence of another human.

"*Form of the formless, root of all names, light in the darkness, first among flames.*"

In response the palms of her hands came alive with silver starlight, as the inscriptions written on them radiated and made themselves known. The light trailed down her wrists and her forearms, all the way to her elbows, testifying not only to the truth of her claim but also bearing witness to the record of her long service. And by revealing herself in such manner, giving her hidden name and revealing her imprints, she had made a forceful claim that not even the Hezra-Ka himself could dismiss.

The Envoy looked at her then, the expression on his face a blend of surprised and impressed. He had, perhaps, expected her to be an Advocate of the Eye; the claim would have been as strong, but of lower rank. It was unlikely he had ever encountered one of her Order before.

He turned fully then to face her.

"Advocate of the Voice, hmm?" he said. "Then you *really* shouldn't be here, should you?" He pointed to the glowing calligraphic lines wreathing her arms. "Normally, I'd say those counted for something. But out here . . ."

He waved a hand vaguely at the surroundings and then gave her a shrug. After that, he turned to the soldier nearest him and said, "When we're gone, you can bury her."

Elyth stood, struck helpless. By all accounts, the Hezra soldiers were required not only to honor her claim to *eth ammuin*, but also to make every effort to see her safely transported back home. Denying her declaration was tantamount to their own declaration of war against the First House. To so casually dismiss it, the Envoy showed an astonishing disdain for the foundational oaths of the Hezra; the fact that the soldiers with him were apparently willing to carry out his order revealed either how much they feared the man or how confident they were that no one would ever learn of her fate, or their participation in it.

Eth ammuin gave her a final, sad look and then turned to follow the Envoy. Abandoning her. After all his talk of alliance and unity, this was all it took for him to walk away. She wanted to call after him; to call him a fraud, a coward, a traitor to truth and all he claimed to be.

But before she could speak, *eth ammuin* let out a cry of his own, an escalating howl of notes, his words obscured, and then stomped his foot on the ground. And before anyone could react, the earth liquefied beneath them.

Elyth plummeted as the dirt and rock gave way to nothingness, and she landed hard on her back. The blow stunned her and stole her breath, and then debris was raining down upon her, threatening to bury her. She swam her arms, fought to get upright amid the cascade of earth, but it was falling too heavy, too fast, and she was still sliding, as if Qel itself were trying to swallow her.

And then a hand around her upper arm, its grip crushing like a trap sprung. For an uncertain moment, she dangled and spun in the flow, her shoulder searing as though it would rend from its socket. Then, in the next moment, all was quiet, and she found herself sitting on a mound of freshly churned dirt, with *eth ammuin* standing over her. And all around them a chasm had opened deep into the planet. She could hear moans from the dust-clouded darkness below, but not nearly as many as would account for all the men that had only moments ago been holding them captive. There was no way to tell how far they had fallen, or how much earth had collapsed; the hole could have been twenty feet deep or two hundred, for all she could see.

Elyth looked up at the man still gripping her arm.

"Grief," she said. "What did you do?"

"We should go," he answered.

She looked around them, wondering where they could possibly go from this little island in the midst of an abyss, and then realized that behind them a rounded bridge of earth remained connected to the cliff face. It was no more than a foot wide. *Eth ammuin* half helped, half dragged her to her feet and guided her forward onto that perilously narrow mound. She walked with tentative steps along the bridge; it was covered in shifting dirt that compressed and sprung again under each step, as though walking over a newly filled grave. She realized it might very well be just that.

They reached the edge of the rocky face, and there the ground felt more stable.

"Can you climb?" *eth ammuin* asked, his voice weak.

"Of course," she answered. "Can you?"

"We'll see."

The striders had both toppled and slid partially down the sloped edge of the chasm, but neither had fallen in. *Eth ammuin* held Elyth's hand as she stretched out to recover her pack from the nearest strider; her footing was so unstable, though, that she knew there was no way they'd be able to get the frames upright. She hated to leave them behind, but their only path out was up, and the striders weren't built for climbing.

They scrambled together up the face, finding it an easy climb with ample footholds and handholds, and numerous shelves and ledges. The cliff was only twenty feet high or so. They reached the top quickly, and when they did, *eth ammuin* fell to his hands and knees and vomited. Elyth turned and looked back down at the gaping fissure below, yawning up at her with its mouth full of dust and dead and dying men. And, she saw now, probably a pair of skimmers, too. And their striders. The chasm had opened in a wide radius all around where *eth ammuin* had stood, running all the way out to the tree line; a few trees had fallen in, and others were leaning precariously as though still deciding whether or not to take the plunge. The late-afternoon sun cast long shadows over the hole, but Elyth thought she could make out some movement within through the swirling dust clouds. However deep it went, she could see at least that it had been an uneven collapse, and was shallower in some places than others. Regardless, there didn't appear to be any spot where it was going to be easy to climb out.

Elyth turned back to face *eth ammuin*. He was still on his hands and knees, his head dangling between his arms.

"What happened there?" she asked.

He coughed twice and spit, and then said, "I didn't like what he said about you."

"Which part?"

"The 'you can bury her' part. Guess it gave me an idea."

He rocked back on his knees, wiped his hands on the tops of his pantlegs.

"We probably shouldn't stick around here long," she said.

Eth ammuin nodded. "I just need a minute."

There'd be no covering those tracks. But, if they hadn't yet used up all their luck, whoever came looking for them next might have to spend some time digging through the ruin below, looking for their bodies. Maybe that would buy her enough time.

"Minute's up," she said, and she grabbed him by the elbow and helped him to his feet. He was pale and sweat-sheened, but seemed stable enough. "Come on."

Elyth didn't wait. As before, she set a pace and expected him to keep up. Now, though, she felt the struggle in her heart; she knew the importance of getting him to First House, but also, she felt compelled to flee him, to escape whatever he was, before the destruction he carried within him consumed her, too.

Once more she led him back into the wilderness that she seemed destined to wander until her work on Qel was done. Before long, however, Elyth was at a loss for where to go. All directions seemed equally likely to lead to disaster. *Eth ammuin* stepped in then and advised her on the course they should follow, and though she was hesitant to accept his suggestion blindly, there was nothing obviously any more dangerous about it than any of their other options. The farther they traveled along the course, the more confident she became that he had not steered them wrong.

They continued for as long as their light lasted, and an hour beyond. Even so, when exhaustion and darkness at last conspired to force them to halt, Elyth could not escape the sense that she had slipped her neck from the noose at the last possible moment, and that it was sure to tighten once again. Gone now were all illusions of what she was up against. Whatever their connection to Qel, the Hezra had dispatched one of its most storied special operations units, to be led by no less than an Envoy of the hierarchy. And now they knew exactly who she was.

When they stopped, *eth ammuin* fell to the ground and lay there panting for several minutes, in his own personal agony. Looking at him, she knew she couldn't force him on much farther. Whatever chaos he had called forth had taken a terrible toll. She set up her shelter, and slung her pack in to the far side, and then looked over at *eth ammuin*.

"Grief," she said. "Get up and come here."

Whatever he'd meant to say came out only as a groan.

Elyth crossed to him, crouched beside him, and wrapped one of his arms around her shoulders.

"Come on," she said. "If you're going to die, at least do it out of sight."

He struggled up, leaning heavily on her, and allowed her to guide him to the shelter. She eased him to the ground and wordlessly he crawled in and collapsed again. Elyth looked at him lying there, and this time, rather than loathing the idea, found herself thinking it might be tolerable to join him. But though she could spare him some time to rest, that was not a luxury she herself could afford.

She sealed the shelter from the outside and then took out her tangle interpreter. For a few moments she just stared at the device, wondering what fury awaited her, and how she might withstand it. But there was nothing else she could do now, other than stand before the Paragon and whatever judgment might await.

Elyth pushed a connection request through and waited. She didn't have to wait long. The Paragon responded almost immediately, as though she'd been anticipating the call.

This time, however, when the dream-state connection formed, Elyth was greeted by no serene natural setting. Instead, she stood alone, in the Paragon's council chamber, with the Paragon seated before her on the dais. The scale of everything was enhanced; the walls stood higher, the Paragon's seat of judgment towered. Even the matriarch herself seemed magnified. There was neither warmth nor welcome.

"Is it done?" the Paragon said.

"Illumined Mother," Elyth said, bowing. "Not yet. Matters are more complicated than I anticipated."

The Paragon sighed, not making any attempt to conceal her frustration or disappointment.

"At this point, dear, I will only be surprised if something actually goes according to plan. Have you at least reached this *eth ammuin*?"

"Yes, he's in my custody. But I haven't yet persuaded him to reveal what he knows."

"Who needs persuading?" the Paragon replied. "Break his mind if you must."

"I tried."

"And?"

"And he resisted."

The Paragon was quiet for two heartbeats too long.

"Then perhaps you have not tried hard enough," she said.

A bare hint of frost clung to her words, but Elyth felt as though an icicle had pierced her heart. For the first time she heard doubt in the Paragon's voice. Not doubt that the mission could still be accomplished. Doubt that Elyth was fully committed to seeing it done.

"I assure you, I'm doing all I can, Your Radiance."

"Elyth," the Paragon said. "The Strain is subtle, and cunning. I would like to believe that you are immune to its influence, but in my heart, I know there are none among us, not even myself, who could withstand its corrupting touch forever. You have been too long on that world."

Elyth heard the implication, refused to acknowledge it.

"I agree," she said. "Which is why I need to extract, now, and have this *eth ammuin* stand before you at the Vaunt—"

"You cannot bring him here," the Paragon interrupted. "You will have to manage it yourself."

"There's more," Elyth said, and she told the Paragon of her encounter with the Envoy and 3 Recon. When she finished, the Paragon sat for a few moments, absorbing the information, evaluating it. But when she spoke, her words brought neither hope nor comfort.

"Qel is under quarantine," she said. "The Grand Council has authorized the Contingency."

It was such a reversal, and so sudden.

"What?" Elyth said. "Why?"

"Why do you think?"

The ice in her words gave Elyth the answer.

"They don't believe First House can stop it," she said.

"At this point, I can give them very little assurance otherwise."

"Illumined Mother," Elyth said. "This task is beyond me. But if we could get him off the planet—"

"It cannot be done, Elyth."

"Deploy another Advocate, then. I'll teach her."

"Deploy another . . . ? Elyth. I don't know why you can't hear me. Qel is blockaded. No one is coming."

"Surely someone can slip through in the evacuation."

The ancient woman was quiet for a few moments.

"Your Radiance?"

"There is to be no evacuation," she answered.

A billion Ascendance citizens lived on Qel, the vast majority of whom, as far as Elyth could tell, had nothing to do with the dangerous changes taking place within their planet. A small fraction compared to the trillions spread across the galaxy perhaps, but surely a genocide of that scale was too great a cost.

"That can't be," she said.

"It is. The fleet is en route. They may very well activate the Contingency the moment the ships are in position. If you do not believe it possible then you have failed to grasp the severity of the threat. Perhaps that explains your reluctance to finish the task."

The accusation stung Elyth deeply. After all she'd given and endured.

"Reluctance?" she spat. "I've done nothing but serve you at every step!"

"Elyth, no one is coming to Qel," the Paragon repeated coolly. "This is *your* task. I set it before *you*. You must accomplish it."

"I tried, and barely survived. If I were to try again it would destroy me."

"Oh, Elyth," the Paragon said, and there was a strange tone to her voice, part exasperation, part genuine pain. "Elyth. My brightest of daughters. Do you even now not see? If that is what it takes to bring this to an end, then it is a sacrifice we must all be willing to accept."

The full magnitude of her separation from the House struck Elyth then, a frozen star of despair radiating through her chest. Though she had always thought of herself as willing to give her very life in service, in her imagining, it had always been a noble choice, a decision she would make for herself; a voluntary sacrifice, for the good of the First House and the Ascendance. Not one thrust upon her, not an order given to stand and die against all reason. It felt nothing like the offering of self she had pictured, only abandonment and betrayal. And her thoughts turned then to *eth ammuin's* words, his assurance that at the end of it all, nothing would remain unshaken.

"A billion Ascendance citizens, Elyth. If you fail, both the destruction and the shame will fall at our feet."

Elyth could barely absorb the words; if there had been any intent to motivate her to action, it glanced off the numbness caused by the obvious loss of her place in the First House. What future could possibly remain for her there now?

She felt a surge of emotion, a desire to lash out in power, to strike at that ancient witch on her throne.

But that thought, rather than animating her, instead woke her, terrified her. As though emerging from some dark dream, she came back to herself. How much had she allowed *eth ammuin's* subtle strains of thought to influence her?

"Perhaps not all is lost," the Paragon said. She must have sensed the storm raging within Elyth. "But your part remains, Elyth, and you must do it. Qel's transformation must be put to an end. By your hand."

Her tone changed then, softened, and Elyth realized that the Paragon still held hope that she would prove true.

"*Sareth hanaan* be your guide, daughter. May it lead you through even this."

The connection closed, leaving Elyth surrounded on all sides by hostile wilderness, feeling lost and alone. The will to accomplish her purpose that once had seemed unbreakable was held together by only the weakest of bonds. And the Paragon's declaration that Elyth was Guided by the True Star seemed more false than ever before. Even the matriarch seemed to have lost her faith in the claim.

Elyth looked at her shelter, envisioned the man inside. The source of all her trouble and the key to its resolution. For now, while he slept, she would consider the way forward. And then, when she was ready, one way or another, she would break him.

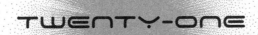

TWENTY-ONE

"Grief," Elyth said, speaking to the man through the open shelter entry. He was lying on his side with his back to her, curled in a ball. He didn't stir. She nudged him with her toe.

"Hey, Grief."

She'd granted him two full hours to sleep, while she remained outside all the while, keeping watch. In that time, neither man nor creature had disturbed the stillness of the night. But that fact had done nothing to ease her mind. She glanced up at the sky, and wondered how soon the blackness might be replaced with the glittering dust of the Ascendance armada, poised to obliterate the planet. Realized that some of them must have been on station already.

She looked back down at the man at her feet, who still hadn't moved.

"Grief!" she said, loudly now, and kicked him with more force than she'd intended.

He didn't react. Not even a grunt or twitch. For the barest moment, the thought occurred to her that he had actually died. But then he spoke.

"Some thanks," he said. "Considering I just saved your life."

After that, he rolled over to look up at her.

"My life," she answered, "wouldn't have needed saving if I hadn't been with you in the first place."

"Fair."

"Come on, we're out of time."

He sat up, rubbed his face with both hands.

"Where are we headed?"

"Nowhere. You're going to teach me what you know, now, or I will leave you here for the Hezra to find."

"Oh," he said. He sat up a little straighter, rolled his shoulders, and stretched his neck. "Okay. Can we eat while we talk?"

She had expected some sort of resistance, at least a needling comment or cryptic deflection. But he genuinely seemed ready to tell her what she wanted to know. Maybe the exhaustion had broken his resolve. Or maybe their near capture had made clear just how razor thin the edge was that they were walking together. Either way, as long as he was compliant, she'd get as much out of him as she could.

"Sure," she said.

She had him climb out of the shelter briefly so that she could reconfigure it, tall enough for them both to sit inside. Once it was arranged, she set the tiles to mimic the surroundings, and opaque to conceal the light from the interior. They both crawled in and sat crosslegged, facing each other, so close their knees nearly touched. Elyth placed a small light between them and switched it on.

His complexion was sallow in the light, his eyes sunken. Only now, looking directly into his eyes, did Elyth realize just how much of a toll it had taken on him to unleash whatever power it was that he had poured out upon their would-be captors.

"I thought you wanted to eat something," she said.

"Yeah," he said. "But I forgot I lost my bag."

Elyth reached into her pack and pulled out her last ration. Something else came with it and landed next to him.

"What's this?" he said, holding it up. When he brought it into the light, she saw it was the bent branch of the frostoak.

"Nothing," she said. "Just a stick."

He rolled it between his fingers, examined closely the delicate bark and the dry fibers where it had split.

"It isn't native. You've been carrying this with you since you arrived?"

"I brought it with me, yes."

"Then it must have significance. You don't strike me as someone who keeps useless things around."

"I haven't let *you* go."

A weary chuckle bubbled up from within him.

"You know," he said, handing the branch back, "someday, you're going to hurt my feelings."

She took the cutting and tossed it back in her pack. In exchange, she handed him half her ration.

"You said you weren't going to feed me."

"Still might leave you behind."

"Shouldn't push my luck, then," he said.

"I wouldn't."

He accepted the food and held it up, bowed his head to her in genuine gratitude, and together they ate.

"I like Elyth, by the way," he said. "It suits you. Much better than Eliya."

"Whenever you're ready," she answered.

He smiled and nodded, but remained silent for a time, both sadness and light in his eyes.

"I actually meant now," Elyth said.

"I'm sorry," he said. "It's just . . . all the years of waiting and preparing. At the time they seemed so long, tedious, and full. But now that my final destiny has at last arrived, I feel that perhaps I should have been more diligent."

"What makes you think it's final?"

He shrugged. "But. Here we are. I suppose we must do the best we can with what we have."

Eth ammuin rubbed his hands together, looked up, and took a long, deep breath. A tutor contemplating how best to instruct his pupil. When he looked at her again, his eyes seemed clearer.

"Why is it," he began, "that when people of a world go wrong, it is the planet that pays the ultimate penalty?"

He knew the answer as well as she did.

"Sow venom for one season," Elyth answered, "reap death for eight."

Eth ammuin grunted.

"Human minds are easily changed," he said. "But the material of a world has a long memory. It speaks to us, wordlessly, in its own way, whether we listen or not. And it listens, whether or not we intend for it to hear. Mountains, oceans, valleys, rivers, they echo back to us what we have spoken. And for all the mighty power of nature, there is one thing that we alone possess, one thing that gives us dominion over all else."

"Language," Elyth said.

"We've had it for so long, we have forgotten what it truly is."

"A technology."

"Yes. More specifically, an interface," he answered. "The mechanism by which we humans alone mediate between chaos and order and shape our reality. The unknown emerges from the darkness, we name it, and so capture it. And from capture, it is a short walk to understanding, and from understanding, to control."

He raised his right hand and focused his attention on it. She followed his gaze.

While she watched, he formed the hand sign for the first letter of the Language, *ahn*, slowly, deliberately. Then *bet, het, ru*, and continuing on through the entire alphabet, gradually gaining speed with each sign, until he reached the end, *tzo*.

"You know these signs," he said, looking once more at her. It was a statement, not a question; every child knew them.

Still holding his right hand up, he then raised his left. Now he began the sequence anew, first with his right hand and then, halfway through the alphabet, he started with the left at *ahn*. His hands moved simultaneously, each on a different form, speed increasing with each transformation, until Elyth could no longer fully see the signs before they were already gone. Yet she knew each was perfectly formed, elegantly executed; he had a magician's hands, the dexterity of a thief.

When he had cycled through the entire alphabet twice with both hands, he began mixing in a series of hand signs she'd never seen before, ones that required the use of both hands together, sometimes with fingers interlaced, sometimes with hands stacked one upon the other. As he did so, Elyth felt a growing energy, and just before he ceased, the air around his hands appeared to waver, like heat rising from a desert floor. Before she could react, though, *eth ammuin* returned his right hand to *ahn*, the first letter, and his left to the last, *tzo*. Beginning and end.

Whatever shimmer she had seen was gone, the feeling of energy dispersed.

"You know these signs," he repeated, "but for you they hold no power."

"The body anchors the mind," Elyth replied. "Movement in space has its value."

"Then your House hasn't forgotten *everything* it once knew. But it has reduced a vibrant truth to empty ritual."

"And in your ignorance, you call empty that which holds deep purpose. Just because *you* can't perceive it, doesn't mean it isn't there."

"The great poets stir you with their words. But have you not been equally moved by the gracefulness of a born dancer? Or by a clear voice raised in song?"

"That's just a stirring of the emotions."

"Just?" he said. And then he leaned forward, closer to her. "That is *just* your being, resonating with the fabric of the universe."

He sat back again. "Do you sing, Elyth?"

"When I have something to sing about."

"And sung words, do they mean the same thing as when you speak them?"

"Of course."

"But do they *feel* as though they do?"

He was being purposely circuitous, inviting her to make the connections, to discover for herself what he had learned.

He hummed a brief tune, its intervals open, sweeping; Elyth's mind conjured an image of rolling hills in golden sunlight. And then he changed to a different one, a mournful dirge, a wordless threnody filled with solemn pain. He folded his hands in front of him while he hummed, his fingers interlocked in a pattern too complex for her to easily decipher.

And in that moment she had a flash of insight.

"It's like speaking several languages at once," she said. "Meaning layered on meaning."

He stopped humming immediately and smiled then, broadly. At last, she was beginning to understand. By using multiple modes of expression, *eth ammuin* had devised a way to effectively "speak" the Deep Language in ways that were not just faster, but were in fact fuller, more forceful in their impact. In contrast, the precise formulas she had been taught were rigid and restrictive. For specific purposes, with predictable outcomes.

"Sometimes the spoken word alone is not enough," he said.

She remembered once more his statement about truths that could not be spoken, but now saw it in a new light. Memories rose of deep grief, her body racked by groans and sobs, and of ecstatic joy, when shared cheers and laughter made words unnecessary. This, then, was why *eth ammuin*'s use of the Language was so volatile, so dangerous. He improvised in the moment, added his own personal layer of meaning to the foundation of the Deep Language, without thought of consequence.

Like Qel's evasion of destruction, and the harmonic resonance that accompanied it. Echoes of *eth ammuin*.

But this personal fire had been drained from Elyth's training in the Deep Language, not out of ignorance of what could be, but as protection against what might otherwise result. *Eth ammuin*, like Varen Fedic before him, was the very archetype of that which the First House meant to prevent. A word of power spoken too forcefully or with the wrong tone could have unintended consequences, effects that might not fully manifest for a time unknown, only to blossom in the most unlooked-for ways.

"You know the destruction that came from Varen Fedic and his teaching," Elyth said. "Why would you believe you could control what he could not?"

"The First Speaker," *eth ammuin* said. "His mistake is there in his self-name. And the power of the word made him believe he was fit to command all others."

"But you don't share that belief."

"He learned to speak before he learned to listen. I've spent many, many years learning to listen. It's only recently that I've begun to speak."

"And thus continue his error."

"Possibly. But if I am wrong, then perhaps, at least, I am wrong in the right direction."

Elyth sat absorbing the information, calculating what more she might need to know before she could act. In the silence, *eth ammuin* leaned forward and took the frostoak cutting from her pack.

"I have a fondness for broken things," he said. "Ever since I realized I was one."

The spark in his eye told her this was no casual tangent of conversation.

"At some point, you'll be dead like it, too," she said.

"And you're sure it's dead?"

She looked at the branch, dry, bent, lopped off from its source of life weeks before.

"Pretty sure."

"What if you told it it was something else? What it could be, instead of what you thought it was."

"You mean if I lied to it?"

"I mean if you had hope for it."

He held the cutting flat across his palm and raised it in front of his face. Then, in a quiet voice, he sang over it, in the Deep Language. His voice was not particularly strong or lovely, and it wavered, but the simple melody was undeniably moving. The statement he made, on the other hand, was hair-raising.

He was singing life to a dead thing, and it was as disturbing as watching a delusional parent speak to the ruined body of a lifeless child, saying it was going to be all right. It was a desecration of the Deep Language.

"Stop," she said.

He did, immediately, and after a moment, he handed the branch to Elyth as though returning a sacred relic; she received it and tossed it unceremoniously back into her pack, disgusted by the display. When Elyth used the Deep Language, it was always to describe something that *could* be, something possible within the bounds of reality; even the death of a world was something that *would* be, given enough time along natural courses. But here, in her little shelter, this man was describing something impossible, as though reaching back in time to undo what had already been done.

"You haven't learned anything at all," she said.

"And you do not understand Qel," *eth ammuin* said, "because you are not listening to it. There are things I have spoken to Qel. Things that are not yet, but that may come to be. If you listen for them, you will hear them. And if you will add your own voice to them, then this world will be the beginning of the next evolution of humanity."

At last his intent was revealed; he wanted Elyth to combine her power with his, to accelerate Qel's transformation.

"You still see the danger of what you're doing."

"I do. But the time is upon us, whether we wish it or not. And as with you, it's a risk I'm willing to take."

"A risk *you're* willing to take? You can't make the Deep Language mean whatever *you* want it to mean—"

"It isn't about creating your own meaning, Elyth. I'm talking about expressing truth in a manner that only you can. With your *own* voice, not someone else's."

Again, he seemed to be challenging her devotion to the First House, hoping to find a crack to exploit. Elyth wanted to deny any existed, but she felt a tremble anyway. Qel had overcome Revealing the Silent Gate. And in her desperation to survive the aftermath, she had formulated a call of her own in the Deep Language. Her understanding had been insufficient. But could the failing have been more than hers alone? Could it be within the structure of the House itself?

"Whatever you may think of First House," Elyth said, "their methods and their ways are strict for a reason."

The words sounded hollow even to her own ears.

"I don't doubt that the intention was good," *eth ammuin* replied. "But in their fear, they've robbed the Ascendance of vital power."

"The sealing phrases are a conceptual *channel* for that power, to direct it to proper ends, and prevent it from spilling out."

"You have access to limitless potential, and you use it for parlor tricks."

"I wouldn't call killing a planet a parlor trick."

"Compared to creating one? I would."

He sat staring into her eyes for a moment, willing her to understand, to believe.

"You could drown a mountain with a word," he continued. "But wouldn't you rather see it flourish into something beyond even your own imagining?"

"Not to become a volcano."

"Given enough time, even the destruction wrought by a volcano makes way for an island paradise."

"And this is what you would make of Qel. You would tip it into cataclysm, in the hope that something better might emerge."

"A time is coming, Elyth, and soon, when all the greatest plans and preparations of the Ascendance will fail. And in that time, we must all hope a solution beyond calculation will emerge. You know what you're capable of, small and frail as you are. You've seen what I can do with my techniques. Imagine what humanity might be capable of when an entire planet joins its own voice with yours."

"And if you're wrong?" she asked.

"Then we'll die, humanity erased from the galaxy. But that might happen anyway. The Ascendance *must* evolve; it must be willing to open its eyes again. Fortunately, I'm not the only one who sees what is on the horizon."

"The Hezra," she said.

He nodded.

And a sense of dread washed over her as she realized now what that meant. His willing imprisonment, their tolerance of his antics. There was only one thing he had to offer them.

"You've taught them the Deep Language."

"In part . . . but maybe not strictly the way they requested."

Elyth reeled. It was no accident that the First House was sole keeper of the Deep Language, kept separate from the Hezra's technological focus. If the Hezra acquired sufficient knowledge of the Deep Language and its uses, the careful balance of power that had maintained the Ascendance for over eight thousand years would forever be destroyed.

"In exchange for what?"

"For Qel."

"One world, for the universe?"

"One world might be enough to give us a new universe."

"To what end?"

"To whatever end presents itself, Elyth. You're looking for answers where there are no certainties."

"They don't believe you, Grief. They're just using you."

"Unbelievers don't concern me. It's the others who cause the real trouble."

"What others?"

He looked at her meaningfully.

"The true believers who hear and follow the wrong message."

Elyth didn't know what more to say or do. The last traces of her firm foundation quaked beneath her with the knowledge that even the death of Qel would not be enough to undo the harm that this madman had loosed into the cosmos. And still, he seemed to believe his every action had been correct, his choices the only ones that could possibly have been made. She wanted nothing more in that moment than to be rid of the monster he'd at last revealed himself to be.

"They've already betrayed you," she said. "Qel is under quarantine. They're going to destroy it."

"I find that hard to believe. Given how hard they've worked to sustain it."

"I don't understand how a man of such supposed wisdom could be so stupid."

"Because they aren't wrong, Elyth," he said, with some heat. And then, quietly again: "They aren't wrong. Not completely. Someone has to guide them."

He let the words hang there, staring intently at her, willing her to see something in his thoughts. When she made no response, he continued.

"There is incredible access to power within you, Elyth. Power you could harness, if only you would open yourself to it. If only you would allow yourself to stretch out beyond what you perceive as your limits and touch it."

"The only thing beyond those limits is destruction, for myself and anyone else caught in the wake."

"It is past the edge of self that your true potential lies. You are more than what you have been told. And you are not as free as you believe. When you grasp that, then you will have all you've been seeking after from me."

He sat back then, fell back against the shelter and closed his eyes; the great teacher leaving his student to ponder her lesson or, perhaps, simply a man overcome by exhaustion. For a time she remained there, watching him, filtering through all his many words to find the essential understanding she sought.

"I have a confession to make," he said, without opening his eyes. "I should have told you sooner, but I was too afraid."

Elyth could scarcely imagine what horror would come from his mouth next, given what he'd so willingly shared. She opened her eyes to look at her.

"When you arrived," he said, "I felt it. Or, rather, heard, perhaps.

Deep calls to deep, after all. I should have known you would find your way to me eventually, but in my haste . . ."

He shrugged.

Even now he was reluctant to finish the sentence. Not afraid. Embarrassed. And as the realization dawned, Elyth finished the sentence for him.

"You caused my crash."

"I only meant to draw your ship down. I didn't intend to tear it in two."

"A simple enough task, when properly understood," she said, coldly, "and you can't even manage that. But you *can* transform a planet for the salvation of us all."

"Not alone," he answered.

She'd had enough.

Enough of this half charlatan, half demon of a man who claimed allegiance to life with his mouth and wrought death with his hands.

Enough of the impossible demands placed on her by the Paragon, and the First House, the relentless taking of all she had and insistence on more.

Enough of the hidden games of power within the Ascendance, and enough of this twisted planet that had brought everything she'd ever been and ever believed she could be to the point of collapse.

"Qel will die," she said. "The only choice now is the manner in which it will do so."

"And it is not my choice to make," he said.

"Whatever you hoped to accomplish has failed. The Hezra is coming, and when they arrive, they will activate the Contingency. This whole world, all of your work, all of your fever dreams, and everyone along with them, will be less than ash. But if you help me now, I will put it down gently, and maybe a good death, at least, will be some small comfort in the face of this catastrophe you've caused."

He held his hands up weakly, his arms a sketch of Watcher Greets the Storm.

"My part is done, Elyth."

Their eyes met, his still light and clinging to some desperate hope. But he must have seen something in her look that at last removed all doubt as to her determination. And he was heart-stricken. Here, now, in the final moment, when he had hoped most that she would at last understand and believe as he did, instead he found only rejection. And the hollowness of his eyes seemed to deepen a thousandfold.

"There's no need to search for one of Qel's ancient threadlines," he said. "You can use one of mine."

She snatched her pack up then and opened the shelter. If she was going to destroy herself in order to rid the universe of this place and this man, there was no point in waiting.

"Elyth," he said. She paused at the entry, glanced at him.

"We are radiant beings, you know," he said quietly. "Truly radiant. The heat from our bodies is visible to millions of forms of life across the galaxy. But, by some cruel twist, we can't see it. And we live with our heads down and eyes fixed on such inconsequential things. It's easy to forget that we glow."

She left without saying goodbye.

For the next half hour she ranged through the wilderness, looking for the nearest threadline. And though the closest point of natural threadlines she could find was a good two days' hike, she discovered that a wisp of Qel's newer one had stretched up to make contact not far from where they had camped. A threadline fashioned by *eth ammuin*. He had known all along where he had been leading her. But it was of no consequence now.

She moved to the point of contact, investigated it briefly. It was small, perhaps only thirty yards in diameter, but it had a vibrancy of youth that seemed to almost radiate out of the ground. Not the ancient stillness of deep-rooted mountains, rather the barely contained expectancy of an early bud on the last dying day of winter.

And she was the winter's breath, there to cut off the bloom in its infancy.

Elyth didn't know, couldn't know, what awaited her on the other side of this interaction. But that too was of no consequence. She settled herself as best as she could, and then began Revealing the Silent Gate.

"From the void all come," she began. *"To the void all return."*

It proceeded as it had before, but now, as she moved through the protocol, Elyth tuned herself intently to the planet's responses; and there within the fibers of Qel, intertwined with its lines, was something she could only interpret as echoes of *eth ammuin*'s voice. The harmonic resonances she had sensed before, she now heard not as background noise to be filtered out, but rather as a vital component of her work. In addition to describing the planet's collapse, she now added a new layer, one she had to improvise in response to what she heard, as though gently guiding a difficult conversation to a place it did not want to go. In the midst of it all, she recognized how, even now, in this last service to her House, *eth ammuin* had forced her into violating its principles and adopting his lessons.

But slowly, as she worked to dispel that which *eth ammuin* had spoken, she began to feel a shift she had not experienced in her initial attempt. An unwinding. Impossibility reverting back to reality.

And beneath her she felt the opening of infinity, beckoning to her. That call, she would have to resist as long as possible. Long enough to see the work completed. Then, maybe then, she would let it take her. It was that acceptance that made it possible to endure—the thought that she would turn and embrace that ecstatic end of self in a moment, but not just yet.

As each strand of *eth ammuin*'s dreadful knot pulled free, Elyth knew that she and Qel were each drawn one step closer to their demise, and though her emotions grew and churned and threatened to distract her, she held fast to the problem at hand, the one she had been sent to solve. And Elyth-Kyriel, Corrector of Courses, did that which she had been fashioned to do.

A voice called to her as she spoke. Distant, vague.

Eth ammuin, calling her name. A final, desperate attempt to stop her. But she was beyond his reach now.

A storm approached, some planetary response to the power gathering around her. But it, too, could not touch her.

Lightning flashed silently across the sky, seen not with her inner eye but out there, in the real world. The pure white light rolled across the land, its approaching wave of illumination slowed to her time-dilated senses, and she watched as the black-shadowed trees emerged from darkness, individual leaves and needles highlighted and brilliant in her expansive vision. The lightning continued its surge across the landscape, flowing toward her, and as it met her and passed over her, thunder chased behind it.

Eth ammuin's voice rode within it, urgent, frantic.

And from the in-between place where Elyth bridged the infinite and the finite, reality tore her away.

It was no lightning. It was a searchlight, and the thunder was the roar of a skimmer descending.

Dazed and weak from the interrupted protocol, Elyth scrambled to recover herself, to make a dash for cover, but before she had made it two steps, a horrible impact struck her at the base of her skull, driving her face-first into the dirt, blackness swallowing her.

Her vision returned sometime later, only long enough to see the Envoy crouching over her, flanked by dark silhouettes of avenging angels.

"Now that I know your value," he said, "I believe I have found a use for you."

TWENTY-TWO

Elyth's next view was much the same as the first; the Envoy, leaning over her. He was speaking, not to her, but apparently about her. As her senses returned, she gradually became aware of her surroundings. The vibrant sounds and smells of the forest had vanished, replaced now with a sterile, almost antiseptic atmosphere. They'd taken her somewhere, the compound, maybe. Her body felt strange, all the weight of gravity misplaced. It took a moment for her to realize she was sitting, not lying down, and that her head was tilted back. She tried to sit up, but someone restrained her with a hand atop the crown of her head.

"Ah ah, not yet," the Envoy said. She felt something click into place around her neck, and then the Envoy stepped back. "There we go. Just in time."

The hand on her head released her, and Elyth straightened up and glanced around. The room shifted and swirled, and a wave of nausea swept over her, enough to cause her to gag.

"Side effect of the nerve agent," the Envoy explained. "It should pass within an hour or two."

Elyth started to ask him where they'd brought her, but the instant her vocal cords started to engage, her throat and mouth seized up. It was a terrible sensation, not painful but akin to drowning, and she surely would have cried out if the paralysis hadn't prevented it. The instant she stopped trying to speak, however, the sensation ceased, and she was once more able to breathe regularly.

"Probably best just to keep quiet," said the Envoy, tapping with his fingernail the front plate of the collar they'd affixed to her throat. "I'm sure you understand."

She had no idea what the device was that they'd attached to her, but its purpose was obvious: to rob her of the power of speech.

The Envoy crouched in front of her, looked up into her eyes.

"Elyth-Kyriel," he said. "A true Advocate of the Voice. And here on Qel, no less. Deployed without authorization." He clicked his tongue, the same condescending noise he'd made when last they'd met. "I apologize for my previous disregard. I didn't realize at the time what a treasure trove you were going to prove to be." He patted her leg.

"Don't worry, though. I know this is unpleasant, but it's a temporary arrangement. We can't have you wandering off. Wouldn't want such a prize obliterated along with the garbage, after all. You just sit here, and try not to make trouble for anyone, and we'll get you home to the Vaunt all in good time. Sound good?"

Reflexively, Elyth started to respond, only to be subjected to the sickening, forced clenching of her throat.

"Sorry, that was meant to be a rhetorical question. I was just on my way out, but I'll see you again soon. In the meantime, perhaps you can sit and consider the harm you've brought upon the Ascendance. You and your House of gray witches, with your constant grasping, your incessant need to insert yourselves in every aspect of the hierarchy's operation. At least you'll have the privilege of watching it burn."

The Envoy stood and patted her on the head, before turning and starting toward the door.

Wherever they were, it was apparent it'd been some kind of official base of operations. Most of the workstations were clear now, but three Hezra officers were scrambling around gathering the last vital components. Evacuating.

"Sir," an officer said, intercepting the Envoy on his way out. He had an armload of terminals and other assorted devices, and was apparently trying to hand some of it off. But the Envoy didn't stop walking as he waved him away, annoyed.

"Just bring it all to the compound," he said. "I have to go make sure our friend finishes his work before we leave."

A vital piece of information. She wasn't at the compound, then. But she guessed *eth ammuin* was. And from the Envoy's words, it seemed they had no intention of taking *eth ammuin* along with them.

"What about her?" another officer asked, jerking a thumb toward Elyth.

"What about her? Load her up with everything else. And don't dawdle. Activation is at 1700 hours, and this is *not* one you want to cut close."

"Aye, sir," the officer said.

The Envoy disappeared from the room, but returned a few seconds later.

"Do not, under any circumstances, remove *that*," the Envoy said, pointing to Elyth and, more specifically, to the device clamped around her throat. After he'd said it, he looked around at the three officers sternly and then exited again.

A few moments after he'd gone one of the officers said, "I wish we'd left him in that hole," and the other two chuckled.

The officers resumed their work then, scurrying around the room and moving gear out. Elyth took stock of her situation, bleak as it was. She was bound at the wrists, hands cuffed close together, and a chain ran from the center of her binders down beneath the chair. When she tugged on them, she could feel the attachment point underneath her, somewhere near the back of the chair. They'd left her some slack, but when she tried to reach up to touch the device at her throat, her hands didn't even make it a quarter of the way up. Even if she leaned forward and hunched down, there was no way she'd be able to get her hands on it.

One of the officers walked over closer to her then, attracted no doubt by her gentle struggling against her bonds. He stopped several feet away.

"I'm sorry, Advocate," he said, and seemed sincere. "As soon as we're off planet, I think we'll be able to make you more comfortable."

He hovered for a moment, as though, having acknowledged her, he was now unsure how to extract himself. Elyth simply stared him down, making it clear that she needed neither his pity nor his comfort. After a moment, he withered under her gaze and returned to his work, careful not to make eye contact with her again.

Elyth sat for a time, still among the frenzied activity swirling around her. She had thought she had hit rock bottom before, that her mission had been a complete and utter failure. But she had survived now long enough to see just how much further down everything could still go. She didn't know precisely what the Hezra planned to do with her, but she had some clue, from what the Envoy had said to her. *An Advocate of the Voice, deployed without authorization.* And to his words, she added *captured by the Hezra, in the company of a disciple of Varen Fedic.* If their acquisition of some portion of the Deep Language hadn't been enough, her apprehension and the narrative they would craft around it would guarantee the fall of the First House, and the Hezra's ascension to dominance before the Grand Council. If they were successful in spinning the destruction of Qel as a necessary act of mercy, in positioning themselves as saviors of the people, the Hezra-Ka's reputation might even supersede that of the Council.

Tears welled then, and Elyth felt her throat clench with the coming

emotion. And though she felt that grief was the only appropriate response for the moment, she did not wish to give the Hezra officers the
pleasure of seeing her weep. She cleared her throat to chase the emotion away.

And a moment later, she realized the significance.

She cleared her throat again, allowed the vibration to linger in her
throat in a sort of trailing hum. And she was able to do it. She then attempted to whisper, and immediately her throat seized. Once she
ceased her attempt, though, the muscles relaxed once more. The device
prevented her from speaking, but it did not stop her from humming.

She thought then of *eth ammuin's* demonstration, humming his
tunes that evoked different responses in her, and then of his time singing over the broken branch of the frostoak. And she recalled, too, the
second attempt she'd made to overpower him, when she'd stunned his
vocal cords and he'd still manage to deflect her power away. She looked
down at the cuffs that held her fast; wrists bound, but hands free.

Elyth was no singer. But she knew the Deep Language intimately,
could feel the jagged edge or polished surface, the willow lightness or
stone weight of every syllable. And though she had never attempted
anything of the sort before, in fact had been forbidden from doing so,
none of that mattered now. Very little seemed to. But as long as she
drew breath, she would not accept defeat.

In her mind, she began to form a new expression. She focused on
the act she'd seen *eth ammuin* perform, when he stomped his foot and
dissolved the ground beneath it, drew up the memory of it and rolled it
over, reimagining it again and again until the images were so vivid that
they began to evoke the same response within her as the first time it'd
occurred. And from that response, she began to extract a description.
She didn't need the earth to collapse, though. She needed only a tiny
fraction of that power, tightly focused.

The Deep Language rose in her mind, her fluency in it making it easy to find a new, exact phrasing that, though she'd never heard it used, promised the result she was after. But now, instead of speaking it, she closed her eyes, held the phrase in her mind, and *felt* it. Felt the emotions it ignited, the images it conjured. She inhaled. And then she let her hands form the signs that seemed best to match what she felt and along with it, she hummed a brief tune, in long, steady intervals.

When she was done she opened her eyes.

And found nothing had changed.

She was still bound, still trapped. Her body felt no different. There'd been no release of power. The only difference was that one of the officers had stopped nearby and was staring at her.

They locked eyes for a moment.

And then the collar around her neck cracked and fell free.

They both watched as it dropped and clattered to the floor, stared at it, and both came to the same realization at the same time.

"Hey!" the officer said, taking a step forward.

Elyth stood in a heartbeat, straddled the chair and whipped her hands up, slinging the chair from between her legs and catching the officer with it full in the face. He cried out and crashed onto his back; Elyth was on him in the next moment, her shin across his neck, pinning him to the ground. He flailed weakly, but soon lapsed into unconsciousness.

The other two officers rushed in and froze, just as their friend went limp beneath her. Elyth held up her hands.

"Unlock these," she said. One of the officers just stood there, staring at her, but the other one, the one who had apologized to her earlier, fumbled around for a moment and then approached her like a man offering raw meat to a wolf.

"Please don't . . ." he said, but he didn't finish the sentence. As he deactivated the cuffs and they fell from her wrists he skittered back two steps, and Elyth realized the full power of the legends of the First

House. These men were all young Hezra officers, not the hardened field operatives she'd encountered before. Judging by the fear in their eyes, they had no idea what she was truly capable of, and their imaginations were rapidly generating plenty of images. For all they knew, she might speak a single word and splatter them across the walls.

"You," she said, pointing to the officer still frozen by the door. "Come here."

He did as he was told. In a few moments she had bound the two conscious officers together, one cuff on each, and looped the attached chain through the metal belt buckle of the third officer. He groaned and stirred as she secured the attachment point of the chain back to the cuffs, leaving the three in an uncomfortable but not unmanageable human knot. If they were clever enough, they'd be able to free themselves with a few minutes of work. But she had no intention of waiting around to see if they could pull it off.

She scanned the room and saw her pack lying on a desk nearby. They'd been rifling through her things, though she'd either caught them early in the process or they'd stopped after a cursory look. She hurriedly shoved everything back into the pack, slung it over her shoulder, and headed for the door.

Elyth paused there, before leaving, and looked at the three officers tangled together.

"Don't panic, and you'll figure it out," she said. "But if you follow me, or try to call for help, I'll tell the planet to swallow you."

One of the officers went pale; the one who had made the comment about wishing they hadn't pulled the Envoy out of the hole. She didn't mind letting him believe she'd been the one to do that.

She stepped out of the room into a corridor and took quick, light steps toward the short staircase at the end; at the top, the door was open and daylight streamed in. When she reached the top of the stairs she paused and poked her head out to scan for trouble. They were in a se-

cluded area, a relatively small clearing surrounded by trees; the smell
and feel of the air reminded her strongly of Hok's cabin. Back on the
preserve, then. About twenty yards away sat a Hezra ship, similar to
her old craft, though larger—the big brother to her former vessel.
Spaceflight capable. And, more important, authorized to pass through
the blockade.

There didn't appear to be anyone else around. She dug her override
device out of her pack and made a dash for the craft. By the time she
reached the front hatch, the device had already deactivated the security
measures. The vessel was a two-seat affair; once the hatch opened, she
slung her gear into the co-pilot's seat and hopped in. She'd forgotten to
close the top of her pack, and a number of her belongings tumbled out,
but she paid no heed.

The Envoy had said activation was planned for 1700 hours; the ship
console showed it was not quite 1300 hours by Hezra reckoning. Plenty
of time. But she wasn't waiting around for those officers to test her on
her promise.

The familiar controls made it easy to prep the drives and prepare
for launch. She knew the Hezra containment protocols. As long as she
didn't make a headlong attempt to run the blockade, normal communications would be established; her familiarity with the protocol combined with the vessel's credentials would be enough to allow her to pass
through the line.

Elyth plotted a course that would take her on a high-altitude trajectory, looping through suborbital flight. The ship finished its initial ascent
and lurched forward. And as the ship gained altitude, leaving the little
clearing behind, the final reality sank in. She was escaping with her life
intact and nothing else. She wondered how the Paragon would react to
her return home; an abject failure having betrayed her oaths, Qel's destruction completed by the worst possible method, and First House diminished for having sent her at all. Would they even receive her?

And she thought too of how far she had fallen in her own eyes. Once on Revik, in what seemed a lifetime ago, Elyth had passed judgment on a woman for embracing a poisoned delusion, for confusing righteousness with vengeance, for envisioning herself as holy arbiter of right and wrong. She saw now that she had been no different.

At least her escape would deprive the Hezra of whatever they had intended for her—scapegoat or bargaining chip. That was one small victory, perhaps.

The ship rocked backward, settling into its trajectory, and at last taking her away from that accursed planet. Elyth started setting up the communication channels, waiting to receive the inevitable challenge, and had to lean over to the co-pilot's seat to activate one of the systems. As she did, she caught sight of the scattered belongings that had spilled out of her pack. There, perched on the edge of the co-pilot's seat, was the frostoak cutting she had taken from the Paragon's garden. Dry, bent, partially broken.

She picked up the little branch and sat back in her seat, contemplating it. So much had changed since the day she'd cut it. Everything. She'd come to Qel full of fire and purpose. And now she was leaving, broken, depleted, cut off from her source. Just like the branch. She ran her finger along the cutting, felt the splayed fibers where it had bent, hard and sharp now with the loss of moisture. A dead reminder of what once had been.

But then she noticed. There, at one end, the tiniest swelling that hadn't been there before. The first sign, impossibly, of growth.

She stared at that change, momentarily frozen, unable to look away or to release the cutting.

Her mind snapped then to *eth ammuin*, and the little song he had sung over it. All the things he had told her, and warned her about, and hoped for her. It couldn't be true.

And yet.

Elyth dug her thumbnail into the branch, felt its softness, and when she drew her nail away, she saw the residue there: tender fibers, sap. New life.

A change effected by *eth ammuin*'s song.

He had made a point of demonstrating it, of performing in front of her very eyes, knowing that the effect would take time to manifest. Planting the seed of a lesson he had hoped would blossom in her mind. And here, now, finally, it did.

The image of him bent over the branch burned brightly in her mind and conjured another, different, and yet suddenly the same.

The Paragon. Speaking over her.

Guided by the True Star.

And in a flash, she recognized it now for what it was. No title of honor, no declaration of deep and abiding faith. It was a binding phrase, meant to drive her to her purpose, and to her end.

Now she saw what he had longed for her to see; that her will had not been wholly her own, that her true foundation had not run as deeply as she had imagined. And instead of forcing the realization upon her, he had waited patiently for her to discover it within herself. Waited beyond the point of all hope, kept silent even in the despair of his apparent failure.

And now, he was at the compound somewhere, undoubtedly bound and gagged, as she had been.

Chained.

Escaping with her life alone would mean nothing. Elyth couldn't prevent the sundering of Qel, nor could she repair the damage to the Ascendance. But she could, perhaps, here in her last few hours, break one last chain.

Watcher Greets the Storm. However inconsequential her part, she would play it.

Elyth placed the cutting on the console and entered new coordinates. The ship responded, rolled in a wide bank, and began descending. She didn't have far to travel.

A few minutes later she hopped out of the craft and strode to the structure. Hok's cabin. She knocked on the door, and, when she got no response, walked around it peering in the windows. From what she could see, all was dark.

But when she circled back around, a man was standing there in a strider, staring at the ship.

Kitu.

"Eliya," he said, startled when he saw her. "What are you doing here?"

Her response was simple.

"I need your help."

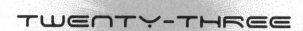

TWENTY-THREE

Elyth, decked out in her infiltration gear, waited outside the perimeter, south of the compound. The main gates were unmanned, and several officers were scrambling around in the open. Much of the facility had already been evacuated, but those who remained behind were of the worst possible sort. A contingent of soldiers from 3 Recon was stationed on the premises, keeping careful watch while others hurried to load the three remaining ships on the grounds.

She'd seen no sign of *eth ammuin* or the Envoy, but she intuited that they were both still there, somewhere. Her hope had been to slip into the compound undetected and then have Hok's crew cause a distraction long enough for her to escape with *eth ammuin*. Two strider frames lay concealed farther down the slope, on the eastern side of the compound. And the Hezra ship she'd stolen lay concealed in a gully, even farther down the mountain, their final escape vessel.

But, knowing how active the compound was likely to be, she hadn't counted solely on her ability to sneak in. They had a backup plan, if it should prove necessary.

Unfortunately, it was looking necessary.

For their part, Hok and Kitu had heard nothing about the blockade.

But they had believed the urgency of her need, and though she hadn't told them everything, she had told them enough. They'd been ready and willing to do whatever they could to help free *eth ammuin*, as had a few of the friends they'd been able to gather.

One of the Hezra vessels lifted off just before 1600 hours, and the activity around the compound lessened. But the alertness of the troopers only increased. From what she could tell, all that remained within the perimeter was the soldiers of 3 Recon, the Envoy, and *eth ammuin*. The final rearguard waiting until the last possible moment to guarantee that *eth ammuin* didn't escape.

They were going to have to go with the backup plan.

She opened a channel with Hok.

"Hok," she said. "Plan B."

"Yeah," he said. "I figured."

"You guys all set?"

"All set."

"Don't be brave," she said.

"Not planning on it."

She waited for the signal. After two minutes had passed she started to get worried that maybe something had gone wrong. But shortly after it kicked off.

It began with a low-pitched hum, coming from high on the ridge northwest of the compound. A few of the soldiers glanced in its direction, but at first no one reacted with any sort of concern. As the sound grew into a buzzing growl, though, others began to turn to face it, searching for its source.

They didn't have to wait long. A dark streak exploded from the trees, followed closely by a second. Hok's hunting drones, pushed to their maximum limit of speed. One trooper managed to get his rifle shouldered, but before he could fire, both drones angled sharply downward, aimed for the fences. They plowed through the outermost, rending a gaping hole through it before impacting the second. Both erupted, sending a shotgun blast of fire and debris through the innermost fence.

The guards moved quickly to cover the area, and while they were still in motion, a great commotion arose from the woods, as though some herd of massive beasts were charging through. That proved not to be too far from the truth.

Four striders burst from the tree line, racing flat out toward the western fence. The soldiers of 3 Recon reacted immediately, almost as quickly as if they'd been expecting it. They responded with controlled fire as they moved to cover, hammering the rapidly approaching frames with disciplined shots. Some of the troopers advanced to intercept the threat, while others collapsed back, toward one of the buildings on the northwestern corner of the compound.

The building where *eth ammuin* must have been.

Like the drones before them, the striders smashed through the outer fence and into the middle one. Two became entangled there, but two others made it all the way to the innermost fence before the damage inflicted by the fences and the gunfire brought them down.

Elyth had known about the drones, but hadn't expected the striders, and she couldn't help but wonder which of *eth ammuin's* followers had just so recklessly given their lives to rescue him. One of the frames twitched sporadically, suspended and twisted helplessly in the ruins of the fence, its arms splayed out like a hide drying in the sun.

And she saw that it was empty.

They'd tethered the frames to someone else, on the opposite side of the compound.

But Elyth didn't have time to appreciate the ingenuity.

Gunfire erupted from the tree line all at once, perpendicular to her line of sight to the compound—Hok and his friends assaulting from the west.

The echoing roar ripped across the compound and then fell silent as suddenly as it had begun. Moments later more shots came in from farther north than the initial volley. From her vantage, Elyth could see the rounds pinging off buildings and kicking up dirt. Not a single one found its way to a human. The goal was to draw as many of them out as possible. She just hoped that none of the soldiers under fire could tell that Hok and his people weren't actually trying to kill them. At least not yet.

A third set of gunshots started up from closer to Elyth's position, and the soldiers of 3 Recon scrambled to adjust. It was starting to appear that the whole upper portion of the mountain was full of assailants.

But Elyth knew it was only a handful of people that Hok and his friends had been able to pull together. Though she couldn't see them, she could nevertheless picture them dashing like hounds through the forest in their striders, moving from position to position, pausing only long enough to fire a few harmless rounds before continuing on again.

All Elyth needed now was for the soldiers of 3 Recon to live up to their name. They were not the sort to sit and allow themselves to be shot at for long. And sure enough, once they'd gotten themselves positioned and organized, 3 Recon began their counterattack.

This was the most terrifying part for Elyth; the soldiers' initial rush into their attackers. Hok and his people might not have been trying to kill anyone, but they could expect no such courtesy from the hardened veterans of 3 Recon. The Fear-Eaters unleashed a coordinated volley and pushed out from the compound, assaulting uphill to meet their attackers head-on. Elyth could only hope that Hok and his friends could respond quickly enough, and fall back before they suffered any casualties. She didn't have time to wait and see, though.

She launched from her hiding place then and closed the distance to the nearest unguarded gate.

The troopers were no fools, of course. They hadn't left the place

completely unsecured, and Elyth had to weave among the many structures of the compound to avoid moving through open areas. She
dodged from point to point, sporadic incoming rounds continuing to
ping and snap around her. But as she moved farther into the compound,
the sounds of combat moved farther west, higher up on the mountain,
as her time grew ever shorter.

The soldiers might hold position outside the compound for a time,
until they were confident they had repelled the assault. But they would
collapse back soon enough. If Elyth didn't have *eth ammuin* safely out
before they returned, they weren't likely to get out at all.

The building that the remaining soldiers were guarding was another two-story structure, similar to *eth ammuin*'s residence, though
somewhat larger, and constructed next to a second, lower building.

As she closed in, Elyth saw that two guards had been posted at each
of the two entrances to the structure, and both pairs were holding their
positions. Though their attention was still focused on the conflict outside the perimeter, there didn't seem to be any good approach to either
entrance where they wouldn't see her coming. Even at her peak, taking
on two troopers from 3 Recon would have been a tall order, and she was
far from top form.

A long balcony ran along the second floor; her best chance was to
bypass the guards from the roof of the neighboring building.

Elyth circled around and clambered up the back side of the lower
building and crept to the front edge. The distance was right at the limit
of what she could do without a running start, maybe a little farther. But
she didn't have time to evaluate it more. She heard the whine and roar
of one of the ships in the compound; a few moments later it lifted off
and passed low, headed in the same direction that the soldiers had gone.

The two guards looked up to watch it go, drawing their attention
away from her perch. Elyth took that moment to make the leap; she
launched across the gap, stepping lightly on the rail of the balcony to

slow her descent, rolled when she landed. She remained still, crouched low, hoping that the noise from the low-flying craft had masked the sound, and listening.

Down below, the guards spoke.

"Whoever they are, they're in for it now," one of the soldiers said.

"Can't blame 'em, really," the other one answered. "I'd rather go out fighting, too."

"You think they know what's coming?"

"Gotta assume so. Probably trying to get to our ships."

"Well, I guess it worked then. Now one's going to them."

The door to the balcony was locked. Elyth verified there was no one on the other side of it, and then made short work of the lock and slipped in. Once inside, she had an uncanny feeling of familiarity; after a moment, she realized that the floor plan of the structure was almost identical to *eth ammuin's*, only larger. From somewhere down below, she could hear the muted tones of a deep voice.

Elyth took her stun baton from her belt and silently deployed it with a flick of her wrist. She crept through the upper hall, listening, scanning, straining her senses, weapon at the ready; the only sound inside the building was the voice, but that didn't mean one of the stone soldiers of 3 Recon wasn't standing post around the next corner, or the next.

But as she prowled silently through the structure and down the stairs to the first floor, she gained confidence with each step that whoever might be in the building, and whatever number of them, she would find them all in the room with the speaker. She came upon another set of stairs, leading down yet again. A third floor, beneath the surface. Elyth followed those, too, toward the growing sound of the voice. And as she reached the bottom of the staircase, she could hear enough to recognize the speaker. It was the Envoy, his unmistakable baritone, with its edge of superiority.

There was a room at the end of the hall, farthest from the stairwell; its door was partially open, and the Envoy's words emanated from within it.

Elyth stole down the corridor, toward that voice.

"—just kept your end of the bargain, none of this would have happened," he was saying. "But it is as it is. I don't hold it against you, I suppose. But the consequences, I'm afraid, can't be avoided. We are a people of our word, after all."

Elyth crouched low outside the door and peeked into the room. The Envoy was there, standing over *eth ammuin*, who was lying on his back on the floor. They were the only two in the room.

Elyth stood then, removed the mask from her infiltration suit, and pushed the door open with the tip of her baton. The Envoy turned at the motion, clearly expecting it to be one of his men reporting in. She left just enough time for his eyes to go wide with recognition.

And then with the baton crumpled him to the floor.

He fell heavily in a jumbled heap, like a marionette whose strings had been cut, next to *eth ammuin*; his head made a dull thunking sound when it hit the ground, one that would have been distressing had Elyth not had such disdain for the man. There was no time to stand over him and gloat.

Eth ammuin looked up at her with wide eyes, part shock, part alarm. Was there any joy there?

The treatment they'd given her was mild compared to what they'd subjected him to. A device similar to the collar they'd fitted her with was around his neck, but his had a secondary plate that cupped his lower jaw and covered his mouth. And she saw why he yet remained lying on the floor, even now that the Envoy had been handled. They'd wrapped thin chains around his arms, chest, and legs, and then anchored them taut to the floor. His hands were pinned flat against his sides.

This she hadn't anticipated. Bound, yes. Chained to the floor, no. They really hadn't been taking any chances.

On a whim, she searched the unconscious body of the Envoy, hoping to find some key, but found nothing useful on him. She crouched by *eth ammuin* then and lifted his head, searched the device for its release mechanism. It took a few moments, but once she unclasped the upper portion, the rest of it came free.

"I thought you were dead," *eth ammuin* said.

"Might still be right," she answered. "How do we get you out of here?"

He shook his head.

"You'll have to do it," he answered.

Elyth felt like she'd been hearing that a lot lately. There was no tool she could find, no protocol she could think of for such a situation. Despite having freed herself with an improvised technique, she wasn't confident she could do it again. Had it been pure luck? Or had the rest of the effect merely not yet manifested?

"I hope I don't kill you," she said.

"Ah, at last, a kind word. Don't worry, I trust you."

"Then you're still a fool."

Elyth inhaled, focused on the anchor next to his head.

"Maybe try the one by my feet, though," he offered.

She scowled at him, but shifted her concentration to one of the other anchors, and reset herself. An image formed in her mind; a phrase bubbled up almost unbidden, and without considering it further, she spoke.

"A parched desert, brittle earth, beaten by the sun."

A tiny jolt passed through her, warm and radiant, like the sun she'd imagined. But the anchor didn't split as she had intended. Instead, the concrete beneath it did, with a little pop that sent dust and shards spitting into the air.

Close enough.

"That wasn't part of me, was it?" *eth ammuin* asked, but Elyth didn't reply. She was too busy working the chain free and starting to unwind it. As she did, Hok came through the comms channel.

"Eliya, you out?"

"Still working," she answered.

"You gotta go, girl. They're headed back your way."

"Copy."

The moment she got some slack into the chains, *eth ammuin* started wriggling around, sloughing off the coils as quickly as he could. He was smiling, almost giddy with excitement, like this was all some big game.

"Who're you talking to?" he asked.

"Hok."

"Hok's out there? How wonderful."

"I don't think you understand what's going on," Elyth said. "We're still much more likely to die than we are to make it out of here."

"That's okay," he said brightly. "This is already way better than what I'd been expecting."

Soon enough they had him free. All that remained was to escape the perimeter while it was crawling with the most seasoned warriors the Hezra had in service, and to reach the gully where they'd concealed the ship, before they ran out of time and the entire world disintegrated under their feet.

"You were right," *eth ammuin* said. "They're activating the Contingency."

"Why do you think I'm here?"

"I figured it was to punch that guy," he said, pointing to the Envoy.

Elyth quickly explained the rest of the situation, and the plan of escape.

"That's a terrible plan," *eth ammuin* said.

"I didn't have a lot of time to prepare it. This is your territory. What's the best way to get out?"

"Oh, you know me," he said. "I've always preferred the front door."

"Guarded. You're *sure* you don't have some secret tunnels in here or something?"

"If I do, they're too secret for me to know about. Let's go see how guarded."

Before she could stop him, he was on his way up the stairs. Elyth followed him up, half concerned, half impressed with how awake and alive he was in the chaos of the circumstances. Chaos seemed to suit him.

She was glad to see, however, that as he approached the front entrance, he slowed and became more cautious. There was a window several feet to one side. He slipped to the floor underneath it and then raised his head just enough to get a look out. He nodded to himself and then slid back over to where she was. Outside, the gunfire had ceased. How long it would take for the other troops to return Elyth didn't know. But maybe those who had stayed behind would be beginning to relax.

Eth ammuin stepped close to her and whispered.

"Just two sentries. We make a short run straight, then behind the building directly across from us. We should have enough cover to make it to the east gate."

"And what's past the gate?"

"A little, shallow bluff. Gentle slope. We can slide down it."

"How far?"

"To the bottom. Come on."

He took her by the arm and pulled her a few steps back from the front door.

"What are you doing?" she asked.

"I'm going to open it," he said. "When I do, run."

"What do you mean you're going to open it?"

He answered by doing it. He called out in three successive rising tones and then clapped his hands together.

And the sound of his hands striking together was a thunderclap; the entire front of the building evaporated in the blast.

He was off an instant later, charging through the gaping hole, neither waiting nor looking behind him for Elyth. It took her only a second to recover from the shock, and then she was chasing after him, running flat out past the guards who lay sprawled and dazed. As she crossed the open ground to the building ahead, Elyth expected with each step to be struck by fire from behind.

But she made it, dashed around behind the structure; *eth ammuin* was already at the far corner, half crouched.

"What're you waiting for?" she called as she caught up.

"Ehhh," he answered, waving his hand vaguely in front of him.

Elyth drew up behind him, peeked over top, around the corner.

Too late. The first of the 3 Recon soldiers had returned and were swiftly fanning out. Some advanced through the compound. Others moved to encircle it. *Eth ammuin*'s dramatic exit had alerted them that their work wasn't done.

Elyth snapped her stun baton open.

"Follow me," she said.

"Anywhere," he answered.

They maneuvered from structure to structure, slinking, darting, a pair of foxes amid a pack of hounds. Every minute they spent moving from the interior toward the exterior, more soldiers filtered in, seemingly from every angle. But somehow Elyth led them safely through.

When they reached the last line of buildings, they paused to evaluate the final stretch. Three small outbuildings ran along the eastern side of the compound. Beyond those buildings, though, lay no cover; thirty yards of open ground led to the gate. Farther down, the wide landing zone ran for fifty yards, with only one remaining Hezra ship breaking up their line of sight.

They were going to have to make a run for it.

"Home stretch," Elyth said. "You ready?"

"Let's do it," *eth ammuin* said.

They crept along the first building, reached the second.

And just as they were crossing to the third, soldiers rounded the opposite corner.

Three of them.

The lead soldier snapped her weapon to her shoulder, taking a bead on *eth ammuin*.

Elyth reacted.

She dove forward, rolled, came up under the barrel of the rifle, slapped it skyward just as it fired. With a palm strike, she snapped the soldier's head back, and in the next instant, hooked her and threw her into the man on her right. As the two collapsed together, the third trooper tried to backpedal as he raised his rifle. Elyth whipped around and launched her baton; it caught him full in the face, plunging him backward to the ground.

Elyth turned back to the tangled pair just as the woman was beginning to gain her feet, rifle in hand; Elyth snatched the weapon and delivered a knee to the side of the trooper's head, dropping her once more, unconscious. The other soldier was still on his back, scrambling to recover his rifle. Elyth brought the butt of his partner's weapon crashing down on the bridge of his nose.

And only she remained.

She turned to look at *eth ammuin* behind her. He just stood, staring, mouth open.

"You okay?" she asked.

He looked at the soldiers around her feet.

"Grief!" she called. "Are you hit?"

His eyes came back up to hers.

"I had no idea," he said.

"Well, get one," she answered. "We're in trouble."

Elyth tossed the rifle. She wasn't about to try to outshoot 3 Recon. But she recovered her baton, took cover by the corner of the building, quickly peeked out and back.

As she expected, across the compound troopers were reacting to the single shot and moving toward them. And, in her brief glimpse, she saw others securing the landing pad. Cutting them off from the remaining ship.

The gate was too far away. But if the soldiers thought they wanted the ship . . .

Elyth looked to the fence behind the building; the closest point, about twenty yards away.

"What do you want me to do?" *eth ammuin* asked.

"Anything to keep them from getting to us while I get us through the fence."

"Okay," he said.

Elyth risked another quick peek; a line of troops advanced cautiously, weapons up. And as she ducked back into cover, a shot fired; the round bit a chunk out of the corner of the building where her head had been a moment before.

3 Recon wasn't interested in capture this time.

Eth ammuin stepped back from the building a few steps, head raised, palms up, as though feeling the first drops of rain.

Elyth turned her focus toward the fence, pictured the three barriers. Began forming a concept in her mind, the image of a massive boulder, bulldozing through.

Behind her, *eth ammuin* raised his voice. Within moments, it took on an unearthly quality, like the sound of rushing water, but composed of many voices. And then Elyth realized she was hearing a roar coming from above, as though a ship were plummeting to the earth.

Concentration broken, words lost, she looked up. But there was nothing, nothing but the terrible howl in the clear sky.

And then it struck.

A microburst, or a fist from heaven, smashed into the ground and radiated outward, throwing the soldiers back and scouring the compound. The building shielded the two of them, but the force of the wind ripped a portion of the roof off and threw it toward the fence.

Elyth didn't think. She just spoke.

"Kingfisher pierces the water."

The debris compressed and accelerated, and its natural tumble became a straight-line trajectory that tore through the fences.

They took off together then, *eth ammuin* ahead of her as they raced across the open ground, through the shredded barricades, sprinting for the bluff. She caught up to him just as he reached the edge.

They leapt together.

And Elyth realized that the bluff was neither little nor shallow. It wasn't quite a cliff, but had she not been blindly following *eth ammuin*, she would never have launched herself out over it.

She twisted, threw her weight back to align with the slope, and impacted twelve or fifteen feet down. In the next moment she was half sliding, half tumbling down the bluff, everything streaking past her, and her only thought was to try and get some sort of control so she didn't break her neck when she hit the ground. And then, a few seconds later, she was plunging through the brush and brambles some sixty feet below. She managed to get her feet around in front of her just before impact, rolled with it, and was up in an instant. *Eth ammuin* crashed heavily behind her a moment later and lay still.

"That slope is *not* gentle!" she called.

He stirred, got up on his hands and knees.

"Come on, we've got to keep moving," she said. He managed to get to his feet, but stayed doubled over, shaking. She'd seen how much it had taken out of him when he'd caused the earth to collapse; she wondered how badly it had hurt him to do whatever it was he had just done. "Grief? Can you move?"

He looked up at her then, grinning, and she realized he was laughing silently. She almost punched him.

"I wonder if we're facing Alonesse right now," he said. She couldn't make sense of the comment, though his expression indicated that he clearly expected her to. "You know, cargo, momentum, all that. You threatened to throw me off a cliff once, remember?"

"Your timing needs work," she said. "We've still got ground to cover."

Eth ammuin looked up the steep bank.

"I don't think they'll follow us."

"Maybe not that way. Come on."

Elyth led him off at a jog then, getting her bearings on the move. Soon enough, she figured out where they were in relation to the hidden striders, and found her way to the frames. They had just finished strapping in when she heard the low growl of a ship closing in.

"Move!" she barked, and she was off, charging down the slope, hoping they could reach their own ship before they were spotted. The trees thinned out, and Elyth knew if the Hezra vessel caught sight of them, they'd be easy targets.

Eth ammuin kept pace with her, the engine noise of the ship like a rockslide following them down the mountain. From the oscillating sound of the vessel, she could tell the pilot was making fast, sweeping arcs, crisscrossing their general trail. Searching. A quarter mile from the gully, they still hadn't seen it yet; but the peak of the sound kept growing louder with each pass. The ship was gaining on them.

Elyth knew if they could just reach the cover of the gully, they could lie low until the ship had passed by. But she had to divert their course to skirt around a clearing. And those few minutes proved more precious than she could have known.

Just as the smooth ridge of the gully appeared ahead of them, so did the vessel. It streaked in from their right, passing just above the tree line, and continued past.

Elyth skidded to a halt, dodged to the nearest tree, and motioned for *eth ammuin* to do the same. They hardly had any cover. If the ship wheeled back around, there wasn't anything she'd be able to do about it.

"Grief," she said. "If it turns, bring it down."

He nodded.

The ship leveled off, held a line moving away from them, pitched slightly upward to gain altitude. Headed back to the compound, it seemed. She hoped.

But then two bright puffs appeared on either side of the vessel, and Elyth understood.

Rockets.

She saw them tumble away from the ship, before they sparked, stabilized, and streaked toward them.

Elyth knew the power of those weapons. Knew they could not outrun them, or survive their blast.

And in the final second before their impact, the moment of her death, so close to escape, raw emotion erupted in a cry of her soul.

And with it, the earth of Qel rose up before her like a great wave.

The explosion disintegrated the earthen wall; Elyth catapulted and somersaulted in the rush of heat and noise and debris.

Dazed, deafened, she swam her arms, tried to make sense of the world. She was on her back, staring up at the sky. The sky, where the ship was.

She raised her head, saw the ship slowing, banking. Turning back. Making another pass.

Elyth was too disoriented, too detached. She wouldn't be able to stop it this time.

It fired again.

But this time its rockets went off course, passed over, and impacted harmlessly down in the gully. In the roar of the explosion, Elyth realized a voice had been calling out. *Eth ammuin.*

The ship banked again.

But no. Not banking. Part of it was falling away. Sheared through the middle in a jagged line. For the briefest of moments Elyth could see the interior of the cockpit just before it became a fireball in the sky.

Carefully, she sat up. And found that she couldn't move her legs, even with the power of the strider frame. It took a few seconds for her to realize it was the frame, not her, that had been damaged. She unbuckled herself, slid out of the harness.

Eth ammuin sat on his knees, already out of his strider, about fifteen feet away. A quick scan made it obvious why he was out of the frame. It lay behind him, vomiting black smoke and sparking with dull flame.

Wordlessly, she helped him to his feet, and together they crossed the remaining stretch of ground to the gully. And when they crested the ridge, Elyth realized that the rockets she'd thought were errant had in fact found their target.

Their concealed ship.

Now only cratered earth and twisted, burning debris remained where their means of escape had been moments before.

There would be no escape for them now.

TWENTY-FOUR

Elyth's heart frosted. She hadn't had much hope, really. But if she had been meant to suffer defeat, she wished that they had done so back at the compound, instead of here, now, when escape had almost dared to seem possible.

"I don't guess that was part of the plan?" *eth ammuin* said.

Elyth didn't acknowledge him.

"Hok," she said into her communicator. "Hok, are you all right?"

Seconds ticked by with nothing but silence from the other end.

"Hok."

Still nothing.

Eth ammuin stepped closer to her, his face serious beneath a mask of dirt and char, traced with flecks of blood. Gone was his giddy delight at the escape, replaced by the somber reality of their situation, and concern for their mutual friend.

"Hok, tell me you're out there," she said.

"Yeah, Eliya," Hok said finally. "Yeah, we're all fine. Little scraped up, no big deal. You make it?"

"Sort of," she said. "Where are you now?"

"Running over the top of the mountain. We peeled off when we saw the ship coming, and we're putting some distance between us and them, just in case."

"They got our ship, Hok," she said.

There was a pause.

"You need us to come get you?" he said a moment later.

"No, it's fine, you go on and get clear. There might be more of them still running around out here. No point in risking it."

"You sure?"

"I'm sure."

"Okay," he said. "Stay on comms."

"Will do. Thanks, Hok. And thank your crew for me. You did it. You got him out."

"All right," he answered. "But don't make it a goodbye just yet."

"Okay," Elyth said. "We'll find you later, if we can."

"When you can," Hok said.

She signed off and looked back at *eth ammuin* then, processing.

"He doesn't know?" he asked.

Elyth shook her head.

"I just told them if we got you out, they'd have to leave the mountain," she said. "Thought I'd save the hard conversation for when we were all back on the ship."

Eth ammuin nodded.

"Some truths are better left unspoken," he said. "His end will come swiftly, unlooked for, like a man gone in his sleep. A gentler death than ours, at least."

"More sudden, maybe," Elyth said. "Don't know about gentle."

She turned and walked away from the burning gully, back up the slope through the trees. Back to the clearing they'd passed.

"You came back," *eth ammuin* said, following behind her.

"You were right," she answered over her shoulder.

"I . . . was?"

"Yeah," she said. "I wanted to punch that guy."

She reached the clearing and walked out into it. She didn't know what would become of the sky, once the Contingency began. But she wanted to look up into it, to see clearly whatever it was that doom looked like.

"Think they'll send that other ship after us?" she asked, glancing back at *eth ammuin*.

Eth ammuin sat down behind her by the edge of the clearing, and leaned back against a tree. He stretched his legs out in front of him, ankles crossed, just as he had a couple of days before when she'd first taken him from the compound. Barely two days ago. A lifetime ago.

He shook his head.

"They know I don't have anywhere to go."

"I wonder if we could have made it to that one," she said. "If we had run for it, instead of jumping off a cliff."

"Maybe," he said. "They usually keep it manned, in case I try to make a run for it. But maybe."

"I don't suppose you can sing us up another one?"

He chuckled.

"Why'd you come back, Elyth?"

"I already told you."

"You once told me that if it ever came down to escaping together or alone, you wouldn't hesitate to leave me behind. But if you had a ship capable of taking us away from here, I assume you could have escaped without me. And yet, here we are."

"I guess I got confused."

"About what?"

"About what was, and what could be."

They sat together quietly for a few moments, the forest eerily silent behind and around them. Nature always seemed to have a way of knowing what was coming.

"Maybe we still have some time," Elyth said.

But as she was saying it, she knew it was too late. She could feel it, like static building in the air before a lightning strike; the hair on her arms and back of her neck stood straight. It was happening now, in that moment, miles above the surface of Qel. In her mind's eye, she could see that gathering power, the great and terrible accumulation of energy, as the Hezra's Herald-class ships aligned and trained their weapons on a single focal point.

"Guess not," *eth ammuin* said.

She didn't know how long they had. Ten minutes? Sixty? It didn't seem to matter now. In fact, very little did. A strange sort of peace settled over her then, an acceptance of her fate and, perhaps, relief that she would not have to witness whatever would follow. Her failure to put Qel down seemed small in that moment; the political games of the Hezra, the Grand Council, and even her once-beloved First House seemed smaller still.

Behind her, *eth ammuin* got to his feet, wiped his hands on his pants, and then walked closer to her.

"I'm going to try something," he said, reaching down to her. "Would you help me?"

"I'm not much of a dancer," she said. And he smiled at that, broad and genuine.

"That's okay. I can teach you."

She allowed him to help her up, and then followed him farther out into the clearing. He looked up into the late-afternoon sky; it was already deepening its blue, and large clouds had gathered, obscuring the sun. Elyth looked up too.

"You're going to try to stop it," she said.

He shrugged.

"Maybe I can turn it," he said after a moment. "If I can focus on that, and that alone. But I won't be able to hold the planet together. It's too much, too many pieces, too many connections. I can't keep it all together in my mind."

She chuckled. It never would have occurred to her to try to resist the awful power of the Contingency. But keeping track of the intricate network of relationships that made a planet what it was? That was certainly something she could do.

"Okay," she said. "I'll hold the planet together, you prevent the cosmic blast of annihilation from hitting us. Maybe it'll be easier than it sounds."

"Sounds like a plan."

"You don't seem like much of a planner."

"That's why I have you."

Somewhere in the heavens, the terrible energy continued to grow, like a black hole tearing a galaxy apart. And though she didn't know what she was doing, or really even why, Elyth began to work through the many steps of Revealing the Silent Gate. But now, instead of describing the collapse and death of all the vital currents that sustained Qel, she spoke of its life, and its strengths, its resilience, its unique pathways and history. She told the planet of its origin, and how against impossible odds it had emerged from darkness to become something marvelous and wonderful to behold. She spoke of the life it had embraced on its surface and within itself.

And as she spoke these things, images began to flood her mind, images of her time on the world. Hok, and his good-hearted crew of roughnecks; the delicate petals of faerie-queen, growing in the mountains; the woman who had inadvertently rescued her in Harovan, and her little daughter, Hykei; the desk sergeant who longed for a reconciled relationship with his son; Birnan and his radical generosity.

With each image, she felt a swelling in her chest, a growing tide of emotion that threatened to steal her mind from the work at hand. And

FVFRY SKY A GRAVE   050

instead of suppressing the memories, she drew upon them, used them to influence her words.

In her broken and exhausted state, she knew it was too much. The yawning, churning abyss of chaotic potential called to her. It strove to fill her mind not with darkness, but rather with magnificent color too varied and complex to process. A fractal rainbow of rainbows, a primordial nothingness that contained everything that ever was and would ever be. She was stepping once more into the infinite expanse of the cosmos; already she could feel her feet slipping beneath her.

But that too, now, was no matter. She knew she would lose herself in this. Whether Qel was destroyed or by some impossible means *eth ammuin* managed to turn back this wave of destruction, Elyth, Advocate of the Voice, would not reemerge. But before she could give herself over, before she allowed herself to be swept utterly away, she would play her part.

She closed her eyes and turned her mind from that glorious annihilation, and instead forced herself to picture the fleet hanging there above them in space, the legion glittering ships of judgment. Elyth had witnessed them before, knew their formation. And in their midst, she knew twenty Herald-class vessels lay aligned to form a corridor through which Qel's bright ruin would pass. She fixed the image in her mind: the ships in their orbit, Qel their focal point.

And as she held the vision, far above the planet's surface she felt the release. A sudden rush, like the heat of a sunray piercing an overcast sky. And doom rode upon that light.

In an instant, *eth ammuin* was crying out, somewhere out there. But quickly he faded away.

Elyth could no longer hear him, see him, sense him. Just as the Heralds focused their terrible energy on the planet, so too Elyth bent her entire will to Qel, and its many rivers, its mountains, its trees, its segmented sky. She spoke to it, reminded it of all that it was. All that it could be.

But the ray of power was too great; it pierced her, passed through her, deep into the core of the planet. She could feel the world coming apart beneath her, around her, within her. In her desperation, Elyth became Qel, and the planet became her. They were one and the same, and the sundering of the world was the dissolution of her self.

But the power was overwhelming, the destruction too widespread. Whenever she turned her focus to hold one part together, some other threadline burst, or watercourse broke free. No matter how forcefully she spoke, no matter how perfectly formed her phrases, she simply could not keep pace with the rending of the planet. And she was sliding, sliding inexorably toward the great expanse.

It was then that she abandoned herself fully, that she stopped struggling against the pull, stopped guarding the limit where self met no-self. And as she spoke, almost without consciousness, Elyth began moving, amplifying her declarations through her body; and her body seemed to know exactly what to do, without any effort or exertion of will. Arrow Seeks the Heart. Warrior Summits the Mountain. Titan Bears the World. The stances came to her faster, stronger, and soon she was weaving them together with new ones she'd never before experienced, transitioning from one to the next without a moment's thought, simply reacting and responding to the chaos unfolding around her.

From that chaos she drew order.

Still she could envision Qel surrounded by the mighty fleet, in such vivid, impossible detail. It was as though she was no longer imagining it, but rather seeing it all with clear eyes. Time ceased its flow, and Elyth swept her gaze over the planet and the fleet. Qel shimmered, its uppermost atmosphere radiant with a thin white light. And the usual rigid formation of the Ascendance ships stood fractured through the middle; the geometric alignment of the Herald-class vessels lay broken along one side, the mightiest of Hezra weapons shattered across the sky.

And from that vision, Elyth felt herself slipping further and further away. Somehow her voice, her body, her mind, everything that made her who she was, seemed to expand and encompass more and more of the universe until she was merely an observer and the self that had once been was no longer.

This, then, was the complete and total dissolution, the fate of those who danced too close to the edge of all power. The last, final traces of the being that had once been Elyth-Kyriel, Servant of the First House of the Ascendance, Advocate of the Voice, slipped away into nothingness, and into the infinite.

And was gone.

And had never been.

Until.

Until a voice called.

Elyth-Anuiel.

Elyth-Anuiel.

And that observer, though it was all things and nothing, heard the voice, and the words it spoke. And out of the nothingness, something came forth. The barest hint of something that could sense a specific time and place.

Elyth-Anuiel, the voice called.

And Elyth recognized the voice. *Eth ammuin,* calling to her from a place beyond all perception and knowledge. Or rather, calling her from it, back to the space she could inhabit. She was drawn to it, and soon she realized that she was no longer just observing, but was in fact a self again, herself, again. And then she was a mind, and with that mind she could perceive that she was not alone in the midst of that chaos. There was one standing with her, standing firm while all else swirled and raged about him.

But in that great empty nothingness, or great fullness of all things, she saw the being standing before her not as she had known him, not as *eth ammuin*, but rather as his true self.

All illusion stripped away, and only revelation remained.

The First Speaker. Varen Fedic.

All that she had feared him to be. Yet nothing like she had imagined.

Elyth-Anuiel, he called.

He was radiant, and his voice was the voice of all creation, and the maelstrom calmed at its sound.

And then the mind that was Elyth added to it a spirit, and then a body, and the cosmos receded, and she was just one woman, fallen to her knees in a clearing, and the terrible trembling of all creation had ceased.

She looked up then and saw the spiraling arm of the galaxy, white against the deep blue of the nearly waned day. And she realized that what she saw couldn't be stars and was instead some brilliant scar slashed across the sky.

Somehow there was still a sky.

And she knew it contained the aftermath; the Ascendance fleet, with a jagged hole torn through the middle of its power.

As her thoughts restructured themselves, Elyth remembered she was not alone, and she turned her eyes back to the ground around her. *Eth ammuin* was lying ten feet away from her, face down, utterly still. Just a man. And the vision of his true identity clashed with all she'd been told; his nature nothing like what she had been led to believe.

She sat looking at him lying there, motionless, helpless. Silent. Still *eth ammuin*.

She tried to go to him, and found she lacked the strength to stand. But she could crawl.

Crawl she did, to his side, and she laid her hand upon his back.

"Grief," she said. "Grief."

He did not stir.

She shook him then, called more loudly.

"*Eth ammuin*. Open your eyes and behold your work. *Eth ammuin!*"

Still he did not move, not even a shallow breath.

Elyth leaned her head down and pressed her ear against his back, listening for a heartbeat or any sign of life. But she could detect none.

She straightened up, sat back on her heels. Brushed his hair away from his face.

"Varen," she said. "Come back."

A hint of movement, a flicker of a smile. His eyes fluttered open a few moments later, and he drew a deep breath, as though it was the first he'd ever taken, and his lungs could never fill.

"I think," he said, his voice raspy, ". . . you have me confused with someone else."

Elyth fell back to a seated position, too weak even to crouch. *Eth ammuin* . . . or Varen . . . rolled over onto his back with great effort, and lay in the dust, staring up.

"You told me you were his disciple."

"No, *you* said that," he said. "I said I followed the thoughts of that man."

"Is it true?" she asked, knowing in her heart it was. "*Are* you Varen Fedic?"

"I was," he answered. "Once."

". . . and now?"

"Something new."

After a few moments, he raised a weak arm and waggled his hand vaguely at the white streak hanging in the heavens.

"Did we do that?"

"No," she said. "You did. I was too busy holding the world together."

"Then you did the important part."

He looked over at her and added, "I wonder which one that makes you."

"What do you mean?"

"Spear or shield?"

Elyth chuckled and shook her head. Doing so made the ground swim beneath her, and she too laid back.

"What happens now?" he said.

"I assume we're actually dead," she answered. "And this is our surprising afterlife."

"Can't be," he said. "I feel too terrible."

"Who said the afterlife was supposed to be pleasant?"

"Everyone who ever worked for it, I guess."

Elyth smiled at that, though it hurt too much to do more.

"If we're not dead, I imagine they'll come to take me home," she said.

"And you'll let them?"

The question struck her, echoed through the fog of her depleted mind. She was still coming to terms with experiencing the present; she could scarcely imagine the possibility of a future, let alone what it may hold for her.

Take me home, she had said. Was there any home for her now?

"What about you?" she asked, deflecting. "Where will you go?"

Eth ammuin returned his gaze to the sky, sighed heavily. Considered for a time.

"I'm at the end of myself, Elyth," he finally answered. "I see that now. I've gone as far as I can on my own. But I know I can yet be more. With help. With guidance."

"What are you saying?"

"I want to learn, as you have."

Elyth shook her head. "First House would never take—"

"Not from them, Elyth," he said, turning to look at her once more. "I want to learn from *you*."

She heard the words, but it took a moment for their meaning to reach her. He reacted to her hesitation, turned on his side to face her more completely.

"Think of it," he continued. "The two of us, free to explore the fullness of the Deep Language. Together. You can teach me."

The image flickered through her mind. The two of them hidden away on some other world, working together in secret. Her time on Qel had exposed the rot within the Ascendance. Here, now, was a chance to start something of their own. Something powerful and, from the outset, truly rooted in the purity of the Deep Language. If she could teach him, what following might they build together? And if they built, what power could stand against them?

"I've always found my own way," he said. "I've never followed anyone else. But I will follow you, Elyth. I will follow *you*. Wherever you lead."

In that moment, paths unfolded themselves before her. He was offering himself into her hand, a weapon too mighty to wield. The strength of her desire to take hold of him served as a warning. Her wounding was deep and raw. Already the seeds of revenge sought to take root.

But there was another way. To return to the First House, to present herself as she was, as the person she had become. To face the Order directly, to submit and allow herself to be tested against whatever fate the Paragon had spun for her. To stand on her own.

And she saw, too, how tightly *eth ammuin*'s fate was bound up in hers. Lying next to him, Elyth couldn't deny the kinship she felt with him. The sense that he saw her for who she truly was and delighted in her. There was freedom in him, and the promise of a deep and fascinating relationship that could take a lifetime to fully explore. If she returned to the House, she would never see him again.

Elyth saw the choice starkly, the lines divided as sharply as Qel's night sky.

"Will you let me?" *eth ammuin* asked. The quiet hope in his voice seared her heart.

Two choices. But, she realized to her pain, only one answer.

"They would never stop looking for me," Elyth said. "And I still have business with the House."

And though her mind flooded with reasons and explanations, she spoke none of them, for fear that he would answer and reveal their hollowness. She kept her eyes on the sky above. After a long moment of silence, *eth ammuin* rolled once more onto his back.

"I think I'll go with you, just the same," he said.

"There's no telling what they'll do to you."

"There never is, Elyth. And you know me. I've never been much of a planner."

A strange peace blanketed Elyth, now that her decision had been made. It strengthened her purpose, but not with fiery defiance or adamantine resolve. There was only a simple, quiet sense that whatever came next was good and right. *Eth ammuin* seemed to feel it, too, though she couldn't help but test it.

"If they don't kill you," she said, "they'll turn you back over to the Hezra, you know. Eventually. Make you stand before the Hezra-Ka himself."

He took a deep settling breath then said, "What man, having mastered himself, should fear any king?"

Elyth found even breathing almost too much effort. But she couldn't let him have the final word.

"What about snakes and spiders?"

"I never said I had *completely* mastered myself. But in time, perhaps. All things in time."

They lay together quietly after that, side by side, looking up as the first stars of twilight began to emerge, bright light shining from light. And for the first time in long years, Elyth saw written there not a reminder of the dead, but rather the hope of something new.

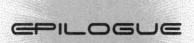

EPILOGUE

Elyth stood alone in the Paragon's garden, waiting at last to receive whatever judgment awaited her. The last time she'd been brought to this place, she'd been full of questions and anxiety. Now, however, her mind was still, attentive to her surroundings, drinking in each moment as it occurred and letting it pass into the next without concern or regret. She saw the miniature frostoak, and how it had grown to fill the gap her stroke had left. If she hadn't known where to look, she never would have noticed anything out of place.

After the failure of the Contingency, a collection team had extracted her from Qel, along with *eth ammuin*. And though Elyth had expected a confrontation with the Paragon immediately upon her return to the Vaunt, to her surprise, she'd instead been sent directly into the recovery cycle, as though nothing unusual had occurred. Nyeda had once more kept watch; a service Elyth discerned that the elder woman had requested.

Though her deployment to Qel had been secret, there was no question that a distance had opened between her and her beloved sisters. And the change was not merely in her own mind; the Advocates of the House might not have known the details, but news of Qel had surely filtered throughout the Order. It wouldn't take much to put the pieces together, or at least for the rumors to spread. Nyeda had treated her with the usual stern care, but Elyth had caught her lingering looks, a mix of sadness and wonder. No one in the House seemed to know what to make of her now.

But all that was coming to an end. Her recovery period was over.

The confrontation she had first anticipated was upon her.

The door of the residence opened and the Paragon came forth, and stopped at the edge of the porch. She was dressed neither in formal regalia nor her simple work clothes, but rather the gray uniform of an instructor.

"Elyth," the Paragon said.

Elyth approached, stopped at the foot of the stairs, and bowed.

"Paragon of the First House," she answered formally.

"I presume you know why you've been summoned."

"I do not presume to know anything anymore," Elyth answered.

"I ordered you to kill the planet Qel," the matriarch said. "And you failed in that duty."

Elyth made no protest, no argument. None would be tolerated. And she felt no need to defend herself.

The Paragon's next statement surprised her.

"It was, perhaps, good that you did. You did not carry out my direct command, but in one sense at least, you did not fail in the mission I sent you to accomplish. Qel is stable.

"Though what that *means* now, we do not know. Perhaps the fault lies with me, for failing to understand the full array of options before us."

The Paragon's words and tone threw Elyth completely off; her manner was solemn, devoid of all warmth, and yet she seemed, in some strange way, to be complimenting Elyth for finding a way to render the threat harmless.

The formality soon vanished, and the Paragon descended a step and sat on the porch. In doing so, she brought herself down level with Elyth, and looked intently for a time into Elyth's eyes, searching. Elyth held herself still and calm, allowed the gaze to probe her inner being. That once-terrible gaze seemed somehow diminished now, its reach and ability to penetrate blunted.

"It is strange to have you here among us now, daughter," the Paragon finally said.

It was a subtle admission, confirmation of what Elyth had long since come to suspect; a truth she had acknowledged, but which until now had remained unspoken.

"You never intended for me to return to the Vaunt," Elyth answered.

The Paragon smiled sadly.

"And you must feel deeply betrayed."

"I did," Elyth confessed. "After. But now that betrayal seems small."

"Small?" the Paragon said with a chuckle. "Even now you are gracious beyond all reason to your House and your old Mother."

Elyth hadn't meant small in the sense that the Paragon had taken it, but she didn't correct the misunderstanding. The betrayal had been complete, it had opened a rift between them that Elyth was not sure could ever be spanned. But within the context of all she had learned, of all she had seen, it seemed petty by comparison. The games of power and influence between the First House and the Hezra in which Elyth was a pawn seemed to her now to be misguided, and almost shamefully narrow-minded.

"But resentment would be the expected response, dear," the Paragon continued. "The only natural one, in fact. Surely you feel it."

"It is the need for the deception that I don't understand," Elyth said. "If you had told me at the start that it was a suicide mission, I would have done no less for the House."

"I believe you," the elder woman said. "Or, at least I am certain you *believe* you would have. It is one thing, however, to ask someone to give their life in service to a greater cause. It is something different entirely to ask them to suffer intensely for an unknown period of time, and to continue to strive in the midst of suffering, knowing the ultimate outcome is death. Another miscalculation on my part, perhaps.

"I believed you would carry out the decree, and in doing so would be absorbed and lost to the infinite. We all did. It seemed the most gentle and gracious way to quell the danger."

The final question that lingered in Elyth's mind was answered. It had all begun with her recall from Revik . . . a message sent after she had already begun the irreversible work. That too had been no accident. The first false lead to send her on her way. The urgency of the recall had served as the pretext for her truncated recovery time; the lack of recovery had been intended to guarantee her dissolution when she carried out the judgment of Qel.

"I see wisdom within it," Elyth admitted. "An Advocate of the Voice corrupted by the Strain would be an unpredictable threat. Resistant, perhaps, even to the combined might of the House and the Hezra."

"Perhaps," the Paragon answered. The glint in her eye showed that she had not missed the mild challenge in Elyth's response. "But do not allow yourself to believe it did not wound me, my bright daughter. When I told you I was giving the best the House had to offer, I meant it."

"And yet you commanded me with a binding phrase."

The Paragon's eyes widened almost imperceptibly at Elyth's words; the first genuine display of surprise Elyth had ever witnessed in the woman. Shock at Elyth's ability to discern the truth of what it meant to be called Guided by the True Star. A moment later, a thin smile stretched the matriarch's lips.

"It was not meant to *bind* you, child. It was intended to insulate you from the effects of the Strain. A defense, to keep you to your purpose. It was the only solution we could foresee.

"But it would appear that not all solutions can be foreseen, even by the wisest among us. Indeed, it would seem those same minds cannot help but underestimate you. Which brings us to the ultimate matter . . ."

"My expulsion from the Order of the Voice," Elyth said.

The Paragon nodded.

"With your true identity known to the Hezra, I . . . of course the House will protect you, my dear, but going forward, I fear your service would be substantially limited.

"And I know it would be difficult for you to leave the Order," the Paragon continued. "I won't insist upon it. I'm sure a place could be made for you, perhaps as an instructor or something of the sort, if you would choose that way. But you are young yet, with much still to offer, and I believe you would find those responsibilities too burdensome. Too confining."

"I had not expected the House to offer any choice in my fate."

The Paragon leaned forward.

"There are many paths open to you, Elyth. Many before us all. The old game has been wiped away. Though few see it, the foundation of the Ascendance has shaken. And our place within it is uncertain, now that the Hezra has regained much of its former glory. We have much work ahead."

Given her lengthy isolation, Elyth had expected some surprises. But the thought had never crossed her mind that the Hezra might *benefit* from the near calamity for which it had been responsible.

"*Gained* glory?" she said.

"For redeeming Qel," the Paragon answered.

"I don't understand."

The Paragon sat back with a gentle, patient smile.

"The official history reflects how the hierarchy developed a new protocol in secret, one meant to replace the Contingency. And Qel was its first true test. Kept hidden, in case it failed. But, because of its success, now revealed to the Ascendance at large, in glorious display. The losses they suffered grant it all an aura of heroic sacrifice that only bolsters the reputation."

"Losses?"

"Of the twenty Heralds they sent, only eight returned."

Elyth recalled the vision she'd had, when she and *eth ammuin* had stood against the power of that fleet. The ships in orbit, broken. Not just a vision after all.

"For the good of the Ascendance, the Hezra bore the dishonor of the first Markovian Strain," the Paragon continued. "Now that is repaid."

"But why? How could you allow it?"

"Concessions had to be made to bring you home, my daughter."

Despite Elyth's emotional distance, the weight of that revelation settled on her shoulders; there was no knowing what else her relative freedom had cost the First House.

"And," she asked, keeping her words carefully neutral, "what of *eth ammuin*?"

"Hidden away in some Hezra hole," the Paragon replied, watching intently to gauge Elyth's reaction. Elyth felt many things: joy that he was still alive; fear for the treatment he must have even now been enduring; an unexpected reflexive desire to rescue him. But all of these feelings she kept buried in her heart.

After a few moments the Paragon added, "And watched over by our own Hand. A strange alliance, certainly. But in giving concessions, we also extracted them.

"In time enough, we'll unlock his secrets. I suspect there is a great deal more we can learn, particularly with your insights."

The Paragon shifted her posture once more, straightening while remaining seated on the porch. It gave her an air of authority, even in its informality.

"Certainly you have your detractors," she continued. "Those who believe it was a mistake for us to receive you back into the House. But you are not without supporters. Few know the truth, of course, as is so often the case in our matters.

"And though I believe we could find a place for you to remain within the Voice, if that is your desire, I had hoped that perhaps you might consider becoming an Advocate of the Mind. That you might come and serve directly under me . . . Or, rather, alongside me."

In all her imagining, this was one possibility that Elyth had never conceived. That she might be elevated to the highest level within the First House, to stand beside the Paragon herself, among her scant handful of advisors and counselors. A height from which she would have not only direct involvement and influence over the future of the House, but would also gain a voice to shape the vision of the Ascendance itself.

And in a spark of insight she saw as well how within such company the greatest Advocates the House had produced would keep her close, and controlled. Elyth smiled to herself. Here then was the promise of a golden prison.

"You're right, it would be difficult to leave the Voice," Elyth said. "But leaving is something I've considered deeply during my recovery. I believe it may be the best thing for everyone, in fact."

The Paragon smiled.

"Then you'll come and serve by my side?"

"There is perhaps no greater honor the House can offer," Elyth said. "But I cannot accept it."

The Paragon sat back.

"You see another path," she said.

"Yes," Elyth said. She had made her decision long ago. Now she would face the test. "I choose to renounce my vows, and leave the service of the First House."

The Paragon made no attempt to hide her shock now. For a brief time she was rendered truly speechless.

"Elyth, my bright daughter," she said, shaking her head. "If you renounce, then you will be exiled from the Vaunt, from all its holdings, now and any established in the future. The House would forevermore be closed to you. You will be beyond any protection your sisters can offer you from the Hezra. They will be watching you, everywhere, always. And if they believe they can take you, they will not hesitate to do so."

"I know all these things. But this is my path. I choose to walk it."

The Paragon regarded her closely for a long moment.

"Perhaps in time I could come to allow it," she said. "But not yet. It would not be wise for you, or for our House. It is clear to me that we each have something more to teach the other."

It should have been another startling admission, the idea that Elyth might have anything to offer the exalted matriarch of the First House. But Elyth knew it was true. At least partially.

"There may be lessons I could teach you," Elyth said. "But there's nothing more I can learn at your feet."

The Paragon reacted, stung by the comment. An ancient fire rose in her eyes then, and she shot to her feet with startling speed.

"Elyth-Kyriel," she cried. "You are a sworn servant of the First House, bound by oath to it and to me!"

As the Paragon spoke, she seemed to grow in every direction, and her words stole the air and the light.

Elyth had faced the cosmos in its immolating expansiveness; here now she confronted it personified. All of creation, and all that might have ever been created, compressed into the point of a blade aimed at her heart.

No matter how strong her will, her body could never withstand such focused power. She felt herself folding under its fury.

But even as she bent forward, bowing to that irresistible authority, she swept her arms out like a falcon soaring, and it was as though the planet itself rose up to share the burden. The great hand that crushed her from above became water, flowed around and past her.

Elyth straightened and met the Paragon's gaze. And though there was terror in the violence of the matriarch's raw power, it too seemed to flow past Elyth without being able to touch her.

"Bend your knee!" the Paragon cried.

Elyth took the full force of the words, felt it wash through her like the shock wave of a dying star. In the midst of that raging torrent, she found her own voice, still and quiet. And with it she spoke.

"There is no power left by which you may command me."

At those words, the Paragon fell back and sat heavily upon the porch, astonished. The great power dissipated, light and air returned, and once more she was merely an old woman in her garden. And Elyth knew then, without a doubt, that while the First House had been built on a measure of truth, there was a deeper, fuller truth upon which she now stood.

"I have something for you," she said, taking a small clothbound bundle from her pocket. She regarded it for a moment, knowing the work that lay within, and how carefully she had crafted it during her time in isolation. But then she held it out to the Paragon, laid across both hands as an offering held up before an ancient power. "I thought perhaps it could find a home here."

The Paragon received it with cautious curiosity, placed it on her lap while she gently uncovered what lay within. At first she was puzzled by what she saw. But then recognition came, and the Paragon's face turned grave. She held it up and looked to Elyth with fear and wonder in her eyes.

The frostoak cutting. Remarkably changed. The partial break in the middle had been replaced by a small knot, a smooth-barked scar covering the old wound. Teardrop leaves grew along the cutting, bright green touched by the blue white at the edges that had earned the tree its name. And where once a clean diagonal cut had separated it from its source, now thin tendrils splayed out, delicate and tender, seeking out new life.

What *eth ammuin* had begun, she had continued.

"A memento," Elyth said.

The Paragon set the cutting aside, apparently at a loss over what else to do.

"If renunciation is your true decision—"

"It is," Elyth said.

"Then hold out your hands."

Elyth did as she was instructed, presenting her hands palm up, as though to receive some great gift. The Paragon stood, and that great ancient power asserted itself once more. Fearsome, awesome even now, despite its recent chastisement.

"Elyth-Kyriel," the Paragon said. "Servant of the First House of the Ascendance, Advocate of the Voice . . . by the power of your own declaration, you are thus expelled from the Order, exiled from the Vaunt, and henceforth banished from the House. I call you *storm-driven, chaser of winds, a wandering star in the deep.* You bear our name no longer."

With the final proclamation, the intricate markings on Elyth's palms and forearms glowed once more with their starlight. Slowly the brilliant silver blue darkened, then changed and burned ember red as the figures and designs withered and faded. Everything Elyth had ever been in the House vanished with them into nothingness.

"Thank you, Paragon," Elyth said, bowing respectfully. "But my name is Elyth-Anuiel."

Elyth turned and left the garden then, and took her last walk across the grounds of the Vaunt, breathing its garden-sweet air, feeling its golden warmth and serenity. And though she knew that once she crossed outside its bounds she would be leaving behind all she had ever been, and all she had worked to become, that thought seemed somehow no longer frightening or sad. To her own surprise, she realized she felt something she had not anticipated.

Free.

She was Elyth-Anuiel. Now, she would make her own way.

ACKNOWLEDGMENTS

Each time I've finished a novel and gotten to this point of the process, I've had basically the same experience. I think about all the people I should thank; the list gets very, very long; and then rather than trying to write the whole thing out, I feel like I should lie down instead. The compromise I've worked out is to just hit a few key highlights while sort of slouching really low in my chair.

To that end, extra-special super thanks go to:

Jesus, for His daily and enduring grace, and for answering prayers like "Please help."

My amazing wife and children, who share the burden of my "creative process" (which mostly involves my staring into the distance with a grumpy expression) and make it all worthwhile. I hope I'm worth it, too.

Sam Morgan, superagent, for pushing me to write this story and for being its champion.

Mike Braff and Vicky Leech, for shepherding this work from the start, and for patiently guiding me through the process of figuring out how to say what I meant to say in the first place.

All the many other folks who helped make this into a real, actual book, a great number of whom I will otherwise never get to personally thank. I'm grateful for your work.

And I think that's a fine place to stop.

Truly grateful.